GREEN MAN'S BURDEN

Anthony Taylor sat watching the wealthy Borden Harper on his multi-vision screen.

"Is there any more news about the—the Greenies?" the interviewer was asking.

"None at at all." Harper dropped his voice to a deep sober sincerity. "We keep on trying. But I'm afraid we are just going to have to face the unpleasant fact that the Greenies are nothing more than human-looking animals...."

Anthony could contain his detestation no longer. Snatching the cushion, he rammed it violently into the speaker-grill, wishing he could ram it down Harper's throat. Harper and the other humans on Venus, milking it of its miraculous beans, using the green-skinned natives to cultivate the crop, because that's all they could be trained to do. They had no language, no human-style intelligence, no cultural potential, nothing.

Anthony grabbed up a dummy piano-keyboard savagely. He struck out a crisp-edged series of chords, double handed, up the keyboard. The notes were sharp, precise sounds.

"Not bad ..." he said, aloud. "For an animal!"

Turn this book over for
second complete novel

CAST OF CHARACTERS

ANTHONY TAYLOR

When he found himself running out of pills, he knew he could no longer pass for human.

MARTHA MERRILL

She seemed to be a beautiful woman, but how long could she keep up the deception?

DR. M'GRATH

A psychiatrist of questionable sanity, he held thousands of Venusians under his sway.

THE OLD MAN

He had the power to wipe out all the human settlements on Venus.

LOVELY

That was the only name she had, for what use did Greenies have for names?

BORDEN HARPER

Though he was the richest man on Venus, he really knew very little about the source of his wealth.

WE, THE VENUSIANS

by
JOHN RACKHAM

ACE BOOKS, INC.
1120 Avenue of the Americas
New York, N.Y. 10036

PART ONE

THE MULTI-VISION screen, a standard installation in all rented rooms, dominated the eye. It was meant to. Anthony Taylor sat watching the slowly changing mosaic of colors, but without seeing them in any real sense. He had just finished a synthetic and tasteless meal in the cafeteria downstairs, and was letting his digestion take care of it, without being consciously aware of that process, either. He had long since learned to ignore insults to his stomach, and suggestions to his eyes, but he couldn't quite ignore appeals to his hearing. Therefore, because the multi-vision set constantly churned out meaningless music and could not be switched off, he had stuffed a foam-filled cushion into the speaker-grills. That served to damp down the offensive noise to the point where he could overlook it.

In his mind he listened to the mighty striding sonorousness of the second movement of Schubert's *Eighth Symphony*, the great "Unfinished." So far as he could discover, no-one had ever produced an adequate transcription of it, for piano. He, Anthony Taylor, was determined to do just that.

As the strong, marching, down-striding counter-point beat in his mind, he laid over it, note by careful note, the nearest equivalent he could think of, within the limits imposed by a keyboard and ten agile fingers. It would be a small miracle if he ever developed this exercise to the point where he could write it out and feel satisfied with it. It would be a miracle of much greater dimensions if the work was ever published. It was extremely unlikely that there were more than ten people in the whole of this modern world who would be able to play it, or would even try.

None of these considerations troubled him, at all. This universe of joyous and beauteous sound was *his* world, the only place where he was completely happy and at home. The noise out there, oozing past the cushion, meant not a thing; was as devoid of inspiration as was the sliding, shifting web of color on the screen. Warmed by his inner music, he felt like someone in a snug room, looking out on a chill and miserable winter.

The mosaic faded, giving way to the careful face of a news-reader, and past the muffling cushion came the announcement: "News of the World, to the World, every hour, on the hour, through the magic of multi-vision . . ." The voice was a whisper, a distantly-sensational catalogue of faraway places, strange sins, crimes and pseudo-crises, to be followed by a rapid-fire succession of advertisements in larger-than-life color, with super-impossible claims, and mind-snaring jingles. Anthony let the stream wash over him, completely absorbed in the near-impossible task of conveying the fugal majesty of a full orchestra within the gamut of a keyboard. Again the news-reader, with a quick explosion of color: "I now hand you over to your local station announcer for your own, more intimate look at the news . . ." he said, and the music all ran together in Anthony's head, and collapsed with a squeal. He sat forward, kicked away the cushion, and paid attention.

"Arriving at London Airport this afternoon, his last port-of-call on a round-the-world shopping spree, Mr. Borden Harper, from the fabulous far-off Venus Colony, was interviewed by our man-on-the-spot . . ." The picture gave way to yet another color-explosion, with engine noises and sounds of gale winds, then became a distant view of passengers streaming across an open plain of concrete. Shift, more color, then a comfortable close-up of a face, tanned and glowing, a strong, smooth, somehow remote face, like that of a patient adult attending to children.

"Nothing special in mind," he said. "Just looking. If I see something I fancy, I'll buy it."

"It must be nice to have so deep a purse."

"It's pleasant, yes. But it's not for myself alone, you understand. I'm shopping for two hundred and fifty other people, my friends, back there."

"Of course. I imagine, Mr. Harper, that millions watching us will envy you and your friends the great wealth, the fabulous luxury, that you enjoy. But it has its dark side, too, doesn't it?"

"That is true. We like it, mind you. Let me not give the impression that we are nostalgic castaways, pining for Mother Earth and the sight of blue sky and stars . . ." Harper shrugged and smiled, tightly, managing to convey just that. "We regard Venus as 'home.' But we are strictly confined to the limits of the domes. A circle one mile across is a world, to us. We do what we can to make it pleasant, but it gets tedious at times. We nibble away at the planet, constantly, but it's slow, uphill work. Venus yields her secrets grudgingly. So we need relaxation, something to keep us occupied. That's what I'm shopping for, something new, a diversion."

"What about the rumors, Mr. Harper, about bean-crop failure?"

"Just rumors. We have our problems, yes, but we'll keep the bean-crop coming just as long as there's a need for it. After all"—his smile grew and became candid—"we depend on it, too. Without the bean-crop, we would be flat broke!"

"How unlikely *that* is," the interviewer permitted himself a chuckle along with the great man, then changed his tone, rapidly. "Is there any more news about the—the Greenies?"

"None at all." Harper dropped his voice to a deep sober sincerity. "We are doing all we can, constantly. We keep on trying. But I'm afraid we are just going to have to face the unpleasant fact that the Greenies are nothing more than human-looking animals."

"It's sad news. They are—completely human-like?"

"Fantastically so. The biologists, anthropologists, and all the other people who study such things consider the Greenies one of the biggest problems science has discovered so far. They've had to revise whole areas of their sciences. It was astonishing enough just to discover a race of beings exactly like us, apart from being green, on another planet. That was fifty years ago, and it's history, now. But the greater shock has come since, as we learn that this seemingly-human creature has no measurable I.Q., has no language, no society, no culture, no artifacts, nothing. It's difficult to accept. As I said, we keep trying to 'reach' them, to understand them in some way, but we haven't much hope. They are the way they are, and we just have to accept it . . ."

Anthony could contain his detestation no longer. Snatching the cushion, he rammed it violently into the speaker-grill, wishing he could ram it down Harper's throat as easily. It was all lies, deliberate and vicious lies. It had to be. It was a conspiracy, with Harper and people like him, and money, and gullible "superior" humans, all involved in maintaining it, and he hated them all with a senseless violence that twisted his stomach and brought bitter bile into his throat. He shut his eyes tight, stuffed fingers in his ears, and fought to regain some measure of calm. Music came to his aid, from the recesses of his mind, and he reached for the Barcarolle from Hoffmann as a thirsty man grasps a glass of cool water.

When he could bear to look again, speakers and voices had gone and the screen shimmered with the everlasting swirl of meaningless color-shapes. In the lower right-hand corner a small square glowed into being, enclosing a black space bearing the words, "You are being called." Anthony pulled in a deep breath, steadying himself, then twitched away the muffling cushion once more, pressed the "Accept" switch, and sat back, tightening his eyes as the strip-lights flared in his face. The screen showed to him, now, a long, lean, knowing face, with dark eyes bright under heavy eyebrows and a black lock of curl draped modishly over its forehead. Gregory Hartford was nothing if not "modish." His sideburns were so long and black that he gave the impression of a man peering between the bars of a cage. Switching on a bright smile, he said, "Hi, Tone. Be at the Cellar, tonight, eh?"

"Don't I always, on Fridays?"

"Just making sure, boy. Got a treat for you, tonight. A thrush."

"Not another singer," Anthony protested, helplessly. "You know I don't like vamping to that kind of stuff, Greg. I'm a soloist!"

"The best!" Hartford nodded, with false heartiness. "But this one is genuine, man. Real pipes, and songs from way back before pops. Your kind of stuff. Classical, you'll see. She's Australian."

Anthony, never very fluent, was completely confused now. "Classical," in Gregory Hartford's lexicon, was anything that called for more than three chords. And, since multi-vision covered the whole civilized world, what did it matter that this "thrush" came from Australia? Or maybe she had a pouch? He rescued his mind from such insane byways, manufactured a resigned smile,

"All right, Greg. I suppose I'll manage, somehow."

"That's my boy. It's all bread, isn't it? Be seeing you."

Hartford's face went away, the strip-lights died, and the idiot-color patterns and senseless music came back. Anthony replaced the cushion, put fingers back in his ears, shut his eyes tight, and dismissed Hartford, his agent and manager, the Cellar, the mystery "thrush" and everything connected with that aspect of his life. He thought, instead, about Borden Harper, and Venus, and the Greenies, and the thoughts were personal pangs.

Fifty years ago very few people had known anything about Greenies, and even fewer cared much. They were obscure, and somehow obscene, parodies of humans, green-skinned animals running silent and naked in the steamy hot forest-jungles of an inhospitable planet. Of scientific interest only, until the advent of the "miracle bean."

Nobody knew, now, who had first found the things, which grew in pods, on stunted bushes, out of the slushy swamp. Venus was rich in new and strange flora, and the beans would have had to wait their turn, had it not been for one or two enterprising field-parties reporting back that they had seen the Greenies eating them. The chemists perked up their ears. What was good for Greenies might be good for humans, and a local food supply would save some of the fabulous cost of shipping supplies all the way from Earth. So they investigated the beans, carefully. Now, almost

9

fifty years later, they were still trying to explain their findings. They could explain, they could measure and show what the bean did, but they couldn't explain how. Once their reports became public, nobody cared much about the "how." The "what" was quite enough to set the public mind afire.

The bean, so the chemists said, supplied two exciting substances. One had the power to mobilize fat. In effect, it made the body withdraw fat from various storage places and move it to the liver, where it was expended as fuel. In short, you ate bean-meal regularly, and you grew slim. Generations of hopeful, wishful and gullible "fatties" had spent millions in chasing many "diets" which had claimed to do just this, and had been defrauded, deluded and disappointed. Now it was hard fact. The second substance out of the bean was a benign antivirus. You ate bean-meal, and you were insured against virus infection of almost any kind. Those were the two substances, and after nearly five decades of hard work, the chemists were no nearer being able to isolate or synthesize either of them than when they began. Only the genuine, Venus-grown beans would work.

Practically overnight, the bean became *The Beauty Bean*, and passed into the loving care of big business. And the Greenies, suddenly, became important. Venus, the whole of Venus outside the shield and armor of a scientifically maintained "dome," was a vicious, strength-sapping, uninviting place, a humid inferno. But that was where the beans grew, and nowhere else. Business wanted beans gathered in large quantities. Business wanted more. It wanted to be able to plant, and grow to order, and harvest, the beans. It wanted a work-force. What more natural than that they should see the Greenies as the obvious answer? Teach them, train them, put them to work, why not?

Anthony shivered as he listed the reasons why not. Much money and effort had gone into the study, and the results were hard. Greenies, for all they looked exactly like humans, were animals, about as intelligent as a dog, perhaps, or a horse, but no more than that. They could be trained to help in cultivating and caring for the bean-bushes, which was something. But it was the absolute limit. Greenies had nothing else, no language, no human-style intelligence, no cultural potential, nothing. They were just green-skinned animals which looked like men.

Anthony got to his feet, moved to a mirror which hung on the wall, and looked at himself. He saw a face that would have been counted as strong and handsome, by any standards, had it not been for the subtly secretive expression. His jet black hair was glossy with health, his skin clear and warmly tanned. A smile, had he been able to force one, would have shown regular and perfect teeth. The white of his shirt clung to and moulded big shoulders and a deep chest. He looked down at his hands—lean, powerful, competent hands, and then back in the mirror he stared into his own eyes. Steady, gray-blue eyes. Only a close examination would have shown that he was wearing corneal contacts, and no one would have had any reason to guess that those contact-pieces were tinted, deliberately, to produce that gray-blue color. That they were designed to hide the real color beneath . . . a blue so dark and vivid as to be almost purple.

Hide your eyes, he thought, bitterly. Hide. Evade questions, avoid too much publicity. Be sure that no one wonders how it is that you're so nicely sun-tanned, although you seldom see the sun and can't bear it on your skin. Never let anyone suspect that you take . . . that you have to take . . . a tablet of anti-tan every twenty-four hours. Be grateful that millions of other people do, for a reason other than yours, and that chemists are, by profession, discreet people. Hide also the fact that you dare not take so much as a taste of sugar in any form, or even a dash of alcohol in a drink, because it will knock you silly. Hide your true self, Anthony Taylor, so that no one will ever know what you really are.

He turned away from the mirror, stooped and caught up from the floor a long box. Laid on the table and opened, it became a dummy piano-keyboard, with tuned and muted metal pieces under the keys. A poor substitute for the real thing, but better than nothing at all. He sat, spread his hands, and struck out a crisp-edged series of chords, double handed, up the keyboard, let his fingers chase themselves down again in staccato runs and trips. The notes were sharp, precise sounds in the little room.

"Not bad . . ." he said, aloud. "For an animal!"

11

To reach the Cellar, Anthony had to run, through sleeting rain, from the nearest Underground station, and arrived with his shabby jacket wet through. Only six of the ten tables were occupied, and the figures sitting there were dim shadows in the half-light that was all the place offered. He spared no more than a quick glance at the nearest as he made his way to the far end, by the rostrum, and found a seat. Strip-lights from the stage cut back the gloom a little, here, showing the chips and scratches in the plastic and gilt decor. A smell of coffee and hot cooking-oil drifted from a side-door as the proprietor bellied his way through carrying a tray.

"Hello, Anthony," he hailed, going by. "A coffee, eh?"

"Please!" said Anthony, but his mind was elsewhere. On stage a thin youth with a blur of black beard and a startling mop of hair was trying to coax a lilt from a lute. The Cellar was hung, about the walls, with ancient instruments of many kinds. Anthony had seen them, had believed them to be ornamental, of curiosity value only. This was the first time he had ever seen anyone try to play one of them, and the result was distressing. Not only was the performer unskilled, he was trying to play something utterly unsuited to his instrument.

In a moment the stout proprietor was back, laying a cup before Anthony and putting one down for himself. Then he slumped heavily into a chair.

"Staff!" he growled. "Because it rains, they are late. Because it rains, I have customers more than usual, and early. Did they think of that? No, I tell you. Does anybody think, nowadays? Same answer. Just like that clown up there," he jerked a huge shoulder at the lute-player. " 'Let me try a tune or two on your lute, Luigi?' he says. A tune! Men had forgotten how to play a lute before he was born. Before I was born, even. Does it worry him? No. 'This is just a different kind of guitar,' he says."

"But that's true, after all, isn't it?"

"Sure it's true," Luigi Gabrielli shrugged. "But he can't play music on a guitar, either. Nobody plays music, any more. They make just background noises, to go with whatever they want to do."

Anthony did not smile, the way other people did when Luigi Gabrielli poured his ridicule on modern tastes. He

12

listened, and sympathized. Gabrielli had been, long long ago, a genuine musician, in a real orchestra. Out of his memories, when he could be persuaded to dip into them, Anthony had had many a clue to old masterworks he would never, otherwise, have heard of.

"Was there every any music written for lute?" he wondered, and Luigi shrugged again, gestured with his cup.

"Who knows? It was the *only* popular instrument, up until sixteen fifty. Then it went out, and our kind of musical notation came in, so if there ever was any lute music written down, who could read it, now, eh? Never mind. You let me take your jacket and dry it. That clown up there will give up, soon. Then you play something for me, eh?"

"All right," Anthony shed his wet garment, held it out.

"Listen!" Luigi took the jacket, but his eyes were on the stage. "You hear?" The lute-player had found a melodic line, and was trying to follow it. "That. Go and show that dolt what he is murdering, would you?"

Anthony mounted the two steps to the rostrum, all his cringing nerves gone, now. This was the one territory in which he was master. He tapped the lute-player on a shoulder, and winced at the resultant jangle.

"Come," he said, simply, and led the way back and round a ply-board flat to where a grand piano crouched in the gloom. It was a genuine Steinway that Gabrielli had rescued from a junk room, years before. Now it was in perfect tune and condition, glossy with the loving care Anthony had lavished on it. He sat, settling himself comfortably. The lute-player stared, curiously, and came near enough to touch the glowing woodwork.

"One of the old cabinet jobs," he said. "Pretty good shape, too. I wonder old Luigi doesn't flog it to a museum, and get a portable. Must be worth a bit, to a dealer."

"It's worth more, as a piano. Listen." He laid his right hand on the keyboard. "This is what you were trying to play," and he sketched the melodic line. The lute-player cocked his head.

"You ain't got the beat, chum."

"There is no beat!" Anthony said, sharply. "Beat is for savages, for the unconscious mind. That music you were beating to death was originally created by Verdi, in eigh-

13

teen fifty, as part of an opera, a story to music. Properly, it calls for a full orchestra."

"You got one of those, too?" the lute-player demanded, scornfully. "What are you, mister, some kind of nut?"

"At least I'm not so crazy as to try to play an instrument four hundred years old that I don't know anything about. I know there are no more orchestras in the world. But there are pianos, and one of the greatest piano-players who ever lived wrote a transcription of that opera piece. The opera was called *Rigoletto,* the pianist was Franz Liszt, and this is the way he wrote it." Anthony put his hands on the keyboard again, sparing a moment to think himself into the mood, to assume the identity of that fabulous, eccentric, flamboyant and cynical old Hungarian genius.

Then he began, meticulously trapping the lilting sounds, the interwoven voices, the competing harmonies, filtering them through his flying fingers. He felt, as Liszt must have felt, an utter absorption in sound, the power to build, mould and control a structure that was at once delicate yet strong, with all the parts fitting together. He built up, he broke apart and scattered recklessly, he caught again and reassembled with dexterous skill, then brought the whole thing to a crashing climax. The following silence seemed thick, saturated with remembered sound.

"Magnificent, Anthony! Just magnificent!" Luigi had come to stand a few feet away and behind, his fat old face aglow with memories.

"Clever stuff," the lute-player shrugged, "but it'll never catch on. It's muddly. Half a dozen tunes all mixed up together. Who wants that?"

"Nobody, now," Luigi sighed. "Put my lute back where you got it, mister. You can't do any good with it." He turned to Anthony, hunching his shoulders in an apologetic gesture. Beyond him, across the empty stage, came Gregory Hartford, leading a girl by the elbow.

"Hi, Luigi! Hi, Tone. Reckoned I'd find you here. Can't leave it alone, can you? This is Martha Merrill. Martha, meet Luigi, who owns this joint. And Tony Taylor. He plays."

Anthony mumbled something, half-rose and sat again, all his defenses in full strength, at once. The girl was medium tall, her hair dark bronze, with metallic glints, her eyes shrouded behind tinted glasses, her teeth brilliantly white

14

against swarthy skin. Her dress, in white elasto-sparkle, dazzled his eyes as it hugged her generous curves. By any standards, this girl was beautiful.

"I hope you can play my kind of music, Mr. Taylor," she said, and her voice was strong, too, with just the suspicion of vowel flattening. From Australia, Hartford had said.

"I can try," he muttered, and Hartford laughed, snapped his fingers in emphasis.

"You name it, sweetie, and he'll play it. I guarantee you."

Anthony wanted to hit him. Casting a sullen look sideways, he saw Luigi, who creased his fat face in wry sympathy, shrugged and went away. Miss Merrill laid down her bag on an empty carton nearby, put on an uncertain smile, and said, "Do you know this?"

Anthony listened to what she hummed, and his eyes opened wide. His fingers felt for the right pitch, sounded a chord or two, and she stopped. Her smile blazed, suddenly.

"You do know it!"

"Yes. By Schubert . . . 'To Music.' Wait. I'll start it properly for you." He thought a moment, then nodded to himself, touched out the simple but arresting introduction. She came in right on cue,

"*Du holde Kunst, in wieviel grauen Stunden . . .*" she sang, with not a trace of effort, but the whole room was suddenly full of sound. Anthony felt a glow. He had read about and heard of voices like "bells," and had always thought the term an exaggeration. Now he knew it was less than the truth. This was magic, a rich full sound that Wagner would have loved. He kept his contribution tender, delicate, well under hers, appreciating that she was playing her voice like an instrument. As it came to an end, he was too moved to comment at all. Hartford filled the gap.

"What'd I tell you, Tone? Is she a nightingale, or not?"

"Miss Merrill . . ." he fumbled for words, looking up at her, "I never knew singing could be like that. So much . . . !"

"Such a voice!" Luigi had come back, and the glow on his fat face gave Anthony a sudden twinge of jealousy. He'd been the only one to bring that kind of fire, before. Now this strange girl with the bell-voice had done it. But the unworthy thought was gone almost as quickly as it had come. Luigi was almost in tears. "Such a voice," he said, again. "Such a waste. Who wants it, now?"

15

"But I don't understand," Miss Merrill's smile wavered. "What's wrong, if you like my singing so much?" Luigi shrugged, a great upheaval of his heavy shoulders.

"I cannot pay you, not what you are worth. And nobody else will pay you anything at all. And you must eat. We all must eat."

"You pay Tony ten," Hartford challenged, suspiciously, "and one for me. What's to stop you paying Martha here the same, eh?" He put a hand on her arm, possessively. "Ten for her, one for me, or I take her away, Luigi."

"Take her away then. But where? Tell me, where?"

"There are other dives. Better ones than this."

"And they pay, for real music? Do they?"

"Well . . ." Hartford hesitated, "Not yet, they don't. But they will, when they hear Martha. Man, she's the greatest, if you like that kind of thing. And plenty do!" Anthony, his gaze shuttling from one to the other, caught an odd note in Hartford's voice.

"You mean you didn't like it?" he demanded of his agent, wide-eyed.

"Oh, it's good. Just like your stuff, Tone. Anybody can tell there's class, there. But it's cold, you know what I mean. No zing to it. Still, I can try somewhere else. Come on, Martha honey. I'm sorry, I thought for sure this would be a good place."

"Just a minute," Luigi spread his hands, and smiled. "Let's not to rush too fast, eh? Be my guests, all of you. We eat, and I talk a bit, and you will see why it's no good trying to sell that kind of a voice, not any more. Ay me, that I should say such a thing, but it is true. Come, what will you have, so long as it comes from a plastican?"

At the table, forking a mass of tomato-flavoured strings of paste, Anthony was puzzled, and said so.

"You know your own business best, Luigi," he said, "but I still can't see why you won't hire Miss Merrill."

She sat opposite him, enigmatic in her dark glasses, paying attention to her plate. She had taken off the cape of her dress, and he saw that her arms, her shoulders and neck, and upper swells of her bosom, all were silky-smooth and glowingly tanned. Made in Australia, and very nice, but it wouldn't last long in the coming London winter.

"You were stupid at school, I think." Luigi said, kindly.

16

"All right, I can't tell you about a piano, either. It's fair. But listen. You too, Greg. We are all friends, why should I lie? This place"—he cast a hand around the dimness—"you think I like it dark, this way? No. But more light costs more money. And I have no more."

"Oh no!" Hartford sneered. "Don't try that story. This place is a small mint. You can't tell me different, either. There's a million little eateries like this, in London, and they all coin the stuff. Don't I know? Don't I sell them gimmicks?"

Luigi smiled, wryly, gestured with a fork. "Look around. Do you see a multi-vision screen? Do you see glow-ads? Do you hear music?"

"That's up to you, isn't it? You could have 'em, if you wanted."

"I have ten tables. I have two staff, one cook, one waitress. And no license. Why? Because, if I put in just two more tables, the law says I must have a license. Then I must have two more staff. I must have multi-vision. It's the law."

"But you get a commission!" Hartford argued, excitedly. "They pay you for that!"

"Sure! And than I get glow-ads, with music, and they pay me for that, too. And I'm rich, like you said. But then I can't have my kind of music any more. Tony, here, couldn't play my piano for me, not in such a noise. You see? So I have only ten tables. I am private. I don't have to have multi-vision and glow-ads. And I don't make much money, either. But I like it this way. I make just enough to be able to afford to pay Tony ten solars to come and play my piano for me three times a week."

"I didn't know," Anthony was distressed as understanding came to him. "You should have said, Luigi. I would have come for nothing, just to play. It's the only piano . . ."

"My ten percent!" Hartford interrupted. "And what would you live on, Tone? National Income hardly pays for rent and grub."

"Mr. Luigi!" Miss Merrill cut into the dispute abruptly. "Why doesn't anybody want real music, any more? It was just like this in Australia, too. Multi-vision everywhere. Pops and commers, jingles and jives, but nobody had any time for the kind of stuff I like. Why not? What's wrong with it?"

"That's a big question, my dear, much bigger than you

17

know, and I don't know all the answer. But I do know most of it. You would like some coffee?" She nodded and smiled and he made signals. "There is a part of it, the coffee," he said. "They can't make instant tea. To make a good cup of tea you must do several things just so, and then wait. Who wants to wait, any more? Who can be bothered to learn how to do a thing right, even to making tea in a pot?"

"No sugar for me," she waved her hand to stop him as he reached for a bowl of plastic-wrapped lumps.

"You and Tony both. That makes you alike, and different. Everybody else likes sugar, likes sweet stuff. Nothing bitter, or difficult . . . or clever, either." He pulled out a packet to offer to her and she smiled again.

"No cigarettes, either," she said. "I don't smoke, don't drink, and don't touch sugar." Anthony felt a strange chill. He pushed it away at once, knowing it to be ridiculous, but it came back. Surely there were millions of people who didn't smoke, or drink, or take sugar. And many of them with that superb bronze tan. And her eyes were probably green, under the glasses.

"We can go back a long time," Luigi sipped at his cup, made a face and put it down. "To the middle of the last century, if you like. Nineteen-fifty, nineteen-sixty, about then. Talent had begun to die. Nobody knew. It was not a spectacular disease, but a creeping thing, like old age. I have gone to the books, just because I am curious. Music, because I know it best, I can give you details. But it was the same for all creative talent. Sculpture, maybe? Polluted by cheap plastic copies of everything good. The creative sculptors? They struggled, tortured themselves and their materials, wire, glass, paper, anything, to find some new way, some new technique. It was precisely the same with painting. Cheap and perfect copies, so who wants originals? Make them different, new, spectacular, but how? Who will pay, when movies and television saturate the mind with rubbish?"

"Rubbish?" Hartford objected. Luigi shrugged again.

"How would you know any different? For a hundred years, now, it has been like this. With music, as I know. Recordings and broadcasts . . . and poverty-stricken orchestras. La Scala, Milan; The Metropolitan, in America; the

18

Festival Hall, here in London; in Germany . . . all over Europe, it was the same. Not one major orchestra could live without subsidy from a government, and when a government is the patron of the arts, the arts die. That always happens. And it died, this time, for good. Because there came Telstar, and then total planetary hook-ups, and all the communications ran together into one lump, for efficiency. Efficiency! Pah!" He picked up his cup again, to rinse a bad taste from his mouth.

"Efficiency means 'I want it now, without having to wait.' Who wants to spend years working, to learn the rules, the discipline? Who wants discipline, anyway? I tell you"—he leaned across to stare at Miss Merrill—"the great ones, like Beethoven, Schubert, Mozart, Wagner . . . they were just channels for music that was real, bigger than them, alive. That is what the discipline is for, to get the 'me' out of the way. I know. I was once a pianist, not so good as Tony, here, but good. Then a violinist. Then a conductor with fine orchestra. But I was too late in my life. The minds are all closed, now. There are no channels left. Now it is all 'me' . . . it is all gimmicks and expressing one's feelings, and release. It stinks!"

"I don't think I quite understand all that," Miss Merrill said, hesitantly. "I know people today don't seem to take the trouble the old ones used to do, but, if you study the old ones, they had a tough time, didn't they?"

"When you sing . . . what is it, you or the music?" Luigi demanded, and she hesitated again. "Which is more important?" he insisted.

"The music, of course."

"Of course!" he threw up his hands. "There you are! Who else, if not Tony, here, would say that, today? Ask Greg. No, let me ask him. What is more important than you, Greg . . . to you?"

"That's a nit question," Hartford snapped, his synthetic grin failing him for the moment. "How can anything be more important than me, to me, hey? You never could talk sense, Luigi."

"Not your kind of sense, no." Luigi smiled, suddenly, dismissing the whole argument. "Never mind. Miss Merrill, I cannot pay you. I wish I could. I'm sorry. Will you do me a big favor, and sing for me, just once more?"

19

"I'll sing for my supper," she said, smiling, "if he can play it. Or maybe something you have in mind, if I know it?"

"Something, yes!" the old man sat back in his chair, eyes half-shut. "You know, when the Soviets came out into the Western world, became partners with everybody else, they talked a lot about quality, and culture. But who can argue with the masses? Offer them the good and the difficult, and they will take the cheap and the easy. There is something wrong with Man. He can talk about good, but it is always too difficult for him to do, even when it seems easy. You said you didn't understand me, Miss Merrill. I think you will understand this, though. I would like you to sing, for me, 'The Last Rose of Summer.' You know it? Good. And then you come back here and sit by me and listen, while Anthony plays something so different. Both good . . . one good-by-itself, the other good-for-showing-off. Anthony, you know what I mean? From the Transcendental Studies of Liszt . . . Mazeppa. . . ?"

Anthony understood perfectly what the old man was getting at, but his attention was caught by Miss Merrill's odd actions. She had taken a sugar-lump from the bowl and peeled it of its wrapper. Now, delicately, she raised it to her tongue for a brief touch, shuddered, put it down, and took a quick mouthful of coffee.

"Shall we go over to the piano, now?" he asked, getting up. She sat a moment, shuddered again, and then got to her feet.

"I'm ready. One extra-special performance, coming up," she said, and he was struck by the new vibrancy in her voice and manner. He could "feel" her by his side as they mounted the two shallow steps and crossed the empty rostrum, through a cone of smoke-filled light, to the ply-board flat which hid the piano.

"Are you all right?" he asked, as she reached for and leaned on the upright batten.

"I'm just fine!" she beamed, clutching the panel. "Give me a note, and I'll show you." He shook his head, wonderingly, went to the piano, touched a soft chord, ran through the introduction, and, from his right shoulder, back there, he heard her begin. With her first strong sweet note, he forgot any problems he had ever had. Almost in awe, he nursed out the harmonies to underlie and augment the

20

throbbing sounds she made, hearing her voice filling the whole room, flooding it with beauty. He knew, too, without looking round, that she was singing with everything, not just her throat, but every nerve and muscle in her whole body. Dimly, in some gestalt of understanding, he knew that this was why she seemed so alive, so vivid. Because she was all of a piece, a completeness. And this, too, was the way he felt when he was playing something especially demanding.

In the hushed silence after she had finished there came a single pop-pop or applause, and then a storm of clapping. Up from his stool in haste, he went to her. "That was magnificent. I've never heard anything like it in all my life," he said. "Just listen to that applause!"

She swayed, unsteadily. He caught her arm, felt a tingle at the touch of her smooth skin. She was shivering like a plucked string.

"Hold on to me. I'll take you back to the table. Can I get you anything? A drink?"

"Just water. I'll be all right." She managed to get down the two steps and to her seat, where she sank down, gratefully. Anthony poured water for her, anxiously, watched her fumble in her hand-bag. She produced a box, popped the lid off, shook out a white tablet, reached for the glass and her hand shook so that she couldn't grasp it properly. In weaving irritation she fumbled off her dark glasses, laid them on the table-top, and reached again. The tablet went on her tongue, the glass came up, she swallowed greedily and shuddered again.

"Hah!" she sighed, and put the glass down. "That's better!" Anthony cast a baffled glance at Luigi, and Greg Hartford, who were just as baffled as he was. Then Miss Merrill became aware of their stares, and laughed. It was a rich gurgling sound, deep in her throat.

"Sorry if I scared you all," she said. "It's not what you're probably thinking. Just sugar. A touch of sugar gets me higher than a kite, and I can sing like crazy when I'm high."

"And this?" Anthony took up the little box.

"Just plain aspirin, mister. See for yourself. Don't ask me why it flattens me out again, it just does." She looked up at him, challengingly, and her eyes were the deepest, darkest blue he had ever seen. Almost violet. Almost glowing, in the dimness.

He mumbled something incoherent. He had no memory whatever of stumbling back to the piano. That was lost in the roaring maelstrom of unbelief in his mind. The grinning teeth of the piano keys, staring at him, broke him out of his daze, made him suck in great chestfuls of air.

Martha Merrill was a Greenie. The thought echoed insistently, almost shouted itself inside his head. A Greenie! He put out his hand, blindly, and the resulting discord made him wince. He shoved the ridiculous thought away, stamped it down into silence. It couldn't be true. It was just a fantastic coincidence. It had to be. In the meantime he was supposed to be going to play something. What had Luigi said? Anthony groped for his disorganized memories, painfully. The Transcendental Studies. Mazeppa. By Liszt. That was it.

For a moment, and for the very first time in his life, the music eluded him, seemed unimportant. Then the discipline of a life-time exerted its power. The hours, months, years, of soaking himself in everything that went with a piano, took charge. He sat up, memories flooding back, firing his fingers. He began to play, and in the first few seconds, everything else had faded from his mind. He became Franz Liszt, at his best and worst. A brilliant, effective showman, a genius deliberately playing down to the common level. Obvious, vulgar and shallow, flashy stuff, but knowing there wasn't one in the audience listening to him who wouldn't have given an arm to be able to play like that, he conspired with the instrument to insult them all on a level that they hadn't the wit to understand.

Then it was done, and the café crowd rewarded him with a spatter of hand-claps as he went back to the table. The place was a little more crowded, now, and Luigi had gone, to lend a hand in the kitchen. His place was taken by a stranger, in a sweeping silver-gray cloak with a high collar. Anthony dropped into his seat, too emotionally exhausted to give more than a glance that way. He looked to Miss Merrill, and something about her expression jolted him out of his numbness.

"Can you really play piano that well, son . . . or is that your show-off piece?" The voice was crisp, coldly confident, familiar. Anthony swung his head round, and recognized Borden Harper, the man from Venus.

"You know who this is, Tone?" Hartford's voice was an unbelieving squeak.

"Yes. I know." Anthony hardly recognized his own voice. All his insides shrunk to mouse-size, had crept away into a hole.

"You haven't answered my question, Mr.—Taylor, isn't it? Are you really a pianist, as good as that last piece you played?"

"I can play," Anthony mumbled. "It's the only thing I can do. It's all my life."

"Didn't I just say that, Mr. Harper? Didn't I? Tone is the best. You name it, he'll play it." Harper ignored the squeak, kept his steady eyes on Anthony for a long moment. Then he shifted his gaze to Miss Merrill.

"I heard you sing, too. I ask you the same question. Was it just a show-piece, or are you really a singer?"

"I asked her to sing that last piece, mister." Luigi had come back once more, was standing between Anthony and Miss Merrill. "I don't know you, but I tell you this. You won't find a better pianist than Anthony anywhere in London. I know. I, Luigi Gabrielli, tell you, having heard the best, from fifty years. And the lady? I can just remember old recording of Sutherland, and Callas, and they were no better."

"I'm not speaking of native talent. A voice, a few pieces, that's not important. I'm after repertoire. Suppose"—he shifted to Anthony again—"you're standing up in front of an audience of music-lovers, who are likely to ask for piano works by Beethoven, say, or Chopin, Mozart, Brahms, Scarlatti, could you play them, as well as you just played that Liszt? And you"—he swung back to Miss Merrill—"could you deliver arias from *Aida*, or the *Magic Flute*, or *Lakhme?*"

"Why? What do you want?" Anthony found his voice, suddenly, harshly. "What are you after, mister?"

"If you two are as good as I think you are, I want you. Call it my whim, if you like. But I can pay for what I want."

"Now you're talking." Hartford became suddenly fluent. "This is where I come in, Mr. Harper. I own these two. Gregory Hartford, agent and business manager. Let's talk money, eh?"

Harper smiled, a chill, hard-eyed smile. He reached into the pocket of his cloak, withdrew a gold-stamped wallet. Then, frowning, he looked up to where Luigi was still standing, belligerently protective. "Signor Gabrielli, I'm taking away your entertainers," he said, evenly. "Will that compensate for it?" and he thrust out a crackling note. Anthony saw the color. It was unfamiliar. The he heard Luigi gasp, and whisper, "A thousand solars! It is too much. I do not pay them . . ."

"Keep it. Mr. Hartford, I'll deal with you this way. See?" He took a second note, tore it across, offered one half. "Take it. You get the other half when you deliver these two, free of conditions, to my hotel. Here's my card, and the address. Have them there within the hour and there'll be one more like that for you. Give me any talk about contracts and percentages, and you'll get nothing. Fail to deliver them, and I'll break you!"

Hartford gulped, and was silent, staring at the engraving in his hand. Miss Merrill found her voice.

"What are you offering us?" she asked, unsteadily.

"Luxury, fame, publicity, the chance to perform before a discriminating audience, and enough in hard cash to keep you comfortable for the rest of your lives, afterwards. A concert tour, I believe they used to call it."

"You mean . . . you want us to go to Venus, with you, when you go back? To perform for your friends?"

Harper nodded. "Precisely that," he said.

Anthony got to his feet, stood on legs that had gone suddenly rubbery. The cafe was a dim blur, just beyond the edge of vision. His stomach heaved and knotted itself. Bile pushed at the base of his throat, threatening to spew up and out. He was walking, blundering into tables, aiming somehow for the door out to freedom, and escape. Someone clutched at his arm, a shrill voice yammered, and he turned, savagely, and shoved. He saw Hartford's wide-open face recede into blur, stumbling backwards. Then he was out, stumbling up concrete steps into the street, and the rain. Wind-driven ice-spray hit his face, saturated his shirt, ran into his eyes, but he tramped on, unheeding, uncaring that sparse pedestrians abroad in that weather stared at him in wonder and gave him room.

In his mind there was a swirling chaos of dark blue-pur-

24

ple eyes, and a lean, hard, smiling face, and scattered words. Fame . . . publicity . . . Venus! Touching *that* word was like thinking of evil. Every time it burst in his mind his stomach heaved again, threatening to come up past his tight lips. Then, somehow, he was in darkness, blundering painfully against a rough wall, wrenching his ankle painfully on an unseen curb, stumbling into a road, and staring around. Blurrily, dashing rain from his face, he saw a distant lonely street lamp and weaved toward it, becoming aware that he was chilled, wet to the skin, and lost. How long had he been walking?

Slowly, rational thoughts came back. He put a hand on the rough cold of the lamp standard and stared about. At this time of night, dark side-streets were dangerous. A quick patter of feet made him whirl, fearfully, and then he wrenched to sudden anger as he recognized the shrill voice.

"Tone! What-the-hell Tone! Wait for me, can't you?"

"You!" he shoved away from the lamp and reached for Greg Hartford as he came stumbling and breathless out of the gloom. "You!" and he took the smaller man by the throat. Hartford squeaked like a rabbit and flailed his arms, clawing at that grip.

"Whatsamatter with you, Tone? You gone crazy, or what?"

"You're not taking me back, to him. You're not going to buy and sell me, like an animal."

"Ease down, will you?" Hartford got his fingers under Anthony's and pried them loose enough to be able to talk. "Who's buying and selling? I'm your agent, ain't I? This is a big deal, Tone. The biggest you'll ever see. What d'you want to run away for? Don't you want to be rich?"

"I don't want to be rich, famous or anything. I just want to be left alone to play piano, my way, and mind my own business. And *I don't . . . want . . . to go . . . to . . . Venus!*" He shook Hartford like a wet bundle of rags with each emphasis, almost screaming himself with the urgent need to get the idea through. "Just go away. Leave me alone. Tell him you couldn't find me."

"Wait!" Hartford pleaded. "Leggo a minute. Let's talk sense, Tone. Let go of me, will you?" He got his throat and jacket free, shook himself, swiped the rain from his face. "Look," he said. "Do me a favor, boy. I done plenty for you, in the past. I've treated you right, ain't I? Well then,

25

just for me, Tone. He gave me a thousand solars, remember? That's more loot than I ever had before in all my life. But I haven't got it yet. I get the rest of it when I produce you, at his hotel. Is that bad? Is that selling you? Is it?"

"I won't go. I don't want to hear about it."

"What's the matter with you? Look, all you have to do is come with me, let me deliver you. That's all. That gets me clear, and the loot in my hand. That's what I want. After that, you can do what you like. You can always say no, can't you? It's up to you, isn't it?"

"I don't want it. I'm not going. I don't want to be famous, a big public figure. I don't want to be rich. I just want to be left alone!"

"Publicity, that's what you're scared of, isn't it?" Hartford's keen senses had not entirely deserted him. "And you think *this* is the way to do it? You're crazy. If Harper doesn't get you, just the way he wants, you'll be the most famous wanted man there ever was, don't you see that?"

The new idea shocked Anthony into acute misery. It was so obvious as to be unarguable. He dropped his grasping hands, and stood, feeling the chill rain seeping through his cheap clothes. Hartford's rat-bright eyes watched, calculatingly.

"It's right, Tone, isn't it?" he said, shrewdly. "You don't use a man like Harper that way, and get off. He's rich, Tone. He could buy London and sell it again, and only use his small change."

"What can I do, Greg?" Anthony's rage had dissolved along with the soaking rain. "What can I do?"

"I think you must be raving mad, anyway, boy, but if you really want to sneak out of this deal, the only way is to stop Harper from wanting you. There's a man who's used to getting what he wants. And he wants you, and the thrush . . . Hold it!" His attitude changed, suddenly, and his lean face tightened as he flashed urgent glances through the gloom. Now Anthony could hear them, too. Shuffling steps, grunts, and the spine-twitching aura of menace. Just out of visibility, figures and approached, perhaps six or seven, threatening shadows.

"Yobs!" Hartford jerked. "Get by the lamp-post, quick!" He moved a hand, and Anthony gasped as a long glittering thing appeared. A knife!

26

"All right!" Hartford shrilled, into the gloom. "Who's to be first, and slip his guts on the pavement, eh? Come on, come on!" he waved the blade in a slow, professional semicircle. Over his shoulder he said, breathlessly, "Get close to the lamp, and scream!"

Anthony stumbled backwards until the concrete upright nudged between his shoulder-blades, but he couldn't scream, couldn't even imagine what Hartford meant. He'd heard of yobs, those faceless, light-shunning back-street runners who came out only at night, to rob for enough to live on until the next night. The unusable, under-equipped misfits that any society will throw up, no matter how carefully it may be designed. But why scream? He stared into the gloom, past Hartford, and felt that the menace had halted at sight of that cold blade.

"Scream, dammit!" Hartford whispered. "Oh, never mind, I'll do it myself!" and he put his head back, lean face staring wetly up into the harsh light, and screamed, a high ululation that split the quiet like an obscenity. Drawing breath, he let go again, and Anthony could hear scuffling feet, knew that the creeping shadows had turned tail, were running away.

"Microphone in the lamp, Tone. There's one in every lamp, down the side-streets. Come on, run for it. The cops will be here inside five minutes, and they won't know us from any other yob. Come on."

Back in lighted streets, with the comforting buzz of traffic and the scurrying pedestrians to dodge, Hartford dropped into a fast stroll.

"Was a yob myself, once, Tone. I know the tricks, and the hiding places. You're only a spit and a jump from that life, yourself, you know that? Living on National Income, just enough to buy food and pay rent, and a bit over, from Luigi. You got no tolerance, boy. No leeway. Nothing to fall back on, if you're sick."

Anthony heard him only dimly. He was still grappling with the fact that Hartford had had that knife handy, all the while he was being throttled, but had not drawn it to defend himself. Why not? And where had that murderous impulse come from? Anthony had not raised a hand in anger, nor even thought an aggressive thought, against any one person since leaving school. It had been his nature to retreat, to evade, to go away.

27

"Know what happens to a yob, if they catch him, Tone? Goes to a clinic, that's what. There's something wrong with him, see? So they shove juice through his skull, scramble his brains, shoot him full of drugs, and then teach him to be good and useful, get rid of all his daft ideas and give him to the Human Employment Office. Of course, he's stupid from then on, but there's plenty of jobs for stupids, like waiting on at table, baby-minding, washroom attendants, barbers, valets, maids . . . personal service stuff. You fancy that kind of life, Tone?"

The barbed hook on the end of the sentence speared through Anthony's mental fog, brought him to a shocked halt.

"Me? What d'you mean? I'm not a yob!"

"You will be, boy. If you get across Harper. He's putting fame and fortune right in your lap, and you're tossing it back in his face. That is going to make him mad, and it makes you—odd. Queer, get me? So the clinic comes next. Where they make queer people into good people, and take out all those nutty ideas about playing pianos from morning till night for nothing. You, Tone. Think about it. And me. What do you think he'll do to me, if I don't deliver?"

"No! Greg, no!"

"But yes, Tone. Harper can do that. Or society will do it for him, if he makes it big enough."

"What can I do, Greg? What? Tell me. You're smart, you know the tricks. What can I do?" Anthony was hardly coherent. Words never came to him easily. Pictures were much more vivid. Pictures and sounds. One vague horror tugged one way. That was the clinic, undefined, and the death of his music. On the other side lay Venus, equally vague and undefined, equally unthinkable. "What can I do?"

"Hang on. Get in there and keep still." Hartford motioned to the shiny-wet blackness of an auto-cab crouching by the curb. "Costing me a fortune, you are." They had come back to the Cellar, now. "Had that cab waiting ever since you ran away. Now stay there, and I'll get the lady, if she hasn't run off too. That would be just my luck."

Anthony fumbled the door open, climbed in the back and settled, wetly, against the cushions. His little unhappy world of uneasy quiet on the fringe of life had fallen to pieces and he felt naked. What could he do? The door

28

opened again, and Miss Merrill came in, head down and knees showing, brushing rain from her bronze hair. Anthony saw that the bronze gave way to jet black where the rain had struck.

"Where did you go?" she asked. "What did you want to run off like that for. Mr. Harper was furious."

"Do you actually want to go to Venus?"

"Are you kidding? I'd go anywhere, twice, for the kind of money Harper's got. And for singing!"

"Is that why you sing, for money?"

"Why not. Isn't that what you play a piano for, then?"

He shook himself away from her, turned his nose to the window. The cab bounced as Hartford got in and slammed the door.

"Your jacket, Tone," he said, tossing the warm dry garment across, "and good luck, from Luigi." Then he fed coins into the slot, dialed the destination from Harper's card, and sat back as the cab growled into smooth motion. "This is a crazy night, all right," he said. "Who said 'easy money'? Been thinking about you, Tone. There's only one way to handle it, so far as I can see. Harper wants you. Why, that's his business. But so long as he wants, he's going to get. So the only thing you can do is make him stop wanting, stop fancying you. Like making a fumble or two on the old keys, eh, boy? Hit a few sour notes. Make like an amateur, you know?"

That just had not occurred to Anthony. It couldn't get into his mind now, even though it was plain enough, and obvious. All he had to do was make discordant hash of a piece, where Harper could hear. But the mere thought of it was a pain, was a kind of death. Take away music, his ability to play . . . and there was nothing left. He was still thrusting away the suicidal thought as the cab stopped, and Hartford was scrambling out. Anthony went into a hazy shadow world, divorced from reality, where his body moved and did as it was told without reference to the shriveled thing that his ego had become. Bright lights and warmth, thick sponge underfoot, obsequious attendants and imperious voices impinged on him through a fog.

Someone took his arm, gently but firmly, directing him to an aseptic whiteness with hot scented steam. Deferent hands tugged at his sodden clothes, tearing them despite the

29

care. Paper-disposals were meant to last a day, or two days, at most. He had been making his last a week. The rain had finished them completely. The shower was good, luxury and clean smells. The towel and the hot-air blast were good, too. Then new, clean, dry clothing, and he returned to reality with sudden urgency, stared into the dull eyes of a uniformed servant.

"My wallet? What have you . . ."

"Your personal effects are on the dressing-table, sir. There was no money. Mr. Harper desired me to inform you that you may have anything you need. A meal, perhaps, and something to drink?"

The servant was male, of indeterminate age, wooden-faced, a nothing. A life, in a uniform, an automaton. Anthony stared, and remembered what Hartford had said. A "Stupid." Cross Harper the wrong way, and that was what they could do to you. Then he thought of something else.

"What time is it?"

"Twenty-two fifteen, sir. Is there anything you want?"

Anthony went across to the dressing table, caught up his wallet, and checked. Identity card; National Income card; one fifty-credit note . . . and, secreted in a pouch in the lining, one foil-wrapped tablet of anti-tan, and an unbroken strip, tight-coiled, holding a dozen. Hiding the torn foil in his palm, he approached the servant again.

"I'd like a drink of something. Fruit-juice, no alcohol. Without sugar. And—" he struggled with embarrassment—"can you get me a packet of anti-tan?"

"I'm sorry, sir. Nothing like that, not in *this* hotel!" The faint emphasis was not lost. Anthony stifled a twinge of terror. Of course they wouldn't, not here. In theory, in open speech, there was no color-bar any more. It would have been impossible, when a tablet of anti-tan a day would bleach the blackest skin to a golden tan. But the bar was still there, on a deeper layer. You could rationalize, on the surface, just as you could buy, from any chemist, the stuff to give you that "pale and interesting look" . . . on the surface. But, deep down inside, no one was deceived. And there could be no anti-tan in this hotel. Naturally.

"Just the drink, then," he said, passing it off. "No sugar, mind." The servant turned away, obediently, and, as he opened the door, noise flooded through. An irate voice, kept coldly in check. Harper's voice.

"I said a piano. A grand piano, a Steinway. I don't care if you have to go to China for it. I want it, here in my suite, quickly."

Anthony shut the door, turned and put his back to it. Harper was insane, perhaps, but he was getting his own way. And Hartford had suggested a way of escape. The thought, as it came back, hurt just as much as it had the first time. Discords, errors, wrong notes. . . . His eyes fell on a slim bright thing, on the dressing-table . . . stirred memories. He went across, put out his hand to touch the bright chrome-steel "key." It must have puzzled the servant, he thought. A box-spanner is hardly the sort of thing one is likely to carry about. There came a peremptory rap on the door and the click as it opened. Anthony swung to see Harper standing there, head up and alert in his silver-gray cloak.

"Ah, our pianist, clean and wholesome again. What's that?"

Anthony tried to hide the spanner but Harper was much too quick in crossing the floor. "It's a 'key.' For tuning . . . a piano."

"Indeed! You know, Taylor, I had doubts about you. To me, you and Miss Merrill, and one other, represent a hell of a gamble, the longest and slimmest chance any man ever took. So, I had doubts. But this"—he gave back the key—"almost convinces me. I'll have a piano for you, in no time at all. If you can play it as well as I think you can, I'll give it to you, as a present when I'm done with you. Now why do you look like that, eh?" The steel-gray eyes narrowed, bored into Anthony's own as he went back a step. "What are you afraid of, Taylor? That I'll expose you as a fake, a show-off?"

"No!" Anthony threw that back at him, instantly.

"All right, then. All I want from you is that you come with me to Venus. You, the little lady next door, and one more person, who will be here by morning. I want you to come, and perform, for my friends on Venus. You will be treated like royalty. You will be paid more money than you have ever dreamed of. I guarantee you absolutely safe conduct there and back. Put it down in writing and I'll sign it.

I can't speak more fair than that. You think about it." He spun, abruptly, as there came a rumble of noise beyond the door, a discreet knock, and then an inquiring, harassed face.

"Mr. Harper, the piano is here."

"Good! Come on, Taylor, this is your moment. Either you *can* play the thing, and you're the man I want . . . or you can't, you're a fake, and I will see to it that you never touch an instrument of any kind, in public, ever again!" The voice was gentle, but crisp, and deadly serious.

Anthony almost cried out at sight of the piano. It was old. It had been frantically dusted, but the finger-marks of age were not to be so simply disguised. It stood, forlornly, in the middle of a room that was glitteringly modern, functional and soulless. It looked as lost as he felt at that moment. The top groaned as he lifted it, propped it up. Ancient smells of varnish and dust came to his nostrils. He slapped the dusty stool, sat, and felt out a chord . . . and his teeth stood on edge. Harper had moved round to where he could watch Anthony's face.

Now he asked, "Out of kilter, is it?"

"You wanted a piano!" the starch-fronted manager protested. "This is the very best we could get. From an antique dealer. Genuine!"

Harper brushed his interruption away. "Can it be fixed, Taylor?"

"Oh yes. It's just out of tune. Hasn't been touched in years . . ." He ran his fingers delicately up the keyboard, came down again in a cascade of double octaves, listening. "Lovely tone . . . a better one than Luigi's."

"That's all I wanted to know." He waved a dismissing hand at the manager. "Fix it up, Taylor. It's yours."

"Don't you want to hear me play?"

"Oh yes, certainly. But I'm convinced already. I was watching your face. You want to understand a man, you don't listen to what he says, you watch what he does. I'm no musician, Taylor. I know a little. That sounds fine to me, but I could tell it didn't, to you. That's good enough. But you square it up. I'll go and see how Miss Merrill's getting along."

The servant came back with a tall glass, wheeled a table to Anthony's elbow, hovered until Anthony sent him away. Then, gulping the tablet and drowning it with the drink, which tasted shockingly different from any juice Anthony had previously had, he carried on with the loving detail of adjusting the sounds of strings, matching them to that "standard" which was built into his whole personality. It was a wonderful instrument, solid and strong, with a depth of tone that was a chest-shaking growl in the lower register, and a shrill, pure yelp in the upper strings, with never a chatter or a jangle in the whole range. By the time he had balanced the whole into harmony, all thought of betraying his love had vanished as if it had never been suggested.

Slipping the key back into his pocket, he began sounding chords and trills at random, caught the tail end of an old favorite as it welled up in his mind, and settled down to play it properly. Liszt again—the man who had gained the whispered reputation of being "diabolic" in his own life-time; who had composed deliberately for complexity, so that even Busoni, contemplating some of the works, had said, "The maestro himself would have to rehearse these carefully." This, 'La Campanella,' began with an innocently simple tinkling theme for the right hand, and a steady striding left hand accompaniment. It was meticulous, precise, but pleasing, at first. Then, as the theme ran out, and started all over again, that leaping right hand motif was knotted over on itself and doubled, but just as clean and crisp . . . a swashbuckling conceit. And then, incredibly, the third time doubled in complexity and speed everything that had gone before, while preserving the innocently simple underlying theme, and one wondered how it was possible. It was sheer technical virtuosity for the sake of it, Anthony thought, as if from a distance, watching his hammering, leaping, jumping fingers . . . but good, too!

The great stamping, finishing chords echoed through the room, faded into echoing silence, and he realized he had an audience. Harper stood by a door, smiling like a man who has just won a bet with himself. By him, Martha Merrill stood breathless and agape, her violet eyes huge.

"That was wonderful . . . but nasty, too," she said. "A sort of clever sneer at everyone. Like a genius bragging."

"He was a genius," Anthony mumbled, "and he was showing off. And he was sneering, because people didn't understand him, I suppose."

"Never mind explaining it," Harper came forward. "You

play like that, where we're going, and I'll be satisfied. More than satisfied. Now, my dear, I'd like to hear you sing something . . ."

Anthony slept very little that night, for all the fine room and the comfortable bed. What sleep he did get was torn and smeared with screaming nightmares of staring faces and pointing fingers, and running, frantically, with his hands over his face. Morning found him sore-eyed, with a thick tongue and a foul mouth, and more than ever determined that he would *not* go to Venus.

"Why not?" Harper demanded, across the breakfast table. "Taylor, I don't understand you. There isn't time to have you psycho-ed out of whatever it is that's gnawing at your subconscious, so I'm going to pressure you, one way or another. I get what I want, and I want you. You can face that, and make it easy for yourself, or fight it, and me, and lose. It will be rough on you, but I'm going to have my way."

"Are you afraid of space-flight?" Martha asked. "Is that it? I am, too, but they have tranquils and stuff, for that, don't they, Mr. Harper?"

"They certainly do," Harper nodded, then snapped his head round as an attendant approached him. "What?"

"A Mr. Austin Willers for you, sir."

"Oh, yes, good. Bring him right up here." The attendant went away and Harper swung his steely gaze on Anthony. "Here comes a man," he said, "who has been flying all night to get here, on my say-so. A tenor, your style, Miss Merrill. I heard him in the United States. He has a trick memory and a freak voice. That's the way he has been handling it. And scraping a living in hole-and-corner clubs. Like you, Taylor. He'll be here in a moment. You have that long to make up your mind. I want all three of you, with me, for Venus. All three, or none. It's up to you, Taylor. Throw me down on this and I wash my hands of *all* of you . . . and I leave it to you to explain, to the other two, how they lost the chance-in-a-lifetime, because of you. Here he comes, now, Taylor. The next word is yours. Do you come to Venus with me . . . or not?"

Anthony stared at the stark tragedy of Martha's face, dragged his eyes away and looked to the door, to the tall, gangling, anxious-faced man who stood there, bare-headed
34

and wondering. And something inside of him shrank to a needle-point ache, then found a hole and hid itself.

"All right," he mumbled. "I'll come."

He sat, alone, in the view-room, looking at nothing. The screens were dead, here. Venus was to be seen from the ventral view-room. That's where the others were. Anthony knew that nemesis was creeping up on him, and the knowledge was enough. He didn't want to sit and look at it. The seat fell away beneath him, momentarily, and he clutched an arm-rest. Someone juggling with the anti-gravs, getting ready to come alongside the satellite-platform. Any minute now the alarms would sound. Venus was out there, somewhere, and getting closer by the minute. The idea hung over him like a weight.

Clang . . . the gong snapped him into a leap of fright. Clang . . . that pitch was chosen to catch the nerves. Clang . . . he scrambled up from his chair, sweating . . . clang . . . into the passage and chrome-railed companionway.

"One minute to course-correction and rendezvous," an impersonal voice warned him. "Passengers will secure to cabins, at once."

At the end of the companionway he almost collided with Martha, and Willers, and that infernal gong began again . . . clang.

"Let me help you," she said, and put a hand . . . clang . . . on his arm. He threw it off, savagely, hardly sane in his . . . clang . . . terror, and the pounding in his skull . . . clang . . .

"Let me alone!" he choked. "Let me alone! If it hadn't been for you . . . *clang* . . . I wouldn't be here. Damn you!" He was almost speechless with . . . *clang* . . . with the effort of holding in his fear. There was . . . *clang* . . . shock on her face. He fended himself away . . . *clang* . . . from the bulkhead, and Willers grabbed at his arm. CLANG.

"Just a minute!" he growled. "You can't . . . CLANG . . . talk to a lady like that!" Without thinking about it . . . CLANG . . . Anthony balled his fist and flung it . . . CLANG . . . against Willers' jaw, saw him reel. Then he tore loose . . . *CLANG* . . . and went retching down the passage to his own . . . *CLANG* . . . cabin. There, sobbing for breath . . . *CLANG* . . . he slammed the door shut and threw himself on his . . . *CLANG* . . . bunk. The automatic mechanism sighed and clicked, the side-wall folded down in a comforting grip of sponge-plastic, holding him safely. The steady clanging was far away, now. After a while it stopped. Strange forces and strains tugged him, physically and mentally. He broke through something inside, and went down into a hot darkness of shame and degradation. He wallowed in fear and humiliation until there was no more left of it, until it had all been boiled out of his system, leaving him dully indifferent.

Everything had gone, his interests and curiosities along with his fears and resentment, leaving him curiously lightheaded and uncaring. He was distantly aware that the ship had come alongside the orbital satellite, that various items of value were being unloaded, and that he was one of the items. In a far-off-way, that bit of information was almost amusing. If it had mattered, he would have laughed at it, as they waited for the shuttle-rocket to come fire-tailing up from the planet below and get them. He was still microscopically intrigued by the thought as he sat where Harper told him to, and watched, through a port, the surface of the planet reaching up to engulf him.

Willers had an angry red bruise along his left cheek-bone. That planet down there wasn't fleecy white clouds, after all, but a seething, mottled greenish-gray, like some gross glob of yeast. Harper was looking at him oddly. Willers was whispering, but Anthony could hear every word, as if his hearing had been tuned up to maximum response.

"I tell you, he's a hop. Nobody acts that way, normal. And you can see the glassy glitter in his eyes. Doped to the ear-lobes, I'll bet . . ."

Willers was obviously much taken with Martha. And why not? She was very attractive, even if she was . . . Anthony's thought-stream dried up, there. Harper was talking, now, like a tourist-guide, and by some freak of the mind, Anthony heard his "now" words laid over all the mixed-up snippets of information Harper had passed on, in odd moments, during the trip . . . the "then" words. Two streams of ideas, related and intertwined, yet distinct, just as brass, woodwind and strings combine to make one "sound" yet each is distinct.

Down there, under that writhing scum were three domes,

each a mile in diameter, fifteen miles apart from each other at the corners of an equilateral triangle. Each had capacity for one hundred "residents," in sybaritic comfort. And such was the freakish atmosphere and surface that, apart from arduous physical journeying from one to the other, there was no contact. Each dome was an island universe in itself. That was "Harper-strings," all sweet hormony. "Harper-brass" had sounded a somber note. The domes were under-com-plement. You could "buy in," if you had enough real money to purchase one threehundredth share of Bu-Bean. But you had to be the right "type," or you'd be wasting your money, and the right "types" were rare. Harper had not been able to define "type" as he used it, but he had mentioned a motto . . . a code . . . in Latin. *Sic utere tuo ut non alienum laedas*—"Be as free as you wish, just so long as you stop short of interference with others, or endanger-ing the general safety." It sounded rational enough.

"Harper-now" was all bright woodwind information. "That atmosphere . . . astronomers wrangled about it . . . probes gave contradictory answers . . . it remained a mystery un-til manned explorations were able to make physical checks. And then they discovered that it is not, in the usual sense, an atmosphere at all. It's alive!" Willers, and Martha, gave the appropriate gasps of wonder. Anthony listened.

"Yes, it is alive, in constant turbulence, apparently boil-ing. It's an ever-shifting sea of microscopic fungal spores. Mushroom soup, you might say. The fine spores ride up on thermals, reach sunlight. They grow, clump, multiply, become too heavy to go on floating. They sink down to the surface, just as endless masses of plankton sink into the sea, pro-viding food for fish life, on Earth. A steady, fine rain of food. And light, too. As you will see, it is not gloomy dark, down there, but glowing with light . . . bio-lumines-cense. And you will find, too, that it is hot, and damp, but quite breathable. In its own way, it's beautiful, what little we know . . ."

"Surely a lot *is* known, by now?" Willers interrupted.

"Hardly anything," Harper insisted. "In fifty years—a planet almost as big as Earth, and with those conditions—hardly anything is known. One small corner, only. Visibility is nil, except where there are trees. For some not-understood reason, the spore-mist avoids tree masses. Radio is useless, except for a crude unmodulated beacon-signal effect, which we use for markers only. Any kind of mobility is arduous. The surface is treacherous. Flying is out of the question. Venus is not hospitable, Mr. Willers. She yields her secrets grudgingly."

The view-ports darkened, now, increasing Anthony's sense of unreality. Harper's flow of information had come like pebbles tossed one at a time into a still pool, only where there should have been splashes, each pebble had melted and been absorbed without so much as a ripple. Now the interior of the shuttle-rocket was lit with a brassy glare like the prologue to a thunderstorm as the craft dipped into the swirling mist. An arabesque of golden yellow whipped past, shifting into pearly-blue, then angry red and pearly-blue again.

"Weird stuff," Harper muttered, over the whine of friction. "It's as if there were distinct colonies of various strains, clumping together . . . hence the shifting colors. That's just speculation, though. We don't really know. That's my point, Mr. Willers. It would take generations of biochemists just to study this atmosphere thoroughly."

It was like diving into an insane artist's palette, Anthony mused, presuming the artist had stirred all his pigments together with a fine frenzy, and then set fire to them. And it wasn't real, any of it. It was just a dodge, a trick to stir him out of his very comfortable disengagement, to get him interested, involved . . . and hurt. But he wasn't to be caught like that again.

Then there came the sudden giant squeeze of braking, the tug at the pit of his stomach, and a shudder through the fabric of the shuttle-ship. And then silence, and a leaden-white glare outside.

"Stay where you are," Harper commanded. "It will take a few moments to get the freight-cans clear. You will know when they open the passenger-hatch, because it will become very hot. Don't let it upset you too much; it won't be for long. When I give the word, be ready to follow me down and out, and stick close, in single file. Taylor, you'll follow me. Then Miss Merrill, and then you, Willers . . ."

The lid came off a giant seething cauldron, gushing odorous steam up through the hatch-way. Anthony felt his clothing sag and stick to him, in the space of one gasping breath. Then he was following Harper, feeling the spurt and drip of sweat from every pore, down a ladder, through an oblong hold in the mist, down a steep ramp, and on to a solid ground. First foot on Venus. It should have been a momentous thing, but all he could think of was the unbelievable heat, and the desperate need to keep Harper's blurred form within sight. Suddenly, darkness loomed up out of the steam . . . another hole in the gray . . . a glare of light, muffled noises, machinery, voices, Martha Merrill jostling him from behind . . . and then a heavy boom of power, and the first breath of comparative coolness.

"The worst is over," Harper said. "We are now within the double-wall of the dome. This is where we keep our outside transporters, and the machinery which maintains our internal atmosphere."

"These walls go all the way up?" Willers asked.

"No. This space is an anchor for the skin of the dome proper."

"Must be thick stuff, to cover a mile circle?"

Most of the mist had cleared, and there was a respectably cool breeze. Anthony saw Harper smiling, heard the satisfaction in his explaining voice.

"No, it's really quite thin. 'Dome' is a misleading term. Think of it as a huge bubble."

"Then what keeps it up?" Willers demanded.

"Just air-pressure." The words came from a squat, muscular man who had approached them out of the gloom. A hard, competent face, Anthony thought, with some of Harper's arrogance, plus a quick impatience. A hard, arrogant body, too, and red hair. This man wore only brief black shorts and soft sandals, and seemed to think that sufficient.

"Air-pressure?" Willers echoed. "But you'd want a hell of a pressure to hold up a bubble half a mile high. How do you breathe?"

"Think again," the stranger advised, with a grin that moved only his mouth. "One tenth of a pound per square inch is all. One tenth of a pound greater than the atmosphere outside. Doesn't sound much, but there are a lot of square inches on the underside of a hemisphere half a mile radius. Total effective pressure adds up to just under three hundred thousand tons. Bord, who are these people? Tourists?"

"Don't ask questions, Barney, not yet." Harper was terse.

He mentioned their names, introduced the stranger as Bernard Lyons, left it at that. To his guests, he said, "In a moment, we shall enter the dome. We call it Prime Base. For many years I have called it home. I want you to feel welcome. I hope your brief stay will be a pleasant one. But I want to warn you: We are not ordinary people, here, and our ways are not ordinary ways. Try to be patient; observe without comment, and save your questions for a later moment. Right now, the first person we want to see is M'Grath. You any idea where he is, Barney?"

"Central Assembly Hall, waiting for you. Where else? Ready to go, now?" Lyons moved across to a great oval door, put his hand on a lever.

"Yes, I think so. Just one more warning," Harper smiled. "It's cold, on the other side. We maintain the internal temperature at a steady twenty-five degrees. Centigrade, that is. Just under eight-five, Fahrenheit?"

"That's not exactly cold," Anthony said, critically, and was amazed at the indifference in his own voice. Harper smiled again.

"Compared with this," he said, "you'll think it chilly, at first." The door-mechanism thrummed, and Harper was right. Anthony shivered as the air-stream leached away the sweat from his body. Then he was shocked out of his indifference as bright sunlight streamed through the doorway. Sunlight, here? He moved forward, lifting his foot high over the lip of the door, and gawked at the sight. Behind him, and to right and left, a great wall of light swept up and away overhead into the "sky." But that was a soft glow, and the "sunlight" was higher still, ahead, and so bright that his eye held back from it. Before him, laid out serenely under the great canopy of light, was a scene that caught at his throat for just a moment.

It was a dream made real. Broad streets, spacious vistas, the gray and white dignity of Greek temples, Roman villas and gingerbread castles . . . all looking exactly as if they had just this minute been soaped, scrubbed and sprayed with perfume and pastel tints. For just one moment, he accepted it all at face value. Then a hard realism he had never before suspected within himself punctured the illusion, and he saw what was really there. Foamed concrete, tinted plastic, chrome and titanium and cunning design . . .

40

all run together into a magnificent fraud, an escape from the overpowering reality "outside."

"It must have cost a fortune," Martha breathed, and Harper shrugged, not displeased at the comment.

"We like it. We don't count cost, here. What we want, we get, even if we have to have it specially made and imported. The flowers, for instance, all come from Earth. Venus has no flowers."

"And the colored air?" Willers demanded. "You import that, too?"

"No. That's local. Residual traces of spore-mist that gets by the filters. We *could* get rid of it, but why bother? It does no harm and it's pretty. Barney, get a car."

Prompted by some instinct, Anthony looked over his shoulder, to the door they had just left. And he saw his first Greenies. A dozen of them, in threes, were bowed under the weight of a series of alloy cans, flat disc-shaped containers three feet across and a foot thick. Bare feet slapping the concrete, they labored to haul the cans to a waiting flat-car and stack them on it. In charge was a tall, towhaired man in a brief kilt, with a bored expression, and carrying a coiled whip. Anthony felt suddenly giddy, as he watched.

They were caricatures of men. Naked as animals, so emaciated that their bones threatened to rip the blotchy green skin, their sunken eyes were almost black, and glazed, without life. Wispy black hair patched their skulls, making them seem the more bony and bald. Their efforts to cooperate were clumsy and pitiful, but every time one stumbled, Anthony saw that hanging whip-arm twitch. As they completed their labor, and shambled away, he was able to let out the breath he had been holding. One of those . . . I'm one like that . . . the thought was a scream in his mind. He jerked away, bumped into Martha. Her face showed that she had seen.

"Weren't they awful?" she breathed. "I should be terrified for my life if I ran into one."

"I couldn't help overhearing," Harper put in. "Your fears are quite unnecessary, my dear. They're absolutely harmless. A problem, to us, but nothing for you to worry about." Another flat-car came sliding up, Lyons in control, and Harper waved them all aboard.

"Yes," he sighed, settling into a seat. "They're a problem. We can't keep them alive long enough to be able to train them to anything worthwhile. They won't eat anything we offer them, won't touch anything except sugar, and they go crazy for that. But they don't live long."

"Surely," Anthony was surprised again at his own voice, "surely they eat the famous beans, don't they. Why not feed them those?"

"Are you kidding?" Lyons demanded. "Talk about pearls before swine! We're here to collect and market the beans, not waste them as cattle-food."

"You might as well learn about our cars," Harper interrupted smoothly. "They are all like this, inside the domes. Our floor is aluminium-titanium alloy layered, underneath. The car is powered so that it rides on electro-magnetic fields. Barney, show them how to operate the controls."

The city opened out as they glided nearer. Anthony saw without seeing, his mind's eye full of shambling green monsters. The car sped on, came to a silent halt at the foot of a magnificent flight of white steps outside what was an idealized copy of a Greek temple. Anthony was struck, all at once, by the fact that there was no one about. Was it some special hour, for everyone to be indoors? What was the time, anyway . . . did they have time at all, here?

"We most certainly do," Harper turned, pointed upwards. "Look there. We are now directly under the centerpoint of the dome. Don't look directly at the 'sun,' but just a shade to one side." Up there, suspended in the void, was a ring of numerals around the central light. They glowed in golden fire, and a dark red arrow-head of flame pointed. "It's a projection, from the roof of the Central Hall, and can be seen from any point within the dome. We keep a twenty-four hour cycle, just like Earth. As you can see, it is just on nineteen forty-five."

"Is it always like this?" Martha asked. "No nighttime?"

"Sunset at eight-thirty," Lyons explained. "Pretty spectacular, it is. We have stars, and a moon, too. You'll see. Come on," he led them up the steps and on to a mighty pillared portico fit for a Caesar.

"Where is everybody?" Willers demanded. Harper smiled grimly.

"They will all be sitting beside their visor-screens, eager

42

to see just what I've brought them from Earth. They are due for a surprise."

"Not just them!" Lyons said, pointedly, and Anthony felt the first small itch of wonder. Harper's single-minded self-assurance was now giving way to nervous tension. The moments ahead were obviously going to be crucial to his scheme, whatever it was. Wondering, Anthony let himself be led along mighty corridors, where all the walls were frescoed, or hung with tapestry and pictures, where there was not a nook or corner but what had a carving of some kind to enhance it. Some of the more famous items he was able to recognize, but most were strange to him. He "guessed" that they were all valuable, and was mildly shaken as Harper halted long enough to explain.

"Reproductions only," he said, waving one hand in an embracing gesture. "We are not squirrels, here. We have them for their intrinsic beauty, not their rarity value, whatever that may be."

They came to the central chamber, a great amphitheatre where tiered seats ran down to a circular space of a hundred feet across. It would have been a fit setting for an empire-shaking debate, or a circus, but was almost vacant now. A great glass-topped table took up only a fraction of the area. A man sat there, quite still, waiting.

"There's M'Grath, now," Harper made for a gangway, was almost running. Anthony felt that sense of urgency grow as he trod down the incline, saw the waiting man put his hand on an instrument-console. Lights glowed, and there were cameras, all pointing into that area. Harper had said "they" would be watching.

The man at the table stood up, impressively. In every sense of the word, he was huge. The top of his completely bald head was six foot three from the ground, and massive, merging without appreciable neck into broad shoulders. From there a loose toga-like garment hung, in capacious folds swelling out over a bulging belly.

"Welcome home, Borden," he said, in a carefully level voice. "You, and your guests."

"Dr. M'Grath . . ." Harper gestured, "Miss Martha Merrill, Austin Willers, Anthony Taylor."

"I'm fat!" M'Grath said, forthrightly. "I say it to save you the embarrassment. I am fat, by choice. It is my way of
43

emphasizing the fact that I am an individual. I ask you, now, to sit, so that I may sit also."

"Dr. M'Grath is our father-confessor, spiritual guide and general wailing-wall," Harper supplied. "More accurately, our resident psychiatrist."

M'Grath shifted his eyes only. "That explains me to them," he said. "I'm waiting to hear you explain them to me."

"You're the psychiatrist," Harper retorted. "You deal in explanations. I'd rather show, by actions. That way, there can't be any argument."

"Get to the point, Borden. Why have you brought these people here?"

"Let me do it my way, M'Grath. I've had a shock. I'm going to pass it on to you, but I want to prepare you, first. Listen, I've been back to Earth. Nothing's changed, except for the worse. I'm glad to be home again. Get that clear. But . . ." Harper paused, and Anthony wondered just what he was struggling with. "It came by accident. In a cheap smoke-and-spit dive in New York, I heard this man, Willers, doing an impression . . . he was imitating an Italian-type singer, for a gag-routine. In his own words, he has a trick voice and a trick memory. I put him on provisional notice . . . for me . . . because he had given me a hell of a turn. Later, in London, it happened all over again. I heard this girl, a hopeful from the Australian outback, trying to sell herself as a singer, a soprano. I couldn't get her alone at that time, so I followed her, and she led me direct to this man . . . and I heard him playing a piano. And that was enough. I knew what I had to do. I rounded up the three of them, and here they are."

"That much is evident," M'Grath sighed. He leveled his eyes on the guests. Anthony thought he looked like a man carrying a world on his back. "I should explain," he said, carefully, "that Borden Harper is *not* musical. Most of us are, here."

"They heard Ricco singing, and Milly Ko playing, as we came by," Lyons offered. M'Grath sighed again.

"We have a plentitude of singers, of both sexes, and all the pianists we need, already. Borden . . . why did you bring these people?"

"Let's start with you," Harper said deliberately. "You're a pianist, aren't you? As good as any, wouldn't you say?"

"I appreciate your respect for my modesty. Yes, I play. I make no claim to entertain. I play for my pleasure, the kind of music your man here will scarcely have heard of . . . nor would respect if he heard it. I fear you've made a gross error, Borden, if you think I am about to change my tastes."

"You're going to change your mind, though. M'Grath, your piano-playing stinks! Now tell me again that I'm not musical, and I don't know what I'm talking about . . . and then I'll have Mr. Taylor, here, *show* you!"

M'Grath sat quite still, breathing slowly. Then he stirred and one finger beat a slow tap-tap-tap on the table top. "There must be some reason for this personal animus, this attack without provocation."

"Medicine isn't supposed to be pleasant," Harper snapped. "But if it's any good, it should work on everybody. If you're scared to try it, say so, but don't twist it into my problem. It's yours. I'm not attacking you, as a person. I'm challenging your standards. At least, Taylor will do it for me. You understand, Taylor?"

"Yes," Anthony nodded, beginning to catch something of what Harper was trying to do. "I think so . . . but where's the piano? I'm not playing that one we heard, just now."

"Why not?" M'Grath asked, with ponderous gentleness. "Isn't it the kind of piano you're familiar with?" Anthony looked him full in the eye, with a strange belligerence.

"You may like playing a piano out of tune. I don't."

"Out of tune? Oh, fiddle-faddle! An excuse . . ."

"Out of tune!" Anthony said flatly, and M'Grath stared. "Indeed!" he said, with an edge to his voice. "This nonsense has gone far enough. Come!" He got to his feet with surprising speed, and swept off in an imperious flutter of trailing robes. This gangway led down and aside, into an ante-chamber, a broad room lined with shelves stacked with tape-spools. In one corner was a visor-screen, looking out into the room. Anthony's eye went to the opposite corner, at once.

"I call this my study," M'Grath said. "And this is *my* piano. Now . . . sir, tell me *that* is out of tune!"

Anthony eyed it with respect. Another Steinway, and a thing of rare beauty, in his eyes. But when he spread a hand, struck a chord, his teeth clicked. He tried another, and shook his head, ruefully.

"Can't you hear it?" he demanded. "Listen . . ." and he struck a single key. "There are three strings, there, all singing together. And arguing . . . can't you hear that?" M'Grath pulled heavy eyebrows down, suspiciously.

"No, I can't. You'll have to be more objective than that."

"That's a start," Harper said. "Go ahead, Taylor. Tune the thing." Anthony groped in the pocket of the fine suit Harper's money had bought for him on Earth, produced the key and damping probe, sat himself at the keyboard. Half of him was keen to minister to the abused instrument, but the other half was confused. Whatever design Harper had in mind was between him and this huge man, and he, Anthony Taylor, was involved merely as an instrument, an extension of the piano itself. That felt wrong. Anthony put the feeling aside, reluctantly, set to work on the strings. Soon engrossed, he could not have said how long it was before he finally looked up in satisfaction, to see an idiot-eye watching him. Cringing from it, he saw another. Cameras had been silently wheeled in, and were now aimed on him, and they were alive. All his habitual hiding reactions stirred him to scramble to his feet and back away.

"All set?" Harper asked, making Anthony whirl, defensively, and then nod, unwilling to trust his voice.

"You are quite satisfied that the instrument is in tune?" M'Grath strode forward, ponderously. "You won't mind if I try it? After all, it is *my* piano!" His open sarcasm was underlined as he rounded the seat and lowered himself without waiting for comment. Anthony watched, fascinated, as he threw back the folds of his robe from his massive forearms, advanced his fingers to the keyboard, and began to play. The room filled with a wild and furious clamor, out of which a melody was barely discernible. Anthony could hardly credit his ears. The fat man was working hard, was intent, his jowly face set in stern concentration. Either he was a consummate actor, or he was under the illusion that he was performing magnificently. Anthony's sense of wrongness grew to an ache as M'Grath brought the piece to its crashing conclusion, sat for a still moment, then looked up.

"Well . . . I won't embarrass you by asking for an opinion, Mr. Taylor, on a piece that you could hardly be expected to know . . ."

"I recognized it," Anthony interrupted, confusion making his voice louder than intended. "You were trying to play a Chopin Etude, one that used to be called the 'Revolutionary Study,' but . . ."

"Trying to play!"

"Look, there's something wrong, here. You don't understand . . ."

"I understand this much," M'Grath thrust out his huge head, angrily. "You have gone beyond the point of excuse. 'Trying' to play, indeed! I yield the instrument to you, sir. Perform!"

"In front of these?" Anthony indicated the goggling cameras. "With all your friends watching. You don't know . . ."

"Perform!" M'Grath thundered. "I cannot imagine what insane scheme Borden had in mind when he brought you here, but it stops, right now, until you have done your worst. And then . . ." he bent a cold eye on Harper. That worthy was grim-faced.

"You go ahead, Taylor," he ordered. "This is why you're here. Go on, play, and leave the rest to me."

Anthony sat, put his fingers silently on the keys, and made a conscious effort to discharge the confusions and chaos in his mind, to replace them with the "mood" of the impassioned exiled patriot, angrily lamenting the sufferings of his homeland . . . and the parallel struck him, all at once. Here he was, a Greenie masquerading as a human, among humans . . . here on his native planet, his home, yet barriered off from it far more savagely than Chopin had even been from Poland. The complex chemistry of frustration, fear and fury flowed from his brain, infusing the music-patterns with new fire. He began to play, savagely, with needle-pointed precision, every note a blow of defiance, every thundering harmonic a blast of anger, the strains and shocks of the past days bursting out of their confinement and shaking him with the fury of their release. So thoroughly did he lose himself in his outburst that he was wet and breathless by the time he reached the end, and it was several seconds before he could establish a clear contact with his surroundings. Then, deflatedly, he looked up, at M'Grath.

The big man stood absolutely still, like an idol. So complete was the blank shock on his face that Anthony half-expected to see him totter and fall. Then a great shudder shook that giant frame, and tears came into those flint-gray eyes. M'Grath sighed, a painful sobbing sigh, put up a hand to his face, shuddered again, and looked down to where Anthony sat.

"My God!" he breathed. Then he swung on Harper. "You damned amateur," he said, harshly, "that wasn't therapy. It was surgery. Brutal!"

"But effective, you have to admit that."

"Not if the patient dies, you fool! I'm not thinking of myself, now. I'm thinking of . . ." He made a sudden dart, moving surprisingly fast for one of his bulk, to shut off the cameras. "The damage is probably done, by this time, but we can, at least, spare them the discussion . . ."

Anthony had risen by this time, driven by something which clamored for expression. "It's all right for you two," he said, stumbling over his words in his efforts to express his humiliation. "You know what this is all about. It's some sort of experiment, for you. But what about me? What about us?" He thought, belatedly, of Martha, and Willers, who were standing by, agape and lost. "We're not just animals, you know, to do tricks for your amusement," M'Grath twisted his head sideways, sneering.

"You! I can't be bothered with you just now. Later, perhaps, you shall have your explanation. And your chance to perform. Harper, am I to understand you right? Have our internal faculties become so deformed, so ingrown, that we can't see our poverty? Is that . . . ?" He broke off and swung his heavy head at Lyons, impatiently.

"Barney, make yourself useful, can't you? Get them out of here. Take them away. Entertain them, anything so long as you get them out of my sight."

Mr. Lyons shoved himself away from a wall where he had been leaning, and nodded, cheerfully. "You know," he said, "I'm no music-lover. It's all just a pleasant noise, to me. But I've heard you play that piece a dozen times, and that's the first time I ever knew it had a tune to it!"

"*That* point has already been made, effectively," M'Grath said, in chill tones. "I am still suffering from the demonstration. I must ask that you take that as an excuse for my poor manners," he swept the guests with an inclusive eye. "Please leave us. Go with Mr. Lyons."

"Did something go wrong?" Willers demanded, as Lyons escorted them back into the amphitheatre-space. "What's this all about, anyway?"

"Don't ask me. Musically, I'm a moron. Me, Bord Harper, and one or two more. Just about everybody else either plays a piano, or sings, or both, but I will say this. I never heard a piano talk like that, before."

"You say everyone plays, or sings?" Anthony caught at that. He had grasped, vaguely, that Harper was exposing M'Grath's conceit, letting the fat man learn, the hard way, that his talent was shoddy. There was, also, the implication that this exposure was taking place before an involved and critical audience. Hence the brutality. But if that whole audience was in the same state of fog as M'Grath, the brutality and the shock would be multiplied. He began to sweat. M'Grath was a psychologist. He was tough. Yet the shock had squeezed tears from him. What might it have done to the others, that unseen audience? What had Harper done?

"I'm scared!" Martha said. "There's something weird about this place. Why is everybody hiding from us? Do we have a plague or something?"

As if it had been a cue, they heard the rapid clatter of feet and a petite, black-haired girl came running down a ramp from the outside upper level. She wore black loose trousers and a brief, unfastened bolero which fluttered in the wind of her hurrying enough to show that there was nothing else underneath. The black stuff was heavily ornamented in gold thread, and her box-cut black hair was held with a single gold band. There was just the suspicion of a slant to her jet-black eyes as she stared at Anthony.

"I'm Milly Ko," she said, breathlessly, "and I want *you!*"

"I don't understand," Anthony hesitated, looking from her to Lyons. "I haven't fixed up anywhere to stay, yet. I don't know what arrangements Mr. Harper has in mind."

"It's all right," Lyons assured, with a grin. "Milly won't eat you. We keep pretty much open house, here. We can always find you, if we want you for something special."

"My hospitality," Milly said, briskly, "is all yours. You can have anything you want. Just ask. But I want you to come and fix my piano the way you did M'Grath's, and then . . . then I want you to play that Etude again, for me. Will you?"

"I suppose so."

"All right. Come on!" She took his arm and he had to step out to keep pace with her hurry. "You have bags, luggage?"

"Nothing at all," he confessed.

"You won't go back empty-handed, anyway," she told him. "That much is certain. I can see what Borden meant by medicine. As soon as the rest of them have swallowed it they won't be able to do enough for you." She steered him almost at a trot along the corridors and out on the steps. "The other two . . . do they play?"

"Singers," he mumbled. "She's a soprano, he's a tenor."

"That Harper! If they are up to your standard, mister, this little dead-and-alive dome is due to erupt."

At the foot of the steps she hustled him aboard a smaller car and sat beside him, seizing the control-bar. At once the car shot away and spun round, narrowly avoiding two more which were converging on the steps.

"Vultures!" she muttered, putting on a broad smile and sending a mocking wave to a blonde girl in one of the cars. "That's Hilda Craven. A soprano, really, but she likes to fancy herself as a pianist. I'll bet she is livid at missing you."

"Is that right you're all musical amateurs?"

"Amateurs! Yes, I suppose we deserve that, now that you're here. Yes, just about everybody plays, and-or sings. My God, what else is there? We've painted all the pictures, carved all the statues, read and written all the books, played all the games. We swim, we exercise, we compete, we argue, but we know all the answers. We know each other, inside out. There's very little point in anything, any more." The furious rush of the car whipped her bolero out behind her. Her skin was silky smooth, her body lithe, her breasts pointed and as forthright as her manner. Anthony shrank from her, just an inch or two, and she noticed it.

"There's sex, too," she said. "Even that gets stale, especially here. We have no taboos about dress, or chastity, or who sleeps with whom. But it doesn't seem to work.

50

When you can have everything you want, you don't want anything bad enough to bother."

"Everything?"

"Anything and everything," she said, wryly. "It sounds like Heaven . . . but it works out more like the other place. There's no thrill of achievement, any more, when you can have anything you want, just by wanting. That's why we all turn to music. Not listening to it, but doing it . . . because it needs effort to make your own, and it's never done, never stale."

"That's because you have to put something of yourself into it," he said, and she gave him a quick side-glance. Her expression baffled him, and he suddenly realized it was getting dark. Overhead, the "sunlight" had almost gone, giving way to a silver glow that conveyed a sense of coolness. The red time-arrow stood at twenty-one. Nine P.M.

"We're here," she said, bringing the car to a stop outside a house that was as subtly Japanese as herself in its slant lines and planes. He followed her indoors. "Plenty of rooms," she made sweeping gestures. "Take whatever one you fancy. There's a shower-room at the end of this passage. There'll be a meal ready in about half an hour. Any food fads?"

"Hardly . . . except that I don't take sugar, or alcohol. Please don't go to a lot of trouble."

"It's no trouble." She twisted out of her bolero, threw it aside, then stepped out of her trousers and threw them after the bolero. Then she stepped to a wall, picked a kimono from a hook, slung it over her arm, turned to him, and then noticed his strained expression. "That's something else you'll have to get used to," she said easily. "We don't bother much with clothes, here. They're a damned nuisance, mostly, and what's the point of covering up, when there's no weather, or indulging in status-symbols, when everybody is on the same level?"

She led him into a side-passage. "I'm going to shower, and then make a call or two, to see how the others are taking it. The piano, *my* piano, is this way." They came to a bigger room. "There it is, and I'm ashamed of it, now. To think that M'Grath has the only in-tune piano on Venus!"

"I don't understand that bit." He touched a key or two, winced at the jangle, and turned to her. "Surely you have

51

pitch-pipes, tuning-forks or any one of a dozen other ways of getting a standard to go by?"

"You *don't* understand, do you?" She shook her head. There was an odd, almost insane glitter in her eyes and anger in the set of her slim body as she stared at him. "We are the Venus Colony." There were capitals in her tone. "We are the richest, the bestest, the most exclusive club there ever has been. Such things as tuning forks, and adjustments are for slobs, for people with humility, people who can conceive of being wrong. Not us!" The savagery in her voice made him shiver. She was baring herself before him in more than body, masochistically exposing the flaws in her values, rending the whole synthetic fabric of the community before his eyes.

He was still uneasy about it as he stood under the shower, with cool, clean water cascading over him, and tried to imagine what it was like for a person to believe himself a skillful, talented musician, and suddenly to find that he is a fumbling ignorant amateur. He saw again the shock it had been for M'Grath, multiplied that by a potential hundred, expanded it into the basis of a whole ethic, for an entire closed colony of people, imagined it suddenly shattered . . . and his mind boggled at the result. He was so engrossed in the size of the problem that he had been rubbing and scratching at a persistent itch for about five minutes before it penetrated his awareness. Then, with a start of sick horror, he realized he was itching all over. He froze, under the stinging spray. The time! How had he missed *that?*

The time, here, was purely arbitrary. How long since he had taken his anti-tan tablet? No way of knowing, at all. He shut the shower off, roughly, seized a towel, went slopping out in search of the room where he had left his clothes.

The itch was painful, now, but it didn't show. He stared at his arms, legs, shoulders, as far as he could see, just to make sure. It didn't show, yet. But he had to have anti-tan, and soon. Martha Merrill! The idea came like deliverance, until he thought it further. *If* she would admit to having any. *If* she had any to spare. And she would run short, too, eventually.

He got to his feet, dried himself, slid into his jacket and

52

pants and shoes, feeling that dreadful mental fuzziness creeping up on him again. The smell of food touched his nostrils. He followed it, along a corridor and into a big quiet room, austere in Oriental simplicity. Three steps inside the door, he stopped. Milly Ko was there, wrapped in a loose green robe and squatting at a low table. Opposite her sat a little man in a black formal suit, with a white collar and string tie. But what caught Anthony's breath was the slim green girl who stood by Milly's side, as still as a graven image in emerald. Naked as a statue, and as beautiful . . . and as empty of life, her eyes like purple jewels, staring at nothing. On his entry, Milly put out a hand, touched the green girl on the thigh with a dismissing gesture. She moved, silent on bare feet, went away.

"You're in time," Milly said, waving. "Sit and eat."

"That green girl," he said, sinking to his knees where she pointed, "you have her as a servant?"

"Hardly. No, I just like having them around, like ornaments. They're pretty, when they're fresh-caught."

"How long—how long do they last?"

"Oh, about a week. You can't feed them, you see. Our food doesn't attract them. Just water, and a little sugar once a day, and they stay." She took a bowl, of wafer-thin china, ladled green steaming stuff into it, passing it across, and he stared at it, suspiciously.

"Is this . . . ?"

"Bean soup? That's right. This must be the one place in the Universe where bean-soup is a prize delicacy. It is, too. That bowlful, back on Earth, would cost you a mint. Try it, you'll never have the chance again, once you leave here."

He tasted, swallowed, and was disappointed. It was indistinguishable from thick bean-soup anywhere. He took a second mouthful, and warmth seemed to explode in his stomach, in a glow that burned all the way out to the tips of his fingers and toes. Then, like a convulsion, sweat burst out on him from every pore.

"There!" she laughed. "That's the way it hits everybody, the first time. We don't often have guests, but I've watched that happen to them over and over. It just shows what an awful state your metabolism is in."

She took up her own bowl and began spooning. He watched her, and hot bitterness swelled up to his tongue.

53

"For this, you hold the whole of Earth to ransom . . . so that your metabolism can benefit?"

"That is naïve saying." The retort came in a flat snap from Mr. Ko, who did not bother to turn his head. "Beans, like diamonds, have scarcity value only. Too many would destroy market."

"But they are *not* diamonds, they're food, and medicine. If they were plentiful, and cheap, that would benefit everybody."

"Fallacious argument. Please think. Large production not possible, without large expense. But even child can see it is not economic to spend much money in order to make product cheap. Also, bean diet increases life expectancy. On large scale, would destroy Earth economy in many ways. So, shortage is maintained, not by us, but by orders from Earth. We obey, they leave us alone."

"You mean Earth dictates your policy?"

"That's right," Milly put in. "Hari is our economic expert, and I can't explain things the way he could, but it's simple enough. We produce. Earth is the market. God, what would *we* do with beans, if we couldn't sell the things?"

It was one more element to add to his confusion, his sense of utter helplessness, of being in the grip of forces he couldn't control. An animal. A pawn in some game. A nobody. Until Milly led him back to her piano and sat him there.

"Poor man," she said, wryly. "You're lost, aren't you, with all this business? But this is where you shine. This you *can* do."

He ran his fingers over the keys, detecting the dissonances, feeling for his tuning-key, setting to work to correct the jangles. On a different level, there was quite a lot in his own mind which needed remedying. His fingers found and began to play, softly, an intricately delicate piece, the while he seemed to stand a long way off and look at himself, curiously. He had been shocked, shaken, terrified . . . purged. What was left? The fear was almost gone, and most of the anger with it. He had gained a kind of numbness. Was there anything else, under that apathy? He thought there was. There was a smouldering resistance, a stubborn conviction that he was not to be broken. Somehow, he didn't know how,

54

he was going to hit back, he was going to *be* something more than just a freak talent, a hired performer.

"What's that you're playing?" Milly asked, and he came back to the presently real with a rush. "Bach, isn't it?"

"That's right. A partita, in B flat major. You know it?"

"Never like that. Bach, to me, has always been a perversely difficult and complicated exercise-maker . . . but that, like that, is music. It sings." A distant chime caught her ear, and she clicked her tongue in irritation, went away. In moments she was back, and he hushed his playing at sight of her face. She was angry, and looked all Japanese.

"Harper is going to throw you to the wolves," she said. "He has laid on a snap concert, in half an hour, in the Central. All three of you."

"So?" Anthony failed to see her reason for anger, yet.

"Don't you see? The others have been getting at him. They won't have it that they are inferior, that their standards have slipped. I know how they feel. I didn't like it, either, but I'm a bit more of a realist than most. I know that we have become a sick, perverted in-group, living in a sugary illusion. I didn't know just how bad we were until I heard you, I'll admit that. But the rest of them aren't going to admit it at all. They want to put you three on a platform, and ask you to perform. They'll toss requests at you, at random . . . and God help you if you fail to identify the pieces, and perform them perfectly."

"Violence?" he asked, and she snorted.

"Nothing so crude. But they'll call you out on stuff you've never even heard of, and then laugh you off the platform."

"I don't know whether you're pleased or sorry," he said, studying her. It was hard to tell. She was bubbling with excitement of some kind, but he had no idea just what. For a moment he had the clear conviction that any drastic, dramatic event would attract these strangely out-of-touch people. "Anyway," he got up, towering over her, "I doubt they'll be able to trip me, and if the others have had experiences like mine, the same goes for them." Behind his statement lay miserable years of playing old broken-down pianos in all kinds of hole-and-corner dives, where there were always two or three bleary-eyed individuals who could recall happier days. "I've been asked for some pretty rare pieces, at times. I'm ready, when you like."

55

"You're a strange man, Anthony," she stared up into his face. "You seem dazed and lost, most of the time, as if you were afraid, almost, but as soon as it's music, you change."

"It's the one thing I know. Are you ready?"

The sense of desperate confidence remained with him all the way to the Central Assembly Palace, not wavering even when he saw the incredibly motley throng which was rapidly gathering. The one thing they had in common, apart from lean health, was the urge to be different. Less than half of them had troubled to wear any clothing at all, and those who had were only half-clothed, or less. His eyes saw, but did not believe. A top-hat, there . . . and another. Scarf and sandals. A fez. A loincloth. Sweatshirt and slacks. An embroidered cloak and high boots alongside bare feet. A nun's habit in shrieking scarlet nodded to a high-school tunic in paper-white transparent veiling. A baby-faced blonde in long black gloves and lorgnette, and nothing else, alongside a man in a violently checked shirt and bowler.

"It could be that Harper's therapy is more effective than mine." He whirled as M'Grath boomed in his ear. "It is sometimes better to cut the knot than to save the string by carefully unraveling it. The cup which cheers is not for you I believe, Mr. Taylor?"

Anthony caught the blast of his breath and shook his head. "No . . . I don't need it," he said. M'Grath took a hearty pull at the pot he held.

"Quite right," he said. "I do. I know what can happen, very soon. It is my duty to bear the slings and arrows of the outraged less-fortunate, but never before have I gone in actual fear. We have anarchy here, Taylor, and there is but a hair-line between that and insanity. Man needs the prop and comfort of others of like mind. You are about to kick that prop away."

"The trouble with this lot," Harper had come up from the other side and was leaning across the piano, "is that they started in at the top, and never had anywhere to go but down."

"I knew it!" M'Grath growled. "You're a saboteur, Borden. You're a self-made man. You hate those who have always had what you had to work for. So you want to smash it all, and just before Harvest, too."

"How close?" Harper demanded. "I've lost track."

"You'll be lucky to last out the hour with your concert."

"Harvest?" Anthony asked, and M'Grath swung on him, waving the pot.

"The gathering of the bean-crop. The time when we justify our existence, Mr. Taylor. A form of catharsis on which we have been relying to preserve our sanity, so far. It has been all the medicine we ever needed."

"You're a kind of doctor, aren't you?" Anthony asked, as his itch nudged him. "You would know . . ." but he had lost M'Grath, now. The big man was waving to Willers and Martha as they made their way down to the central arena. Aside, he said, "Those in brown coveralls, out to the edges, are the off-duty technicians. I had hoped we would be spared humiliation before them. Ah well, we might as well begin." He put up a massive palm for quiet.

"There is no prepared programme. You call it, our guests will try to deliver. What do I hear?"

Anthony sat himself, and Willers came close, to bend over, calling Martha with a jerk of his head. "This is a snap," he whispered. "I've done this a million times. You get a lot of shouting, and you pick out the ones you know. Nothing to it. All right?"

Anthony looked up at him, saw that his anxious look was completely gone, now. For the first time, he felt a kinship with this gangling American. Martha, too, looked ready for anything. The mood was catching. He smiled back at them. "I'll start, then," he said, and stood up to move and stand beside M'Grath. Out of the crowd came a shout of "Scriabin," and he pin-pointed the source, fingered the man who had called, asked him to specify. A tall man in a wild red robe.

"*Flammes Sombre* . . . if you've ever heard of it!"

Anthony nodded, bowed cordially, moved back to the keyboard. It was good start. Tension came into the audience, and utter silence, as he used a moment to think himself into the mood for this darkly exciting piece of complex polymetric polyrhythm . . . allegretto, with the treble in six-eight, against the bass in two-four . . . and he began, carefully, confidently and with jewel-like precision. His conclusion brought an explosive "Bravo!" from the rapt audience. M'Grath was wrong, Anthony thought. It is primitive rhythm which drives men mad. Music, real music, has

57

charms above the primitive. He wondered if it was an original thought. Martha stepped forward, managed to catch a request for something from *Lucia di Lammermoor,* and he nodded, gave her the introduction. She had absorbed the magic of the moment, too. All her life went into her creation of the woman driven mad by the knowledge that she was expected to marry a man she didn't love . . . and that she had just come from stabbing him to death rather than agree.

Moved as he was by her performance, Anthony couldn't help noticing the sheen of sweat on her face and arms, the more than fervor she put into the music, and a horrible suspicion sneaked into his mind. It festered while Willers felt for and got a demand to produce . . . it would be Ricco Milano, of course . . . the famous lament from *Pagliacci.* Then, as the lanky American was tearing at their heart-strings, a strange rustle spread through the throng, a whisper, and then a mass exodus, on shuffling feet.

"Well I'm damned!" Willers gasped, as he finished. "I never had an audience do that to me before." M'Grath surged forward, heavily unsteady.

"No criticism of you, sir," he mumbled. "The Harvest came sooner than expected. This is the time when we sally forth and garner the products of our industry. This is the one moment not one of us would miss."

"I see. You collect the beans, eh? I'd like to witness that. It will be something to brag about. Can I?"

"Of course, but be quick. Join up with anyone."

"Aren't you going?" Anthony demanded, reaching for Martha's arm, but his question was for M'Grath. "Do you, too, need this catharsis?"

"More than any. Yes, I shall go, as soon as I can shake off this bleariness. I have methods. Excuse me . . ."

"Just a minute," Anthony still held Martha's wrist. "You're the doctor, the medicine man. Can you do something for me?" M'Grath looked a heavy-eyed question at him, and he gathered his courage. "I have an itch . . . very bad . . . all over." He felt the sudden twitch in Martha's arm, and knew he had guessed right. "It's nothing to worry about. I know what will fix it, if you can get it for me."

"I have a fairly well stocked medicine chest," M'Grath

nodded, heavily. "I may be able, if it's not too unusual. You know the cause, you say?"

"No, I didn't say that. I know what will fix it. Anti-tan. Can you get me some?" Again Martha's wrist jerked, and she pulled loose. Anthony did not dare look her in the face. He kept his eyes on M'Grath, who was dully silent for a long moment. Alcohol warred with his intelligence.

"Anti-tan? You want me to supply you with anti-tan? I'm afraid that's one drug we neither keep nor have any use for, here. It is all we can do to maintain pinkness, with artificial ultraviolet. We don't need it, you see . . ." His thick voice faded away into mumbling as his wits began to churn. He stared at Anthony, and the light of comprehension grew. With it came an unpleasant hardness. "You—you *need* anti-tan? You're—"

"Never mind what I am. You won't give us any, then?"

"Both of you? Indeed!" M'Grath drew himself up, unsteadily, to his full height. "We have none, and that is the truth. I'm sorry . . . sorry for the pair of you. You hear me? I say I'm sorry!" Try as he might, he couldn't make his voice sound sorry, and, as he swung around and lurched away, his shoulders shook . . . but not with regret. An enemy, Anthony thought, in sinking despair. This will give him payment for humiliation. But what do we do, now? He turned to Martha, met her blazing eyes.

"You have your nerve!" she hissed. "How dare you tell him . . . let him think that, about me? Now he thinks I'm —I'm a Negro, and so do you!"

"No I don't" he said, grimly. "I don't think anything of the kind. But you itch, just as I do. And you take . . . and need . . . anti-tan. How long since you had any? How long? Look, there's no point, any more, in trying to pretend. How long since you last took a tablet!"

"I don't know," she wailed. "I've lost track of the time, in this mad place. I've lost mine, or mislaid it somewhere. I'm always losing it, or running short and having to make a mad dash to the nearest drugstore. And I couldn't ask anybody, could I? Now everybody will know!"

"How long since you first started to itch?" he pressed her, as they made their way restlessly out of the great hall.

"I don't know. It started, I think, when we were getting off the ship, but I thought it was just the heat . . . and then

59

it kept on. What am I going to do?" Her voice was ragged, now, as full realization crept over her. "What am I going to do?"

"What are *we* going to do?" he rephrased it, and she looked at him, her violet eyes wide and unseeing. She would have to be told, he thought. The truth, which was a thousand times worse than the fears she had now . . . but how to tell her? He caught her arm, suddenly, drew her aside into a room lined with glass cases.

"Tell me," he said, urgently, "just who do you think your parents were? Do you know?" As she hesitated, he pushed the question a bit closer to home. "Did either of them have anything to do with . . . Venus?"

"With Venus?" she was startled out of her shakes, for a moment. "What on Earth are you talking about?"

"You believe either your father or your mother was colored —was dark-skinned, don't you?"

"Must we discuss it? All right, if you must have it, yes. It was my father. I don't know anything about him. Mummy would never talk, she just wouldn't tell me. There! Satisfied? Not but what everybody will know, soon." He had turned away from her, combing his mind for some set of words that would break the truth to her gently. He had read a line on a metal plate three times before it clicked. He looked around, at the others, in dawning comprehension. This was a Hall of Records, of a kind. The metal plates were dated, carried lists of names. He caught her wrist again.

"There ought to be something here," he muttered, reasoning out the sequence, doing simple arithmetic in his mind. Names, honorable degrees in any science you cared to name . . . and so many of them bore the final notice, "L P D"— "Lost, Presumed Dead." A history of Man's struggle to win Venus, all here in memoriam.

"What are you up to, now?" she demanded, angrily.

"You're not colored," he said, abruptly. "No more than I am. At least, not the way you think. Not any color you'd ever imagine."

"Have you gone stark raving mad?"

"I think not!" He was peering at the cases, quickly, until he found the one he wanted, that he knew *had* to be. Then he halted, turned to look at her, and caught his breath.

60

For the concert, she had chosen a scarlet cape, and the briefest possible skirt in the same color. Against the vivid flame, there could be no mistake. He looked away, at the wall, saw a great mirror.

"I'm not crazy," he said. "Come and see for yourself. Come on!"

He took her by the shoulder, more roughly than he intended, thrust her face to face with the mirror and stood behind her. "See for yourself . . . you're green!"

He watched her, saw her face go blank with shock. Her hand went to her face, shakily, and then to the soft curves of her shoulder and throat.

"Oh no! It can't be. There must be some mistake!"

"No mistake. You're a Greenie, a half-breed Greenie, just as I am."

"It's not true. It's a joke of some kind, something we've eaten," she stared at herself frantically. "It can't be. I don't want to be a Greenie . . . an animal . . . I'm not . . . I won't!" She fought him as he took her arm and led her back to the case where the all-important record was kept.

"Look there," he commanded, harshly, "and then argue." His finger led her eye to a line of graven script that read, laconically: *Dr. T.O. Merrill.* Following that there ran a string of degree credits and then the stark phrase: *Lost in jungle on study-tour; wife and baby daughter returned to Earth.*

"Baby daughter . . . you," Anthony said. "The date is about right, too, isn't it? Isn't it?" She stared, speechlessly, her lips moving as she read the cruel words over again. "You were born right here on Venus. And so was I. Look!" His finger moved, skipped lines, came to rest. *Dr. Eleanor Taylor . . . died in childbirth, in jungle. Dr. R.S. Taylor, husband, returned to Earth with infant son.*

"Infant son . . . me. Dr. Sherwood Taylor was my father. I've known, all the time, that I was a Greenie. That's why I didn't want to come."

She broke and whirled away from him, but he caught her in two steps. "Where will you run to?" he asked, harshly. "You're green, and getting greener every minute. You ran out of drugs a bit sooner than me, but I'll be right there with you in a short while. Greenies . . . both of us."

Her lips were purpling as he looked at her. So were
61

her nails. In an odd way, the green tint flooding to her skin made her more beautiful than she had ever been. But Green.

"Oh God!" she said, dully, "what are we going to do?"

PART TWO

"IF WE STAY," he said, suddenly ice-calm, "they'll come back, and find us . . . as Greenies. And you can guess what that will mean. The only other thing is to run for it."

"But where?" She gave back his own question. "Where can we go?"

"Out . . . out there in the jungle. It's our home, after all. This is our native land. If the other Greenies can live out there, we can!"

"But it's jungle! It's hot, and misty, and dangerous. We don't know anything about it. We'll get lost!"

"And we'll be torn to pieces if we stay, Martha. Already we have hit these people in the talent. What do you imagine they will do when they find out what we *really* are?" He could feel her sagging, as he gripped her arm.

"It's hopeless. We can't just run off into the jungle."

"All right!" He let her go with a quick twist of his hand, so that she almost fell. "You stay, and face them. I'm going. . . ."

"No! Anthony, don't leave me. Don't!"

"Make your choice, and be quick. Stay . . . or run with me."

She turned, her eyes sweeping the quiet room, seeking some solution to a thing that had none. He saw her catch a glimpse of herself in the mirror, and blanch at what she saw there. Her hands went to her breasts, and then she held them out, fingers spread, and stared at them as if they were new. But they were her own, and green.

62

"We don't seem to have any choice, do we?" she whispered, coming towards him. "We can't do anything else."

"None that I can see. All right, come on. Quick!" He led her out of the hall, and the temple. The city, so far as they could see, was deserted. "A car . . . there!" He pointed and ran, had it humming by the time she scrambled up by him. "Cover yourself as much as you can, with that cape, just in case we meet anyone." He set the car skimming, and after a false start, got himself pointed to one of the exit-gates. It was open, he saw, as they swooped close.

"All right, so far." He shut off the power and they got down. "But from here, we're afoot." He led her into the great open door, and the glare-lit compartment inside, made for the outer door, looking hastily for the controls. "Nobody about," he muttered, pressing a button, and jumping as the quick zoom of power came from behind him. Then he saw that the inner door was swinging shut, and cursed his nerves. Got to keep calm, he urged himself. No point in panic, not now. There's a whole world out there. Then he gasped, and heaved for breath, as the outer door cracked and the heat washed in. Martha gripped his arm, frantically.

"We can't go out there," she wailed. "It's dark . . . and hot. . . !"

"We haven't any choice!" he snarled, and put his foot over the coaming. She hung on to him. He turned, savagely. "Come on . . . or let go. . . !" He could see her eyes widen in panic, but she came, stepping high. Three paces from the door they might as well have been in a steam room. He went ahead, putting on a boldness he didn't feel, but as helpless as a blind man, sweat clogging his breath. Then, faintly through the dull white glare, he caught a hint of brightness.

"Searchlights!" he said, remembering the Harvest. "Over that way," and they began to tramp, cautiously, seeing the brightness grow. Then, little by little, it broke apart into several sources, into great milky shafts of light, hanging in mid-air. A great lemon-yellow pillar of fire grew out of the mist. A tree. Then there was another, rose-red glowing. The searchlight glares grew plainer, and they could hear yells, and laughter, and screams. He took her hand.

"We'd better be careful, now," he warned. "Take it very

63

easy." They edged forward, and came across the bulk of a car, then another, and circled past them. Now he was able to pick out ghostly figures, in the thinning mist, and he could see that they were ranged in orderly fashion, some six or seven feet apart, in between the glare-colums, but on the shaded side of the light. Gripping her hand tight, he moved closer, close enough to see what was going on. "We had better watch this," he muttered, "we might learn a trick or two." Over to the right there was a burst of laughter, the snap of a whip, and a hoarse scream.

Then he caught his breath as a trio of shambling green figures blundered out around the bole of a bright blue giant tree and into the glaring light. Each had cradled in skinny arms a treasure of bean pods. Faces contorted into blindness because of the light, they shambled forward, and a shadow went to meet them, became a white man, in black shorts, with a yellow plastic bag over one shoulder. He put out a rough hand to grab the nearest Greenie by a skinny shoulder, and used his other hand to snatch the pods and stuff them into his bag. The Greenie whimpered, went to pull away, but the man aimed a casual kick at those spindly legs, the Greenie howled and hopped, and the man went on with his plunder.

Anthony shifted his gaze to where a second shadow had moved out, intercepting another of the helpless trio. A female, this time, with a pod in her mouth, as well as fullarmed. The man, naked as Adam, slashed the edge of his hand across her throat, so that she gagged and disgorged. Then he, too, began to grab and stuff, while the dazed female stood, trying to swallow, and retching.

The third Greenie had taken fright, had turned to run back into the dark. Anthony groaned as he saw a third shadow step into the harsh glare. With only a twist of cloth about her loins, and a whip twirling in her hand, this was a blonde woman he had never seen before. Setting her feet apart, she brought her arm over, the lash licked out, and the Greenie screamed. Another lashing stroke caught its foot, and the blonde walked up the taut line, reversed the whip-handle, brought the stump-end down with a crack on that patchy-haired skull. Then, calmly, she collected the pods, for her bag.

"Get a good look," Anthony advised, savagely. "See how

64

they treat the Greenies . . . how they would treat us." He could feel Martha shivering, but he was steady. Indignation could wait. He fixed his attention on the bags. He meant to get one. They were valuable, even to the Greenies. "Wait here," he hissed, "until there's a full bag. Then *we* take it!"

"Why? They aren't worth anything, to us. Not now."

"The Greenies value them. We're going to have to live with Greenies, and like it." More shambling green figures broke from cover, and the Harvest went on. Anthony saw, with sick hate, that the blonde woman seemed fond of her whip, using it at every opportunity. Soon her bag was full.

"Now!" he said, giving Martha a shove. "Here she comes, loaded." His eyes followed her into the gloom. Then he was up to her, seeing her surprise, her quick gasp and attempt to shout, which died as he hit her, a smash on the jaw that jarred his hand and arm right up to the elbow. Ruin my fingering, he thought, crazily, if I were a piano-player any more. He stooped to grab her bag, heard a scuffle at his back and wheeled round. The man in black shorts had trapped Martha, was holding her close and peering. Anthony took two long steps, swung his arm, and lashed out again, enjoying the vicious pain of the blow, as the man sank down without a sound.

"You all right?" he demanded, flexing his fingers. She nodded, stupidly, looking down at the prostrate man. "All right, then. Grab his bag, quick!" He went back to the blonde woman shoved her over with his foot, got her bag, slung it over a shoulder, went to Martha, helped her to shoulder hers. "Now, come on . . . let's get away from here."

"But where?" she wailed, as he plunged off, turning his back on the glare. "Anthony. . . !" He slid, stumbled to one knee, got up again, waited, and she came up, out of the gloom. "I couldn't see you. . . ." she gasped. "Where are we going?"

"How do I know?" he snapped. "Who cares, anyway? We have a whole planet. We just go, and keep on going, that's all."

He took her hand, and they went forward together, slipping and staggering, into the slimy, greasy-wet inferno, into a multicolored nowhere.

Going nowhere. Nowhere to go. The words went round

and round in his mind. Just keep going. Keep going. Until you drop. And then, what? The glowing mist swirled, lazily, round him, ever changing, ever the same. Shreds of shifting color came and went, glowed and passed by, tempting the mind to build figures and phantoms, peopling the silence with a myriad things.

And it was a silence, such as only cloying, sound-swallowing mist can make. His feet made no sound on the spongy slippery moss. Nothing seemed to live or move, out there . . . nothing . . . until he became aware of fugitive touches, now and then, against his ankles. Little things, scurrying away into the safety, making no sound. All he heard was the drum-pounding of the blood in his ears, the rasp of breathing, and the click and chuckle as he swallowed. He moved in a bubble a yard in diameter, and everything else was a dream. He had the softness of Martha's hand in his, and he could see her as a blur, by him, in the haze, as they blundered along together. But all else was insane nightmare. The ground under his feet, spongy and wet, was even, like a table. Now and again he caught his foot in a stunted tangle of something, a bush, possibly, but that was all. No break in the monotony. Nothing. Just walk, and keep walking.

He felt for the bean bag, seeking the fastening, and his fingers skidded on the slimy surface as he tried to get it open. Then, when he had succeeded, he took out a pod, sealed the bag again. A black and yellow thing, about three inches long, banana-shaped. On Earth, this would have kept him in luxury for years. Right now, he had to open it, eat the contents, and be nourished, or it was worthless. He gripped it, squeezed, and it burst open at one end, like a three-cornered mouth. There were four black-and-red beans inside. He shook one into his palm, took a deep breath, and put it into his mouth. He bit on it.

The texture was fibrous and woody, like a nut. The taste was acid-sour, flooding his mouth with saliva. He chewed, cautiously, then swallowed the juice. It stung his throat, sending quick tingles along his arms and legs. He chewed more, reducing the fiber to a pulp, and gulped it. Then he waited. In a moment, his stomach roared at him, making him shudder. But he could feel the dragging weariness and lassitude drop away.

66

"Here!" he said to Martha, roughly. "Get one of these between your teeth."

"Ugh! It's bitter," she complained, but chewed, obediently. They shared the remaining two, finding them not quite so bitter on the second taste.

"We shan't starve for a bit, anyway," she sniffed, more cheerfully. And they resumed their journey with a lighter step.

"God in Heaven!" he suddenly gasped, as the featureless mist right behind them was rent by a monstrous, gargling scream.

Martha's hand clamped on his like a vice. They swung round, peering into the swirling gray. The hideous noise came again, like the blast of an angry steam-whistle, magnified by a hundred times.

"There," she said, and he could see it, too, a great dark mass, looming up . . . black . . . no, it was green, a dark, glossy, olive green . . . a huge, blunt-snouted thing, weaving and questing, as big and round as a man's waist . . . and stretching back enormously, into the mist.

"It's a snake, or a worm, or something of the kind," he muttered.

"Can it see us?"

"Lord knows. I can't see anything that looks like an eye.

The blunt-pointed snout swung, and came to an uneasy rest, pointing right where they stood. In some awful way, it knew they were there. Then Martha screamed, uncontrollably, as a cluster of lamp-like eyes, glowing purple, opened in a circle about the great head, and stared at them. She flung herself round, and Anthony felt his knees turn to water as he stared over her shoulder into that ring of eyes. Then, from the center, yellowly, a great gaping mouth opened, peeling back, and that gargling scream came again, deafeningly, borne on a hot stench of breath.

The next thing Anthony knew, he was running, senselessly and terrified, from that gaping mouth, and the ring of razor-edged teeth he had seen within it. His breath burned in his throat, and the bean-bag bumped awkwardly across his back, hammering him, as he ran, and slipped, and slithered, skidding down to his knees and scrambling up again, forgetting all else in his blind need to escape the horror. His imagination felt the hot breath of it on his neck, the shudder of the soggy ground under its ponderous body, and he fled, gasping, sobbing, squandering every last ounce of energy he could find, to get away. Something caught his foot, so that he went sprawling in a heap. Cursing, he fought up to his fee and ran again . . . and the dark ground fell away under him. He fell and slid, scrabbling at the slimy moss, over an edge, into gray nothingness . . . into a smashing blow at his middle, a bursting flame in his head . . . and then, nothing.

He lay in glorious, cool comfort, deliciously at ease, in the quiet of a shady grove, close by a tinkling fountain. At his side knelt a lovely maiden, smiling on him, and every now and then dipping her fingers in the crystal water, to sprinkle the cool drops on his forehead. He was only pretending to sleep, and she, knowing it, was teasing him.

"Come, beloved, open your eyes," she called, but he would not. Somewhere, in the distance, an orchestra was playing the ballet music from Faust . . . and he knew that if he did wake up, something dreadful would happen.

"Awake!" she cried, impatiently, flicking water in his face. He rolled his head aside. "Wake up!" she insisted, in a different kind of voice altogether, and the splash of water was vigorous.

Anthony opened his eyes, and groaned as ache sliced through his daze.

"My head!" he moaned, and tried to sit up, cringing from another knife-slash of pain across his middle. "What the hell . . . ?" Martha sat back on her heels and watched him, anxiously. Fighting the wrench in his stomach, he sat all the way up, looked round. It wasn't a grove at all, but a dark, dim-lit hollow. He saw the distant standing-flame of trees. There was no mist. And no snake-worm.

"What happened?" he mumbled, not daring to open his mouth too wide, in case his stomach revolted. "Where's the thing . . . the snake?"

"Up there, somewhere," she pointed round and up, vaguely. "You went right over a cliff. I thought you were dead."

"Yes, I remember that." He nodded, and then groaned, wishing he had kept his head still. "I was running like hell, thinking it was after me, and then down I went." He frowned, looked at her, searchingly. "How did you get here? How did you find me?"

"The snake . . ." She shuddered. "I saw it coming, and you yelled, and I was rooted. I couldn't move, at all. It just came—all mouth and eyes—and I waited, gave up . . . and then it went straight past. Knocked me over. There must have been a mile of it!"

"It certainly was big. What then . . . ?"

"It just went past me. Never saw me at all. And then, when I saw it going by, I knew it was chasing you. So I ran after it."

"And what would you have done, if you'd caught it? My God, do you realize what you're saying?" He stared at her. "Suppose it had caught me, and then waited for you?"

"I never thought of that," she said, blankly. "All I knew was, if I kept after it, I was keeping after you . . . and I daren't lose you. So I ran after it. Then it sort of stopped. And I got scared, then. I thought it must have . . . caught you. So I stood as still as I could. And it coiled back, and went away. And I went along—it leaves a groove, you know —and I fell over the edge. But I landed in some bushes, so it wasn't too bad. Then I found you, all in a tangle, around a little tree-stump. I thought you were dead, at first. Then I saw the water—"

"Water? It wasn't *all* a dream, then. Where?"

"Over there, look!" He twisted round, painfully, and, in the half-light, he saw the oily-rippling edge of a sheet of water that stretched away, a long way, into the gloom.

"I managed to drag you down as far as this. And then I got some water, with my cape, and threw it over you. I'm so glad you're not dead!"

"So am I, for the moment," he said, wryly. "I owe you my life, for what it's worth. I wouldn't have given a snap for it, back there. Let's hope there aren't too many of those about. I fancy we'd be just a couple of bites, for him." He shifted, painfully. "Still, water's something to be glad of. I could do with a big drink." He gathered himself, made the effort, and got to his feet, swaying but managing to keep his balance. He felt her hand on his leg.

"I don't think we'll be able to drink it," she said, unhappily. "It's cramful of little fish-things. Millions of them. And they bite. Look!" She put out her arm for him to see. It was covered, up to the elbow, in red splotches.

"Hell!" he growled. "You shouldn't have done that, not

69

just to get water to throw over me. I'm going to take a look."

He set off, weavingly, for the water-edge. In the last yard, he sank to his knees and crawled, until he could peer down into it. Then he saw that the oily blackness was illusory. The water was clear, enough so that he could see the bottom, and the masses of hair-like, waving weeds. But, even as he put his head down, there was a sudden flurry, and a shower of darting neon-lights, spearing through the dark. Shifting his weight on to one arm, he dabbled his fingers, and winced as he felt the instant sting of needle-sharp teeth. The water was alive, now, with sparkling flames.

He tried to imagine gulping a mouthful of that, and groaned. A bead of sweat ran from his chin and splashed into the water. Wringing wet with sweat . . . and parched with thirst . . . it didn't seem right, somehow.

"What are we going to do?" she whispered, as he sat back, to think. The pain in his head was abating a little. He rubbed it, feeling the greasiness and slime in his hair. To get clean, cool, and inwardly moist . . . it was a crying urge. There had to be some way.

"You were splashing me," he said. "How?"

"I dropped the edge of my cape in the water, then shook it, to get the fish out. And then I wrung it out, over your face."

"Let me see!" he held out his hand for the cape, to feel it. Plastic, still a vivid red, crimped to give a fleecy feel, and wet. He shook it out, to find that it was an almost perfect square, a yard a side. A cord threaded through it, one third of the way from one edge, made it possible to wear it as a coat, or a cloak with a hood . . . but he saw it only as a spread-out sponge. Setting himself on his knees, he swung the cape out, let it flap into the water, drew it out, shook it, and stood up, to wrap the soaked material around his head. It felt good. He did it again, and had rinsed the worst of the slime from his head and face. Once more, but this time he held the cape high, balled it, and squeezed, sucking greedily at the drops as they fell on his face.

"Best we can do, for the moment." He passed the cloth back to her. "You have a go. It's worth it, just to feel cool and partly clean." She took the cape, did what she had seen him do, and he left her to it. Looking round, he saw where she had lugged the two bean-bags, and went for them, to bring them to the edge of the water. The effort tied his abused stomach in knots, but he felt better for it, after the twinges had subsided. Next thing, he thought, were his clothes. He was still cumbered by jacket and pants. A quick glance showed him that Martha was busy, still, with her shower-bath. He stripped off the garments, dipped them in the water, shook them vigorously, and they came out much cleaner. Then, as he wrung out most of the water, he argued with himself.

Habit said he should cover himself again, but the tremendous improvement in freedom and comfort made him hesitate. Who was to care, here? Except Martha, of course. He squinted across at her, again, to see that she had peeled off her clothes, too, and was luxuriating in the dribble of water over her nakedness.

"Don't look round," he called, gently. "But I'm having an argument with myself. I don't want to swelter in these silly clothes. Do you mind?" She held still for a moment, with the dripping cape over her head, then brought it down, and turned, facing him.

"I certainly feel better, this way," she said, frankly, "and it can't make any difference to anyone but us."

"All right, then." He rolled his clothes up small, compressing them as hard as he could, so that the water squirted out. "I'm going to pack mine," and he unfastened a bean-bag, got out another pod, and made a space to stuff in his bundle.

"Come and eat"—he waved the pod—"and if you'll rinse out your things, I'll pack them with mine."

She came to sit by him, stretching out her legs. He burst the pod, handed her a bean, took one himself.

"Nice color, green!" he said, stretching his own leg alongside hers.

"Oh don't!" She shuddered. "I think it's awful. Every time I look at it, I just can't believe it's me. I hope they come for us, soon!"

"Who?" he asked, blankly.

"Why . . . somebody from the dome, of course. They're bound to miss us, and send out search parties."

Until she said it, that aspect of the business had not occurred to him. He sat silent, chewing, and thought about it. It was difficult. All at once, the colonists, and people in general, seemed remote and unreal, as if they belonged to another world. In a way, they did. But there was no getting away from the facts. He and Martha would be missed. But would they send out search-parties? Could they? He thought back to what Harper had said, about the meager amount of exploration that had been done, and how difficult it was. Where would they begin?

"I don't think they'll bother. . . ." The words were on his tongue, but he held them back. "They" would have to bother, wouldn't they? It was that, or provoke a devil of a fuss . . . and that wouldn't suit them, at all. He chewed it over, along with bean-pulp, until he grew tired of it.

"Come on." He got up, feeling the refreshing tingle of the bean-stimulus working against his weariness. "We might as well move on. Can't just sit here."

"Why not?"

"Because . . ." He hesitated, then, "Because we need food. Solid food. The beans are only a stimulant. We can't live on them, alone."

"Oh, very well." She got to her feet, and stood while he helped her get her pack comfortable. Then she slung the red cape over one shoulder. "It can't make much difference, one way or the other, can it?"

He caught up the other bag and flung it into place. Step by heavy step, he tramped on through the half-light, with Martha's hand in his. He lifted his feet, one after the other, stubbornly, slithering and stumbling along, skirting always the uneven edge of the dark water, making wide circles round the more soggy parts, and passing, all the time, the endless series of great fire-trees, of every imaginable color.

He wondered about them, about the rare branches he could see, high up, as they looped away into the overhanging mist. If you could climb one, you'd get up into another world altogether, he mused, a world of branches, leaves, and a gray cloud of light. Possibly fruit, of some kind.

Food! The thought made him look up, and shake his head. If there was food up there, then they would surely starve, for no one could climb those giants without some sort of help. The lowest branches he had seen, so far, were all of twenty feet overhead.

Then Martha fell heavily to her knees, and on her face,

with the heavy pack pinning her down. He bent to help her, and almost fell on his face by her side, in his weariness.

"We're a couple . . . of fools," he gasped, shoving her pack aside, so that she rolled over and began to suck in air, hungrily. "No idea how long . . . this damned twilight . . . no time-sense, at all. . . . Must have been going for hours and hours. . . .We need to sleep, that's the trouble!" He got her arms free of the straps, and she sat up, wiping the ooze from her face.

"Sleep? But where?" she breathed.

"Anywhere." He waved a tired arm. "Help yourself."

"But"—she looked round, fearfully—"one of us will have to keep a look out."

"For what? And to do what?"

"I couldn't just lie down, here, and go to sleep." She shuddered. "I just couldn't, that's all!" Too weary to argue, he shuffled out of his pack, took the red cape, and plodded down to the water to wash. She was close behind him, as it unwilling to let him get more than a yard or two away. He said nothing, giving all his attention to as thorough a wash as possible. Then he gave her the cape, shambled back to the bags, thumped one into the semblance of a pillow, and stretched out, letting the weariness have its way. His last conscious thought was of a pain in his inside . . . an emptiness.

He woke, suddenly and all at one, with the fleeting impression of a hard thump of some kind, quite near. Something falling . . . a footstep . . . what? He kept quite still, becoming aware of cramps and stiffness, a filthy taste in his mouth, and a deadness in his right arm. But no repetition of the thumping noise. He opened his eyes, cautiously, and the first thing he saw was the top of Martha's head, where she had snuggled close, her cheek resting on the crook of his arm. He extricated himself, delicately, sat up, creakingly, and looked around.

Then he saw it. Less than a yard away from his head. A great ovoid, an oversized egg-shape, bigger than his head. It sat there, quite still, and glowed with a red light. He stared at it, waiting for it to move. Or had it fallen? It kept quite still. He gathered his legs beneath him, carefully, and stood up. Still it didn't move. He took a step, then another . . . and put his foot to it, rolled it over. Now he could see a dimpled base, like a navel of an orange. Greatly daring, he stooped, got the weight of it, and lifted. It was heavy, with a rubbery feel. It was a fruit of some kind, surely? His grumbling stomach overrode his caution. He dug his nails into it, and the rubbery surface broke and peeled back, like an orange, and with a similarly acid-sour smell. He sat down in a squat, began ripping off the thick peel. Inside, the thing was full of needle-pyramid shaped segments . . . yellow . . . with the texture of water-logged sponge. He freed one, looked at it, took a breath, and bit into it. The juice overflowed, dribbling down his chin and on to his chest.

It was good. Squashy banana-lemon . . . that was the nearest he could come to naming flavor. He swallowed, and then woke Martha.

"Don't ask," he said. "Just eat, and be thankful."

They ate, greedily and with gusto, until they could eat no more, and there was still almost a third of it left. He put the almost empty husk aside, and they got up and went on.

The water-edge had suddenly taken a long bend, and the trees were well back, leaving a broad patch of level shoreline, studded with bushes of a kind they had not seen before. It was habit, and caution, which made them steer clear, but Martha did not keep quite clear enough. The swinging end of her cape brushed against the pointed tip of one spiking leaf, and she screeched in sudden terror as the whole leaf sliced down to the ground like a chopping blade, dragging the cape with it. For a moment, she teetered, off-balance, and he grabbed her, frantically. Then she was free of the cape and staggering against him, gasping.

He stared, over her shoulder, at the bush. A little way off he could see another, just like it. A stout center stem, and a mass of outstretched blade-like leaves, like the spokes of a sun-shade. But this one, here, had been triggered by the touch of the cape, and all the blades were down, slicing into the ground.

He pushed her aside, gently, and went as close as he dared, to study it. Those leaves were all about a yard long, slim like swords, and stiff, and they had all snapped down, edge-on, so that the needle-sharp tips were buried in the

74

soft moss. He tried to imagine what the effect would be, should some small animal blunder into this thing. A touch . . . and down would come the blades . . . and the prey would be sliced like mince-meat. Then, presumably, to decay and form food for the roots. He shivered a little at the thought, and took hold of the edge of the cape, to try to free it. Then something else occurred to him. The plant, if it was a plant, was developed in one direction only, to strike down. Logically, it would resume its outstretched state in a while, provided there was no further stimulus. So he had only to wait, and the blade-leaves would lift up again.

But, suppose he could hold one of those blades—the one which had caught the cape—and hold it down? He got down on his knees, then on his face, and put out both hands, wrapped in the folds of fleece, and pressed firmly on the tip of the leaf. And prepared to wait.

"What are you doing?" she asked. "Come away from there. It's dangerous. You'll be hurt."

"It's all right," he said. "Get back, and stay quiet." He could feel the tip begin to lift, under his fingers, and he pressed down. The real danger was, now, in two things. First, the leaf-blades were like razors, and might cut through the plastic fleece, and second, the vicious plant might just have another trick up its sleeve. That thought made him grin to himself. A plant, with sleeves? Then he was amazed at his own ability to laugh. I've never really *lived*, before, he thought. Not like this. All these years, I've been shut up inside myself, looking out, afraid.

Now . . . and the leaf-tip began to lift more strongly. He could see the rest of the leaves twitch and lift out of the moss, and the sturdy main stem beginning to bow, stiffly, under the unaccustomed load. He hung on, feeling the cords in his wrists and arms aching as he applied all the pressure he could, at this awkward angle. The whole plant twitched and stirred, strongly, and the leaf he was holding began to bend, like a spring, and quiver. Then there was a splitting crack, and he bumped his face on his arms as the leaf fell limp. The next moment, he had shifted his grip, muffling the cape to give him more purchase, and set to work, tugging and twisting, until he flopped back,

75

holding the broken thing in his hand, a trailing strip of tendon-like membrane dangling from the inward end.

"Got you!" he said, reversing it, and seizing the thick end. It was sticky with sap, but he didn't mind that. Getting to his feet, he hefted it, swung it, and it felt fine. Now he had a weapon, a three-foot razor-edged blade. Primitive, no doubt, and clumsy, but he felt like ten men with it.

"I'll bet you ripped that cape all to ribbons," she grumbled, retrieving it from the ground and shaking it out. But she was wrong. The tough plastic was unharmed.

"I've got a real weapon, now," he said. "I don't feel helpless any more."

"How can that thing make any difference?" she asked. "Suppose we should meet another of those great worm-snake things? What good would your sticker be, then? And you can't cut anything with it, because there isn't anything to cut. *And* it's just something to carry."

"I shall be carrying it, not you!" he retorted, stung by her lack of enthusiasm. "Come on, we might as well push on," and he led off ahead, not holding her hand, this time.

His mind was looking ahead, now, wondering what the next thing would be. A little whispering refrain grew in his mind, repeating itself, although he felt sheepish every time he stopped to analyze it. *Anthony Taylor . . . King of the Greenies!* He could hear her squishy footsteps at his back, and her breathing, but he kept on, steadily, peering around, almost in the hope that something, anything, would turn up that he could meet with his new sword . . . just to test it. Then he heard her grunt, and stop, and the slap as her pack hit the ground. He halted, went back.

"What's the use?" she demanded, angrily. "Where's the sense in it? We aren't getting anywhere. For all we know, we may be walking round and round the edge of a pond. I'm fed up, dragging myself along, on and on, and I'm tired. I'm hot. I'm hungry . . ." and she began to cry, standing there, looking into nowhere, her shoulders drooping and the tears creasing through the grime on her face.

"Have a bean . . ." he said, helplessly, and she brushed his hand aside.

"You and your filthy beans!" Her voice cracked with weariness and rage. "You—I believe you *are* a Greenie, after all. You seem to like it, here. I want to go home . . ." and she

crumpled into a sobbing heap by her pack. He stood looking down at her for a moment, then shrugged out of his
pack, let it fall by her side. Of course she was tired, and hot,
and hungry, and afraid . . . and he couldn't do anything
about it at all, except leave her alone for a bit, in the hope
that she might get over it. He stuck the sword leaf into
the moss, firmly, took up the cape, and went down to the
water, selecting an overhanging edge.

He knelt for a moment, watching the seething mass of
darting flames under the surface, then he shook out the
cape, let it fall into the water, jerked it out, shook it, and
wrapped it round his head, feeling the coolness trickle down.
Swinging it free again, he paused a moment, to watch. All
at once the swarm of tiny fire fish flew apart like splinters
in front of an axe-blade as a long blue flame whipped past.
Life is a feast, and every one of us is guest, and dish. He'd
read that, somewhere, long ago. It certainly seemed to
be true, here. He swung the cape, holding on to a corner
. . . and something flared and leaped, in an arc of blue
fire. There was a violent tug at his fingers, almost dragging
him in . . . and the cape was gone! He caught just a
glimpse of it, disappearing into the dark depths.

"Hell!" he mumbled, staring stupidly at his empty hand.
Then, as the full magnitude of the loss came to him, he
stood up, feeling sick. He would have to tell Martha, on
top of the way she was feeling now. He turned, shrinking
from the task, but knowing it had to be done. He took
one careful step, to go back to where she was still slumped
by the bags . . . and froze in sudden unbelief. She lay still,
in the glare of a giant flame-orange tree, and from behind it came a slithering, silent hideousness that made his
heart stop and his blood run icy. It made his stomach heave,
just to see and be unable to believe. A mass of ropy snake-
like things, each as thick as his wrist, each with a gaping,
three-cornered mouth at the tip, each seemingly stemming
out from a bloated central bladder-like body—all the fifteen-
foot members writhing and crawling, so that the eye was
baffled as to which way "it" was moving, as a whole. And
it was gray-white, like the underbelly of a snail.

Breaking from his sweating horror, he stumbled forward,
into a run to get to his sword-leaf. "Martha!" he yelled. "Martha! This way! This way!" Her head lifted at his call,

but the many-snake heard him, too, and its sluggish writhing quickened. Then it made sound, a multi-toned whistling scream. He saw her look back, over her shoulder and up, at the gaping mouths that were so close. And she screamed— a full-lunged, senseless, wrenching scream—and again, her whole body shaken by the absolute surrender to blind terror. Then he was skidding and slithering to a breathless halt, to snatch at the sword-leaf, and on again, madly, leaping over her where she had fallen back, to stand and slash at the hydra-headed nightmare.

He felt the blade bite deep, and the whistling grew to a scream. He slashed again and again, with all the strength he could find . . . and again . . . and spat, blindly, as yellow-green ichor squirted and spouted all over him, his stomach heaving and knotting at the stench, and he went on chopping and slashing until his arms ached and the breath roared burningly in his throat . . . long after the thing was ruptured beyond harm . . . until it was nothing more than a dismembered shambles of feebly twitching yellow-green meat, all around his feet. Then he threw the blade aside, and was sick. Painfully, disgustingly and helplessly retching, the tears burning his eyes, the little refrain came back to mock him in his helplessness. *Anthony Taylor . . . King of the Greenies!*

At last his stomach could throw no more. Shakingly, he straightened up, spat the acid from his mouth, took a shaky breath, and went to where Martha lay still. As best he could, he examined her, and as far as he could tell, she was unmarked. Just a faint. She would come round, in a while. He stood up, and choked on the smell that came from the smears on his own skin. He looked about, found the blade again, staggered down to the water, crouched, and swished it until it was clean, watching the shooting arrows of flame, under the surface.

Water—millions of gallons of it—and he couldn't get any. The King of the Greenies was due to die of thirst, because he couldn't figure out a way. What would a Greenie do, now, he wondered, dully, watching the ceaseless dart and sparkle of the fish. A feast . . . and a dish. An idea struggled to make itself known. He fumbled with it, got to his feet again, went back to where she was still unconscious. Biting back his revulsion, he speared up a

78

few lumps of the chopped body of the snake-thing on to his blade, went back to the water. Crouching, he gripped a piece, tossed it in . . . waited. Within seconds the dark surface was boiling with activity where the meat had splashed.

"That's me, if I fell in," he muttered, and made haste to splash his hands and face in the deserted water close by the edge, daring to duck his head right under, for a breathless moment. A careful wait, another dripping slice of meat, and he slid his feet in, scooping handfuls of water as far as he could go. He felt better. Not good, but better.

If only there was some way, now, of taking some to where she lay. But, he shrugged, she could come here. He got up again, went back to her. She lay as if asleep, so peacefully that it seemed a pity to disturb her, but the smell was overpowering, now that he had got himself clean, and the moss was alive with little wriggling worms, of all shades of yellow and gold, converging on the minced carcass. Maybe they did eat only dead meat, he thought, and then again, maybe they didn't. She had to be moved. He knelt, took her hand.

"Martha, Martha, wake up!" he called, urgently, and she stirred. "Come on. Wake up!" He patted her cheek, and she smiled, opened her eyes, and sat up.

"I've been asleep!" she said. "I had such a funny dream, Tony. Such a funny dream. Can we go home, now?" She looked at him, expectantly, and her look, her voice, her whole impression, was that of a child of six or seven. He sat on his heels, holding her hand, and gaped, the wheels of his mind grinding to a halt at this shocking change in her.

"Are you all right?" he asked, stupidly, and she smiled again.

"Of course I am, but I'm hot and tired, and I want to go home, now!" Then he knew, saggingly, that this was not Martha Merrill, at all. Something in there had snapped, had failed under the shock, leaving an amiable, half-witted child, blank-faced and docile. His wits circled, aimlessly, like a flight of birds at a gunshot. What to do, now? He realized he was still holding her hand. He squeezed it, reassuringly.

"Can you get up?" he asked, and she laughed, and scrambled to her feet.

"Are we going home, now? Is it far?"

"Not much further," he said, as cheerfully as he could manage. "But I think you should have a wash, and a drink, first. Yes?"

"That'll be nice," she nodded, gravely. "I'm ever so hot and sticky." He took up one pack, indicating the other. She hoisted it, willingly, and followed him to the water-edge. The dismay in his mind was subsiding, now. The damage, whatever it was, was done, and there was no help for it . . . but it might be a blessing in disguise. At least, she didn't seem to be frightened any more.

"You stand just there," he instructed, indicating a spot close to the shallows, "and when I say 'Now,' you step in and splash yourself, very quickly. All right?" She nodded, wide-eyed, got herself ready, and he lobbed another stinking piece of meat into the water. "Now!" he said, and leaned over to help shower her with water as she stood knee-deep. It was grotesque, and yet it was a moment that would live with him as long as he lived—the sight of her kicking and splashing the water over herself, and laughing, delightedly, like a child. "Right. That's enough. Out you come, quick!" he ordered, helping her on to the bank. "Now, we'll have a bean-feast, and then we'll push on."

As they sat and chewed, in silence, he tried to peer out over the water, wondering how far it stretched. It might be just a pond, it might be a lake, or even a sea. Anthony sighed, inwardly, as it was borne in on him just how much he didn't know about his home planet. And no way of ever finding out, now. Unless and until they met up with some natives. . . .

Why hadn't they met any Greenies yet? Surely this would be the sort of place to find them?

"All finished?" he asked. "Let's get back to the trees."

They made their way clear of the edge, and set off again, at a steady tramp, on and on, keeping the water always on their left.

On they went, steadily, through an endless monotony of slithering wetness underfoot, pillars of fire on the right, the dark stretch of the water on the left, on and on, into the heat, the clammy dampness, into what? Where are we going, he wondered, and why?

The questions went round and round in his head like an

idiot chant. With a sudden jerk, he caught himself upright and realized he had been nodding . . . tramping in a doze. He shook his head, angrily, dashing the sweat from his face with the back of his hand. And then Martha was down, on her knees and her head bowed, heavily.

"I'm tired, Tony!" she whimpered, in that little girl voice. "I can't go any more!"

"All right," he said, and felt an enormous wave of weariness sweep over him. "All right. You just settle down, there. I'll get some water, and we will have some more beans . . ." But he was talking to himself. She had fallen asleep.

He dropped his sword-leaf, sank down on his knees, and then slid down flat, turning over to look up into the glowing gray mist, up there. For the very first time, he let the idea of defeat, failure and death become a reality . . . and faced it. This is the way it ends, he thought. Face it. Stop trying to dodge it. Barring a miracle, this was the end. And he still had a choice, either to go on struggling, stupidly, to the very last quiver, or to lie down and accept it, sanely, with what dignity he had left. Anthony Taylor, King of the Greenies . . . A joke, that's what that was. He could see the funny side of it, now.

A small, strange sound had been tapping gently on his ear for some time, trying to make itself known. Now, in the half-world between sleep and waking, he heard it. The chuckle and plash of water. What was so strange about that? There was a damn great lake of it, only a few yards away. And then a splinter of curiosity nagged him, restlessly. He heaved himself to his knees, then to his feet, and went staggering and shambling in the direction of the sound.

Up a gentle rise, so that he had to fall on his knees and crawl to get to the top, and then he looked, blinked his eyes tight to drive away the blurring of fatigue, and looked again.

The splashing was quite loud, now. It came from a tree, at least, it looked something like a tree. But, although it flamed just like all the rest, this one was a mass of rippling, changing color, the waves of glowing light rising and spreading up from its squat hole. And it stood squarely in the middle of a fountain. A veil of falling spray and drops ringed it round like a sparkling curtain. He got to his feet, and went slithering down the slope towards it, nervously because of the weirdness of it . . . yet eagerly because of the craving in his mouth and throat. Coming close, he put out his hand, into the falling spray . . . and shivered. It was cool! With great daring, he stepped bodily into the downpour, and shivered again, luxuriously, wriggling as the water coursed down over his face, his chest, down the hollow of his back, trickled down his legs. He put his head back, shut his eyes, opened his mouth. The spray was clean, cool, and, to him, like wine. Weariness fell away from him along with the sticky grime and sweat.

Martha, he thought, I must get Martha here! Shaking the wet from his face, he went up the slope at a heavy run, and back to where he had left her. She was still asleep, like a lovely child. He got her arm around his shoulder, and half-carrying her, went back, up that slope and down the other side, scrambling and stumbling, until they were under the cool shower. Holding her by the shoulders, he watched, and waited, saw her shudder, and open her great violet eyes wide.

"It's raining!" she said. Then, as he laughed, she laughed, too, and put up her face to the spray.

He stepped back into the cool water, wondering. This spray, now . . . it had to serve some sort of purpose. There was no sign of it lessening, so the tree must be getting water as fast as it was throwing it away. He moved round the circle until he found the lake, only a few yards away. He stepped clear of the spray enough to see that the downfalling water had cut little pathways in the moss, and was running back into the main body of the lake. It would seem, then, that this tree was drawing water up, from the lake, by its roots, and then just squirting it out, up at the crest, somewhere. But why? And then he remembered the swarming fish-life, and could see, in imagination, the little fire-darting things being sucked in, and digested, in some way.

But what did it matter, anyway? Call it a fountain-tree, and be glad of it. He put his head back and drank. Then he took Martha by the hand, led her clear of the waterfall, to where he had dropped the packs, and made her sit, while he got out another bean-pod. Plenty more of those, he thought, popping it open and handing her a bean. She took and chewed, obediently, and he had a sudden twinge of worry at the utter blankness of her face and eyes. He was

82

reminded of those other Greenies, back in the dome . . . so long ago, it seemed . . . and they had been dead-eyed, too. Staringly vacant. Was this a part of some inevitable process, part of becoming a Greenie? Would he go like that, in due course, and then be condemned to wander, aimless and pointless, and uncaring in this everlasting twilight?

He pushed the awful thought away, shivering. Not that! Then, as he chewed and pondered, he became aware of something else: the feeling that he was not alone. Thinking back, curiously, he realized that he had not felt "alone," at all, any of the time since they had found this lake. Always, there had been that unspoken conviction that he was "among friends." The idea made him smile, sourly, even as he brought it to the front of his mind and examined it. Among friends? For all he knew to the contrary, there wasn't a friendly heart within hundreds of miles.

And yet, the thought would not go away. It was exactly as if, at any moment, someone might step out from behind one of those trees—that one over there, for instance . . . And he froze, quite still, on the instant, staring.

She was not quite as tall as Martha, and a shade slimmer, perhaps. Her glossy black hair was long, down to her shoulders. But where Martha was pretty, this girl was a poem, a glorious completeness of design and form, curves and lines . . . of sheer, vibrant healthy life. She stood quite still, but it was the breathless stillness of arrested motion, with the promise of darting life in every inch of her stance. Smooth-skinned, quite naked, yet he had never seen anyone look less undressed. Her eyes were wide, the same deep violet as Martha's, and steady on his. Her blush-purple lips were parted in a faint smile, which faded to a frown as she stood, silent. He had the feeling that there was something she had expected him to understand, and was disappointed because he didn't. He moved, cautiously, got to his feet. Martha had not seen. Her head was turned the wrong way, watching the sparkling water.

He stood up, went slowly, step by step, towards this strange vision, as if afraid that some sudden action would startle her away. She stood quite still. Her frown had faded, and the little smile came back, showing white teeth. Then, as if a choir had chanted all at once, he knew she was not alone . . . that there were others with her, many others.

He stopped, and looked round, but he could see no one. Then she moved, for the first time since she had appeared to him. All in one sinuous movement, she twisted, turned and stooped, then swung back and up, facing him, and in her hands was another of the flame-red fruit with the banana-acid pulp. Thrusting it out at arm's length, she let it fall, with the very same thud that had woken him, the first time. He knew, then, that the first one had been put out for him . . . and it was obvious, when he thought of it. If it had fallen from a high tree, it would have burst like a bomb.

So she, and her companions, must have been watching, and trailing, all the time! He looked up from the red fruit, and she was gone. The place was as seemingly deserted as it had always been. The impulse to run, to call out, came and went in two successive heartbeats. He went forward, picked up the fruit, and carried it back to where Martha was sitting. What possible chance did he have of trying to catch her, in this gloom? And what would he do with her, anyway? He sat, and began ripping off the peel, methodically. The natives are friendly, he thought, with a wry grin. So far, at any rate. And if that was a blank-eyed, non-intelligent animal, then he, Anthony Taylor, was a one-legged centipede!

But what was the next move? He fed Martha with segments of the fruit, took some himself, and settled down to think very carefully. A lot would depend on his getting the right answers, here. Assume, first, that "they" had been watching, all along. Yet they had not shown themselves. Why not? Caution, possibly. But they had helped, with food, twice. Friendly? It seemed like it. And wasn't it just possible that this "feeling" he'd had, about going the "right" way was due to them, also? A sort of herd instinct? And they hadn't tried to steal the beans, as they could easily have done.

But, he took the other side. They hadn't helped at all with the spider-snake, or the blade-bush, or any other hazards. Their help, if you could call it that, had been negative, except for the fruit.

"Maybe we've had to prove ourselves," he mumbled. "If we'd been chopped by the bush, caught by the snake-thing, or chewed up by fish, they'd have just written us off as stupid. Maybe we've qualified, now."

"What did you say?" Martha asked, sleepily, and he grunted, settling his shoulders against his pack.

"Nothing. Just talking to myself. You had enough."

"Mmmmm!" she wriggled close to him, her eyes already closed again. He could feel sleep tugging at his own eyes, and this time there was no need to fight it, or feel afraid. The natives were friendly. Just as he was slipping away into comfort, it came to him that he was taking this very much for granted, as if he had "known," all along, that it would be like this.

All at once, out of nothing into full alertness, he was awake, and a tug of urgency made him sit up. Time to be moving . . . as plain as if someone had shouted it. In the same instant he saw a dozen figures, possibly more, moving through the hissing spray from the water-tree. Just a glimpse, and then they were gone, leaving that insistent urge to be moving. He got to his feet, and then he saw the green girl, standing, watching. She turned, moved a step or two, looked back. It couldn't be more plain. He stooped, shook Martha, got her to her feet, took her hand, and started to follow. Around the spraying tree, and then down a shallow gully, to the water-edge. The girl stood, waiting. There, beside her, bobbing on the dark water, was a huge flat shape—a leaf, dark purple and the shape of a spearhead. The main rib, where it had been hacked from its parent tree, was as thick as his wrist, and curled up. From there to the pointed tip, the thing measured some twenty feet, and little more than six feet wide at its broadest. He went close, leading Martha, and the green girl, light-footed, stepped out, on to the thick rib, and crouched, to look up at him.

He saw the whole thing sag, slightly, and curl up. And sweat broke out all over him as he realized what was intended. This . . . was a boat? This flat, frail thing? On that seething water? But the girl kept quite still, one hand holding on to a stump-root. He went along, until he stood about the middle, got out of his pack, stiff-armed the bundle, lowered it, carefully, and the green girl edged back, to balance the weight. He put Martha's pack alongside his, up towards the point, and the leaf sank a little more, the edges curling up. His hand was clammy as he took Martha, led her, obediently, to the edge.

"Step lightly," he muttered, "and squat, by the bags." She

did as he said, without question, settling herself to face the green girl, who was now holding the upsprung edges at the stern end. Taking a deep breath, he stepped in and went down into a crouch, facing the green girl, clutching the edges, watching for her next move. The leaf-edge, in his fingers, had a rim, a thickening, and was flexible, but firm.

Now what, he wondered? There was no sign of an oar, or paddle, and sails would have been ridiculous, in this constant calm. He was miserably aware of the water, no more than three inches away from his fingers, at the edges. The thick end of the rib had curled, now, until it was almost upright. The green girl set her back against it. Then she leaned and reached, her hands apart, grasping the edges, and shoved out against the water. In quick time she pulled herself back, gripped and shoved again, pulled back and shoved, and then did it all over again . . . a three-stroke movement that made a bulge and sent it rippling along towards herself. She kept on doing it: reaching forward and rocking back in three quick shoves, and he saw that the effect was to "squeeze" the frail craft through the water.

They were moving. Already the dark shoreline was out of sight, and only the fading glow of fire-trees remained to tell him where they had been. Squinting round, gingerly, he could make out faint shapes, and the spread of fiery ripples, to show that there were other boats, ahead. Then he brought his attention back to her, noting the rhythm of her movements, and the lift and spring of the flat sheaths of healthy muscle across her shoulders, chest and stomach as she worked. Then he saw, too, the full sheen of sweat on her skin, and roused himself. This was all wrong, that he should crouch, nervously, while she slaved to carry him. He gripped the edges anew, watching her. If he could start that bulge, from where he was, in time to pass it along to her . . . He counted, in his head, her reach and press, and pressed out . . . shifted his grip, pressed, shifted and pressed . . . and his face was close to hers as she reached and took the thrust from him.

She gave him a fleeting smile. He rocked back, falling easily into the swing of it . . . and now he could see the spreading vee of their wake, in lines of liquid fire. Not bad, he told himself, for an animal. And he had a wry moment as he wondered what the colonists would think, if they could see him, now. It gave him a mild shock to realize just how long ago it seemed since he had thought about "people," at all, and how remote the past had become, like a dream from some other life. But it wasn't long before those idle thoughts were scraped away by the ache. It began in his forearms and fingers, and he concentrated, as he had been taught, at the piano, long ago, on relaxing, on not seizing hold too hard, on using only such muscles as were absolutely necessary. The ache spread to his shoulders, to his chest, and then his stomach, and the great thigh-muscles, more and more insistent as the repeated effort became harder and harder to make. And he was working for breath, too, pulling great gasps down into his lungs over a throat that felt raw and sandy. Shaking the sweat out of his eyes, he could see that the girl was rocking and thrusting steadily, still, her calm face expressionless and withdrawn, her eyes half-closed. She was glossy with sweat, but to all outward appearances she seemed good for hours of this, yet. He set his jaw, grimly, determined not to be outdone by a girl.

Then the stupidity of the thought struck him like a kick in the face. Pride? What the hell was he doing with pride, here? On the instant, he gave one last weary shove, put up his palms and tried to pantomime his fatigue. The girl stopped as he did, gave a small, weary smile, and sagged back against the stern-post, letting herself go absolutely limp. Now he could see that she was breathing just as heavily as he was, and he was glad he hadn't driven himself too far. Slumping into the bottom, he let his head fall on his knees, and his stomach growled at him, reminding him of the bean-bags. They were believed to be precious to the Greenies, weren't they? Now was a time to find out. He squirmed round, gingerly, wincing against the protest of his muscles. Martha was fast asleep, curled up like a kitten. He tugged at a bag, carefully, managed to get a pod free, and wriggled back.

He held it out, touching her gently on a knee. She opened her eyes, and looked at him, but made no other move. Again there was that wondering, puzzled look, as if he was failing to understand. He scratched his head. Then, on an impulse, he popped the pod open, shook out two of the beans, put one in his mouth and held out the other to her with his finger-tips.

"For you," he said, foolishly. Her eyes widened. That faint twist of a smile crossed her face as she craned forward, bared gleaming white teeth, and took the bean from his fingers with a neat bite. Then she sat back, and chewed, thoughtfully. And then, in a soft, almost hushed voice, she said, distinctly, "Thank you!"

The pod fell from his fingers and the frail boat rocked perilously, at his shocked surprise. "You spoke! You can talk, and English, too."

"Yes," she said, with careful, odd intonation. "I understand this talk. You, also?"

"But of course!" he said, and then caught himself, for there was no "of course" about it. He was as green as she, with nothing to show that he was anything else. How could she be expected to guess?

"This is incredible." He choked and coughed on bean-fragments, gulped them out of the way hurriedly. "How . . . where did you learn? Who taught you?"

"We go on, now," she said, swallowing and putting her hands to the edges.

He shrugged, pushed aside the questions that surged to his mind, and set himself to join her. But there was one thing.

"You have a name? What do I call you?"

"I am called Lov-lee," she said, shaking the long hair back from her face and smiling.

"Lov-lee." He copied her pronunciation, and grinned. I'm with Greenies, he thought, continuing to row. I'm a Greenie . . . I'm accepted. That much is obvious. And, if the rest are like her, then they are intelligent . . . human! Where are we going? How do they find their way? So many questions kept him busy that she had stopped her rowing before he noticed. Then a quick glance over his shoulder showed ed him that they were gliding into the black mouth of a tunnel at the water-edge. A tangle of vinelike fronds brushed across his back as he bent. He heard Martha mutter, felt her sit up . . . and they were in blackness as tangible as velvet. He could see the twin violet lamps of eyes . . . Lovely's, and then Martha's, as she sat up.

"Keep very still," he warned. "We're in a tunnel. It's all right."

"We're nearly home, now," she whispered, as if she knew.

"I hope you're right," he said, but so softly that she couldn't hear. A few more moments of the blackness, and then there was the growing light of a pearly glow, and they slid out into thick mist, so that he couldn't see anything, not even Lovely, who was no more than a foot away from his face. The boat jarred, gently, and was still. He felt Lovely scramble out, and her touch on his arm. He crouched, gave his hand to Martha, helped her out, warned her to stand still, then passed her a bag, took one himself, and got out, on to wet warm moss. Blurredly, he saw Lovely seize the leaf-boat, to drag it up high out of the water and turn it over. The mist was patchy, tempting the sight one moment, blanketing it the next. Still, if they were to be afoot, they might as well get into harness. He helped Martha into her pack, shrugged into his own, stuck the sword-leaf into a strap fold, and waited. Lovely loomed up, her hand out.

"Come . . . !" she said, simply, and was gone again, into the gray glow.

"Hold on!" he called, keeping his voice as calm as he could. "I've lost you. I can't see a thing." In a moment, she was back, her face close to his in the mist, that puzzled expression in her eyes again.

"You cannot see?"

"Not in this stuff, I can't." And she was gone again, with just the echo of a word. "Stay . . . !" And he peered vainly to try to see where she was. Was this his failure? Was he supposed to be able to see, through this stuff? She could, pretty obviously, but how? Did she have a built-in radar, or X-ray eyes, or what? And, as the moments crept by, he wondered if she had gone off and left them? Just as he was beginning to consider this as a possibility, she was back, a dark shape in the gray.

"Hold," she said, and pushed something into his hand. He seized it, a slim, flexible, cord-like something, and gave it a turn round his knuckles. Off she went again, and the cord came taut, pulling him. He took a better grip on Martha's hand.

"Come on," he said. "We start walking, now." The underfoot was slippery and wet, and, by the feel of it, led slightly up hill. He had the feeling of a slope on either side, as if they were climbing the valley of a little stream. And it seemed hotter than ever, or was that just an illusion, because of the thick soupy mist? He plodded on, heavily, with Martha a gentle drag on his left hand, and that enigmatic cord dangling in front, coming up taut every time he slowed down the least bit. He imagined the slim, lithe green girl striding on ahead, setting this cracking pace, and marveled. She must be every bit as worn as he was, yet she didn't let up. And she was quick in the wit, too. He knew, as positively as if she had shouted it, that she had been surprised by his inability to see in this soupy stuff. It must have been a completely new problem to her. Yet she had met and solved it in a matter of moments.

He felt the thing in his hand, investigating it with his finger-tips. It was a root, or a creeper of some kind. Not a "made" thing, anyway. And that gave him something to think about in real earnest. Intelligent people, anywhere, made things. Tools, weapons, ornaments, clothing, artifacts of some kind . . . didn't they? Or was that just one kind of intelligence? And could you call that boat a "made" thing . . . or not? And, come to think of it, what had *he* ever made?

Onward, still uphill, and steeper now, but no let up in the pace. He urged his weary limbs to keep going, one step after another, feeling Martha as a growing drag, but the girl on the forward end of that cord had sinews like wire and leather, and no idea of the word "rest."

"I'm tired," Martha whimpered. "Can't we stop, now?" But the dangling cord showed no inclination to stop.

"Damn this place," he mumbled. "We've been on the move every blasted minute since we landed . . . going, going, all the time, and never getting anywhere. . . . No sense in it . . ." And he was just in time to check himself from blundering into Lovely, who had stopped, ahead of them. "What now?" he demanded, blearily, as she turned and touched him.

"Now we go down," she said, pantingly. "The path is small, and I cannot be with you. But I will wait, at the bottom." Then she stooped into a crouch, and seemed to vanish into the mist at his feet. The cord in his hand was limp.

"Can we rest, now?" Martha whispered, sagging where she stood. "I'm tired, Tony. I want to rest!"

"All right," he said, backing off a bit. "You squat here and rest, while I investigate."

He slipped out of his pack, holding on to the cord and looping it. It was about nine feet long. Casting it out in front, he followed, cautiously, and went on his knees when it seemed to tug at him. Then his groping hand found an edge, and a blank. He felt down, getting down on his chest. A rough wall-face. A cliff! But where was the path? He swung the cord, felt it touch something. The swirling mist-veil parted a moment, and he saw it, no more than four feet down, and no more than eighteen inches wide, either. He lay still, visualizing it long after the vapor had closed in, and liking it less every minute.

But, he told himself, grimly, the more I think about it, the less I'm going to like it . . . and there isn't any other way but down there. So we might as well get on with it. He coiled up the creeper again, wriggled back to where Martha sat.

"There's a path," he told her. "And it will be all right, if we're very careful. I'll fasten our packs together."

He freed the straps, made a belt of one, buckled it about her waist, made another for himself, linked the remaining two, hauled them tight around the two bags, and took up the creeper. Threading it through the bag-straps, he knotted one end to her belt and the other to his own.

"Now," he said, "we'd better start. Come on." He urged her to her feet, led her cautiously until she reached the edge, made her kneel, and then wriggle backwards, while he held her wrists. To his immense relief, she found firm footing while still breast-high to the edge.

"All right, now. Stay still." He moved along, lowered himself over and got his feet set. The path dipped sharply, as he scrambled along, dragging the bags. "Follow the rope!" he called, and waited until she was close to him. "Now, hang on and keep still again, until I've moved and got set." And so they went, alternately, groping and fumbling, down into the mist. To his relief, what had seemed nightmarish in prospect, became monotony in effect after the first few minutes. In that mist, they lost all sense of height. Their world shrank to a small thing, a bubble in

91

space, bounded by a rough wall and a jagged path. He shuffled on, half-turned, and his shoulder met solid rock. A dead end. He waited for her, until there was a loop of cord, and gently lowered the bags over the edge, crouching down. They rested on something. He turned, let himself over, groping, and found another ledge, zig-zagging back from the first. Helping her down, he went on again, meeting and parting from her in the mist.

Then, dully, he noticed that they were not parting any more. He could still see her, right out to the full stretch of the cord. The mist was thinning. Again the path broke and doubled back on itself, giving him a moment to look down. There, below and out, was a haze of colors, of blurred glowing lines and patches. Down they went, yard by yard, to see that these were trees, and then there was no mist at all, but a clear, faintly-tinted glow, a haze. The tree-tops came near, until they seemed close enough, almost, to touch, and the down-dropping track, angling to and fro, brought them into a different kind of world from any they had seen, so far. They stood and looked across into a network of fiery beams and struts, branches and great flat leaves . . . and life, running and leaping, crawling and chattering.

They began the trail once more, weary despite the brief rest. They had descended, below the level of the lower branches. The scene had opened out into haze-color distance, and Anthony could see a huge valley, with standing fire-trees, the distant glint of waves on a lake-shore, a dark mossy slope . . . and people. Green people, a great host of them down there.

Straight down, as much as he dared to look over, the foot of the cliff gave on to a gentle slope, about thirty feet or so below, and there were people here, too, a dozen of them, stretched out, resting. He could discern great bundles, net-like, containing various-colored fruits and berries—at least, they looked like berries—all in a pile. He straightened up, thoughtfully. That might be the party they had come with, those mysterious ones in the other boats. Lovely ought to be there, but it was impossible to identify her, at this distance. All at once, he was impatient to be down, but he fought the impulse. This would be a damn silly time to slip, to make a mess of things. He waited for Martha to inch her way close.

"Hang on," he said. "Don't look now, but we have an audience. Keep still a minute while I unfasten this line. I think it will be safe to let the bags drop the rest of the way." He took the two ends of the creeper, slid the bean-bags over the side, let them hang steady, then released them, watching them go down with a slap on the dark green turf. One bounce, and they were still.

"Now"—he gave her a grin—"let's go, with a bit of style!"

"There must be nearly a hundred of them" she gasped. "All watching us!" He went ahead of her, as steadily as he could manage, until the track was no more than a small jump down to the turf. That jump cost him the last bit of starch in his legs and he swayed as he turned to help her down. Then in a silence that he could feel, he led her to where their packs had fallen. He saw the dark hollow of a cave-mouth, and an old man squatting before it. An old green man, his skin still glossy, but his face lined and grooved with the toll-marks of much living, his hair faded until it was the color of antique silver, his great purple eyes broodingly calm.

A girl crouched by his side. Anthony recognized her at once, and was grateful for her smile, but his gaze came back to the old man, and was held there in fascination. Those eyes held nothing of a smile, or welcome, or anything except deep curiosity. And power. Anthony stared, and the ground under his feet suddenly began to tilt and reel. Feeling control slipping away, he tried to speak, but his mouth refused to work, his throat was dry, and the ground came up and hit him in the face.

He was stretched out in the dark, flat on his back. Voices grunted close by. As he came more awake he felt a headache unlike any he had ever known. Just for a moment he had the image of probing fingers that had reached inside his skull, seeking for what they might find. The vision went as quickly as it had come. He stirred, got to his knees, and saw the dimness of the cave-mouth, began crawling towards it over a mossy surface. His hand brushed and fell on a soft bundle, like a plastic sack of some kind, with odd angular objects inside. He groped awhile, then abandoned the thing, whatever it was, and crawled on, out into the glowing light. The scene outside was changed only in that the gathering of green people had dispersed. The old man sat where he had been, as if he had become part of the picture. And Lovely sat by the old man's knee. Anthony paused in the cave-mouth to listen, but he could make nothing of what they said, and he added this mystery to the growing total of disjointed information about his own people.

For he was more than ever convinced, now, that they were a people. In the past hours he had seen too much to believe otherwise. Now, obviously, he was listening to them speaking their own language. But that girl had spoken English every bit as good as his own, if oddly accented. He moved, crept out of the cave-mouth and stood. The girl turned, smiled, and waved him to come close. The old man's eyes shifted, following him as he went the few steps, and settled down on a knee. Anthony made a bold but natural assumption, and put it into one word.

"Chief?"

For one breathless moment there was no response, then the old face broke into a stare of utter amazement, transforming it entirely from its age-old calm. Those deep eyes blinked and grew wide.

"You, also, speak this tongue?"

"It's the only one I know."

"As I told you," the girl said. "And they were wandering, not knowing, when we found them. Are they not a great wonder?"

"Indeed!" the old man nodded. "The woman also speaks thus? But her eyes are as ours. Yours are not." He looked at Anthony. "Never have I heard of, nor seen, one of our people with eyes of that strange tint. What are you?"

"I wish I knew," Anthony sighed. "There's such a lot I don't know. I feel that I am one of you, and yet I can't be sure. My father was an Earthman. At least, that's what I've always been led to believe. And I don't know how much you understand of what I'm saying, anyway. You know what an Earthman is—a human?"

The girl smiled and said, "Earth is a planet of the Solar System very similar to this one, which the humans call Venus. The humans came here with much difficulty in strange boats to be friendly with us and to teach us, also learn from us. But this atmosphere"—she pronounced the word with great care, and made a sweeping gesture around and above—"is not good for them. They call it hot, and it makes them quickly tired. Many of them die. We think they will go away when they are all tired."

She said it very simply, like a child reciting a lesson, but her words were enough to churn Anthony's wits into hopeless confusion. The implications, alone, made him reel.

"Who told you all that?"

"It is a true saying?"

"Some of it is, yes. But the rest of it is utterly false. Who told you? Who taught you to talk like this?" He half-knew the answer before the old man spoke, and yet the words were like blows.

"There was a human here. He lived with us. He was a friend, and he taught us to speak his tongue because he could not learn ours. He died."

"Died? When? How long ago?"

"What is long?" the old man asked, his old face calm again now. "This was a great mystery to us, when Doctor spoke of it. Of days and weeks and time. This we do not understand. Before this one was a child, Doctor came." He indicated Lovely with a grave nod. "With him, also, came a woman. His woman. Both were very tired always, but they talked much, and taught us to talk to them. Then the woman began to swell with child, as our women do, and it was a bad thing for her, just as it is with our women. Doctor said we should hunt the bean for her, and we did, because she was good. Always, before that, we had given the bean only to men and women, never to young ones, or any who fall sick, or are with child, because it would be waste, and beans are few. But Doctor told us to crush beans and make juice of them, for the sick and weak. And it was a good thing. Now we do it always. You have brought many beans, in the two bags."

"Oh those!" Anthony had almost forgotten his treasure. "You can have them. Share them out among the rest of the people."

"That is good." Lovely smiled. Anthony returned her smile, but was impatient to hear the rest.

"The human woman had her child, but it was dead," the old man went on. "This happens also with us, many times. Doctor was angry. Other humans came in a machine, with special things to eat, but the woman was sick in her head, I think. Two of our women were with child. This was one of them—" he nodded to Lovely again. "The other one would have died, because the woman died as she delivered. But Doctor was there, and took the baby and gave it to his woman to care for. Then he gave the child some of the special things to eat, and became pink, like a human. This was a great wonder to us."

"Wait! Wait!" Anthony implored, trying desperately to fill in the gaps in the laconic narrative. "The human woman took a green baby and gave it something to eat that made it white, you say? A boy baby?"

"No. It was a female, like this one."

Anthony was dashed for a moment, but only a moment. Memories flooded back, enough to tell him the rest of it. "The white woman became well enough to be able to leave, to return to the other humans, didn't she?"

"That is right." The old man nodded. "But Doctor stayed with us. He was very sick, and there was not enough space in the machine for him. He stayed. The machine was to come again for him, later. But it did not come. Then, when this one was become a woman, ready for mating, he died."

The picture was so clear, now, that Anthony could have put a name to the shadowy figure of the "Doctor." But the clarity had brought a new confusion. The mention of machines argued some kind of communication with the Domes. But those people back there had insisted that they knew nothing of educated Greenies, had made it quite clear that they knew the green people as animals, nothing more. He struggled for an answer of some kind. Could it be that there were two factions? One the scientific, seeking for reason, and the other the superstitious, shrinking away from these caricature humans? Could that be why the machine had never come back to rescue the lone man? Anthony imagined him stuck here, enduring the heat, waiting and waiting, never knowing what happened to his wife, and her substitute child, the baby that she had dosed with chemicals to make it white. That would be some variation of anti-tan, of course. A girl-baby, taken back to Earth by a half-demented mother, and allowed to grow up believing herself colored. As she was, but not the way she had believed.

"What happened to Doctor?" he asked. "To his body, I mean?"

"Scavenger worms!"

"And there nothing left, then? Nothing at all to show that a man lived and died here?"

"Oh yes!" Lovely broke in. "Doctor had a writing. A book. I will get it for you." She scrambled up and stooped to plunge into the cave, returning in just a moment or two with a slimy plastic pouch, smaller than those which held the beans, and clear. As he took it, Anthony could see, dimly, the outline of a black-backed notebook. On opening it he saw, also, that there was a battered briar-wood pipe, gray with fungus, and a plastic lighter. He touched a fiberglas stylus from which the ink had long since departed, and then a very small glassite envelope. It held two spare flints for the lighter, and a coiled lock of golden hair. Anthony touched them all gently. Strange things for a man to treasure and keep in his last moments. He took the notebook and opened it. Only the cover would move, and even it peeled back reluctantly. The rest, the pages of script, were rotted into a solid soggy mass. But the cover was enough. Just inside, the inscription was still legible: *T.O. Merrill.* Anthony closed the book again.

"The girl who was with me?" he asked. "Where is she?"

"She is with our women. She sleeps." The old man frowned very slightly. "There is something wrong with her, in her head. Also with you, but not the same. These are mysteries. You can explain?"

"I can explain this much. This man"—he indicated the pitiful remains—"sent his woman away with a baby of this people. A female baby, as you have said. The girl, she who came with me, is that baby, grown up. Her name, and this name, are the same."

The old man's face was as expressionless as mossy wood. "This is good. She has come home. But you?"

Anthony was puzzled. Surely this old man had the wit to put two and two together and find the answer for himself. Then he recalled his colored contact lenses, and smiled wryly. There was no possible point in keeping them in place any longer. He reached for that small envelope, which would serve as well as anything for a place to secure the fragile things. Then he touched a finger-tip to his tongue, and then, delicately, to his eyes. For a few moments he had to sit with his eyes shut until the involuntary tears ceased. Then he was able to lift his head . . . and gasp in astonishment.

What had been a dim half-light was now pearly radiance, and all colors were startlingly vivid, seemingly imbued with their own flame. It was as if he had been color-blind before, but could now see with new eyes. Then he caught wide-eyed amazement on the faces of the other two. The expression on Lovely's face, in particular, was a glow that made him suddenly warm and uncomfortable. Then, just as before, it gave way to that fleeting look of disappointment, of something he ought to be, but wasn't.

"Now you are one of us," the old man said. "It is good. You will stay, be with us. This one shall be your woman. She found you."

"Oh now, wait a bit!" Anthony drew back in instant rejection. He saw the glow on her cheek, a gentle flush of purple, and knew it for what it was, but the swiftness of the decision was too much. "Hold on a bit," he repeated. "There's a lot to be sorted out, first."

The old face was bleakly calm, and Anthony wondered how he could ever have believed that expression to be one of understanding. He saw it now as absolutely autocratic, a power that expected no argument, nor would bow to any.

"You are asleep in your head. So, also, is the woman who came with you. This is because you have lived all your life with the humans. This, I know. Doctor, also, was like this. But he was human, an Earth-man. You, and the woman, are of us and like us. We will wake you up."

There was no menace in the tone or the words, but Anthony cringed, inside, from the implications. Whatever it was the old man meant, he didn't like the sound of it one little bit. He got up from his kneel, took a step back, and then something made him look round. Where the scene had been deserted and quite quiet, the mossy slope down to the water and the distant groves of standing trees barren of people, he now saw a host. They were all at a distance, all merely standing and watching, but they were there. And he had seen nothing in the way of a sign or command, but he knew beyond any doubt that the old man had summoned them. He turned his head back to look at Lovely, and saw her smile, a smile of reassurance.

"Come and sit again," she said. "There is nothing to be afraid of. We wish to help you. I think you are like a small child which has not yet learned how to live properly."

"I suppose that's true," he admitted, "but I don't like the sound of that 'wake up' business. I'm not asleep. There's nothing wrong with me!" He squatted, fighting his nervousness. "I'll admit Martha isn't quite right in her head. I can tell you how that happened, because I was there—"

He broke off, catching his breath as a sudden chill struck him. In the same split-second the old man reached out a long arm to touch him. The peacefully glowing scene dissolved from before his eyes as if a curtain had fallen. He knew that he was under water, several feet down, drowning, gasping for breath, panic-frantic at the knowledge that a myriad needle-toothed carnivorous fishes were within seconds of ripping his flesh to streaming ribbons. He cringed before the first agonizing wave of bites. Strong arms groped and seized him, held firm, lifted. He came up out of the living water, snorting for breath, feeling the scrape and burn of swallowed water, gasping deep and thankful breaths . . . and then, as inexplicably as it had come, the vivid nightmare vanished . . . and he was once again in the tranquility of the little grove, with Lovely on one side, and the old chief on the other.

Even if that had been no more than an illusion, it had been real enough to leave him gasping for breath now. "What was that?" he panted. "What happened?"

"You know quite well. You shared and experienced it."

"But I *don't* know, damn it! You keep assuming things that just are not true!" He fought to overcome his growing sense of helpless frustration, to make himself calm. "I had the illusion of falling into deep water, of not being able to swim, and then being pulled out. It was a trick of some kind. Because I am *here*. I did *not* fall into water. I *can* swim!" He glared at the old man, striving to break that brooding know-all calm. "It was a trick. You did it. I want to know why!"

"I do not know what you mean by 'trick.' One fell into the water and was in danger. We helped him. You also."

99

"But how? And who was it?"

"You want a name, I think," Lovely murmured. "This is the way of Earth talk, to have names. We do not have such words. The man who was in danger, which you knew about, if you met him you would know him, I think."

Anthony caught back the rejection which came to his lips, and frowned. It was true, what she said, now that he thought back. He would know that man beyond all doubt, because, for a brief moment, he had *been* that man. Again, the implications were enough to spin his mind into stumbling confusion.

"You understand now," the chief murmured, "that it is true, as I told you. You have the strength and power of a man, but you are asleep inside your head. You have learned too much of talking with the mouth, and nothing of touching with the inside."

"That's enough," he muttered, getting to his feet. "Enough. I want to be alone for a bit, to think. You're going too fast for me."

"You are afraid?"

"No, not the way I was before. I'm just all mixed up. I need time to sort things out in my mind." He turned away to walk down the slope and Lovely appeared by his side.

"I will come with you. I am your woman, now."

"That's another thing that goes a bit too fast for me," he protested. "Don't think I'm objecting to you as a person, mind. It's just the idea."

"It is not like this, on Earth?"

"What do you know about Earth? How much did the Doctor tell you? And more than that, how much did you understand?"

They began walking slowly, and she tilted her head on one side in thought before she replied, "Doctor told us much, but only in words. Earth people have only words, like this? Nothing else?"

"What else is there?" His mind refused to make the step that he could see looming ahead. He wanted her to say it for him. "You use words, don't you?"

"Not like this. Words are not true. Listen, this is a word—water." She pointed to the glossy ripples just ahead. "Water—it is just a noise."

They went the last few steps over blue sand. She stepped

ankle-deep into the small surf and kicked a rainbow splash. "This," she said, "is water!"

He had caught her arm, urgently, without thinking. "Careful, you'll be bitten!"

"Not here." She put her hand on his, where it was gripping her arm, and glanced a few yards along, where several small children were splashing in the tiny wavelets. "This water is safe."

He felt foolish, and then acutely aware of the silky skin of her arm, the warm grasp of her hand, and her nearness.

"Water is a something, a feeling, a touching. Not a word. You feel, inside. Just then, you were afraid for me, and now ashamed, and excited. How do you speak that in words?"

He eased his hand out from under hers, struggling with his embarrassement. "How do I say what I'm feeling, you mean?"

"No!" she strode away from him abruptly, straight into the water, and turned again when she was waist-deep. "Now!" she called. "This is how I feel," and in that instant he had the conviction that he was waist deep in cool water. It was no illusion, but a perfectly valid sensation, complete to the gentle swirl of currents past his ankles and toes. And then it was gone, so abruptly that he almost fell. His face must have betrayed his astonishment, for she laughed. Her teeth were like a white flame against the purple of her lips and the glowing green of her face, and he knew, in that moment, that she was the loveliest, the most desirable woman he had ever seen. My woman, he thought, and the thought was like a fire in his veins, magnifying all his fears and confusions a hundred-fold.

On the impulse he waded into the water after her and she laughed again, and bobbed down, right under for a moment, then came up and shook the water from herself like a dog.

As he came near she challenged him gaily, "How do you speak this, in words?"

"I don't know. Lovely, you shared your feelings with me, then."

"Yes." She nodded, smiling.

"Can you also share in my feelings?"

"Sometimes. Just a little bit. When they are very strong, or simple. Mostly I feel just a mix-up, as if you are not

101

happy. But now it is not like that. You are feeling good, strong for me, that I am your woman. It is very pleasant. I am glad. . . . She paused, and he forgot her as he saw a small company of green people, men and women, marching steadily by the foot of the rock-wall, going in the general direction of the original cave, and, presumably, the old man, the Chief.

In their midst was Martha. Catching sight of him she smiled and waved her hand. "Tony! We're going to play a game. Are you coming with us?"

"I'm coming," he called back, and turned a hard eye on his companion. "What's this game she's talking about? Do you know?"

"I think we will go ahead and talk to the old one, that one you call Chief. He will explain."

She led the way with long rippling strides that took them ahead of the placid marchers. The old man sat exactly as he had been before, as if he was an unchangeable part of the scene.

"We are going to wake her up," he said, as Anthony threw the question at him. "She is all shut up in her head. You, also, but you have started to open. With the woman, it is different. She has known a great fear."

Anthony stared at him, and then guessed. "This woman told you?"

"She let me see. It is almost the same. When you killed the many-snake. There was great fear, and she fled and hid inside her head. Now we will help her to find out that there is no danger any more and she will come out again." If the words were crude and simple, the diagnosis was profound and accurate. Anthony wanted to know how, but the old man shook his head.

"We spoke much of this with Doctor. It is not possible to speak words for feeling-thinking. Doctor said like this—" The old man stretched out his hand and splayed his fingers. "One person is like a finger, but many fingers together make a hand. Hand joins to arm, to brain. Brain is the focus for all, unites all. I am like such a brain. Many people think, one and one and one. Through me, many can think together. This is what I am for. Every tribe has one person like me. A focus. When I am dead, it will be her," and he nodded to Lovely.

102

"Every tribe? There are many tribes like this?" Anthony asked.

"Very many. Doctor spoke much to us of numbers, and how to count. A tree has many branches, many leaves. All trees spring from the ground and are joined. I am like a tree. I am joined to other trees. But enough, all is ready for the awakening. You will help." He looked round and saw now that Martha stood all alone in the center of a great circle of silent and impassive green people.

"What do you want me to do?"

"Speak to her. Help her to remember that part that she has chosen to forget. We will do the rest." He felt a moment of rebellion.

"You don't know what you're doing. If you wake her up, make her normal again, she'll be worse off than before."

"What do you want?" the old man asked woodenly. "If she remains like this, who will care for and protect her, find food for her? You?" Again the words were simple and profoundly significant. In that moment Anthony knew that he was in the jaws of a trap from which there was no escape. He could barely hope to survive in this alien environment. It was out of the question for him to support anyone else, let alone someone as helpless as Martha was in her state. But—and it was a great "but" in his mind— if she were restored to normal awareness, and found herself in the midst of a horde of Greenies . . . He shivered at the thought. The old man's stare was as flat as a brick wall. Unwillingly, Anthony made his way into the center of the circle, and took Martha by the hand.

"Let's sit down, shall we?" he said. "And let's talk. I want to see how much you can remember. Will you? It's a kind of game." She nodded and squatted on the turf, tucking up her long legs. It was a shocking experience to see her like this, a beautiful mature woman, but with the wide-eyed stare of a child. He mentioned names. Austin Willers. Borden Harper. There was no flicker of recognition at all. Nothing. He shifted in time, tried another approach. Yes, she recalled coming down the cliff-walk, the mist, and a vague something about a boat, a water-tree.

"That was ever so nice!" she laughed. "I liked that. It was cool!" Over her shoulder Anthony caught the old man's eye, his grave nod. On the instant he could "feel"

103

again the pleasant sensation of the cool shower. He sensed that all the silent crowd were joined with him and Martha. It was an odd feeling. He approached the next effort cautiously.

"What happened just before that, before we found the water-tree?"

"I don't know." She wrinkled her pretty brow. "I was asleep, I think."

"Feel sleepy now. Remember the little frog-lizard? And then when I went to wash, with the red cape? And then . . ." In his own mind the hideous memory of that foul crawling thing was very vivid. She seemed to catch it. She jerked upright, like a doll on strings, and screamed mindlessly, senselessly, pointing. Again and again the crazed screams erupted from her throat and the scalding strength of her fear washed over him, hurting, wrenching at his stomach. Much as he ached to reject the pictures which came to his mind, they came nevertheless—the hissing, the crazy slashing and chopping, the evil stench. He seized her hand, felt it clenching and shivering in his, and she went on screaming, over and over, like a mechanical thing. Sweat sprang out all over her body until she glistened. And then the tide began to ebb. The screams weakened, died away, became gasping silence. She sat, staring at nothing, shivering.

"It's all right," he soothed. "All right. All over. Finished."

"It was a nightmare. Wasn't it?"

"No, Martha. It was real. But it's done and finished with. I killed the thing. You're all right now, all safe."

"Where is it?" She still stared at vacancy, still shivering.

"All gone. Some of it I threw in the water. The rest, why we just left it. That was a long way back and a long time ago."

"I can still smell it."

"No you can't. That's just imagination." Her hand slipped out of his suddenly and she swung to stare at him. Then her stare licked round the circle of silent watchers, and he "felt" her mind snap shut so violently that it was a blow.

"Greenies!" She came up to her knees and then a crouch. "Greenies! Hundreds of them!" She started to run, so abruptly that he barely managed to catch her arm. She flung off his clutch instantly but staggered into a sprawl and he dived, catching her by the ankle to bring her flat on her face.

104

"Hold still! There's nothing to be afraid of. These are friends!"

"Let me go!" She kicked her leg and scrabbled at the moss.

"Don't be a fool! You've been here a long while, perfectly safe. I tell you, these people are our friends!"

"Let me go . . . !"

"You've been cared for, fed, looked after and restored to sanity by these people. Don't ruin it all, now."

All at once she went quite still, face down. He relaxed his clutch, and on the instant she was free and away, up on her feet and running like a deer, straight between two stolid green men and down the slope.

"Martha!" he yelled. "Stop!" And then some of his rage spilled over on the mute audience. "Why the hell don't you help? Do something!" He bit off the rest as he saw no response, and started running after her down to the water-edge. She had plunged in up to her waist and was wading. He skirted the shore to keep abreast of her.

"Be sensible!" he called pleadingly. "There's no danger, nothing to run away from. At least give me a chance to explain."

He saw her turn and come wading out again. He waited for her. She came directly towards him and he extended his hand in reassurance. Her face was blank until she was close.

"Greenie!" She spat it at him, bringing her hand across and down, her fingers splayed like talons. Half-blinded, tears flooding his eyes, he reeled back and felt her brush past. By the time he could see again she was well away up the slope, making for distant bushes. A snatched glance showed him he was still not getting any help from the silent crowd. He ran. He didn't want to. He had no idea what he would do if and when he caught her. He wished vainly for the moral courage to stand, to just let her run, let her decide her own fate. But he ran, just the same.

Freakishly, the mist-veil that covered the land, lifted aside long enough to let him see her and, looming up out of the swirl to her left, a truck, a great headlamp-eyed monster, hopeless-wheels churning at the moss. She ran forward, arms waving, shouting, but the truck snorted past within feet of her, totally indifferent. She spun to pursue

105

it. He saw it duck sidewall-deep into swampy ooze, the wheels completely disappearing, and then it righted itself and surged competently on. The glowing mist swept down just as he saw her plunge after, and lurch to a stop, hip-deep in ooze.

"Martha!" he yelled, running crazily, "lie down flat and swim it!"

"Keep away from me!" she screeched instantly. Mud sucked at his feet. In two more steps he was up to his knees and sinking.

"Lie down!" he shouted again.

"Keep away, you Greenie!" she screamed. "Keep off!"

He heard her thrashing about. Taking his own advice he threw himself forward and began a desperate swimming action, ploughing through the sucking ooze, spitting it out of his mouth and straining always to keep in touch with her. By perverse instinct she had thrown a wall around her thoughts and he could no longer "feel" her. But he heard her laugh. Or screech. He couldn't be sure which. He had no breath to spare for calling out. He squirmed on by painful inches, spreading his arms to feel, to grope, trying to touch her. He kept on, even after she had stopped thrashing about, after she had fallen dreadfully silent.

Then he "felt" the keen wrench of her agony as she breathed water instead of air, as she choked . . . and died, not all at once as he had imagined it would be, but little by little, the way a crowd breaks up and disperses, as the multitude of complex interdependent processes which go to make up living faltered one by one and became still.

Then, when all was still and silent, and there was only a great hollow echo in his mind, he floundered round and dragged himself to where he could feel solid resistence under his elbows. Then he heaved himself up out of the slime, crawled out on to the wet warmth of moss, and lay there, empty.

At last, like an automaton he lurched to his feet and began to walk back. Because he could think of nothing else to do. Ten steps and he fell heavily to his knees. Brainless effort got him up to his feet again. Two more steps, and he fell once more, flat on his face, numbly surprised that he had felt no bump, had felt nothing, could feel nothing now except stupid comfort. Why not just leave it at that? Why bother with more?

He let go his last finger-nail of effort and slumped mindlessly. Then the darkness of his thoughts flooded with a vision of the quiet valley, the bright glow and color, the placidly moving green people. And Lovely, who seemed to be looking at him, holding out her arms. A pleasant dream. He let himself slip into it.

He woke in the dark, muzzily aware of pleasure only a breath away, of a gentle caressing warmth that was more than just a physical touch. Half-remembered thoughts rippled and spun, not quite in focus. Vague memories of a long and staggering walk through mist, with the strength of many to uphold him, and security wrapping him round . . . the security which held him now, at this moment. Security and contentment. The thought suddenly snagged like a hang-nail, hurting. He stirred, and a warm thought soothed him at once. He knew instantly who it was and rejected her so violently that she squirmed away from him in the dark and sat up, the violet moons of her eyes glowing reproachfully at him.

"You were happy then," she said. "Now you are angry again. Is it better to be angry, or sad, always?"

"I will not"—he said it very distinctly, convincing himself—"be an animal. I will not relapse into blind and stupid contentment, uncaring. I will *not!*" Which was fine to say, and she gave no argument, but it left him facing a blank against which all his righteous resentment seethed in vain. He felt the weight of unrighted wrongs bearing down, the burn of unjustice, the nagging urge to *do* something. But what?

She kept a discreet distance, patiently, and began to hum a snatch of melody.

"Where did you hear that music?" he demanded, dreading her answer.

"What is 'music'? Doctor did not tell us that word."

"You mean . . . you *have* no music? No singing? You were singing, just then. That, what you were doing, making sounds without speech with your voice, that is music. Where did you hear it?"

"When the other woman died, and you were very

107

sad, many voices shouted in your mind, all together. And many other sounds, too. I heard, because I was listening for you, because I am your woman. I heard. No other person on Venus has ever heard such things, this which you call music."

"No one? Ever?"

"None," she said, and where he would have doubted anyone else, he knew that she spoke true. That was a secondary implication, that with a people who exchanged "thought-feelings" as freely as this, what one of them knew, all would know. So they had no music, his people. It was a mind-staggering thought. And a valuable one, too.

"You liked it?"

"It was very wonderful. More than anything I have ever known. A great mystery. You can do that many-sound again, in your mind?"

"As often as I like. And others." He danced a dainty Mozart minuet for her, and sensed her instant rapture. It gave him a feeling of power, and he knew it to be real. Music hath charms, he thought, and a small spark of jubilation began to glow in him, walled with caution, but alight.

"It was wonderful," she whispered. "I have never known anything like such feelings. Colors and sounds and patterns, so beautiful. I am so glad I am your woman." He seized on that, too, with instant ruthlessness.

"What does that mean, that you will do things for me?"

"For you, anything. What you want, I want."

"Good!" The fire began to burn in him now, threatening his caution. "Tell me, what the old man does . . . you can do it? You can reach out and be in touch with others, other chiefs of other tribes?"

"What he does, I can do. When he dies, that will be my function."

"All right!" He stirred, got to his knees, pointed his head to the glow that was the mouth of the cave. "Come on. You and I are going to see the old man. I want to tell him a thing or two, and I need your help."

The old green man was still sitting where he had been, as impassive as a sun-dial. Anthony squatted before him, ordering his thoughts.

"I've got some very important information for you," he

said. "I want you to listen carefully, and then pass it on to all the people. Understand?"

"I will hear, first. How important?"

"This much. The humans have told you false. One did, at least. They come here to take over your planet. They destroy you, slowly at first, but more and more. In the end, all green people will die. They must be stopped. We must fight them, now!"

The old face twisted into a ghost of a grin. "You say this like a child afraid of shadows, using strange words. What is 'take over'? And how, if it was true that humans are dangerous, do we stop them? What is 'fight'?"

"Humans are friends," Lovely murmured, at his elbow. "Doctor said so. Also, when you went away to earth, they cared well for you. How can you say they are false?"

Anthony had expected something like this. To the old man he gave a thin smile. "Friends? Doctor told you, I'm sure, how friends behave, among humans. How they shake hands?" And he offered his right hand. The old man kept his faintly derisive smile, and put out his own hand in response. It felt leathery but firm in Anthony's grip. He took a good secure hold, and put on just a bit of pressure. The old man's grin faded. He tried to pull his hand away, but Anthony held on, increasing the pressure very slowly.

"You are hurting my hand."

"Yes." Anthony nodded, meeting the old eyes quite openly. "My hand is strong. It has done much work, much training. I can crush your hand to a pulp, old one. What can you do about it?" And he increased his grip-pressure, very slowly. He had no real desire to hurt this impassive old man, but it was the only immediate way he could devise to make his point, so he proceeded slowly, giving the chief time to reason his way through what was an entirely novel situation to him.

"Why do you seek to injure me?"

"That's my business. What are you going to do about it?"

The old face twitched, eyes shifting, seeking some answer. The grip went on increasing. Lovely stirred, hesitating but unable to hold herself.

"You must not do this thing!"

109

"You keep quiet. I'll ask when I want you. Let *him* handle it."

The grip went on increasing. Anthony knew the old man must be in very real distress now, although his face showed little of it. He would have given much to be able to see into that old mind, but he dared not even try. Instead he squeezed harder. And harder. And then, all at once, it was as if an enormous yet invisible vice closed in on him. In three dimensions it shut in on his arms and legs, his body, his heart, lungs and throat, a great and strangling pressure. Instant panic bloomed in him, but he fought it off. To move his head a fraction was a labor, but he made it, to mumble to Lovely, "Now! Now I need your help. What he does, you can do. Help me!" For a drawn-out moment the peaceful scene blurred in his vision and the black night of death was close as she hesitated in bewilderment. Then he felt the constricting pressure ease off, and saw the old man's face stiffen, saw sweat break out on him. Around the three, all in utter silence, there grew a tension that was unseen yet palpable enough to lean on. Even though he had been hoping for and expecting something like this, Anthony was awed by the sheer power that crackled round him. He relaxed his crushing grip.

"That will do," he gasped. "It's enough. Stop!" The tension disappeared like a burst bubble. He was drenched with sweat and laboring for breath. The old man stared at him, nostrils flaring.

"You play with things you do not understand. That is dangerous."

"On the contrary, I understand very well. You were threatened. You took action. That is what I meant by fighting. You *can* fight. You can do this to animals. She did it, when we came over the water in the boat."

"No," she contradicted. "It was not the same. All I did was to make our sea-brother take a different path, away from us."

"You could do that to humans, too. Or crush them, as he would have crushed me. That's what I want."

Now the old man's eyes shifted to Lovely. "Why did you do what you did, for him. This power, the gathering, is not for that! If you try it again, others will shut themselves off from you and you will have nothing."

110

Before she could reply Anthony staked his all on a gamble. Reaching out, he took her wrist. "Give him this. Give it also to all the people of this tribe," and in his mind he built up the blaring fanfare of trumpets from the Prelude to the second act of *Lohengrin,* the most arrogant burst of music he could think of at short notice, Wagner at his defiant best. He saw the old man's eyes open very wide, and all the rest of him freeze utterly still.

"That is why," he murmured, when it was done. "I, too, have power. Try this, for contrast." And he "played" the sugary-sweet *Barcarolle* from Hoffmann, giving it overtones of sybaritic delight that Offenbach might have envied. He saw that Lovely's eyes were closed in rapture, that way out on the fringes of the glade the green people were standing as if hypnotized. Then, when his mind was silent again, he met the old man's eyes.

"Because of that," he said, "she will do as I wish. For that, so will all the people do what I wish. It is a great power."

Instantly, with no need for words, he knew the old man was against him. He knew that countless centuries of traditional and unquestioning belief refused to be overthrown. He knew that the fight was only just begun, that he had yet to win this old man to his cause. A house divided must fall, he thought. It was something, just to have shown this old man that force existed and could be used. It was something to have shaken him with a new kind of persuasion. But Anthony felt, instinctively, that he was doomed to failure unless he could bring this old man—and all the other old men—over to his side. And that prompted a question, something he needed to know.

"Doctor taught you many things, human things. Did he teach you to count?" He held up a hand to illustrate. "I have five fingers. Do you know what that means?"

The chief sneered and stirred. "We learned this thing, and the words. Ten of ten is a hundred. Ten of hundreds is a thousand. And so on. Hundred of thousands. Millions. Because Doctor wished to know how many people we were. This was important to him, although he never said what it was good for. Earth people have many curious ways. But they are not a danger."

"I'll get to that in a minute, I hope. Wanted to estimate

111

the total population, did he? And you were able to count and tell him? How many?"

Anthony expected a large fingure, a meaningless figure, but he reeled as the old man said, "Three hundreds of millions!" It was pointless to argue the figure. Even if the old man was out by a factor of ten, it was still a number to bewilder the mind.

"You mean adults, like us?"

"We do not count children," the chief said scornfully.

"And you're in touch with all of them?"

"Of course!"

Of course. It was devastatingly simple for the old man, but enough to fill Anthony's mind with fog. A fraction of a percentage of that vast horde would be more than enough to wipe out the human colony, to tramp the domes flat and to stamp into oblivion all their works. Just a fraction, if he could get them, appeal to them, stir them up, set them marching. But could he, up against the old men?

"With so many, and the humans are few hundreds, why do you permit them to remain?"

"They do no harm."

"But this is your planet. They're interlopers. They have a world of their own!"

"They do no harm! Three small enclosures is nothing!" The old man began to show signs of boredom. Anthony felt the flame of his resolve flicker and dwindle among so many immense concepts.

"What about your people?" he demanded. "Your brothers? The humans make slaves of them, treat them as animals, beating, flogging, poisoning, making them work, killing them. Don't you care about that?"

"This is false!"

"You mean you don't know? You don't know that your own people, *my* people, are being exploited and killed, like brainless animals?" Lovely put a gentle hand on his arm. He turned angrily to her.

"A tree bears much fruit," she said. "Some of it, not much, may be bad. It rots, withers, and falls from the tree. Do you expect the tree to stoop and pick it up again?" It took several seconds for the ruthless commonsense of what she had said to sink in. Those green people who fell prey to the human population of the domes . . . were defectives?

112

The urge to deny it died on his tongue. This people knew far more about mental deficiency than he would ever know. He had to accept their statement, sour as it was. The flame flickered lower as he searched desperately for a lever to move their indifference.

"The humans take away great quantities of your beans," he said. And in that instant, with that simple statement, he knew he had won. The battle was by no means over, but he had his lever. Their stiff masks of outrage told him all he needed, even if he had not been able to "feel" the horror in them.

"You know this?" The old man's face was as bleak as weathered copper ore. "You know it, for sure?"

"I know this. Long ago the first humans discovered the bean and took some back to Earth. There it was found to have many wonderful properties, and now they prize it greatly. To them it gives youth, health and new life. In their need for it they made the domes, put the people there." He whirled on Lovely. "You were watching as I ran after the woman Martha. You saw, through me, the strange machine which passed? In that were humans. They were looking for the bean plants. Those they find, they take up by the roots and transport to the area near the domes, and plant them. There they have much space, full of bean-plants. Because they do not know properly how to care for and protect the plants, they capture those of our people that you call 'rotten,' but who are still clever enough to do this work."

"But even the spoiled-brain ones will pick and eat," the old man argued. "Even a brainless animal will do this."

"Oh yes, they do. At least, they get all ready to do it, when the time of ripening comes. But then the humans leave their domes, come out into this atmosphere, which they hate and which is too hot for them—as Doctor must have told you—and they snatch the ripe beans from the hands of those who gather. They whip and flog and beat, to make them yield. And then they collect vast quantities of beans, in bags, and—you saw the bags which we brought." He waited for that to sink in. "You saw! Martha and myself took a bag each away from the humans who had, in turn, taken the beans away from your brainless ones.

113

That was why we had to run away, because we were only two against many."

"You say they make the bean grow in great quantities?"

"Oh yes. They gather the young plants and make them grow to yield a crop. Then the plants die, but they go out and collect more, in their machines. And they will go on doing this, because the beans are greatly prized by the other humans, on Earth. On Earth there are five thousands of millions of humans . . ." He let the words drift into silence.

The old man made an utterly indescribable sound, but there was no need to translate it. The meaning was clear.

"We must stop them. You are right. It must stop. But how? You will tell me how."

They squatted silently on the surf, wrapped in a halo of pearly mist. *Just we two,* Anthony thought, *but behind us a thousand, or a million if necessary.* It was a strangely comforting thought. In rare moments of stillness like this, he was able to dwell on the rapid transformation that had come in his fortunes. From all points within a grand circle roughly one hundred miles in radius and centered on the domes, green people were on the march. A slowly plodding, steady swarm of them, continually in touch, occasionally inspired by melodies, they moved in on the unsuspecting human colony. Anthony had found a common factor between his own people and humans on the level of emotional reaction to music. March melodies, whether from *Tannhäuser, Aida,* or Schubert's *Marche Militaire,* or even the fiercely nationalistic *Marseillaise,* all evoked a similar response. He couldn't be sure whether the charm was in the non-verbal reaction to rhythm, or, as he suspected, due to the fact that he was transmitting, all unwittingly, his own sentiments along with the music. Whichever it was, it worked, and the sense of masterful power was intoxicating. But now he was more intent on something quite different.

Lovely squatted by his side, as silent as he, but her attention was cast away to a distant point. On his instruction she had spun a web of close espionage, searching with a thousand eyes and ears, and now they had netted the fish they sought. She stirred.

114

"It comes nearer, coming this way. Soon we will be able to hear it for ourselves. Shall I try, now?"

"All right," he agreed. "I'm sorry I can't help. Wish I could."

She hushed him with a gentle touch, understanding quite well. This was a moment to make him realize his ignorance. He knew that she was reaching out, trying to sense the humans who were within the swamp-car which was rolling their way. Although the very act itself was meaninglessly foreign to him, he could see readily that there had to be a difference between this, and her ability to contact and influence the sub-intelligent responses of some animal. Animals she had known all her life. A roaring thing of metal and power-drives, with glaring lights, porthole eyes, churning wheels and possible weapons was so totally alien to her as to make it a nightmare to visualize. How much more difficult then to reach through that to the minds of the men inside? She snorted a quick breath, and gripped his arm again.

"It is no good. I can feel nothing but confusion. Two men, I think. Or perhaps three. I cannot even be sure of that. It is useless."

"Never mind. We expected snags, remember. We'll just have to try our second-string trick. Call up the worm."

She nodded, a wavering jade figure in the mist, and he sharpened his ears, getting ready to run. This tactic could be dangerous. Far away over there—he could manage *that* much by himself—a quick-footed knot of green men were coaxing and taunting a giant worm, like the one that had scared the life out of him before, on the plain. Into its vegetable-mind they were insinuating the suggestion that there was a large and delicious source of food somewhere quite near. Tantalizingly near. Now, under the direction of their "chief," that intuition would become strong, and the worm would plunge off, seeking to fill its great maw.

He heard the distant gargling bellow, and the growing boom of the swamp-car's engines, simultaneously, from different sides. Beneath him, the damp moss trembled to the heaving approach of a gigantic body. He kept quite still, trying to sense the thing coming. He got a blurred feeling of hunger, of great urgency, and eagerness. Then, out of the mist the huge head loomed up, ringed with violet lamp-eyes. He knew a madly irrelevant moment of wonder,

115

that with eyes all round its mouth, this thing would never know whether it was the right way up or not. If it had a "right" way up. But it certainly knew which way it was going. Eighty feet of it rustled by him, almost in touching distance, the massive leather-plated barrel of its body all of nine feet thick. And then he saw the swamp-car, dark and roaring, its goggle-eyes spearing twin beams of light.

Caught by the hard tension of the moment he forgot entirely the dizzy confusion of seeing with his own eyes, and sensing through the little band of people with him, both together, the fractionated feeling of being in several places at once. Leaping up, he plunged after that voracious great thing, saw its blunt head rear and strike massively, at the car, and heard the dull thump of the impact. The worm-head bounced, drew back. A hideous scream blasted the mist as it swung round for another try, the slow curves of its body rippling round into a trapping circle. There came sharp dagger-flames and the spit-crack of a turret-weapon. Anthony fell flat, shouting a warning, knowing that the others had hit the moss as fast as his own reflexes had taken him. Head up, he watched, saw the weapon stammer again and saw large chunks of meat exploding from the worm's carcass.

Some kind of fragmentation projectiles, he guessed, but there was no need to guess about something much more immediate. One of the drawbacks of empathy was its two-way effect. He could "feel" those great tearing wounds, even as the worm felt them . . . dimly, because its sensory capacity was slight, but he felt them, and groaned at the pain of them, just the same. The huge head lifted and flailed down again, flat on the top of the car, hammering it into the soft surface. Then the gouged body flowed massively over the car, beating it deeper down, the blunt tail adding a final hammer-blow as it went over. Back around came the head, insensate now with pain and all-important hunger, and arrowed down, gouging into the soft earth, burrowing under the car, heaving it into the air. Anthony spared a shivering thought for the humans inside as the vehicle lifted and slammed back, upside down, crashing into the soggy surface. The weapon was silent.

Somehow, Lovely was at his side, touching his arm. "Inside," she said, "they are dead, now." And he snatched at his instant anger, remembering that for her, unconsciousness equalled death. He wanted live specimens. If they were only unconscious, that would do.

"Have them call off the worm," he said. "And six or seven will have to help upturn that car and get them out of there."

The combined strength of many arms rocked the hapless vehicle, got it swaying, heaved it over. Irrelevancies touched him again. Without training, these people could work in perfect co-ordination instantly, every man knowing exactly what to do, and what all the others were doing. Such potential was breath-taking. He thrust the thought away as he saw the armored access-doors. How could he open those, with bare hands? His violent urgency abated in the need for rational thought. There must be some way to open them from outside.

I'm beginning to think like a savage animal, he thought, and the thought chilled him. In a moment he had the trick of it, found levers and handles and heaved them. The car lay on its side. Through the opening door he could look in and down. Glaring light made him squint. Seat-cushions, shiny with plastic, made a tumbled confusion. Scratch-pads, scribbled sheets, a package of cigarettes, a flask of something, all in a dismal heap against the far wall. In the driving cock-pit was one man, and strapped in the control-seat of the turret-weapon was another. No more. Only two, hanging from their straps, but breathing. And bleeding. He saw it all in one frantically urgent study. Then he flung the door wide and dropped down inside. Lovely was right after him, catlike and wide-eyed.

"They're not dead, only stunned when the car went right over. Help me undo these straps . . . No, have the gang tip this thing further, all the way upright. Yes?" She nodded gravely, and he felt the vehicle lurch.

It was still a trifle alien to him to have orders passed without so much as a sound, but his rapport was growing with every effort. The man at the gun was bleeding from a simple skull-wound, but the driver was in worse case. By appearance, he had tried to push his face through his console-panel, despite his safety-harness.

Two black eyes and a broken nose, and associated bruises and strains, Anthony thought, and then wondered how he

117

could be so instantly sure. The car came down on its hope-less wheels with a thump.

"They're coming round. Now's your chance to work on them."

"I am trying," she murmured. "It is difficult, like speaking words that have no meaning. A confusion." He stepped clear, as far as the small confines of the car would allow, and watched. Both men wore the minimum of shorts, and sandals. One was sandy-haired, the other dark, both about thirty. He knew them to be the technician grade, and wondered, for the first time, just what *they* thought about this fairy-land of their wealthy employers. Where did they stand in the question of exploitation? He noted, belatedly, that each man wore a gun-belt, and was wryly amused at the thinking behind that. Imagine plunging out into the mist to tackle a worm, with that thing!

Then the man in the weapon-chair snorted, groaned, and lifted his head, shook the black hair out of his eyes, stared round. Even as he saw the two green figures his hand went back, down and up, all in one fast movement, and Anthony reached for the wrist holding that gun. He did it without thought, by sheer reflex, knowing that death stared him right in the eye, only a finger-pressure away. Without bothering to know how, he wrenched that wrist up and a-way.

The weapon went off, in that metal confinement, sounding like a bomb, but the bullet flattened itself vainly on the ceiling. Deafened, frightened, and suddenly savage in his new-found power, Anthony applied a "squeeze" and the black-haired man stiffened, his face purpling, eyes bulging, locked in an invisible grip. Then, staggeringly, Anthony felt the power wane and weaken. It was a distinct sensation of ebbing strength.

"No!" Lovely said distinctly. "You must not kill!"

"You saw what he was going to do to me! And then you, after that, you may be sure. Why shouldn't he be killed?"

"I do not know any why. I only know it is wrong to kill like this."

For a futile second he raged against her sudden awkwardness. "What I want, you want. Remember, you said this?"

"I said it. But not now." Her jaw was stubborn. "It is wrong to kill."

Frustration boiled in him, then it went as suddenly as it had come. This was no time to argue with her näive moral sense, or to wonder whether empathy had anything to do with her stubborn refusal to lend him power. His wits, hardened by many trials, found the way to turn this impasse to his own wishes. He eyed the black-haired man grimly.

"You heard what the lady said? And she is a lady, even if she's green, and naked, don't forget that. She just saved your life. For the moment, that is. Drop the weapon. You too!" He spun on the sandy-haired man, who was beginning to stir in his seat. "You might as well know what you're up against. There's only two of us here, but there are as many thousands as you care to name outside and all round, so don't try anything stupid."

The man in the driver's seat groaned, put hands to his face to feel, very delicately, of his wounds.

"I've got 'em," he mumbled. "A couple of Greenies talking English."

"It's no illusion! We're real. She objects to having you killed, but she couldn't stop me from tossing the pair of you outside, and letting you try to walk back to base. And that would be the same thing, wouldn't it?"

"What d'you want?" the black-haired one asked. "Who the hell are you, anyway? No, shut up, Hoby, this is real. I've seen this one before somewhere. Look, my name's Shaw. Mike Shaw. That wreck there is Hoby Wilson. Now who the hell are you? And can we have that door shut, because this heat is cooking us. No tricks, this is straight." Anthony smiled without mirth, and pushed the armored door closed. He heard the air-conditioning plant humming, felt the temperature begin to fall immediately. Lovely shivered, but it was with pleasure rather than trepidation.

"No tricks," he echoed. "Metal walls make no difference to us. I am Anthony Taylor . . ." He hesitated and then, without any uncertainty at all, he added, "King of the Greenies!"

Shaw started, and stared. "Taylor? Not the missing piano-player? That Taylor? But you were—you are . . . Weren't you a white man, a human?"

119

"Was I? Does the color of the skin make so much difference? Yes, I was as white and human as you. Now I'm a Greenie. That ought to make you think a bit. And while you're thinking, there's this to add. Where do you stand? What's your attitude?"

"What d'you mean? How do I feel about Greenies?" Shaw rubbed his sore head and frowned. "I've no hard feelings one way or the other. They look like people to me, but the biologists reckon they're not. Me, I'm an electronics technician. Who ever asks my opinions on that kind of thing?"

"You must be nuts," Wilson snarled. "This is just a trick, a glorified talking parrot. Everybody knows Greenies are just dumb animals! You've seen plenty of 'em! What's the matter with you, gone soft in the head?"

Anthony had swiveled his gaze to Wilson and so missed Lovely's gesture, her pointing finger, her blazing scorn.

"I can touch your mind," she said. "It is a crawling thing, sick with ills and fears, a smell! We have people like this, too, but we do not accept them as whole. We judge them defective. You too, I think."

Wilson twisted his blood-stained face into a bare-teeth menace, dragging at his gun exactly as Shaw had done. Anthony felt her pressure strike him as if he shared in the fringe of it. Wilson got the whole of it, the full impact of her wrath, and his struggling figure seemed to wilt and sag in the driver's seat.

"Hey! Hold up!" Shaw cried. "You said it was wrong to kill, remember?" And Lovely's accusative finger drooped. She took in a deep breath.

"You are right. I can feel you, too, but you are not as he is. And this has troubled me. Anthony . . ." She shifted her worried violet eyes to him. "This I have been thinking ever since you said we must strike, and drive out the humans from our planet. Just as we are not all the strong, so it must be with humans. Not all are bad."

Anthony sighed. "There is no time now to explain this to you properly. There is truth in what you say, but it is not as simple as you think."

"Just a minute," Shaw interrupted. "You have to be kidding! Drive us out, away from Venus? How the blazes do you reckon to do that? No offense intended, believe me, but you're naked, and defenseless. You're just sitting up and begging for trouble if the big boys in the domes as much as suspect any such move. Like I said, I'm not taking sides in this, but if you started wiping out humans, then I would have to object, like it or not."

"What's more," Wilson sneered, getting over his moment of fear. "Even if you did knock out the domes, and all the people in them, how long d'you think it would be before Earth struck back, eh? And then where would you be, mister?"

Anthony stared at him, at Shaw, and then swung his gaze round to Lovely. He could see and feel her bewilderment. He sighed. "It's true. If we struck at the colony, if we inflicted damage, even the few who do not believe that green people are animals would be swung over to the desire for revenge." As he said it, he sensed that she didn't know the meaning of the word. "Revenge means, quite simply, if you hit me I will hit you afterwards, only harder. Don't try to understand, just accept that."

"You mean they don't know about revenge?" Shaw was frankly incredulous.

"Do you think they'd have stood by and let their own people be abused like animals, otherwise? They—I mean 'we'—believe that any adult person should bear his own responsibilities, that co-operation is the right way. . . . Oh, what's the use?"

"Is it true that you collect our bean-plants and take them away, to grow, and then take the beans away to Earth?" Lovely's voice was stern.

"I'd be a fool to deny it." Shaw jerked his thumb to the rear of the car, indicating a sizeable pile of immature plants, each sealed in a plastic sack. She stared at them, feelings churning. Her evident distress triggered a desperate idea in Anthony's mind. To Wilson in the driving-seat he said, "Start up. Head for Dome One. Prime Base, as you call it."

"Drop dead, Greenie!"

"You're a fool. More guts than brains. Once more, start up, or I'll toss you out and let you walk home. And she won't object to that, because to her it would be no hardship at all. It wouldn't be killing, in her terms."

"Go ahead and toss me out," Wilson snarled. "Where

121

would that get you? He can't handle this thing. You'd be stuck just the same."

Anthony smiled, with no humor at all. "Now you're taking me for a fool. If Shaw can't drive this thing he's more stupid than I take him for. I can drive it myself, come to that. You're still being deceived by the color of my skin, but that's your problem. Make up your mind, quick!"

"Don't be a damn fool, or a hero, Hoby. Get going. What's to lose?" Shaw swung round in his seat and got up, oddly awkward. "You can have my seat," he offered, and Lovely smiled at the gesture, making him turn delicate pink. She accepted, settling herself on the resilient cushions and savoring the new sensation. Motors coughed and hummed into life as Wilson settled down to his job with a bad grace. Anthony, balancing himself against the pitching of the floor, went to look over his shoulder.

"I can also read a marker-beacon," he murmured. "Just in case you had any more crazy notions. That thing . . ." and he jabbed his finger at it as it pulsed and died on the panel. "See you follow it!" He went back to sit by Shaw on the padded side-seat.

"I hope you know what you're doing," Shaw caressed his bruised head and scowled in sympathy. "Like I said, I don't want to take sides, but it's no more than fair to warn you that you're heading into a bomb, going back to the domes. If you are Taylor, you've been missing a hell of a long time, and there's been seventeen different kinds of panic-call about you, and the dame. The top committee is fit to do murder, and not fussy about whom they pick."

Anthony hid his chagrin. This was an aspect he had overlooked in his nebulous plans. He had so long been accustomed to think of himself as a nonentity that it had never occurred to him he would be missed, or that the missing would be an occasion for uproar. The germ of a notion tried to get rooted in his mind but was swamped by the thought that this was just one more complication to the deadlock.

"Deadlock!" He said it aloud. Shaw eyed him curiously, and Anthony smiled a sour smile. "My people have been abused, exploited, treated as animals and worse. And yet, if we try to take action to correct the mistaken impression

122

it will immediately be construed as a threat, a menace. I don't want that. None of us wants it."

"What *do* you want, anyway?"

"Immediately? That the present state of affairs should stop, that the green people be accepted as equals. Different in many ways, but equal. This is *our* planet!"

"I wish you luck." Shaw sounded sincere but troubled. "I can't see how you're going to do it. You're bothering me, even, just sitting there and talking like a white man, when I can see you're not. Maybe if I shut my eyes it would be different. I could be wrong, but my guess is the only way you will do it is by force. That's something we humans understand."

"And the result? You know what would be the outcome of that, only too well."

"Dead right," Shaw muttered, his eyes going appreciatively to Lovely, and flicking away again every time she rewarded him with a smile. "One thing we humans are very good at, and that's force. Look, I'd better move up front with Hoby, keep an eye on him. I don't want to know what scheme you're planning. It's better that way, I reckon."

As he staggered away, Anthony leaned across to her to murmur, "The others are still in touch?"

"Yes. They follow. What are you thinking?"

"It would be better if you didn't know until I've worked it out more. In the meantime there's something that can be done." And he put his head close to hers to explain exactly what he wanted. Lurching along in the powerful car, surrounded by the sophistication of human technology, it was eerie to realize that as fast as he could formulate the designs, hundreds of thousands of distant green people were responding, moving, preparing to carry out his wishes.

Her eyes widened as she absorbed what he was saying. "It is so huge?" she wondered. "And yet so easily destroyed as you say? That no more than a breath holds it up?"

"Like a bubble on the surface of water." he nodded. "Natural forces like this are understood by humans, and used by them. This car, the cool feeling, the lights, all are natural things which the humans have taken and used for their own wishes."

"They are wonderful beings. I am glad we will not be

123

against them. This is 'cool,' this feeling of being in water, but dry?"

"Right. You like it?" He watched her face, and could share her pleasure in this utterly foreign but exciting sensation. "Inside the domes it is like this all the time. On Earth, most of the places on Earth, it is like this, also. That is one of the reasons why Earth people wear clothing, and why they dislike our climate."

"Cool. Dry. Clothing. So many new and exciting things the humans have. And we have so little."

He frowned at that, his memory telling him of the sad fate of the primitive savage who learns to yearn for the superficial sparkle of civilized life. But, he corrected himself quickly, these people were not primitive, not mentally. And they did have something, something very valuable to certain other people.

The car roared on, dipping and plunging, tearing blindly through the pearly mist, warned of obstructions by its sonar, and led as if on a string by the beacon-marker. Anthony schooled himself to be patient, to avoid worrying about troubles before they came. From time to time he set himself to "play" selected pieces of music for the unseen and ant-like throng out there. They liked marching melodies and dancing rhythms, and no performer was ever so eagerly listened to, or so keenly aware of audience reaction.

After a while Shaw took over at the controls to let Wilson come back and sit and light a smoke for himself. His face was a gruesome sight, what with the puffing around his eyes from the blow, dried streaks of blood, and the gobs of antiseptic and soothing jelly Shaw had smeared on him as temporary medication. He was in pain, too, as Anthony could tell without having to make the effort to "contact" him.

"Should be sighting the dome in about an hour," he growled. "You'll get yours then, Greenie. That's what I'm waiting for. You'll get yours."

"Why do you hate us so much?" Lovely asked, and the simple question seemed to infuriate the injured man.

"Damned uppity animals trying to act like humans. You've got the edge right now, all right, but just wait till we get in!" His senseless anger was an ugly thing, but it prompted Anthony to reflect again on his tentative plans.

124

He went to sit by Shaw. "You've probably guessed that I'm planning to get into the dome," he murmured. "And I'm going to. But where will that leave you? Will you raise the alarm? I can't expect you to try to pass us in."

Shaw frowned at his instrument board, struggling with a decision. "You want a hell of a lot of trust from me, Taylor. I don't know. You could fasten us up with something, give us an alibi in case you flop. I reckon you will. Flop, I mean. But suppose you do rope us, and then go ahead and slaughter a couple hundred humans? How am I going to feel, afterwards?"

"I'm sorry for you. I can't help, except to say that it is not my intention to kill anyone unless I am compelled to."

"Doesn't every revolutionary say that?"

"I suppose so," Anthony sighed. It was true. This was a revolution. But if he had any say in the matter, it was going to be different from all the others that had ever been known.

He left Shaw and went to the rear of the vehicle, searching among the equipment for enough stout plastic line to serve. Then he nodded to Lovely, who had been watching him. By this time the need for detailed explanation between them was slight. Wilson never had chance to make a sound. Only his eyes betrayed his rage, and fear, as the invisible bonds held him long enough for Anthony to rope him securely. Then the car was run to a halt long enough to make Shaw similarly helpless, and Anthony took over the controls. The marker pulse was very strong now, flooding the whole of the indicator quadrant with each beat, and the sonar picture was plain. In a little while the milky headlights gave back a reflection that could only be an artificial surface, a huge plane of smoothness, rearing up.

"This is it," Anthony breathed, and Lovely crouched by his side to peer through the viewfinder screen. She was shivering, and for the first time in his experiences with her, the rapport was broken. She had shut herself off from him. Intuition told him why. She was afraid. It was one thing to contemplate this alien environment from a distance, but something quite other to be confronted by the reality of it. She was afraid!

He wasted no time in reproach, or anger. Instead, with pressing urgency, he asked her, "When you hunt, out in the mist among dangers, do you ever try to make yourself unseen, to make suggestions in the mind of the animal threatening you such that it cannot see you?"

The question caught her attention away from the picture of out there, made her pretty brow wrinkle in thought. "What does this mean? How can it not see what is there?"

"You made the worm think it was pursuing food. You made it see what was not there. Can you not do the same now? We will be going inside, to pass among many humans. You know how to touch them, now. Can you make them *not* see us?"

She rejected the idea at once, as he could tell by her face. Snatching a glance ahead, and at the panel, he knew there was an entrance-lock quite close now. Once again desperation drove him to inspirations he would never have contemplated in saner moments.

"Never mind," he said. "Leave it to me. Just give me the power, as I need it, and let me channel it."

He cut the motor to a crawl, and then to a stop as he saw the entrance-port begin to cycle open in response to the built-in signal from the car.

"Come on, out," he said, "and follow me. Do as I do. You are a white human woman, returning from a short journey. Think that. Believe it. Believe it strongly!"

He scrambled out into the suddenly oppressive heat and headed for the slowly-opening door, knowing that she was at his heels. In his mind, as strongly assured as he could make it, was a personal image of himself as he had been the last time he had gone in by such a door. White, human, clothed, and with a white woman. Believe it! he ordered himself. Believe it, project it, assume that everyone within eye-shot accepts it! He strode into the space between the walls, into the harsh glare and the grumble of busy machinery. A small knot of technicians some distance away gave him an indifferently curious glance and returned to their work. He bit down on a sudden elation. It worked, but it had to be kept working. He took her hand, halting her for a moment.

"See this," he urged. "See it well, and pass it to the others." In brief gestures, augmented with mental pictures, still struggling to maintain the illusion of human appearance, he explained to her the double-wall arrangement and the

126

purpose of the machines, gave her a clear mental image of the great ballooning wall of plastic which rose from this space. Not so far away now a horde of green people, each armed with a razor-edged sword-leaf, absorbed the information as fast as it was passed, and began to arrange themselves in a certain order. Smothering his doubts, Anthony led her now to the inner door.

"Do not be distracted by anything that you see. Just follow. Do as I do, and do not break the flow of power, whatever happens."

She seized his hand. "Anthony . . . I am afraid. It is so huge!"

"I know. Be afraid all you want, there's no shame in that. But believe in me; believe that you have every right to be here; believe that everything is going to be fine; believe! Remember that three hundred million of your people are depending on you, and through you and me, at this moment."

The door hummed open and he stepped over the sill, leading her in. He felt again that sudden shiver as the cool dry atmosphere leached away the thin film of moisture from his skin. Then he heard her gasp, and felt sympathy. The first look at this fairyland had shaken him. How much more would it stagger her, who had never known anything remotely resembling it?

"It is so beautiful," she breathed. "So beautiful. And real? It is not a sleeping-picture?"

"A dream, you mean?" It had never occurred to him to think that she dreamed, and the small astonishment threatened his mental control for a moment. Then he put it aside for some other time. "This is another thing Earth people do. They take dreams and try to make them real. But they seldom succeed so well as this." He left it at that, not wishing to point up the fact that this sweet-cake-and-icing picture was more illusion than anything else. He led her to a nearby floater and was handing her aboard when a startled roar made him swing round, stomach knotting in sudden panic.

"Hey! Taylor! Where the hell have you been?" It was the forthright and red-headed Barney Lyons, staring-eyed and indignant. Anthony met his eye, torn between elation at this confirmation of the effectiveness of his illusion, and sinking chagrin that of all the many people in this dome they had to run right into someone who knew them. Them? Lyons came close, nodded to Lovely.

"Am I glad to see you two safe! And is there going to be one hell of a stink about this! No, never mind the explanations right now. Just hang on." He climbed up on the floater beside Anthony. "I'm taking you to Bord Harper, right away. And M'Grath. This, I want to see!" He spun the car and sent it skimming along a wide lane, a route Anthony recognized only too well.

He felt Lovely's clutch on his arm and put his hand on hers in reassurance. "He believes me to be as I was," he whispered. "And is taking you for the woman who was with me before. Don't bother about it now. I had not meant it this way, but it is all to the good. Is the other operation all ready?"

"Not yet," she breathed, "but very soon now."

"Good! Just be confident. All is going to come out fine. You'll see."

He heard Lyons mumbling into a communicator, but he was much more engrossed in trying to guess just what awaited them as they slid to a halt before the great central assembly building. As they reached the top of the great flight of stairs he cast a quick glance backward and saw the first wave of scurrying float-cars in hot pursuit.

M'Grath was as massive, and as thunderously impassive, as ever. By his side Borden Harper stood angrily, containing himself with an obvious effort. He repeated the question Lyons had asked, as the trio hurried down the ramp-stairs to the central ampitheater.

"Where the hell have you two been? You'll have to bear with my language, Miss Merrill, but I feel it's justified. Talk, Taylor. Four weeks ago, in the middle of Harvest, you vanished. We turned the entire colony inside out to look for you. We've had cars out combing the local area, even though we knew it was pretty futile. We've had the damnedest communications from home. Your colleague, Willers, shipped out three days ago, and what he'll say when he reaches Earth I shudder to think. So, by God, you're going to talk, and it had better be good, or you'll regret the day you ever were born. That I can promise you."

"I've done that a few times already," Anthony said, feeling a sudden wave of savage elation, a surge of confidence. "Your threat doesn't scare me one bit, Harper. Nor anything else you can do. Not anything!"

"One moment!" M'Grath put a massive hand on Harper's arm to still his angry retort. "I sense something different about our errant piano-player, a new arrogance. What did you find, out there, Taylor?"

"What have I found? Myself. And three hundred million green people. Not animals, Harper. People! People who know why you're here, what you're doing and why. Work it out for yourself how they feel about it. I'm saying no more now. I see you've sent out a call, and that the crowd is gathering. When I do talk, it will be to all of them, not just you."

"You're out of your mind," Harper snarled. "You couldn't have lasted a day out there, not on your own. Somebody put you up to this. Somebody's using you as a tool!" He swiveled his gaze to Lovely. "Are you in on this too, Miss Merrill?"

"She is with me in everything," Anthony said, taking her hand.

"Call it my conceit," M'Grath rumbled, "but I pride myself I can detect the sound of sincerity, and that, while no guarantee of accuracy, should give us reason to pause and be cautious. The figure intrigues me, too. Three hundred million! Taylor, are you saying that you have succeeded where our best scientists have failed, that you can communicate with these sub-human—"

"Your *best* scientists?" Anthony interrupted, raising his voice over the growing hubbub of the gathering crowd as they settled around the tiered seats of the great hall. "Biologists, perhaps? But you're a psychologist. You should be aware that even the cleverest scientist cannot communicate with an imbecile, an idiot, or a mental defective. How would an alien judge human beings, if all he ever met were the inmates of an institution for the sub-normal?"

M'Grath's jowly face grew a sudden perplexity and he would have spoken, but Harper was too impatient to wait. "Whoever's using you to drive a wedge in between us is due for a big shock," he said. "I know only too well just how the majority of people back home hate our guts—

how they'd like to see us broken. And this little stunt hasn't helped any. But we've got a card to play, the sensible ones among us. We'll find out just who cooked up this notion, and smash him. And Earth will have to lump it. Because without us—no beans!"

Anthony felt Lovely's hand twitch in his. All unwittingly, Harper had said the one thing needed to make her determination assert itself again. He turned to see that the auditorium was almost full, that there were more here than there had been for his music recital, so long ago it seemed. This time none of them wanted to view by device. They wanted to see this in person. Even the sober-clad technical staff had come in droves.

Harper stepped to the fore, raising his hands. "You've all heard, that's obvious. Here are the precious couple all the fuss was about. Safe and sound. Unharmed. I assume that, like me, you are all glad nothing has happened to them. But, getting that out of the way, you'll want to know just what did happen? I think I know. I think this was a put-up job by somebody, or some group, right here in our midst. Somebody with funny ideas about shaking up the present arrangements. That's what I think. If that turns out to be true, we'll know what to do, I reckon." He paused to smile savagely at the many-voiced growl of anger that grew out of the crowd. Anthony pressed the trembling fingers that lay in his own.

"Now, as never before," he whispered, "I need your belief, your trust, your power. Just give it, all of it, and let me channel it as I decide."

"There will be no killing?"

"No. That I promise. Some may die of fright or folly. For them, I cannot be responsible. But there will be no killing."

"All right!" Harper waved a hand. "Let's hear what they have to say, first of all. Let's play this thing fair. Taylor, you have the floor."

Anthony went forward two paces, leading Lovely with him. To Harper, he said quietly, "I presume the other domes are watching this? By land-lines of some kind?"

"You can bet on it. You've got your audience. It had better be good!" Harper said, stepping away to one side.

Anthony turned to face the eager throng. "I am Anthony Taylor," he said, "King of the Greenies."

And this time he knew it to be true, sincere, and it made him feel curiously humble. The words fell into a silence, then exploded into a great shout of derisive laughter, underneath which was a distinct note of savagery. He waited for quiet.

"The green people have no concept of 'kingship,' or of any other kind of ruler, in your sense," he said, sweeping them with a curious gaze. "But they *do* have co-operation. And they do have, at last, a supreme spokesman—myself. I think they will overlook my use of the word 'king.' I speak for them!"

"You're as green as they are," some wag shouted, "if you believe that!"

"Quite true. I am as green as they are. As you can see!"

And he cast off the illusion that had wrapped him and Lovely with false appearances. It was surprisingly difficult to do, to strip himself, physically, mentally, figuratively—and irrevocably—before that hostile throng of eyes. He was surprised and ashamed to find that, far away at the back of his mind, he had clung to a fragment of insane hope that he would one day be white again. To pull that out and throw it away was like losing a tooth. But he did it.

In the stunned silence he turned to look at the girl by his side, and was struck by the change in her. The transformation was as delightful as it was unexpected. In this dry and cool atmosphere her skin had lost its sheen, its oily sleekness. Now it had a peach-bloom glow of radiance like velvet and silk in delicate combination. There was an added lift, a buoyancy in her shape, too, and her long black hair that had been heavy and clinging was now a dark lustrous cloud about her glowing face. Where she had been lovely before, she was ten times more so now.

It was just a glance, but it helped to bear in on him the difference that could come to his people, the transformation that could happen to all of them, given the right circumstances. The knowledge stiffened him against the sullen roar of the frightened mob, for that's what it was, now. He put up a hand.

"I am green. I speak for all the other green people. You will do well to listen, before it is too late." The implied

131

threat got him silence. "I am here to tell you that your time on Venus is almost done."

He saw Harper start forward furiously, and raised a hand, pointed a finger. Harper stopped as if he had run into a wall. His face purpled as he fought to move. The audience hushed in astonishment. M'Grath tramped forward—and was frozen in exactly the same fashion. Barney Lyons, quick to learn, kept still of his own accord. The death hush in the audience held for ten seconds then snapped into a roar of outrage.

Anthony turned and spread his hands—and there was stillness and silence, immediately. "I'm not going to explain. There's no need. I hold you all helpless. Just me, because I speak with the voice, and the power, of three hundred million green people like myself. Now you will listen, and those who are watching within the other domes will do well to listen, too, because what I have to say includes them.

"I am green. I was born on this planet. All my life I have known I was green. Never have I believed myself an animal. I *knew* different. Now I know that this is also true of my brothers, out there. The green people you have met, the only ones you know anything about, have been defectives, the castoffs and failures, the only ones stupid enough to be caught by your drugs and temptations. The rest have kept away, have ignored you, have not wanted to know anything about you.

"What does it matter to them that you have taken up a small area of their planet? That you have built yourselves a phoney fairy-land to hide in? What do they care about Earth? Or Earth-people? Why should they? They were quite happy to ignore your puny miracles, your tawdry empire, until I told them of something else that you do. *I* told them. Hold *me* responsible. I told them that you have been, that you are, and that you will go on, stealing away their bean-plants. You uproot them, wherever you find them. You force-grow and strip them, and then uproot more. You ship the beans back to Earth. As of this moment your depradations have taken but a tiny fraction of the whole, but you will go on, like a creeping disease, a blight. And know this, that the bean is not just a fancy food to my people. It is life and death to them. When they learned, from me, that you were stealing away their life-needs, it was then

132

they decided the time had come to remove you. That time is now!"

He could feel their combined resentment, their anger. This clutch that he held on them was his own making, for the first time. Lovely supplied the raw force, the gathered energy of thousands, but he was channeling it, and he felt what his victims felt. He knew, beyond all doubt, that he could not kill by this method, that he couldn't even hurt without being hurt himself. That was the hidden snag in this gamble.

"It would be pointless if you all spoke," he declared. "I will release one to speak for you."

He glanced at Harper and shook his head. He chose M'Grath. "You can talk," he said. "Don't waste it in argument."

"Admirable advice," M'Grath grunted. "I'd give a lot to know how you spread the invisible glue I seem to be steeped in. But, man, you must be insane! You can't hope to get away with this. Naked savages, regardless of how many or how intelligent, can't hope to win against technology!"

"I expected that argument. I've arranged a display that might convince you otherwise."

He made a tiny gesture to Lovely, who nodded in return. In another place a silent, waiting line of green people, perched high on an anchor wall, spaced a meticulous arm's-reach apart, moved as one. Razor-edged sword-leaves bit into tough plastic, through one layer and then the second. Blades moved from left to right, slits joined up with each other. The precious cool dry air gushed out in a gasping gale. The green figures dropped silently down over the pyramided ranks of their brethren and vanished into the mist. Anthony faced M'Grath, quite steadily.

"I have just destroyed Dome Two," he said. "The plastic balloon has been slit completely around, at wall level. I've pulled your house down about your ears, M'Grath. One of them, at any rate. Ring up and find out!"

Confirmation was obvious on the fat man's gray face as he came back to the platform. The audience knew without need of speech, and writhed in their prisoned silence. Anthony felt their instinctive fear giving way to equally instinctive rage and resistance.

"It will take some hours for the envelope to collapse all

133

the way. Enough time for the inmates to protect themselves. No one need be hurt. In fact, given time, the whole thing can be put up again. But that is just a small sample, M'Grath, of what we *can* do."

"You caught us unawares, that time. Next time—"

"What next time? What can you do against a silent enemy who can do this—" and Anthony put a throttling squeeze on the fat man's throat without lifting so much as a finger himself. "Must I say it again? Three hundred million. And this is *our* planet. What I am doing, they can do also, any and all of them, at any time. Men in atmosphere suits, with guns, can fight this?" He let M'Grath choke awhile, and then released him, to watch him heave for breath and massage his throat.

"You preach an effective sermon. I'll take your word for it. I'll even agree that you have made a point. But I'm not all men, Taylor. If you know anything at all, you must know that mankind has never been ruled by cold reason, or commonsense, that there is no such thing as a hopeless cause, to the average man. Throw us off this planet—as I admit you *can* do, and have every right to do—but whatever the ethic, there will be the bloodiest outcry ever, from Earth. Mankind will come back in force. Perhaps to fail, to die by the millions, but no reasoning I know will stop them. Tell a man he can't, and he'll die trying to prove you wrong!"

"I know," Anthony sighed. "I was a man, once." He reached for Lovely's hand, drew her near to him. "You have her to thank that I saw this a long time ago. This is one of your primitive savages, M'Grath, one of the people I can speak for. She will do anything I ask, except kill."

He turned to the crowd again, raised his voice. "I grew up on Earth. I wanted to wipe out the lot of you, when I realized just what you were doing. That's the way I was taught to think, as a man. Hit back! But my people taught me something else. It is better to work together, to co-operate—as brothers."

"How can we co-operate with you?" M'Grath demanded. "What have we to exchange? On what level can we possibly meet?"

"I've been thinking about that, but perhaps Lovely can tell you." He smiled to her and she blushed.

For the first time since entering the dome she ventured to speak aloud. "This is cool, and dry, and a bright light. These things I have never know before. They are good things."

M'Grath regarded her thoughtfully. "Succinctly put, my dear. But you are only one. How do you know the rest of your people would approve such strange things?"

"What I feel, all feel, all know. And it is good!"

"Good God!" M'Grath swung his wide eyes on Anthony. "Does she know what she's saying? That you have some form of total telempathy?"

"It's quite true. Complete community of emotion-feeling-experience. It shook me when I found out. It's not on a verbal level, of course."

"No? No, of course. That's education, personal-trained response. Obvious! Good heavens! Do you realize what this will do to all our accepted theories of mental processes?" M'Grath caught himself suddenly. "But it is out of the question. We cannot possibly provide controlled environment such as this over the whole planet. If that's the kind of co-operation you want, we're stopped before we start."

Anthony felt an urgent prickling at the fringe of his attention, a struggling for notice, out there. "Who?" he asked, lifting the blanket of restraint, and an eager-eyed man broke forward from the ranks of the technicians.

"Never mind who I am," he said urgently. "There are others who will back what I say. We can modify this climate. This is something we've thought about for a long while among ourselves. It wouldn't be too tough. The plans have all been worked over a dozen times. Humidity is the main thing, and there are a dozen ways to lick that, to reduce evaporation from open water surfaces. And there are just as many ways to lick the fungus dust, too. Enzymes, clotting-agents, precipitants, all sorts of things. It would take time, sure! And money. But it could be done."

"Why hasn't it been done, then?"

"Don't ask me. The ideas have been submitted several times, but they got shelved, passed-over. I guess somebody didn't want to know, wanted things to stay the way they are. You can guess."

"Thank you." Anthony turned his stare on Harper, lifting the restraint. "Let's hear you on this. Is it true?"

"Why should *we* waste time and money making the

135

whole damn planet fit for any snot-nose to live on?" Harper snarled. "If your damned Greenies want it so much, why don't they do it for themselves? And don't think you're on top, Taylor. You might fool M'Grath with a bit of jargon, but not me. You daren't lay a finger on us, and you know it!"

M'Grath sucked in a breath, but Anthony halted him before he could speak. He turned to Barney Lyons, who had kept a discreet silence so far.

"I believe you have ways of seeing, from here, what is happening outside, outside the hall, I mean. Have you?"

"Yeah, sure. We can scan any part of the interior from here, and throw it on that screen there. That what you want?" He stepped to a console at one side of the central area. "Where d'you want to look?"

"A main entrance. Any one, or all, just as you like."

Lyons touched a switch that dimmed the lights a trifle, and the screen glowed into life. And the aghast humans moaned with one collective voice as they saw what the cameras revealed. Green people, no matter which view Lyons shifted to, there were green people, thronging in silent march. Thousands of them, filling the broad avenues, casting appreciative glances up and around, but moving steadily forward.

"And those are but a very tiny fraction," Anthony said. "Just a few. At a thought from me they would cut down this dome, too. With no effort at all they could stamp this fairy-land of yours into oblivion. And what would they lose, Harper? They were happy and contented before you came. If I gave the word they would obliterate all sign of you. It wouldn't take long. And then they would vanish back into the mist where they have been all this time, where you never knew they were, and where you'd never find them again. As for your punitive expedition"—he eyed M'Grath—"you have your point, but how would Earth people exact vengeance on an enemy they couldn't find? It's a big planet. And *would* they? Would they arise in wrath to avenge the elimination of a group of parasitic and selfish exploiters? After all, you have exploited humanity just as much as you have *my* people."

"Hey! Not all of us!" came a cry from the audience, to be joined by others, into a clamor.

136

"There's your answer, Harper. Do you want me to take a vote on it?" He turned back to the restive audience. "You're all free to speak, just as you feel. What do you want to do —stay here and fight that?" He gestured to the marching hordes, and then to the first flow of green people emerging into the hall where they were. "Or run home back to Earth and tell them that you were kicked out? Or do you want to stay, and help, and co-operate with us?"

"How can we co-operate?" M'Grath demanded, through a swelling hubbub of argument. "It will take years to transform the climate, and a fantastic amount of money, men and material. That's bleeding us of our resources. Altruism can go only so far. What do we get out of it? What's in it for us?"

The sentiment found many echoes. Even Harper regained calm enough to agree with it.

"A deal is a deal, Taylor. I'm damned if you'll twist my arm, but I might do a deal with you. Honorable terms of some kind."

"What could be easier?" Anthony met him with a level stare. "You can bring us medicine, physical knowledge. We can give you knowledge about the mind. But there's one thing above all that we can do together. Show us how to make two beans grow where only one grew before. It's that simple. Give us the agricultural know-how, the science, and we'll do the growing. And we share the crop. That way nobody loses."

Harper's face betrayed, without any call for mental powers, that he gagged on the thought of losing his comfortable monopoly. In the audience there were a handful who shared his resentment. But by far the majority let it be known in no uncertain terms that they liked the proposition. Harper had to yield.

"Have it your way," he growled. "You've called the tune. On your head comes the responsibility for passing on the tricks, the know-how, the training of all these—" and he flung his arm in a sweep to encompass the pressing crowd of green people. "We can deliver. How do we know you can keep up your end, and pass the skills along in a proper manner?"

"Nothing simpler." Anthony smiled, a great sense of relief flooding him. He took Lovely's hand again, saw her eyes
137

glow with understanding. "You said I called the tune. Let me show you how appropriate that was."

He raised an arm, and got silence in a moment. It was an intently expectant silence, as something of the immense power he wielded communicated itself even to the awed humans. This was a treasured fancy, something he had dreamed of for a long time. And he knew that all over the planet, far and wide, breaths were being held now.

To M'Grath he murmured, "This is the most expressive piece I could think of, for a moment such as this. Listen!" And he brought his hand down in a gesture.

With a unanimity no human choir could hope to copy, the assembled green people raised their voices in a great shouting sound, the electrifying "Hallelujah Chorus" from Handel's *Messiah*. Hardly had they roared into the third bar when there was a rustle, and Anthony saw the human audience scrambling to its feet, and joining in lustily. Now his dream was complete, and he, too, sang "Hallelujah" along with the rest.

WAS THAT THE KEY TO A WORLD FORGOTTEN?

One explorer had already disappeared on the primitive planet, Kappa. So the day that a second Terrestrial, Jones, ran away after drinking the sacred Kappan water that he had coerced the natives into giving him, the remaining planetologists meant to find out just what was going on.

Questioning the aliens only deepened the mystery. For they said that what Jones had drunk would enable him to communicate with his animal ancestors. It was their most precious and sacred possession.

But how could it affect a person never born on Kappa, a person without such "animal" ancestors? What had really happened to Jones and the other man—and what would happen if either of them managed to bring this incredible liquid back to Earth?

Turn this book over for
second complete novel

FRED SABERHAGEN has had stories in several science-fiction magazines. An Air Force veteran and a bachelor, he lives in Chicago and claims to enjoy "karate, chess, and science-fiction conventions, besides such more peaceful activities as writing and looking out for the right girl."

His previous novel for Ace Books was THE GOLDEN PEOPLE (M-103).

THE WATER
OF THOUGHT

FRED SABERHAGEN

ACE BOOKS, INC.
1120 Avenue of the Americas
New York, N.Y. 10036

I

I<small>N THE DREAM</small>, a faceless figure paced after Boris, holding out distorted hands whose fingers writhed like menacing snakes.

No, Boris told the figure. It's not me you want. Those are your hands, not mine. And then he realized he was waking up.

The girl named Brenda was bending over him; he lay on his back in the bottom of a little sportboat, pulled in to the shore of a tiny river island. The light of an alien sun came dappling down through alien trees to reflect from the quiet water and shimmer on Brenda's laughing face and dark brown hair. Boris was blond and bony and tall, with innocent blue eyes in a rough face; he thought now that Brenda was his opposite in every physical detail.

"I don't mind your dozing off," she told him. "But must you have nightmares?"

"I guess I must." Boris stretched luxuriously. He tried to remember the dream, but it was already slipping away. "Was I making noises?"

5

"What was it about?"

"I think it was about my last job."

Brenda became sympathetic. "Where was that?"

"Oh. Light-years from here."

"Of course. But what happened?"

"A man on my crew opened his helmet when he shouldn't have. Something got in and began eating at him."

"Oh, horrible. I wish I hadn't asked. Will he—be all right?"

Boris felt a trace of amusement at her concern for someone she had never seen. "The medics saved him. He's getting a new face built."

Brenda watched him silently for a long moment. Then, with some hesitation, she asked, "Did they blame you for it?"

"No." Boris sat up in the boat, making it rock soft ripples into the quiet river. He looked around him at the peaceful green wilderness. Hayashi was a planeteer, not an infant; he shouldn't have needed warnings and leading by the hand.

Once, years and planets ago, Boris had been young and green; and a planeteering scheme of his, thoroughly approved by the higher-ups, had led to the drowning of a number of men. Now—why should he recall an old disaster on this pleasant afternoon? And why did Brenda ask him if he had been blamed—did he look guilty? He was far from being a failure.

He needed this leave. Lately he had felt tired and stale.

He grinned at Brenda. "Enough about nightmares!" He caught her by the arm and pulled.

A minute later, the communicator chimed from under the dashboard of the little sportboat.

With a little gasp, Brenda pulled away from him. "It must be important, or they wouldn't call."

"I suppose." Boris reached around her and touched a switch. "Brazil here."

A male voice shouted excitedly at him, telling some confused story about a killing. Boris let the babble go on while he disengaged himself fully from Brenda and got the boat moving away from the island into open water. Accelerating downstream at the top thrust of the sporter's water-jets, he could see, a couple of miles ahead, the insubstantial-looking forcefield screens that shielded the tiny colony of Earth-descended people.

6

"Is that you, Morton?" Boris put practiced calm into his voice. If he remembered correctly, Don Morton was the colonist now standing routine defensive watch; and if serious trouble had popped up, Morton might be forgiven some overexcitement. For ten rather peaceful years now, there had been a colony of Earth-descended humans on this lonely planet of Kappa. No doubt the colonists were beginning to think they understood the place.

"Yes, it's me. This is the defense tower."

"Now what's happened? Start again, will you?"

"It's Jones," said Morton's voice, gaining some self-control. "He went crazy here. Now he's run away."

"All right, hang on. I'll be there in two minutes."

All Boris knew about Edmund Jones was that the man was, like himself, a planeteer. Jones had said he was spending an entire leave here on Kappa, pursuing a semi-professional interest in anthropology. Boris was on leave too, but only stopping over on Kappa, waiting for a ship that would carry him home to Sol.

Boris and Jones had started out this morning on a picnic with Brenda and another unattached colony girl named Jane. Jones had a standing request to be notified at once when any native medicine men visited the colony, and Morton had called Jones on his boat radio about noon—a shaman had arrived, and started to set up camp near the colony's main gate.

Certainly Jones had not been drunk when he left the picnic, and hurried back, with the displeased Jane, to see the witch-doctor. That gave him less than an hour to somehow get in shape for going crazy and running away.

The sportboat skimmed over the calm brown river, between shores of growth that was just a bit too open and pleasant to be called jungle. Something in the sun and air of Kappa gave to chlorophyll in leaves a greener-than-reality postcard look. The planet might make an excellent site for a big colony, thought Boris, if it had not so many human natives, and if it lay in a different direction from Earth. As it was, dust clouds and permanent atomic storms peppered the section of galactic arm around Kappa, making C-plus travel uncertain.

Boris slowed the boat, passing the riverside landing field where shuttles came down from visiting starships. The field

was empty now. Just ahead, the colony's forcefield opened a gate in itself where it swept out into the river. Boris drove through the gate, docked, gave Brenda one farewell pat, and strode toward the defense tower, which was a neglected-looking building near the center of the small compound. There were only a couple of dozen structures here, built of native wood and stone and glass, inhabited by fewer than three hundred people. All the Earth-descended on Kappa lived here, while automated machinery ran mines and farms and ranches for them, out in the zones of Kappa's grimmer climates, where intelligent natives were few or none. The Space Force, with its planeteers and research teams, was gone from Kappa, moved to Earthman's expanding frontier. The colonists were people who liked the life of an isolated small town, or they were not likely to remain long on Kappa. They maintained a foothold here for Earth, and made themselves comfortably prosperous. Kappa had never offered them more than incidental and occasional danger.

But now, Boris found half a dozen men, and Jane, gathered in the little room atop the defense tower. They had crowded around Morton's sentry chair and were watching his viewscreens.

Pete Kaleta, the colony's pudgy mayor, was saying, "It all looks normal at the silver mine; he went in the other direction anyway. Oh, Brazil, glad you're here."

"What's it all about?"

They looked uncertainly at one another. When no one else seemed eager to speak, Jane began, "Eddie—Mr. Jones—hardly said a word all the way back here in the boat. But he didn't seem wild or anything. Just thoughtful."

Boris asked, "So, what happened when he got here?"

Kaleta took a deep breath, and spoke, "A pair of men from a tribe just west of here arrived, right after you four had left on the picnic. They started to set up camp just outside the main gate. One of them was wearing a witch doctor's face paint, and he said he wanted to see Jones—Jones has been talking to all the witchmen. So, Morton here got Jones on the radio. Jones came back in his boat, put on a ground-suit, and walked out through the main gate."

"Put on a groundsuit?" Boris asked. "Why?"

Kaleta gestured nervously. "He didn't say. I suppose he

8

wanted to impress the natives; or maybe just to have the radio handy."

The big viewscreen in front of the sentry chair now pictured the area just outside the main gate. Bright bits of fabric, scattered boxes and primitive utensils littered the grass. In the foreground stood a native pack animal, placidly grazing. Heavy leather straps hung broken from its back; someone or something had torn the panniers from its sides and scattered the contents.

Don Morton, a powerfully-built young man, swung round in his sentry chair, and took up the story: "Jones went out there in the groundsuit. He said hello to the natives. I wasn't paying any attention to what they said. I'm not sure Jones even had his suit radio on then." Morton looked at Boris belligerently, as if expecting to be accused of something.

"All right, go on."

Morton hesitated. Jane said, "I came up here to watch. The Kappan outside was offering Eddie a drink. He poured it from a funny kind of bottle—I've never seen one just like it before. And then Eddie did radio in, and said something like: 'Hey, better have a stomach pump ready, just in case.' He didn't drink whatever it was right away. He still had his helmet on, and was standing there talking."

"Morton, I wish you'd called me," said Mayor Kaleta, staring into the viewscreen.

Morton shifted nervously in his chair. "Well, anyway, I called up the infirmary, and got Doc, here."

Doc pulled thoughtfully at a heavy mustache. "What that stuff was, I can't imagine. I wouldn't expect a small amount of any Kappan drink to have much effect on an Earthman —unless it was meant to be poison. You know, Kappans and Earth-descended are remarkably similar in their biology; I've seen experimental skin grafts made to take from one to the other. Anyway, I did get a stomach cleaner ready, just in case. Since he asked for it."

Morton took up the story again. "When I finished talking to Doc, Jones had his helmet off, and was starting to drink, from a little cup. He took a sip, and then he stood there talking for another minute. Then he tossed it all down. Then, in another minute, he and the Kappans were arguing. I was just starting to really pay attention when I guess he must

9

have shut off his radio. I don't know what the fight was about."

Morton looked at Jane. She said, "Well, I saw him step forward, shouting at the Kappans, I guess he was threatening them. They backed away from him; they looked like they were frightened and surprised."

"Jones grabbed at them," said Morton. "He knocked them down behind those bushes there. I suppose he might have killed them; you know the power in those suits. Then he tore the baskets off the pack animal, and scattered the stuff, as if he was looking for something. By that time I was already calling you, and the mayor."

Mayor Kaleta seemed much worried, but he had nothing to say for the moment.

"What kind of suit did Jones put on?" Boris asked.

"Heavy ground armor," Morton answered. "We keep two suits of it ready, just in case. We've never needed it."

"Ugh." It seemed to Boris that things just might get much worse before they got any better. He decided to put on the other suit himself before going out to investigate.

Jane said, "And Eddie found the bottle, where the Kappans had put it away, all wrapped up. He took another little drink, in a hurry, and then he set the bottle down in the grass, as if it was something precious. Then he came back to the gate."

"What?"

"Oh, yes." Morton had an angry look on his face. "He radioed: 'Open up the outer gate, you fool. I need a rifle.' Well, I didn't know what the hell was going on. When he came back like that, I thought he must have some good reason. I mean, he's a planeteer, isn't he? He's supposed to know what he's doing in—strange situations. Right?"

Boris said, "Well, let's find out how strange the situation is. So you opened the outer gate, and he came in again?"

"Right. And I opened the little door to the arms room, and he went in and got an energy rifle. We keep two of them handy, like the suits. And then he trotted off without another word, heading west."

Jane added, "And he picked up the bottle and took it with him."

The silent mayor had one hand over his eyes.

"I'd better get out there," said Boris. He adjourned the

10

meeting to the arms room at the main gate, where he could get himself into the remaining suit of heavy ground armor while the talk went on.

So, it seemed that Jones was running amok, with equipment that would make the average man as dangerous as a troop of saber-wielding cavalry. And Jones was not an average man, but a planeteer, with all the skills of the professional interstellar explorer.

Boris was a chief planeteer himself, when not on leave for rest and recreation as he was now. So it was logical for the colonists to call on him in an emergency like this one, and let him take over. Set one to catch one.

Possibly, he thought, Jones is still rational. It's just that he's discovered something that makes it right for him to man-handle a couple of natives, arm himself even further, and run off without a word of explanation. Boris couldn't imagine what such a discovery might be.

"Anything else peculiar around here lately? Unexplained?" he asked, while a couple of the colonists helped him into the armored suit.

"Things have been pretty dull," said Kaleta.

"Since Magnuson disappeared," said Doc. When Boris looked at him, he amplified: "An anthropologist named Emanuel Magnuson. Used to work for the Space Force, spent most of his time out in the hills near Great Lake. He was supposed to leave when the last of the Space Force people pulled out, but he vanished. Looked like some carnivore might have gotten him."

"But you weren't sure?" Boris probed. "Could the Kappans have done him in?"

"We've always kept on good terms with them," said Mayor Kaleta, looking at Doc. "The Space Force seemed to be satisfied it was just animals killed him."

Doc shrugged. "Magnuson was a strange one, in some ways. He'd argue his theories. . . . How's that fit?"

"Okay, now." Boris brought an arm in from one suit sleeve and fastened his helmet from the inside. Then without further delay he headed for the outer gate. For all the suit's weight of metal, walking was easier in it than without it. Its limbs were driven by servo-mechanisms which followed the movements of the man inside, and were powered by a tiny hydrogen-fusion lamp.

11

As he passed the arms rack, Boris took down the remaining energy rifle, and checked the charge. Such a weapon was effective against heavy ground armor at close range. If it should ever come to that.

When the main gate shimmered open for him, Boris went out and saw the scattered Kappan goods, and the grazing phlegmatic animal. It would be nice, he thought, to find tracks showing that the two Kappans had departed the area at a speed impossible for seriously injured men, and to find Jones sleeping off his strange intoxication behind a bush. Sometimes, Boris had noticed, the world was not nice.

Kappans were a leathery-skinned people, with very wide-set eyes and bulging foreheads, grotesque by Earth standards. The first man Boris found in the bushes was quite dead, with the insects at him already. The appearance of his head suggested he had died of a blow from the power-driven arm of a groundsuit.

Boris's helmet radio brought him a collective gasp from the people in the defense tower; they were watching through the TV eye that rode on his shoulder.

"That's not the witch-doctor," someone commented.

Boris turned up his suit's sensitive air mikes and kept searching, now holding the rifle ready with the safety off. When he had moved on a few more yards, he caught the sound of ragged breathing. The second Kappan had crawled under a bush to hide. The wide-set eyes were open, and from behind oozing blood and witchman's paint they followed Boris.

"Send out a couple of stretcher bearers," he radioed. "And someone tell me a few soothing words to use."

Boris stood with two or three others beside the hospital bed in which the injured Kappan lay. While Doc was still giving the man emergency treatment, Brenda was acting as translator for Boris.

"He says, as soon as Jones had smacked his lips over the drink, he demanded to know where it came from. Jones was being initiated into the—Kappan witchdoctor's union, I guess you'd call it—so they told him the truth; it comes in trade from the western hill people, near the Great Lake. Jones demanded more of the drink; they tried to stop him from tearing up their goods, but he just knocked them aside."

"What was in the drink?"

The Kappan hesitated for some time before giving his short answer. Brenda glanced around at the blank faces of the others present, frowned, and translated, "He says: 'The Water of Thought.' "

"What's that mean?"

No one knew. "I've never heard of it," said Kaleta, who had just come into the infirmary. "And I've been here eight years, always in contact with the natives."

"Maybe this guy's making it up," said Morton, shaking his head at bedside.

Boris said, "Well, an Earth-size planet holds a lot of secrets. I'd be out of a job, otherwise." He drummed metal fingers on the groundsuit helmet he was now carrying under one arm. "You're all sure there was nothing in the Space Force survey reports about such a drink, or poison, or whatever?"

Everyone nodded or murmured assent. "I'm sure," said the mayor. "We practically memorized those things."

"Then maybe our pal here is lying about it. Or, it's something new."

Brenda asked. "He says its old. The Water of Thought lets a man communicate with his animal ancestors; very powerful medicine. He can tell us about it now, because we've saved his life. No one ever reacted to it the way Jones did; he says he guesses Earth-descended men are just different."

"If only I'd reminded Mr. Jones of that fact," said Doc morosely. "You people had all better clear out for a while. He needs rest."

"Two anthropologists," said Boris, thinking aloud as he walked to the door. "One vanishes near Great Lake, and the other runs toward it. It is west of here, isn't it? Or is there another Great Lake?"

The colonists gave each other the quick searching looks of people who have known one another for a long time.

"There's just one Great Lake," said the mayor finally. "I don't see any connection, though, between Magnuson and Jones."

Brenda was thoughtfully silent.

"Excellent man in his field, he was," said Morton, closing the infirmary door behind them. "Magnuson, I mean."

13

Time was passing, but something in the air was a little fishy.

"I've got to go after Jones," Boris said. "If any of you know anything that might help me, I'd better hear it."

Mayor Kaleta shrugged irritably. "We're telling you all we know, Brazil. No doubt you're right; someone must stop Jones, or there's no telling what he'll do, what he'll involve us in with the natives. Frankly, I'm glad you're willing to take the risk of going after him. I don't want to send a lot of untrained people, not knowing what he's up to with that suit and that rifle, or what the natives might . . ." He looked uncertainly back toward the infirmary door, behind which lay the injured Kappan.

"You're right," Boris said. "Better keep your people here inside the defenses as much as possible. I'll need a copter, though."

"Right. I'll see that one's ready." Kaleta hurried out.

"I'm as good a pilot as there is around," said Brenda.

II

FROM AN ALTITUDE of two thousand feet Boris could follow with binoculars the trail Jones had left, straight as a fanatic's lunge through bush and swamp and an occasional cultivated field, toward the western hills that were still fifty miles and more away.

Jones might be napping as he traveled, or unconscious, or even dead. The semi-robotic suit could be set to balance itself and walk, or even run at twenty miles an hour, holding to a course and steering itself around major obstacles. With its recycling systems and emergency rations, it could keep a man almost comfortable for a week, and functioning for a month, while he stayed sealed in.

Boris saw no signs along the trail that Jones had had more trouble with the natives. Any Kappan who saw his suited figure pace by would be likely to stay clear; he had knocked down rows of small trees that stood in his path.

"What do we do when we catch up with him?" Brenda asked coolly, sounding not at all like the girl who had been giggling in the sportboat a few hours ago.

"You set me down on his trail before then," Boris an-

swered. "This copter makes too good a target for that rifle of his, even at this altitude."

"You think he'd shoot us down?"

"We'd better think so." Boris watched Brenda's profile. Something about the colonists' behavior still bothered him, and he shot a sudden question, "What was this Emanuel Magnuson like? The other man who vanished."

Her eyes, watching the terrain and air ahead, clouded briefly. "I think he was a fine man. He was nice to me and to Jane—oh, in a fatherly sort of way, though he's not really old. But there's something so—intense about him."

"You speak as if he might be still alive."

"Well, I get the impression, sometimes—I don't know."

"Tell me."

"It's like a feeling in the air, around the colony that Dr. Magnuson didn't just die in a simple accident. I don't recall anything definite ever being said. Do you know what a small town's like? Or maybe we're unique."

"It puzzles me a little why you stay here, gal."

"Oh. My parents died here; I've just stayed on. All the people are my family and friends. Jane and I are the two orphans; maybe we're spoiled." She glanced over at Boris. "Sometimes I—we—get restless. We took a trip out once—"

Business came first, and Boris interrupted, "Better start down now; I don't think he can be more than three or four miles ahead. See that second meadow up there? Aim for it, but when you get halfway there peel off to the right. We'll take a little evasive action, just to be safe."

Suddenly the accustomed drone of the copter's engine was gone; in the heavy silence Boris looked overhead to see the jet-spun rotor idling to a halt. In his stomach he felt the familiar start of free-fall. His hand moved instinctively for the copter's controls, but Brenda's fingers were already there, doing the proper things.

But to no avail. The engine was dead; Jones must have hit it with a jolt from his energy rifle. The copter tilted forward, and forest replaced sky in front of Boris, trees coming closer in a long hard rush. The machine was not dropping quite like a rock, but you could hardly call it a glide.

"Bail out!" Boris yelled at Brenda. He reached to take what control was left out of her hands. "I've got the suit!"

Her fingers were already tightening the parachute straps

15

over her coverall, but she hesitated momentarily, her wide brown eyes looking into his, perhaps to see if he was being gallantly self-sacrificing. A cool one, this girl. Then, with her chute ready, she popped open the cabin door and leaped out, just as Boris was ready to shove her.

With his metal arms, he fought the controls until the steering column bent. And the trees were upon him.

Bounce and bang. Bounce again, and smash. He held his arms in front of his faceplate, until he had shocked and jolted to a halt. Blessed be heavy ground armor!

Boris's seat belt was holding him, upside down, among splintered branches. The copter was a mass of torn metal around him; it would never fly again. The afternoon sun shone through a fine haze of leaves and sawdust, still drifting and settling.

Taking inventory of his sensations, Boris found nothing worse than a couple of bruises; so he began to break his way out of the wreckage. It had been a frustrating day up to now, and there was a certain satisfaction in bashing obstructions aside. When the way was clear, he dropped with a clanging thud to the ground. He retrieved his rifle, and saw with relief that it was undamaged—Jones might be coming around for another shot.

After getting his directions from the sun, Boris moved off through the thin forest at a fast lope, toward the area where Brenda should have come down. In a few minutes he spotted the bright cloth of her parachute spread on the ground.

"Boris!" Her voice came from above him. She sat twelve feet high in a tree, clasping the trunk. Her face was pale. "My ankle's hurt," she said. "No, I'm all right, really; I climbed up here. I thought I might see where you came down."

"Well." Boris allowed himself a grin. "Your knight in shining alloy is here now. Looks like we're in pretty good shape; with this suit I can carry you back to the colony in five or six hours. Of course if I have to wear the suit I won't enjoy the task nearly so much."

"What about Mr. Jones?" she asked.

What a girl. "Just let me check his trail; I'll be back in about five minutes. He can keep running west all night if he wants to; but I want to make sure he's not lurking around here to take another shot at us. Suppose you come down from

that tree and hide in a bush, and I'll call your name when I get back. My suit's number Two—see? Jones has number One on, I guess."

"Okay, go ahead. I'll be all right." Brenda started down from the tree.

There seemed little point in trying to tell her what to do if he didn't come back, so without further delay he moved out through the woods, going as quietly as possible in his bulk of metal. For a minute he waited, just out of Brenda's view, watching to see if Jones appeared near her. Jones might have seen the chute come down.

Jones did not materialize, so Boris moved on. Where he expected Jones's trail, he found it—a line of brush and saplings trampled down and bent toward the west. Boris followed the trail for a hundred yards, and noticed hopefully that it began to waver. Soon it looped around as if the man making it was no longer certain of his directions.

And then Boris saw a silver gleam ahead—Jones's suit, fallen on its faceplate in low grass. Boris let out a little sigh of relief, and moved forward, watching alertly—

"I've got a rifle on you, Brazil," said a voice behind him. "Freeze in your tracks."

There seemed to be little future in any other course.

"Now drop the rifle and take off your helmet."

He did.

After a moment Jones came walking around to face him, well out of reach but easily close enough for the energy rifle he held to puncture Boris's armor. And the weapon stayed center-aimed at Boris.

Jones was as tall as Boris, and heavier. He sported a short black beard; more dark hair grew thickly on his bare massive forearms, and from the throat of his coveralls. He looked happy.

"Well, what's the matter, Jones?" Boris asked. "I'd like to hear your side of this." He made his voice a trifle loud, for Brenda might by now have decided to follow him.

Jones showed white teeth, and looked Boris's suit up and down with an expert eye. "No sidearms, eh? Fine. Sit down against that tree over there and I'll tell you my side, as you put it. I'll kill you, if need be, but I don't want to kill you. I've thought of a much better way."

"That's good to hear," said Boris, sitting down as directed.

17

Then he nodded toward Jones's fallen armor. "Neat ambush."

Jones ignored the compliment. "Brazil, I've tasted the Water of Thought—that's what the witchman said they call it. And I've come to know—" Jones paused, then gave a little shake of his head. "There's no use my trying to explain. I wouldn't have believed anyone who'd tried to tell me. You'll have to taste it yourself before you'll understand." He walked to the fallen groundsuit, and from somewhere inside it he brought out what could only be the medicine man's bottle.

"Maybe I *can* understand," said Boris smoothly. "I'd like to try. You tore up those people's property back there, and ran off, just to find more of this Water of Thought?"

"I did more than that. I killed someone, didn't I?"

"One of them."

"Ah. But I had to, they were keeping me from the Water. You'll see, when you taste it. Nothing could mean more to me now than it does, not food, or relief from pain, or women, or anything else. I sound like a madman, don't I? You'll see how it is." Jones put a hand to his forehead. His face and eyes looked as if he might be developing a fever.

Boris thought rapidly. "Jones, do you have a family?" Had something shown of the guilty married man when Jones during the morning's picnic put an arm around Jane? How long ago the morning and the picnic were.

"Never mind my family!" For the first time, Jones showed a hint of inner conflict. "I won't see them now for a long time. Maybe I'll never see them again. How can I, when the Water of Thought is here on Kappa?"

"All right, so you want more of this Water of Thought. Most likely it'll take a large expedition to find where the stuff comes from."

"Oh, no, Brazil." Jones chuckled. "No. You're not sweet-talking me back to the colony. They'd just stick me in the infirmary, and wouldn't give me any more Thought-Water if they had any, which they don't. Right now, the only way I can get along with another Earthman is to convert him to my way of thinking." Jones held up his stone bottle. "You will be my first disciple."

Keep him talking, thought Boris. Maybe the stuff will wear off. "Jones, are you religious?"

Jones accepted the question as relevant. "You know I wasn't."

18

"And now you are? I don't understand."

"You will." Still keeping the rifle ready, Jones used his teeth to loosen the carved top of the bottle. Removed, the cap made a little drinking cup. He set down the cup and very carefully poured it half full of clear liquid from the bottle.

"This is God, Brazil. That's what I mean. God's in my little bottle here." It was only with great evident effort that Jones was able to keep himself from drinking the contents of the cup. But he set it gently on the ground, and backed away, holding the bottle and the rifle. "Now drink that!" he ordered. "Move forward slowly, and drink it."

"If I take any, there'll be less for you."

Jones bit his lip. "It's an investment, to get more. That's the only reason I can stand to give it away. With two of us, in ground armor, working together, the Kappans will never be able to keep us from getting at the source of the Water; one man alone can always be tricked or trapped somehow. Now drink! I'm in a hurry. If I must, I'll kill you and go on alone."

Boris stood up and walked slowly forward; he had heard the threat of murder in voices before. But experience gave no protection against the cutting edge of fear.

"Let me just walk away, Jones," he said loudly. "Even without my groundsuit, I could just walk back to the colony." Maybe Brenda was listening, wondering what to do and would accept the hint. He added more quietly, "It would take me a couple of days, and you'd get away."

Jones just moved the rifle muzzle slightly, motioning toward the cup. It would be plain suicide to try to rush Jones. Swallowing the Water of Thought might be suicide of a different kind, but it seemed that if Boris drank he would at least keep on breathing, and there was always hope while breath lasted. In three or four days the cruiser Boris had expected to ride home to Sol would make planetfall on Kappa; it would have the men and equipment for a massive search.

Boris decided to risk one last argument. "Jones—"

"One more stalling word and you're dead."

Boris bent down, reaching for the cup. He noticed that his fingers were still steady. As if that meant anything.

"Brazil, if you *spill* even one drop, I'll take time to kill you slowly, before I go on."

19

Carefully Boris picked up the cup. The liquid in it was as clear and thin as spring water, or raw corn whiskey. A subtle, slightly fishy odor rose from it.

"Drink!"

As a man threatened with drowning would clutch for physical support, so Boris tried to clamp a mental hold on sanity. He hoped Brenda would somehow know enough to run from him if he went mad. The fluid in the cup rose before his face, a tidal wave to sweep his mind away. I am the master of my fate—

"Drink!"

Boris sipped. It had an alien tang, not unpleasant, but with a ghost of fishiness. He swallowed the half-cupful of the Water of Thought, and found it pleasantly cooling to his throat.

Boris brought his hand down with the empty cup, careful not to spill a drop. He tried to brace his mind against the overwhelming lust for another drink, which any second now would hit him.

Jones relaxed, sure of himself, slinging the rifle over his shoulder. "Brazil, I'll pour you another little shot, if you like. You don't have to rush me for it. It might spill, and we wouldn't want that, would we?" His chuckle had an obscene sound.

Boris felt a moment of mental confusion; but it seemed to pass. He still had no craving for the Water of Thought. Could he hope to be immune? He would play along with Jones. He would hold out the cup, and when Jones reached toward it he would grab—

And then Boris discovered that he could not move a muscle.

He still breathed, and obviously his heart was still beating. He didn't feel numb. But he couldn't move. He felt sweat break out on his forehead.

Jones stepped closer to him. "What's the matter with you? Brazil. Look at me. Answer me!"

As if with a life of their own, Boris's eyes swiveled obediently to look at Jones. Boris's voice said: "The matter with me is that I can't move."

"Hah!" said Jones, in a kind of incredulous snort.

"So, you can't move without being ordered," said Jones,

three minutes later, pacing back and forth. "You can't be faking. If you were faking, you'd pretend to feel the way I do. I'd have fallen for that. Then you'd take me by surprise, and drag me back to the colony." Jones shuddered. "They'd keep me there, alive, but without the Water. They'd try to *cure* me."

Jones grabbed the cup from Boris's statue-hand, and rationed himself a tiny drink. He swallowed it, gasped, and stood for a moment with his eyes closed. Then he carefully capped the bottle again. "Oh, put your arm down," he said, in preoccupied annoyance.

Boris's arm relaxed, but his eyes still helplessly followed Jones, who had begun to pace again.

"You don't have to watch me all the time!" Jones barked. Then, in an apologetic tone, he added: "Look—you can stand easy, or whatever you want to call it. Just don't try to attack me, or run away, or disobey me—or communicate with the colony. Outside of that you can move anyway you like. All right?"

Boris's neural circuits seemed to close again.

"I guess it'll have to do," he said. The paralysis had left him so shaky that he sat down and closed his eyes. He hoped Brenda was hiking for the colony by this time. Probably, though, she would spend the approaching night in a tree somewhere near here. And it seemed likely that the colonists would come searching this way in the morning, and spot her parachute, if she remembered to spread it out. Boris wished he knew more about Mayor Kaleta and the other people back there.

"Well, maybe this is all right!" said Jones, suddenly pleased. "Yes, I think so. You'll have to help me, and when we find more of the Thought-Water I won't have to share it with you."

Opening his eyes, Boris saw that Jones was climbing cheerfully back into his groundsuit. If Boris moved quickly, he could beat Jones to one of the rifles. Boris decided to leap for the weapon, grab it up, and kill Jones if need be. But he could get no farther than the thought; his body would not even consider starting any such course of action.

At least I still have my sanity, he thought. *But what use is it, and how long will it last?*

21

Jones resumed his westward march, and Boris, by his order, walked beside him. I am a semi-robotic man, Boris thought, walking inside a semi-robotic suit. That makes one whole robot, plus a little extra machinery. Plus a little something else, all that is left of me. Or might the little something else be an illusion?

Darkness found them on the first steep slope of the western hills, and there Jones called a halt. Ahead of them lay a hundred thousand square miles of rough forest-covered country, almost completely unexplored.

"There'll be more copters looking for me, sooner or later," said Jones, turning his faceplate up to the first stars of the Kappan night. "So we'll light no fire. And we'll take turns standing watch, just in case. Wake me in about two hours, or sooner if you see anything I'd want to know about."

So Jones lay down to sleep; and Boris found himself unable to do anything but stand guard against his possible rescuers. How long could his slavery last? Surely any drug would wear off in time.

But two hours passed, and he awakened Jones. Then Boris drifted off into a daze of sickly dreams, in which he had to fight with a child's thin arms against an overwhelming faceless Something—

Jones was shaking his suit to awaken him. It was dawn and Jones had watched for more than two hours. Fifty or sixty feet away a figure stood, motionless, partly hidden by mist.

It's a man, was Boris's first thought. It's a short Kappan savage without clothes. It was less than five feet tall, male, with grayish leathery skin and a heavy growth of dark hair at crotch and armpits, on the forearms and lower legs.

Standing up slowly, open hands spread out, Jones made the planeteer's gesture for greeting primitive people. With a bobbing, somehow apelike motion of its upper body, the figure half-turned away from Boris and Jones. Its arms were muscular, but short, not apelike. It hesitated, as if on the verge of flight, looking back over a shoulder at the two men. Boris imagined he saw intelligence in the pale eyes, and then imagined he saw the lack of it. Jones gestured again, and the creature turned and sped away into the mist, running easily like a man.

"So," said Jones, as if not greatly surprised. "The Kappan hominid does exist. It was carrying something in one hand."

22

"Yes, I believe it had a rock." So might Earth's first tool-maker have looked, thought Boris, a million years ago. "It *was* pre-human, then?"

"Can't say, for sure." Briefly Jones was a planeteer again. "The survey missed them completely. Only in the last couple of years a few stories have leaked out of these hills. Other Kappans live around here, too. They call the hominids the Forest People."

"Our survey missed a whole tribe? Or maybe even a species?"

Jones took off his helmet and rubbed his neck. "I'd say they're a separate species; from what little I've heard I don't think they're men. Sloppy work, sure. But look at this country around here; you can see how survey crews would miss a lot. High-crowned tropical forest. No way to see under it, really."

"That's right."

Jones surveyed the morning sky again. "Trees'll help to hide us—we'll need that." He picked up his rifle and adjusted the vernier for a fine beam. "Think I'll try to get us some meat for breakfast. Why don't you start a little fire?"

Boris began to look for wood. "That was a neat shot you made yesterday."

Jones looked at him blankly. "What?"

"Hitting my copter."

Jones blinked. "I never saw your copter after it started down. Didn't you just land it?"

III

BRENDA WAS AWAKENED by the sound of a copter's engine. She had dozed off in spite of everything after tying herself into a tree a dozen feet above the ground. Now the sun was up, burning away a low ground mist. The sky was clear.

The copter was circling slowly, a few hundred feet above her head. From the branches of her tree she had hung the bright cloth of her parachute, making a marker visible for miles.

Brenda waved; the copter circled once more, and then started down to land a little distance away where the trees were thinner. Brenda unknotted the belt with which she

23

had secured herself to the tree, and climbed down. Pain stabbed her right ankle, and now she could hardly stand on it. She remained where she was, clinging to the tree trunk, until she saw Kaleta coming toward her from the landed copter. He was carrying a machine pistol, and looking around him warily.

"Mayor Pete! Am I glad to see you!"

Something was wrong with the way he looked at her. "Where's Brazil?" he asked.

"He went on after Jones, yesterday before dark. He said he'd be back in five minutes, but he never came. I couldn't look for him—my ankle's hurt. Something's happened to him, we've got to get more people out here and start searching, right away."

"Hm. We've got to find him, all right. Can't you walk? Here, lean on me." They started to the copter.

"I'm sorry, Brenda," the mayor said, watching her limp. "I didn't intend—well, now you're in this, I suppose. There's nothing to be done about it."

"What's up?" Don Morton demanded, leaning from the pilot's seat of the copter. Jane sat beside him, looking small and frightened.

"Brazil's gone west, I guess," said Kaleta, motioning in that direction with his gun. "After Jones, or with him."

"I don't like it." Shutting off the copter's engine, Morton hopped out. "Why couldn't we have had a couple of more energy rifles?" he complained, as if to himself. He slapped his own holstered pistol. "I don't know about these things—against one of those suits."

"Are you going to call for help?" Brenda demanded.

"No," said Morton. "Shut up and get in the back seat."

Brenda had seen Don Morton in ugly moods before, but this was the worst. She kept quiet for the moment, and climbed up into the rear of the copter. Jane helped her up, and came to sit beside her, while the men talked to each other in low urgent voices.

"What's going on?" Brenda whispered.

Jane was near tears. "Oh, Brenda, honey, I'm sorry. I knew Don and Mayor Pete were up to something. I guess I knew it was smuggling. But I didn't know that business yesterday had any connection with it. And there I was, telling everyone

24

just what Eddie did outside the gate before Don could hush me up. I thought he was going to kill me, later."

"Smuggling? What?"

"That—damned drink. It's some kind of drug . . ." Jane bowed her face into her hands.

Right now, to Brenda, the important thing was that Boris still needed help; she would not let herself believe him dead. Intending to call the colony herself, she reached forward to the copter's radio—found that all power was off.

"Please, Mayor Pete! Don!"

The mayor would not meet her eye. Don Morton held up the copter's power key, showing her he had it; his smile was ugly indeed. "Just behave," he said. "The good mayor and I will do our own searching."

"You're not drinking much from your bottle," Boris commented, when he and Jones were on their way again, striding up a long slope through open forest. After a breakfast of roast meat Jones had taken a single swallow of the Water of Thought; he had otherwise been content with the ordinary water in his suit's canteen tank.

"I know something about drug addiction." Jones smiled faintly, behind his faceplate. "This is something different from any addiction I've ever heard of. In fact, I'm not an addict, in the sense that I don't suffer physically if I don't drink the Water. No, the effect seems almost purely—mental. I can't describe it. I don't think any doctor could—or any poet. All I know is that nothing else will matter to me, for the rest of my life."

"How did you come to take the first drink?" Boris asked, and felt the ghost of humor at sounding like someone interviewing an old alcoholic.

"Why, I wanted to get in good with the witchmen." Jones laughed, without humor. "I told you I know something about drug addiction. I'm here on Kappa for Space Force intelligence. The crime syndicate's taken an interest in this planet lately, and we've wondered what the attraction was. Some kind of exotic dope seemed a good bet, but I swallowed the stuff myself before I suspected that I'd found it. All I really wanted from the witchmen was information about the tribes in these hills, and to try to get a line on Magnuson. He's in-

volved somehow. Nobody ever really believed that the wolves got him."

"He worked for the Space Force, didn't he?"

"Yes. Towards the end he spent most of his time arguing with his boss. It seems he wanted to make anthropology an experimental science. He had theories about reinforcing natural selection, and weeding out the unfit. Of course the Tribunes wouldn't let him test any scheme like that on a Kappan tribe."

"So you think he went into hiding here? To work in secret?"

"That's what SFI thought. Now, I think he might have tasted the same thing you and I have." Jones looked at Boris. "It hit you one way and me another. There's no telling what it might have done to him."

In the afternoon Boris and Jones passed four Kappans, who stood in a group at some distance, watching them. These were not hominids, but tall spear-carrying warriors who resembled the men of the tribes nearer the colony. Jones waved at them but when he got no reply he made no move to approach them.

"They don't seem too much surprised by our suits," observed Jones thoughtfully. "They've had some contact with Earthmen. Maybe Magnuson."

"So, what do you do now?"

"We just walk on some more. Let ourselves be seen."

At sunset, Boris and Jones dined again on fresh-killed meat. And again Boris was left to stand the first watch.

Boris had not asked a second time for his freedom. It was not something to be given him, it was something he would take when he was able.

He would try now, with all the will that he could muster. Jones slept. Boris picked up a rifle. Experimentally, he tried to aim the weapon at Jones, and found that he could not. There was no struggle with himself; his hands and arms simply refused to make the required motions.

He threw the rifle down, and looked up through the treetops at the stars. Killing Jones, or threatening him, was not the answer anyway. The trouble was inside himself.

Boris faced in the proper direction, drew a deep breath, and willed himself to walk quietly away, back toward the

colony. But his feet would not move. After a long time he sat down.

Again Jones's shaking awakened Boris to a cool and misty dawn. What had looked in the evening twilight like another valley, he now saw to be a lake, at least two or three miles in diameter. Much of its surface and shoreline was obscured by the morning haze.

Eight Kappan men, armed with spears and wearing loincloths, stood about twenty yards off, watching stolidly, not much impressed by groundsuits.

Seeing that Boris was awake, Jones slowly stood up, making the peace gesture. Boris imitated him, willingly. He welcomed the natives, on the theory that any random change in his predicament was likely to be for the better.

Some of the Kappans imitated the peace gesture. Then the tallest one stepped forward, and spoke in the language of Earth's colonies and Space Force:

"You men of Earth, why do you walk here?" His voice was accented but quite plain.

Jones answered, "We are looking for a man named Magnuson. We are the enemies of his enemies, so we would be his friends."

The tall warrior raised his arm as in a wave to someone on a distant hill. Then he said, "Wait. Magnuson is not far. If you try to use your far-speakers, he will hear them, and then you will not find him."

"We will wait," said Jones. He turned to Boris. "If Magnuson has radio equipment out here, that means he's getting help."

Boris came to a decision. "Jones, I don't think you're my worst enemy on this planet. I'd better tell you something. You know accidental failure of a copter is very unlikely. If you didn't shoot at mine, someone probably sabotaged it."

"So. Probably our smuggler didn't want you to catch me. Wants us both out of the way. Who do you think it was?"

"Probably the mayor. Another thing—Brenda was with me in the copter, and she had to parachute. She's back there somewhere with a twisted ankle."

Jones turned away. "What's all that to me, now?" he asked. "If my own family means nothing, what do you suppose Brenda means?"

27

The warriors still leaned on their spears, watching impassively. Perhaps half an hour passed, and the morning mist lifted slowly into the greenish Kappan sky, revealing most of the lake's shoreline. About a mile and a half away, along the shore, the huts of a village became visible. The settlement straddled the mouth of a small river and was almost concealed under the forest's edge.

In the direction of the village, but much closer, another Kappan warrior appeared on a hilltop, waving his arms.

"Walk," said the tallest warrior in the waiting group. He had circles of red paint or clay daubed around his thick arms, and his flint-bladed spear was longer by a foot than those of the men with him. Now he motioned with it toward the distant village. Jones and Boris started in that direction; the Kappans followed.

Seen at close range, the village was surprisingly well built. The houses—structures too elaborate to be called huts—were of dressed logs and shingles, even a few of stone. Stone paths were laid out neatly, and a central building which appeared to be a temple was built half of smooth-cut stone and half of elaborately carved wood. Boris was certain that other villages of the same or tributary tribes must be nearby; there were not enough dwellings visible here to support the social superstructures implied by the temple.

Perhaps the Space Force survey, ten years before, had not even touched these people. The whole planet would of course have been mapped by aerial and orbital photographers, but quite possibly ninety-five per cent of the surface had received no further attention than that.

A little mob of village children formed, and men and women came out of the house, seeming calmly curious, as Jones and Boris drew near. The people of the village wore robe-like garments, and their gestures were gentle. They were of the same stock as the eight hard-muscled warriors, but obviously of a different class or caste.

The tall spearman with the red-circled arms now came to the front of the procession, to lead Jones and Boris through the village. Boris's planeteering eye judged that the warriors were not conquerors here, for they moved courteously enough among the soft-robed people.

Spanning twenty yards of quiet river was a wooden bridge that thumped and squeaked under the weight of groundsuits.

Just ahead was the temple building, and now a lean and shaggy Earthman, wearing worn coverall and boots, appeared in its doorway. He had the bearings of a leader, a chief, and the robed villagers there deferentially made way for him.

Jones halted a few yards from the man, and bowed slightly. "Dr. Magnuson."

The man returned the nod, and cast quick, appraising glances over Jones and Boris.

"Gentlemen, you puzzle me. You've been walking for at least a day in this area, but you've made no radio contact with the colony."

"Magnuson, they say your enemies are theirs," the tall warrior informed him.

Jones smiled. "That's right, Doctor. I've come to prefer your way of life."

Boris thought the appraising eyes were puzzled. But they moved calmly enough over to him. "And you, sir?"

"He's drugged," Jones cut in. "Never mind him for the moment. Magnuson, can I speak to you alone right away? It's urgent."

"Why not?" Magnuson gestured toward the entrance of the temple.

Boris followed Jones inside; Magnuson came after them. The interior was dim, divided into several rooms, and held nothing immediately startling to a planeteer's eye. A couple of the soft-robed men were there. Magnuson said a word to them, and after hesitating for a moment they made graceful gestures and went out.

Magnuson turned to Jones. "Now?"

"I want the source of the Water of Thought," said Jones in a deliberate voice. "And I want it right away."

"So." Magnuson hesitated thoughtfully. "Once I wanted very much to find that myself. I should still like to, but—May I ask you what your reason is?"

"I don't want to steal it, or smuggle it. I just want some for myself; I can live with any arrangement that guarantees me a steady supply. A few mouthfuls a day, at a minimum. But that minimum I mean to have, make no mistake. I've killed men already for the Water. You know the power in these suits?"

"I'm not a fool," said Magnuson shortly. Not a man to be bluffed or easily frightened, Boris thought.

29

Magnuson went on, "Some of the Water of Thought is available, in this village. I'll undertake to guarantee you a mouthful a day, if you work with me."

"Where does it come from?"

"The warriors capture it, somewhere upstream along the Yunoee, the river in the village. They make periodic raids, and bring it back with them in pails." Magnuson gestured at some pot-like containers piled against a wall. "I don't know more than that. I've made myself a person of some importance here, as you'll see, but I'm not yet privy to the tribal secrets. I am in some ways a dictator, but not yet a full member of the people. Perhaps I shall be soon." He smiled suddenly, with surprising magnetism.

Jones looked about him. "You say there's some of the Water here in the village? Show me."

A tiny frown creased Magnuson's brow. "Remember, it's a sacred thing to these people."

"Show me."

Magnuson hesitated briefly. "All right. Come in here." He led them through a door behind a stone altar, into another room, a windowless place, lighted only by a few oil lamps on low stone pedestals. Half a dozen of the robed priestly men were here; two of them lay supine on a mat of woven branches, and Boris was not sure that those two breathed.

"They've drunk the Water of Thought," said Magnuson, indicating the two with a gesture. "Kappans claim to experience racial memories under its influence."

It seemed to be all things to all men. Boris spoke up: "What did it do to you, Doctor?"

Magnuson's vital eyes flicked at him, unperturbed. "Nothing, really."

"Where is it?" Jones demanded.

Magnuson bent, and, from the floor against one wall, lifted another mat. A sunken vat, of bathtub size, was revealed. The liquid in the vat seemed black in the dim light.

Jones took a step forward. "You mean, that whole tubful is —the Water?"

"Yes. You see, the priests here try to keep a stock—what are you doing?"

Jones had dropped to his knees beside the sunken vat. He pulled his helmet off and tossed it aside. Turning to Boris,

he ordered: "Brazil, watch them. If any of them start to do anything dangerous to me, kill them. Say you'll obey me."

Boris's hands moved to unsling his rifle, and his finger flicked off the safety. His chest forced air up through his throat, and his throat and his mouth made a word of it: "Yes."

Jones bent over the vat, and there was a stir among the watching Kappans. Magnuson gestured sharply, and said something, and the robed ones muttered but stood still.

Jones dipped a finger into the vat, and raised it to his mouth, tasting. A moment later he had stretched himself prone on the stone floor, and was thrusting down his head to drink.

Boris had to watch Magnuson and the Kappans, to see if they might be going to do anything dangerous to Jones. Their faces were not pleased at what was happening. There was a bubbling sound; Boris wondered what would happen if his master drowned himself.

At last there came a louder gurgle, followed by a gasp, and Boris looked down. Jones rolled over on the floor, his armor clanking on stone, his whole head wet, his eyes moving like a baby's, chasing things unseen by others. For an instant Boris thought that the man had been poisoned, but then he saw that Jones's ecstasy was of pleasure and not of pain.

Jones cracked the stone floor with a metal fist. "Brazil, let them kill me if they want to!" A moment later he sat up. "But no, don't let them! I can drink again tomorrow, and the day after, and every day, for years and years." As if his body was a new thing to him, Jones got unsteadily to his feet, and leaned for support against a carven temple post.

A lamp sputtered. Everyone else in the temple was silent while Jones's gasping breath slowly returned to normal.

His eyes came back to look at the others. He said, "Magnuson, there's plenty here for both of us. We have no quarrel."

"I don't use the drug, but you're forgetting the owners. My friends here will not allow you unlimited wallowing in that vat. No. I told you it was sacred."

"We'll see about that."

"I suppose in those suits you could destroy this village, but that won't help you find the source of the Water. Not if you kill the whole tribe."

"I don't want any more killing, but I'll do anything to find that source." Jones let go of his support.

Magnuson moved two paces away, and stood for a moment with his back to everyone. Then he spun around. "You say you'll do anything. Will you join this tribe? I'm supposed to be inititated soon. The ceremony can be held a day or two from now."

"What'll I gain?"

"Once initiated, we will be entitled to the tribal secrets. These people will help us and defend us like brothers."

"Might be a good idea."

Magnuson nodded. "I'll explain the details presently. Right now things will be easier if you'll leave the temple."

Jones looked down at the Water of Thought in its dark vat. "Funny. Now, when I try to imagine the source I can almost see a green, peaceful place. But it's like a half-forgotten dream." Abstractedly, Jones moved to the door and slowly out of the room.

"It's not good that he should drink so much of it." Magnuson shook his head, looking after Jones. Then he put a hand on Boris's suited arm. "You must follow his orders?"

"That's right."

"When did you first drink the Water of Thought . . . both of you?"

Boris thought back. It seemed a year. "This is the third day."

"I drank the Water once myself, and in five days its effects had left me. I give you this hope now; I trust you'll remember me when I need help."

Boris could not let himself start hoping. "What did it do to you, Magnuson? What was the effect that passed in five days?"

"It brought me here." Magnuson looked round the temple. "To more important things than drugs." His sudden magnetic smile flashed again. "Come. You are my guests tonight, and we will have a feast."

IV

GREAT LAKE, south of the village, mirrored half the greenish sunset in its calm water. In front of Magnuson's hut, torches were lighted, a low table was set up, and platters of food

were prepared. Acting as cooks and waiters and furniture movers were Kappans who wore neither the warrior's loin-cloth nor the priest's robe, but a kind of kilt. The kilted men and women alike wore their hair in long braids.

Magnuson emerged from his dwelling and addressed Jones cheerfully: "I would suggest that you and Brazil get out of those suits, if you want the people here to accept you. Anyway, you must remove your helmets to eat."

"All right, we can't live sealed in forever." Jones's eyes were still distant, and his face had a feverish look again. He had spent most of the day sitting alone, as if preoccupied with thought. "Let's relax for a while, Brazil."

A minute later, the empty suits lay with the rifles on the ground. Five seconds after that, the necks of Boris and Jones were ringed by a dozen spearpoints. Boris, at least, was not greatly surprised.

Magnuson was pleased, but also worried. He chided the spearman in their own language, and pulled gently at their arms. The ring of flinty points widened by four or five inches.

"I'm sorry to frighten you," said Magnuson. "Still, my Kap-pan friends have the right idea. You must be subject to me here, not I to you. More than your lives or mine is at stake here. Man himself. Yes."

Red Circles, who seemed to be chief of all the warriors, appeared, and smiled to see the groundsuits and weapons separated from their owners. Red Circles held a brief dia-logue with Magnuson, then issued a few sharp orders. The ring of threatening spears dissolved. Teams of kilted workers carried away the groundsuits and rifles.

Magnuson excused himself briefly. "I have a short radio message to send, and I'd better do it before our planet's Heaviside layer makes it difficult to maintain privacy." He nodded at the sunset. "Soon enough, the colony and the galaxy will know where I am. But not just yet." He went into his house.

In a minute, Magnuson was back. "Gentlemen, shall we dine?" He motioned them to the table. "Believe me, I mean you no harm. There is suffering enough."

With a slave's fatalism, Boris squatted on a mat at the low table. He was halfway through his portion of the roast meat when he heard a copter.

33

Beside him, Jones jumped up shouting, "Our suits! Bring them back!"

But Magnuson simply got up and walked away, not showing any great excitement. The copter's sound slowed and died abruptly in the darkness as if the machine had made a radar landing nearby. In a few minutes Magnuson was back, and Boris was not astonished to see that Pete Kaleta walked with him. Don Morton and Jane were more of a surprise; and then, stopping Boris's heart for a second, Brenda walked into the firelight, her hands behind her as if they were tied. She limped badly, but seemed otherwise unhurt. The relief in her eyes when they discovered him tore at the raw wound of his helplessness.

Kaleta stopped in front of him. "I meant you no harm, Brazil. Or her. I didn't expect your copter would fail that suddenly. I'm no expert at sabotage."

"No one's meant me any harm yet on this planet," said Boris. "How far behind you is the Space Force?"

"I meant I didn't want to kill you." The mayor stared thoughtfully at Boris; the stare was all the worse in that it did not seem intended to frighten.

Magnuson suddenly noticed Brenda's bound hands. He yanked a knife from a sheath at his belt and cut her free. "There's no need for this damnable business!" He hurled pieces of cord away.

"Who said you could—" Morton's move toward Magnuson was stopped by Red Circles' spear leveled at his chest. Morton stepped back, his hand going to the holster at his side.

"No!" Kaleta grabbed at Morton. "Take it easy. We can't afford— Take it easy, will you? We'll talk this over later."

"Go ahead, tough guy," said Jane to Morton. "Get us all killed."

With a little shudder she moved away from him, toward the table. "I see supper's ready. Are we all invited?"

"You are indeed," said Magnuson. He looked big, standing protectively beside little Brenda. Beside him she looked very young, rubbing her freed hands, her brown hair hanging loose around her face.

"Thank you," she said to Magnuson. Then she looked across the table at Boris. "Are you all right? Our *mayor* came and *rescue*d me this morning, as you see."

"I'm alive; I'm drugged," Boris told her. Brenda's eyes went wide.

Magnuson sheathed his knife. "Let's all have something to eat," he said, calmly. "Then we can talk."

While eating, Boris kept a planeteer's eye turned on the Kappans. None of them were sharing Magnuson's table tonight, yet Boris thought they might at the next meal. Their relationship with Magnuson seemed to be a complex one. The robed priests deferred to him, the warriors defended him, and the kilted workers served him. Yet he had said they would not tell him the secret of the source of the Water of Thought; not that he seemed much interested in it. Such a relationship might be possible only between people of different planets.

From across the table, Brenda was appealing silently to Boris for some reassurance if not help. He found himself resenting the way she looked at him. He wanted to scream at her that he was helpless, that there was nothing he could do for her whatever happened. But he kept his face calm; that was all he could do.

Jane was a frightened girl and showed it, looking from one face to another for some sign of hope.

Kaleta and Jones and Morton were all dining in poker-faced silence.

Even now, relaxed, Magnuson had the bearing of a chief. He ate sparingly, though with evident enjoyment. At last he wiped greasy fingers on a cloth handed to him by a kilted worker-girl, and belched with healthy satisfaction. The worker-chef smiled at this sign of approval.

"On Kappa," Magnuson began, "Eden is here and now."

At Boris's side, Jones raised his head. He turned his face, with an odd expression, down the table toward Magnuson.

Magnuson gestured at the villagers nearby. "Oh, for these people, and for the rest of their species scattered around the planet, Eden of course has passed. But, for some creatures in the wilderness near here, its time is now."

The Kappan night was deep around the torch-lit table, and the night insects had awakened. Jane giggled in nervousness, and Morton ostentatiously yawned.

Magnuson looked at Jones. "I told you that something more than our individual lives is at stake here. We find ourselves privileged to aid the forces that created us, to become

35

the conscious, willing tools of evolution. I mean that the Kappan hominid is on the verge of becoming man, and chance has given us the opportunity to help."

Red Circles had been leaning on his spear, a few yards from the table. Now he stirred restlessly.

Magnuson looked over him, as if accepting a challenge implied by the movement. "What are the Forest People, Red Circles? Are they men?"

"They are enemies or slaves, Magnuson."

"But when some of them become men, full men like you and me, what then?"

"Magnuson you know they are our enemies. I have seen you torture them, and it was good. Now these others from Earth will help us kill the grown Forest People and make the young ones slaves. And we will hide all of you, when your enemies come flying to find you. All this will be good."

Magnuson sighed with weary impatience. "Red Circles, I do not mean to kill the Forest People or to make them slaves, and you well know it. You have learned new speech from me, with great skill. Can you not learn more? When the Forest People have become full men, like you and me, it will be wrong to kill them or keep them at work by whipping them."

"Yes," said Red Circles calmly, not arguing. But not giving way either, thought Boris.

Magnuson looked round at his fellow Earth-descended. "How many men and women, do you think, upon how many planets, have lived out the lives of baboons, among groups of less-than-men? How many with the spark of humanity in them have spent their days and years grubbing for insects beside their animal fathers and brothers? I tell you it is happening here and now on Kappa.

"Tomorrow we all go up the river to the Workers' Village. The chiefs have decided that a new temple is to be built, and the stone quarry up there is busy. You will see the hominid used in the quarry. They are beasts of burden, but among those beasts I fear that there are slaves."

"Helping the poor slaves is all very fine," said Pete Kaleta to Magnuson. "But you know what we want."

"I sent you some of the Water of Thought," said Magnuson shortly. "I've paid you for the radio and the other things you sent me. For your silence about me. As if you didn't want silence."

36

"Yes, you gave us a little of the stuff, just a sample. Well, the people in the Outfit want more. I understand they like something with a real kick to it. Don't look so disgusted. You knew who we were doing business with. Now I swear to you, Magnuson, I mean to deliver the stuff we've contracted for." Kaleta looked around; Red Circles had walked away, and no other Kappan was listening. "That's going to mean a lot of Thought-Water. We'll give you a share of the profits. You can spend it working with these hominids, if that's what you live for. But understand you're going to help us deliver the Thought-Water."

Magnuson looked at Kaleta and Morton as if they were filth on his supper table. Then he turned to Jones and Boris. "Gentlemen, I have quarreled with the Space Force. Daily I violate its somewhat narrow-minded rules governing anthropological research; but I still respect it and I respect you. When I see such as these . . ."

"Don't get tough." Morton's voice was cold. Then he smiled over at Jones. "I understand you'll make a good customer for the Water from now on. Stick with us, and we'll see you're taken care of."

Jones stared back. Then he put his face down in his hands on the table.

In the small hut where he and Boris were quartered for the night, Jones poured himself a sip of the Water of Thought. Then he sat silently clutching his stone bottle, which seemed nearly empty.

"You look sick," said Boris.

"I am. Magnuson hasn't given me any more of the stuff yet. It may be killing me, but I don't mind if it does. If only I wouldn't imagine strange things." Jones stretched out on a sleeping mat, still holding the bottle tightly.

"What sort of things?"

Jones did not answer. After a little while he seemed to sleep.

Boris sat cross-legged in the little hut's open doorway, looking out at the fire-spotted village night. He wondered where the groundsuit and rifles were being kept. Not that the knowledge was likely to do him much good. Against a nearby tree there leaned a warrior with a spear, visible in silhouette, probably watching Boris.

37

Kaleta and Morton had not seemed to be worried about the Space Force. Doubtless the cruiser was late, and before it got here the smugglers planned to have a barrel of Thought-Water stowed away, and no inconvenient witnesses on hand.

The rest of the colonists were probably staying close to their firesides, and thinking with admiration of heroic Mayor Kaleta, brave Don Morton, and fearless Jane whatever-her-name was, all of whom were trying to rescue Brenda and Boris from the berserk killer Jones. Probably Kaleta had ordered the rest of the colonists to stay home, even if the rescue operation became protracted.

On the other side of the village common, a slender figure appeared beside a small fire. It was Jane, looking about as if hoping to see someone.

Boris found himself free to stand up and walk from his hut. Jane watched him coming, and smiled tentatively when he drew near.

"How goes the plotting?" Boris asked, moving up beside her at the fire.

"Not too well, I think." Jane's voice was like her body, small but firm. "Don and the good mayor have walked out to the copter; they're going to radio back to the colony that all's well with us but that we haven't found you or Brenda yet. I suppose you're worried about Brenda?"

He thought it was best kept hidden. "Sure, not to mention myself. How about you? Should I worry over what might be done to you, or what you might do?"

She gave her nervous laugh. "Both, I guess. You mean, which side am I on. Well, I'd like to be rich and to get off this planet with Don. Or someone. But I don't want to hurt anyone in the process. Isn't that a laugh?"

"No."

"No." Her eyes became sympathetic. "Boris, what's happened to you?"

"I drank the Water of Thought. I lost my—free will." Boris's voice cracked. He realized suddenly that he was close to breaking down. He had lost count of the days and hours of his helplessness. "I have to follow Jones's orders. If he told me to stick my head in this fire, I don't doubt that I'd have to do it."

"Don't say that!" Jane took a step toward Boris. She gripped his arm, as if to save him from the flames.

38

Having her do that was more help than he would have thought. "I'll be all right." He put his hand over hers. "Are you involved in this dope-peddling? Not yet, eh?"

"No." Jane let go of him, and shivered, and spread her small hands to the fire for warmth. "But I'm afraid of Don. Why haven't you asked me about Brenda?"

"How is she?"

"All right. Asleep. Boris, you don't think I'm ugly, do you?"

"You're certainly not ugly. Under normal conditions, I might well be chasing you around the fire."

"But as it is, you just worry about Brenda. Oh, I'm her friend, really, Boris. But I have this streak of envy when she has something or someone I don't have. Maybe that's how I got started with Don. He was after her though she was too smart ever to be much interested in him."

"What kind of guy is Morton?"

"Not a nice guy. He can be mean, very mean. Boris, I've been—well, I've been living with him, you might say, on and off, for a year."

"And you never knew what he and Kaleta were up to?"

"I was afraid to ask, I guess. But I didn't know it was anything this bad!"

"But you knew it was something."

"I found out little bits of things from Don. Dr. Magnuson made himself vanish out here, and then he sent a Kappan he trusted to Don at the colony, telling Don there was something up that might make money and that he needed help from Don. He knew what my Donnie boy is like, all right. Magnuson scares me."

"What kind of help?"

"Oh, radio equipment, so he could tell if anyone was searching for him. Other things, some scientific equipment. I don't know. You ask a lot of questions."

"It's about all I can do."

"I know, Boris. I wish it wasn't so. Then Don had to cut the mayor in on things. He's greedy too."

"So they're using Magnuson and he's using them. Interesting. Anyone else in on it?"

"No. Oh, you mean Brenda? She never knew anything. I'm one of those females who *can* keep secrets." She gave him a cold bright smile.

Boris returned it. "So here we are. You still think you

39

might get rich and get away from this planet and not have dope-peddling on your conscience—or murder. But in your heart you know the Space Force is bound to uncover all this sooner or later, because so many people are involved. And when that time comes you'd like me as your friend."

She put her hand on his arm again. "I'll do what I can for you. Yes, for Brenda too. But I can't do much." Jane raised one finger, to trace the line of his jaw. "You know, I could wish you were under *my* control, not Eddie's. But Don will be coming back. I'd better go; good-night."

When Boris was almost back at the door of his own hut, he realized that a man was standing motionless in the shadows beside it. It was Magnuson.

When Boris stopped, the doctor took a step forward, cleared his throat, and said self-consciously, "I order you to stand on your head."

"What?" Boris almost giggled with the sudden relief of apparent silliness. Then he understood. "Oh, a test. No, Doctor, I don't have to obey your orders. Only Jones's."

"Good. Then you will not obey Morton or Kaleta. Will you step into the hut?"

Inside, three warriors held Jones. His arms were bound, and there was a flint knife at his throat.

"Jones controls you, and now, as you see, I control Jones." Magnuson was not boasting; he was miserable. "Oh, this is all horrible. But I must remain in control, and there is no other way for me to do it."

Jones spoke without moving his head. "Brazil, he wants you to get into a groundsuit and disarm Morton and Kaleta. Wait until they finish with the radio and come back to the village. Shouldn't be too hard a job."

"It should be a pleasure." Boris looked from Jones to Magnuson. "You don't need to compel me to do that—just give me permission."

"I hate to use you as a slave." Magnuson was suffering. "But I have done worse things. I know you'd escape me in a moment if you could. Perhaps you'd kill me. I must control you in the groundsuit and get you out of it again. I hope that soon I can convince you that I do the work of Man. But . . ."

There came a muffled clanking at the door of the hut. Red

Circles and three others bore a groundsuit in, carrying it across bending spears.

Jones gave precise orders. "Brazil, put the groundsuit on. Disarm Kaleta and Morton, but don't hurt them if you can help it. Then come at once back to this hut and take off the suit." He glanced at Magnuson, who nodded. The flint knife was taken from Jones's throat, but not any great distance.

"I think I will be the one to take the weapons from the two Earthmen," said Red Circles.

"No." Magnuson looked steadily at the war chief. "They will be on their guard, and you might have to kill them, especially if you went alone against them."

Muscles bunched along Red Circles' jaw. "Magnuson does not say that I might fail."

"I know you better than that. But as bad as they are, I do not want the two Earthmen killed. I mean to give them the chance to prove themselves true men."

Red Circles seemed to understand, if not agree.

Magnuson stared briefly off into space, fascinated by something only he could see. "Like a baptism," he mused. "It might wash away past sins."

Boris, getting into the suit, thought he understood. Magnuson had said that all of the Earthmen present would become members of this tribe. Then the "baptism" he talked of would be an initiation ceremony.

"There may be some shooting," Boris said to Magnuson. "Better see that the village people keep their heads down."

"Yes, that's right." Magnuson hurried out of the hut.

"One thing," said Boris to Jones.

"What?" Jones opened his eyes. He had seemed to be resting, almost oblivious of the Kappans who were still ready to kill him at a moment's notice.

"Let me make sure Brenda's safe."

"I'll have them bring her over here so you can see she's healthy—when you come back here and get out of that suit."

And that had to suffice; Boris went out of the hut. Outside, he met Magnuson and strode beside him across the village common, wrapped now in the familiar fluid power of a groundsuit but as helpless as ever.

"They'll come back to the village along that path," Mag-

41

nuson whispered to him, pointing in the starlight. "The copter is in a clearing over there. Remember, no bloodshed."

"I want none."

"Of course. Good luck." Magnuson moved silently away.

I don't need it now, thought Boris, watching the greater darkness of the path where it emerged from the forest. He would need all the luck he could get, later, when he tried to resist his orders, when he tried to keep the suit on and pick up Brenda and carry her out of this mess.

A flashlight appeared, far down the path. Moving expertly in the bulky suit, Boris took shelter behind some bushes. He turned up the sensitivity of his helmet's microphones, and picked up a low murmur of voices.

"—anything fatal to Brenda, at least not right away. That'd be a terrible waste." Don Morton chuckled.

"Let's get the *business* settled." Kaleta sounded angry. "We'll be lucky to manage that, without playing around."

"All right, all right. Anyone who's dead or missing can be blamed on Jones, when there's an investigation."

"*If* we can get the Kappans on our side. But we go along with Magnuson until we find out where this Thought-Water comes from."

They were very close to Boris now, and evidently caught the gleam of his suit in the bushes. The flashlight in Morton's hand swung suddenly to shine straight on him.

"Who?" Kaleta demanded sharply.

"Me," said Boris, and plunged after Morton, who had turned and was running back along the path toward the copter. Morton heard the metal footfalls closing in, turned, and fired. Bullets whanged off the armored suit before Boris got a grip on the barrel of the machine pistol, yanked it from Morton's grasp, and flattened it into uselessness.

"Come along." With compelled gentleness, Boris took Morton's arm and towed him back toward the village. Morton made choking sounds, of rage or fear or both, but offered no more resistance.

The good mayor had been smart enough to raise his hands and stand still. Boris plucked Kaleta's firearm from its holster, and squeezed it into junk. Then, gripping one man's arm lightly in each metal gauntlet, Boris marched his prisoners back across the village common.

Magnuson met them, an escort of warriors at his back. His face showed relief. The two girls stood beside him.

"I'm all right, Boris," Brenda called to him. There was hope in her eyes again.

Nothing would be easier, now, than to rage through them all, knocking them aside until he had Brenda safe in his metal arms; then, to run with her, spears bouncing from his back, trees crashing under his feet, carrying her safe through the night to the sheltering forcefield walls of the colony.

. . . Boris began to remove his helmet, and then his suit. He could not even try to disobey.

V

IN THE MORNING, again transmitting his orders through Jones, Magnuson had Boris again put on a groundsuit, and then drag the other one to the river and throw it in, together with the energy rifles.

"We are going upstream," Magnuson announced, when the rest of his prisoners had been assembled. "A couple of miles north of here, at the Workers' Village, there are some things I want all of you to see. Probably we will stay there tonight, and tomorrow go upstream again, another mile or two to the Warriors' Village. And there we will see, all of us, whether we are acceptable to the spirit of man."

"You're out of your head," said Morton.

"I know you think so, now. But come."

Magnuson led the march upstream, with Red Circles and an elaborately robed chief priest at his sides. Boris, still wearing the groundsuit, followed, with Brenda and Jane. Then, sullenly silent, came Kaleta and Morton. After a few more priests, a band of warriors brought up the rear, with Jones secured among them, gagged so he could shout no sudden orders to Boris.

The path between villages was a well-worn trail but steep in places and fairly difficult. It zigzagged uphill among boulders and under overshadowing trees, and skirted rapids and falls. Boris helped the girls over the rougher places. He found he could hardly speak to Brenda. Her eyes were sympathetic, not accusing—but still it was harder and harder for him to meet them with his own.

After about a mile, the slopes smoothed out, and the trail wound beside the Yunoee through cultivated fields in a broad flat valley. Trees were widely scattered here; a scouting copter could have seen the procession, spotted the Earth-descended people and the glinting groundsuit. Magnuson kept looking up and around at the sky, but there was no searching copter.

A few kilted field workers looked up from their labor or rest to gape at the procession as it passed; and soon another cluster of huts and small buildings came in view ahead.

The Workers' Village, like the Temple Village, straddled the narrow Yunoee, but instead of a temple it held shed-like buildings where logs and stone were worked and stored. A kilted worker-chief came forth to greet Magnuson and the other two village chiefs as equals. The six new Earth-descended people caused much polite curiosity among the workers.

Again Boris was ordered out of the groundsuit, and it was carried away to some hiding place; then Jones could be relieved of his gag. Magnuson's prisoners were casually watched. After talking until mid-day with the other chiefs, Magnuson came to share a meal with the six other Earth-descended. He ate quickly and sparingly, as usual, then rose to speak.

"I have persuaded the other chiefs to begin the annual rite of passage tomorrow night. When this year's class of young Kappans face their test, all of us will go with them." He smiled happily at the two girls. "You will go to the women's earlier ceremony, of course. Things will be much easier for you than for us."

Kaleta jumped to his feet. "What are you getting us into?"

"Why, Mr. Mayor, I am giving you a chance. Not to enter a tribe of savages, no. Though if you survive, you will find the tribal secrets open to you, and these warriors sworn to defend you as their brother. But I give you a greater chance. If you can prove your own humanity and your own manhood, to yourself, I think you will care less for peddling dope."

"And if I can't—prove myself—to you?"

"Not to me, Mr. Mayor, to the tribe. I'll be beside you, undergoing the same things. And if we fail? Why, we will die—deservedly."

Kaleta sat down as if his legs were suddenly too weak to
44

hold him; his plump face was grayish. Morton sat beside him, smoldering silently. Boris found some satisfaction in watching the clever operators as they revised their opinion of the crackpot who wanted to be a savage, bumbled around with theories, and could be somehow disposed of when the time was ripe.

Magnuson turned from the table. "Come along, all of you. I'll show you something of my work."

He led them west from the village, at right angles to the river's course. The path was wide and dusty, as if worn by the dragging of heavy objects. After a quarter mile's walk, staccato shouting and the cracking of whips could be heard from a short distance ahead.

The path emerged from the forest, and spread out to form a grassless area that rimmed the edge of a quarry-pit. Dust hung in the air. Kilted workers shaped blocks of stone with saws of copper or bronze, the first metal tools Boris had seen in Kappan hands.

The workers took time out to stare at their visitors, but stone cutting and metal tools were not what Magnuson meant to show.

"There," he said, and pointed.

Up over the lip of the quarry-pit, through a haze of dust, beasts of burden came into view, a pair at a time, gripping a rope with their human hands, hauling upward with all their strength. There were eight of the short, two-legged beasts in the team, and they dragged uphill a sledge weighted with a single stone block. Under the flicking whip of a kilted over-seer, the hominids moved their load with a straining slowness, but without outcry. Their naked leathery skins were pow-dered with the dust of the quarry. One of the two females in the team was pregnant.

Moving a few paces forward, Boris saw other hominid groups toiling in the quarry. He had seen slaves before—men abused and brutalized upon a score of planets. This sight before him now was somehow different—he could not decide at once if it was worse, or not as bad. These hominid faces showed nothing, no gleam of human hope or hate, fear or resentment. For all their human shape, the creatures seemed to be not apathetic men, but animals. Their five-fingered hands hung limp when not curving to grip a rope or flatten-

ing to push stones. The kilted men with whips barked their orders in repeated monosyllables, as if to horses.

If these beasts were the once-human product of some brainwasher's art, the the most evil men of the galaxy might learn new skills on Kappa. But no, thought Boris. These two-legged beasts have never been men.

Jane had turned her face from the sight. But Brenda watched, and Boris saw that there were tears in her eyes.

"It is not as simple as it seems," said Magnuson to her gently. "If they had the bodies of horses, and you saw them given food and water and rest, you would not weep for them. They are given those things."

"But they're not horses," said Brenda.

"Weep for those who are not. That's the point, yes. One in three, or one in ten, must bear in his brain the spark of humanity, and that spark has never been fanned."

"Why do you say they must?" Kaleta asked.

"Well, they can hardly be anywhere else on the evolutionary tree. In the wild state they use weapons—to fight the villagers and no doubt in hunting. I'm no biologist, but their brain capacity seems adequate for abstract thought. Apes will now and then use tools, but their brains are smaller, and their forelimbs are needed primarily for travel, whether brachiating or walking. Only man and his immediate ancestors habitually stand erect. Come this way. I'll show you my laboratory."

Magnuson led his party away from the quarry, along a narrow path that curved through the woods for a hundred yards and came to an end at a big, new-looking cabin. At one end of the building was a pen of upright logs, like a prison stockade.

In the stockade were eight hominids. The one female and one of the males looked old and completely crippled, obviously unable to haul stone in the quarry. The remaining six were younger males, all more or less healthy-looking, though one of them was minus a hand. Looking at the six more carefully, Boris saw that each of them bore the scar of some serious but now healed injury. Probably primitive ropes broke often in the quarry, and heavy stones slipped and slid and fell.

A water trough ran into the pen. "Dry again," sighed Magnuson. He took up a pail, and began to fill the trough from

46

a nearby well. "I can't get the villagers to feed or water a hominid that does no work. They give me the ones that are badly injured in quarry accidents, and first aid and Earth drugs save some of them, as you see. Red Circles will not understand that my treatments are not meant as torture. There. You were all thirsty, weren't you?"

Inside the pen, the hominids clustered along the trough, cupping up water in their hands, or bending over to slurp noisily. The one-handed male drank, then turned and reached out between the logs of the palisade toward Magnuson. Magnuson touched the gray leathery hand, as if knowing that was all the creature wanted.

"Have they any speech?" Jones asked, staring with an odd expression at the hominids.

"No. Oh, the villagers say that the wild adults have a language of their own, but I doubt that it's more than a system of warning cries such as monkeys use. Though I've never gotten close to a wild adult myself."

"But they *must* have speech. Don't they? I can remember—" Jones stopped speaking, abruptly. He stared at the hominids as if they frightened him; they were paying him no attention.

Magnuson shook his head, watching Jones carefully. "No, they have no speech. The young ones are captured when they wander away from the wild troop, brought here and trained like horses or dogs. I've tried to teach these a few words, but I think none of them are psychically ready for symbolic thought. So I mean for the six young males to go with us, tomorrow night, into the rite of passage."

Boris was not surprised, having followed Magnuson's thought this far. He tried to picture members of three intelligent species being initiated into the same primitive tribe—he didn't yet know what the initiation would be like, but he could imagine it. Still, he refrained for the moment from arguing.

Jones was surprised. He asked, "Will the villagers stand for it?"

Magnuson nodded. "Just barely. Oh, perhaps all six of these will die in the ordeal, for no mere animal can pass through alive. But in pain and shock is man born, as an individual or as a race. If the ordeal awakens none of these six to manhood, why I must try again; I must somehow get time

to try again. In the end I must succeed. Then I shall have made man, and what civilization does to me will not matter."

Morton laughed. "You'll play hell starting a tribe with those. Six males."

Magnuson was unruffled. "The female is not so important." He bowed, smiling, to the girls. "Until civilization is attained. And even then a psychic difference remains between the sexes, which we ignore to our cost. Civilization abandons the rite of passage, and enfeebles the race. Eventually we must return on our home planet to the ordeal, to the weeding-out. Only males who can prove their manhood should survive and reproduce."

Magnuson's Earth-descended audience was silent, angry or fearful, some of them half-believing him. Magnuson ignored them. The one-armed hominid still stood at the palisade, thrusting his hand and stump out between the logs. Magnuson touched the gray hand again.

After feeding his hominids, throwing leaves and roots from a bin into the pen, he beckoned to his visitors. "Come inside, all of you."

Most of the interior of the large cabin was a single room, floored with stone slabs. There were village-made worktables and shelves, and a scattering of books, papers, chemical and electrical apparatus.

"I took a chance, stealing this for you," said Kaleta, pointing to a microscope under a dusty plastic cover. "Why'd you want it, if you're not working with the Water of Thought?"

"I was interested in the Water, at first. Drinking it brought me here; but here I have turned to more important things. Yes. Now I've almost entirely given over the physical and chemical sides of research. But here, here's an interesting bit of physical evidence."

From a table Magnuson picked up a skull, of somewhat less than adult Earthman size, but of a brain capacity probably sufficient for intelligence. The teeth were omnivorous, human-looking, and noticeably worn—probably a quarry-beast that chewed a lot of grit with its rough food. The jaw was short, heavy and almost chinless. Below a receding forehead the supraorbital ridges stood out boldly, joining together between the eyes.

"What do you say of it, gentlemen?" Magnuson spoke to Jones and Boris.

Jones, briefly a planeteer again, took the skull and turned it in his hands, looking at the face, the sides, and the top of the cranium. "I'd say it fits the type of standard, galactic pre-sapient hominid. Rare, but not astonishing."

"Right. Now, tell me, upon how many planets has the transition from beast to man been observed? The achievement of sapience by the standard hominid, or any other form?"

Jones shrugged. "It's never been observed but that's not surprising. If you want to talk technical evolutionary theory, it's an instance of the automatic suppression of a peduncle. The beginnings of all things tend to be out of sight and out of reach."

"Right again." Magnuson nodded, smiling and intent. "But here and now, upon this planet the rare moment is before us, or it will be if we choose to create it. And I so choose."

Jones put down the skull, and leaned wearily against the table. "All this has ceased to concern me, or I'd argue with your methods."

"Then argue. You will soon be concerned again with the rest of humanity. I've told you that your slavery to the Water of Thought will probably soon be over."

"If I'm soon dead." Jones displayed a sickly smile. "If I argue with you, will you refill my bottle?"

"No. But I can promise you that you'll drink the Water of Thought once more. We all will when we enter the initiation ceremony."

Kaleta and Morton almost jumped at Magnuson, cursing him and demanding explanations; Boris came near joining them.

"I tried to have you all exempted from drinking," Magnuson said. "But the chiefs refused. They gave in to me on letting the hominids participate, so I could not press this other point."

Only Jones had relaxed. "Then I won't argue. I'll accept as true any theory that brings me more of the Water."

"If you won't argue, I will," said Boris. "Our going through a paddling to join some half-wit fraternity is not going to prove anything, except that we'd rather suffer than die. Neither will it prove much about your hominid pupils here, as far as I can see. If you can't educate them now, a torture

49

session won't make them any smarter. What's wrong with just letting them alone, to go to hell in their own way? That's all the Space Force wants, and for once I agree with my bosses."

But it was no use, he was not getting through to Magnuson; they were thinking in different co-ordinate systems. Boris had expected an argument to fail but he had to try.

Magnuson faced Boris more in sadness than in anger, or perhaps controlling his anger well. "Oh, yes. I am—what is the phrase?—a do-gooder? I interfere. My interference in evolutionary processes has been forbidden on this and other planets. I remember the words of one Tribune—he said my work would be cruel, cruel to animals and men. As if hominids and men were not already on the anvil of evolution! The only mercy granted the hominids now is their ignorance of what lies just beyond their reach. Cruel! Perhaps that Tribune would forbid a woman to give birth, because the experience would traumatize her child."

"Well. I can't stop you." Boris picked up the hominid skull from the table, and on a hunch turned it upside down. The *foramen magnum* had been enlarged by crude hacking into a gaping hole, large enough to have permitted extraction of the brain.

Magnuson was smiling at Boris's discovery. "Yes, more evidence of proto-humanity. When a hominid dies in the quarry, or in my pen, the others cut or break open the skull, and devour at least part of the brain. Unpleasant, yes, young ladies. But still, as a twentieth-century anthropologist wrote: 'Nearly the most ancient human trick we know.' "

Boris sat in the sunny common of the Workers' Village, while Brenda stood behind him, massaging his tired neck, and kilted and kiltless children goggled at them.

"How's your ankle?" he asked.

"Not bad. Afraid I can't run for help, though."

"I can't do that or anything," he said. "I've tried."

"You will be able to, you will. Sometime."

"Magnuson thinks Jones and I will recover in another day or two; I suppose just in time to drink more of the stuff. But Magnuson isn't trusting me in the groundsuit any more."

"That's a good sign. Maybe he's right."

"I can't afford to start hoping." That was a shameful thing

to say to a brave girl but Boris said it. He could feel himself hitting bottom.

Quartered that night in a hut in the Workers' Village, Boris dreamed again. He was a hominid, dragging a heavy sledge up the side of a quarry-pit. He felt a whip. Planeteer Hayashi was behind him, pulling desperately with one hand at the monstrous growth upon his face, and lashing Boris with the other.

VI

IN THE MORNING there was a breakfast of fruit, stewed meat, and fresh-baked bread. A pair of robed priests arrived from the lower village, and helped Magnuson lead his six young hominids from the pen, after first roping them together like mountain climbers. Then the procession of the day before, enlarged by hominids and priests, moved upstream again. This time the groundsuit was left behind, so Jones was not as closely guarded.

After a mile the flat valley pinched in again, becoming a gorge through which the Yunoee tumbled. Again the trail became difficult; but the journey was short.

The Warriors' Village, at the influx of a tributary creek, straddled the Yunoee like the two settlements below. The warriors' huts were roughly made, and crudely shingled with thorny bark.

Here, the villagers' greeting was a screaming mob-scene. Boris put protective arms around Brenda and Jane as howling warriors leaped past them, brandishing knives and clubs.

It was the roped-together hominids who drew the brunt of the threatening uproar. It took all the shouting and gesturing that Magnuson and the robed witch-men could manage to keep the hominids from being assaulted and probably slaughtered. The hominids cowered and snarled, huddling in a group ringed by screaming warriors and squaws. It took half an hour for Magnuson to get his pupils into the village to the comparative safety of a pen that had been built for them.

Boris had little worry to spare for hominids. But he was relieved when the village women took gentle custody of

Brenda and Jane and led them away, evidently to some ceremony where males were prohibited.

Kaleta and Morton whispered together. Jones paced the village restlessly. Boris sat down in the abandoned hut where he and Jones had been billeted, and tried to keep out of trouble.

He had been there only a few minutes when a shadow darkened the green brightness of the doorway, and Morton stepped in.

"Brazil, you're still under Jones's orders, huh?"

"Yes. But I can defend myself if need be."

"I didn't come in to start a fight." Morton seated himself on the earth floor. "Look, do you know anything about this initiation business Magnuson's got us into?"

"Not this one in particular. I've seen 'em on other planets."

"What's the best way to get through one?"

"You're asking me for help? When do you plan to murder me?"

"All right, so I've got a lot of nerve. I said I didn't come in here for trouble, but you don't scare me a damn bit, colonel, or whatever the hell you are. You don't have your tin suit on now."

Jones came in. "What's this all about?"

Morton stood up. "Maybe *you'll* tell me something about this initiation thing. After it's over you'll want me around to help you fill your bottle."

Jones's cheek started twitching. "There's no secret about getting through. Just grit your teeth and follow orders, and don't try to fight back. As Brazil said, it's like joining some half-wit fraternity."

Morton nodded slowly. "That's about what I thought. And it might be pretty rough, right? Suppose we tried to get out of here, today or tonight. What do you think our chances would be?"

"Just about zero," said Jones. "And I don't want to get away."

"Sure, you'll do anything to stay near the Thought-Water." Morton thought for a moment. "Well, I agree, for once. I've gone through a lot already to get my hands on it. I'm not gonna quit."

When Morton was gone, Jones sat down, his cheek still twitching, and pulled his stone bottle from a coverall pocket.

"Brazil, you're lucky. If you're cured, you're a free man. If I'm cured, I'm still a murderer. You know if I lose the Water now, I won't have anything."

"You think we'll be cured?"

"Magnuson thinks so, and he's so sure of everything. Right now he's arguing with the chiefs again. They still don't like the idea of initiating his six hominids, but he's insisting, and he'll probably win. He's quite a man."

"He is. But what chance will his hominids have in an initiation?"

"Almost none. They won't know what it's all about. They're just simple, ignorant people."

"People?"

Jones raised the dry bottle to his mouth, holding it vertical to drain any last possible drop. Then he hurled it across the hut, and began to laugh, in quiet near-hysteria.

"They're people," Jones said. "I'm mad, but I know. Don't ask me how." Then he collapsed, laughing or sobbing.

Boris sat quietly looking out into the green Kappan sunshine.

Somehow, the day passed and most of the night.

In the dark pre-dawn, Boris found himself suddenly awake, listening to a distant rumble of drums, and to a howl like that of whirled bull-roarers. Across the hut, Jones too was awake and sitting up. Before either could speak, the hut was filled with warriors, masked and painted as Boris had never seen them before. He was jerked to his feet and dragged from the hut with Jones beside him. Their escort joined another little swarm of warriors surrounding Morton and Kaleta, and the whole mob moved out of the village, taking the path that climbed yet farther upstream beside the riverbank. Magnuson was there already, going in the same direction under his own power, holding the lead end of a rope which the six cowering hominids gripped like blind men traversing a place of danger.

There was much howling and jostling. Boris staggered and scrambled and was pushed along. Torchlight fell on frenzied or frightened faces, on night-black river water and the white curl of rapids. Half a mile ahead, the sky was lighted by a huge fire, and from there came the sounds of drum and bull-roarer.

The steep riverbanks fell away again as the place of the fire drew near. The procession moved on into the glare and heat of the flames before halting. The young villagers who were candidates for initiation were here already, in kilt or robe or loincloth, frightened but trying to be stoic. The five Earthmen and six hominids were pushed into their group. The drums were very loud.

"Tell Brazil that he is free," Magnuson shouted to Jones. "Until he has passed through the ordeal, or failed it, he must act for himself. Tell him!"

"All right." Jones turned to Boris. "So be it. You're on your own, sink or swim."

Boris hated both of them. He was not property, not a robot to be turned off or on. And at the moment, any talk of his having freedom was a bad joke. The hands of half a dozen warriors were on him, pulling off his clothes. Each candidate was first stripped, then draped with a net-like garment of tough fibers, weighted with fist-sized stones. Someone thrust another such rock, painted with a crude design, into Boris's hand, making sure his fingers gripped it tightly.

"Hold on to your rock at all costs," Magnuson was shouting at the other Earthmen. "To drop it means to reject the use of tools, and you will be killed."

The candidates were pushed into a ring, scorchingly close around the fire. A warrior thrust a cup under Boris's nose; he drank, and the Water of Thought was cool and familiar in his throat. Jones gasped, and drank; they had to tear the empty cup away from him. The hominids gulped, like so many thirsty animals. The young villagers swallowed the drug with reverence, tasting it for the first time. Magnuson and Kaleta and Morton were now somewhere on the other side of the fire from Boris.

Someone screamed and a dance began, the candidates circling the fire, the warriors keeping pace with them in an outer ring, flourishing weapons and leaping between a village youth and one of the hominids, in the firelight, to the roar of the drums.

Boris jigged and hopped in the inner ring, doing what seemed to be expected of him. Somehow the hominids were moving with the others, not dancing, but at least keeping their relative places in the ring. What would the Water of

54

Thought do to them? At least it had not paralyzed Boris again; he felt nothing from it yet.

One warrior leaped in from the outer circle, and slashed lightly with a small knife across the chest of one of the young villagers, who gave no sign of pain or shock. Then the man whirled back to his place in the outer ring, and others danced in, each to single out a different victim.

Boris felt a sudden sharp gouge on the back of one leg, and managed to keep himself from showing any reaction. The man who had wounded him now spun dancing past in front of Boris. He was masked, but Boris recognized Red Circles by his size and his painted arms. It was a compliment to be favored with the personal attention of the war chief, though not one that Boris could fully appreciate.

The creeping hypnosis of the drums and the dance began to grip Boris, and he knew that it could help him. He let himself move into it, gradually, while holding part of his mind clear and ready to take control.

Screaming hell broke loose; the warriors had started to torment one of the hominids. Boris turned in time to see the victim react with the simple directness of an animal, striking back with the sacred rock it held in its fist. In the next instant, the hominid's body seemed to sprout spears like porcupine's quills. Then it was only a gory and lifeless thing, being dragged away.

In the next moment, another hominid fought back and died. And in the next, another. Between the explosions of violence, only seconds elapsed, but Boris found himself able to think as if leisurely minutes were passing. The hypnotic influence of the dance had brought him to a state of observant detachment; he felt he was able to calculate long plans between throbs of the hammering drum. He saw the warriors with torture-knife and killing-spear, getting rid of their hominid enemies one after another, killing them within the rules of the ordeal, but with hair-trigger good will for the task. He saw Magnuson, standing still, arms half raised, ignoring his own fate, watching while all his work and his hope died on Kappan spear points.

And with this detached clarity and tremendous speed of thought, Boris saw the fifth and sixth hominids still standing in their places behind Magnuson, while the fourth was dying before Magnuson's eyes.

55

Those last two hominids still stood, moving obediently with the circle, holding firmly to their ritual rocks, while one warrior jabbed at them with a point and another scorched them with a glowing stick. The two hominids watched Magnuson like dogs, and they obeyed him like trusting men, amid this violence and death. And Boris saw two warriors look at each other, look and come to silent agreement. They thrust with their spears, and the fifth hominid died, not by the rules of the rite of passage, but by racial murder.

Then the two murderers saw Magnuson turn toward them, and they moved away as if ashamed, and so the sixth hominid still lived, under Magnuson's watchful eye.

To Boris, all these things seemed to hold deep mystical significance. He knew he was sliding deeper into the hypnosis of rhythm and pain and the Water of Thought and whatever else might be here at work; he knew it with the corner of his mind that was still normal but kept shrinking into less and less importance. Boris was not frightened now. Mayor Pete Kaleta hopped past him, glaring wildly, muttering his terror, but that meant nothing to Boris. Even Red Circles had become an unimportant figure, who now and then approached bringing unimportant torment.

The fifth hominid had died unjustly, killed by murderers who were false to the tribe and false to the spirit of man. Some time Boris would tell the story and see the murderers punished. Some time in the future. But there was no future, really; this dance was eternal.

The figure of Magnuson drifted past, dancing mechanically, bending to look at the stained earth where his hominids had died, then looking up again, eyes prayerfully following the lone hominid survivor.

It was the young hominid with one hand.

Magnuson should be praying, now. There should be some atheist's prayer to the Spirit of Man that he could say.

Let us call you down, Man, from your abode of evolutionary law. Let our fire and the sound of our drum bring you down through this planet's night to enter the brains of those who dance for you. Make us all men. Make us all men. Boris could almost see the Spirit now, brooding in the rolling heat above the tongues of fire, coming and going with the heartbeat of the heaviest drum.

Then there was a disturbing noise to give his mind a

foothold, and he fought his way up from deepening trance, pushing spirits and dreams away. One of the village adolescents had cracked and gone wild, had screamed and tried to run from the torture and the dance. And spearmen, ruthlessly obedient to the law of the ritual, forced their weapons home. The young Kappan died with a bubbling scream. Magnuson did not care about this one; Magnuson did not take his eyes from his hominid. But Boris saw the corpse dragged away. The sacred rock had fallen from the boy's hand, and a man kicked it into the fire.

Don Morton danced past; Boris was vaguely surprised to see him still alive. Morton's eyes were glazed and he shouted incoherently. He did not blink when a warrior jabbed him.

The next thing Boris realized clearly was that the dance was over; the sun was touching the eastern horizon; and he and the other survivors were being led through the gloomy woods in torchlit silence. Was the ordeal finished? Not likely.

Boris heard one awakening bird, and then found himself entering the mouth of a cave. His head still echoed with the now-silent drums, and his minor wounds blended into one pervasive ache, but it was not over yet. He was herded forward with the others into damp stony silence.

The twisting passages of the cave linked together chambers so big that in some of them the torchlight died out without revealing all the walls. Feet shuffled behind Boris and ahead of him, and from somewhere came the sound of trickling water. His throat burned with thirst, but there was no use hoping for a drink.

The procession of candidates for manhood wound to a halt inside another big chamber. Here each candidate was made to sit in a separate niche among the rocks, isolated from sight of the others. Boris sat down with relief; there was a moment of rest and peace.

Magnuson walked past him, croaking, "Do not move from where you have been placed, under pain of death. Do not move from where you have been placed—" He went on, repeating the warning, evidently for the other Earth-descended.

Sitting in his rocky niche, probably carved out many generations ago, Boris could see no one. In most directions, his field of view extended hardly farther than his arm could reach. Directly behind him was a shadowy opening between

rocks that looked as if Something might crawl out of it at any moment; directly in front was a large open space. Niches and folds and stalagmites surrounded the open space like rows of seats round an arena; and now in the arena there gathered half a dozen robed medicine men, carrying torches and chanting.

As they chanted, the witchmen were extinguishing their torches one by one, so the darkness grew up a leap at a time. Boris waited, fatalistically ready for whatever might come next. He sat tailor-fashion, holding his sacred rock on one knee, while the other stones tied to his net-garment dragged wearily down upon his shoulders.

Only one torch still burned. The medicine men were lighting what appeared to be small shielded lanterns from it, while the rocks of the cave leaned and swayed with its light. And now the priest-chief, wearing the biggest mask of all, appeared in the arena, chanting his own song, an animal-skin robe dribbling wet in his hands. He raised the robe above his head, and brought the night down with it, putting out the light. The last syllable of the chant died with the sputtering of the torch. With sight gone, the sound of trickling water seemed louder. And now Boris could notice that the air in the cave was fresh and that it moved subtly past him. Probably there were several exits. A clever man might crawl through this darkness, find a way out and be miles away in the woods before his tormentors missed him. A man who thought himself clever might easily crawl into a trap and get himself speared to death. Still, escape was now a possibility, but a faint one; and things were not that desperate yet.

At least Boris found himself able to think like a man again. Had his free will really been restored? Did Magnuson think that the ordeal would help to cure him and Jones—

A hideous scream tore through the blackness, echoing and re-echoing like a frenzied animal leaping from one wall to another of its cage. Boris kept himself under control and sat still. There was a shuffle of movement nearby and the sound of heavy breathing. Somewhere a Kappan boy began a hesitant, groping chant, as if inventing prayer.

Boris's eyes grew slowly sensitive in the darkness. Now he could detect a faint blur of light across the upper part of the cave.

"Brazil? Magnuson? Anyone near me?" It was Jones's voice from somewhere nearby on Boris's right.

No one jumped at Jones to kill him for speaking, so Boris judged it was safe to answer. "Brazil here. What's up?"

"Good. Listen, Brazil, some of these guys with the spears may have taken a drug to sharpen their night vision. Before this started I heard one of the women saying something about it."

"One of the women?" Talking was rough on the dried-out throat, but it might help the cause of sanity.

"Yes. From what I heard, the women have their initiation in this cave, too. None of them ever get killed; Brenda and Jane are probably having a feast with their new sisters right now. How long have we been in here?"

"I don't know."

No one else seemed disposed to join the conversation. Talking too much might be dangerous. There was silence for a little while.

"Brazil, you don't think I really wanted to leave my family, do you? Leave everything I had and everything I was? Maybe you wanted to be a slave to this Water of Thought but I didn't."

Boris's head jerked around. He stared into the darkness, toward the invisible Jones. "What do you mean, maybe I wanted to be a slave?"

"Well. Some people do want to get rid of all responsibility. It occurred to me."

Boris felt a great hollow rage. *There's no truth at all in that*, he thought. *Not in my case. I wasn't tired of being responsible for myself.*

God. It couldn't be true, could it? He shivered, sitting still in the damp, moving air. Suppose the Water of Thought pushed an Earthman's mind whichever way it happened to be leaning, making a fatal obsession out of what had been only a potential weakness.

Was this realization the cure that Magnuson had predicted? Or was it the cure, but Magnuson didn't realize it—

From off among the rocks came a sudden weak flash of light—one of the dark lanterns flicked open for an instant. There was a startled gasp and then a return of darkness and silence. After a timeless interval another lantern flashed in another part of the cave, accompanied by the sound of sud-

59

den movement and a cry of fear. Boris made his muscles relax and tried to keep his mind on things other than thirst or danger.

Perhaps it was well that he did, for the next light that flashed was aimed at him, and he saw that between him and the lantern crawled the figure of Red Circles, knife in hand. In the next instant blackness had returned. Don't move, Boris reminded himself, under penalty of death. He would like to crack Red Circles on the knuckles with two or three pounds of sacred rock, but that might be considered bad form.

But instead of the now-familiar pain of Red Circles' dull bone knife, the lantern beam came again, still aimed at Boris. Red Circles was not in sight. Five feet in front of Boris, on the cave floor, was a large cup that seemed to be full of water. The light went out again.

He was not to move from where they had placed him; and they would know, somehow, if he did. But Boris's memory held the sight of the cup, full to overflowing, a little water sloshed out onto the stone floor as if the cup had just been hastily set down. Boris's thirsty throat argued that no one could notice a difference if a mouthful of water were taken out. But his brain knew it was some kind of a trap. The cup might even be poisoned. If he had to, he could go for a long time yet without drinking. And he had to.

He shifted and stretched his fingers, which were growing stiff from gripping the sacred tool-rock; it would not do to drop the thing by accident. Then he gave a little jump, and cursed, as Red Circles jabbed him nastily from behind, out of utter silence and darkness. Boris felt sure it had been Red Circles again; he thought he could recognize the technique by now. He kept himself from trying to kill Red Circles.

What price free will now?

From somewhere in the cave there came an animal sound, a growling and snuffling that spoke plainly of a prowling predator. Boris's intellect insisted that it must be only a warrior doing imitations, and Boris kept his intellect firmly in control.

Soon, from close in front of him, came the faintest possible sound, as if someone were examining the cup, or removing it.

Unmeasurable time hung in the cave. Its darkness swarmed with ghosts of sound, like the murmur in a man's ears of his own bloodstream. Like the imaginable sounds inside an ant-

60

hill whose inhabitants sought a way to climb out toward sentience. Growing louder in the mind, a whispering that might have been blind cells, evolving, pre-conscious but desperate to grow, to find the way to Thought. . . .

This was worse than the dance. Boris wanted to leap up, to fight, to run away; but he made himself sit still. When the animal snuffling came again, it was almost a relief.

Boris heard Red Circles coming to stick him again, behind the rocks to his left rear. It was a very faint sound of movement, but Boris heard it. How good it would be to turn and smash the sacred rock into—

"Boris?" It was a tiny ghost of a whisper, but he knew immediately that it came from Brenda. Great God Support of Physics! He wanted to whisper to her to get out of here, but his dry throat choked.

"Boris, it's Brenda. I can see, a little. Do you need water?"

"Yes," he got out, in a faint whisper. "But—"

She was moving away already, crawling in almost perfect silence, apparently going to get him a drink. She must be mad. But what was he to do, call her back, start an argument with her?

Then Jones's voice came again from somewhere on Boris's right.

"Brazil, I did want to. I've thought it out, I've faced it."

"Jones? What's that?"

"I did want to give up everything. I sit here in the dark and I can see into myself. I left Kitty and I left my work and everything else I had. I wanted to be a fanatic, to give up my whole life for something, and I did. For the Water."

"It—may work out." Boris was listening for Brenda, expecting every moment to hear the sounds of her capture or murder. He wondered if any of the warriors who must be listening could understand his talk with Jones. Boris flexed his legs, getting ready for the hopeless running fight that seemed inevitable. At least that might give Brenda a chance to escape. But how had she gotten in? And where was she?

"It'll work out, Brazil. I'll tell you how it will. I gave up everything for the Water, and now it's given me up. I'm cured." Jones's voice was dead.

"What?"

"That last drink we had, starting this business. It tasted

61

the same, but it meant nothing to me—it had no effect. I'm dead, Brazil. My life has gone for nothing."

Boris was listening and listening for Brenda, sifting every whisper of sound. He almost shouted for Jones to shut up. "Maybe so, Jones," Boris said.

"Maybe so. Listen, Brazil, they put a cup here, right in front of me. I wonder what's in it."

"They set a cup here but I didn't taste it."

"No, you wouldn't. You're not the kind to give up your life for somethingl. Nobody's ever understood me. My wife or anyone else. If I thought this cup had the Water in it, and that I might feel it again—"

"Can't you keep quiet?"

"Quiet? Quiet? Gods of Space, I'm dead, and you say keep quiet. Brazil, I'm putting you back under orders, right now. Don't move unless I tell you, and don't lie to me."

Boris heard a sound behind him, and knew somehow that it was Brenda coming back, bringing him water. He was afraid to try to move. His freedom had been only an illusion, and had flickered away into nothing at a word from his master. Boris could do nothing for Brenda, for himself or for anyone else. Whatever happened was not going to be his fault, no, not this time.

Jones said, "Brazil, is your cup still there? Taste it and tell me what it is."

"I don't know if it's here."

"Boris." It was Brenda's whisper, from behind him. Boris realized suddenly that they must have given her the Water of Thought during the women's ceremony, and that it must have unbalanced her in some way that brought her here now trying in this mad fashion to help him.

Jones said: "Brazil, I order you."

"Boris." She whispered his name again, and this time one of the warriors heard. Boris could vaguely see the man's upper body as he passed nearby, turned at the sound of Brenda's voice and approached to investigate, soft-footed as a cat. In ghostly silence the warrior passed so near that Boris could see he carried a short spear, and was going to probe with the spear for Brenda.

Boris moved, without thinking of whether it might be possible—this terrible thing called freedom was his again.

He should have used his sacred rock, but for some reason

62

he set it down before he rose up silently behind the warrior. Boris's left hand shoved low into the Kappan's back, and his right whipped around for the silent-killing throat attack. Boris was stiff and weak, and the man was not properly caught. He still had balance enough to twist around and gasp in air, getting ready to yell. Boris drove a hand into the man's throat, preventing an outcry, and then grappled for the spear.

A second later the silhouette of the warrior's head bent backward; hands had reached from behind him to scratch and pull at his face. Boris managed to wrench the spear away, spun it end for end, and drove it home. A dying weight sagged away, sliding quietly to the floor of the cave.

Then Brenda had Boris by the hand, kissing his hand, and tugging on it at the same time, pulling him away. He let her lead him. The only hope now was to get out of here quickly, by whatever way she had sneaked in. Other warriors would already be approaching to see what had caused the scuffle.

Behind Boris, a far louder struggle exploded in the darkness. Jones's voice bellowed, "Brazil! There is no cure! Obey me! Fight for me!"

Lantern beams were springing alive, centered upon Jones. He had captured a spear, and was fighting like a berserker. Another spear had already been thrust through his body. One warrior lay at his feet, while more of them closed in.

There was nothing to do but go with Brenda and get out of here. Boris followed her insistent tugging, away from the lights and the struggle, under an overhang of rock that forced him to stoop, into still deeper darkness.

"Brazil, fight for me! I'll have the Water—before—"

Jones's voice died away, and the sounds of fighting with it. The faint reflected glow of the lanterns vanished suddenly from Boris's vision. *Jones is cured*, he thought suddenly.

Brenda released Boris's hand and crawled ahead of him. The way became a tight low passage through which Boris could barely escape. He lost the rocks from his net-suit, and he lost a little more skin, but he got through, still gripping his captured spear in one hand. After perhaps another hundred feet of crawling he could hear insects, and then he saw a crevice of comparative brightness, like the night sky.

There was room now for him to move beside Brenda. "This way out is the women's secret," she whispered. "One of them

showed it to me today. And I took some of the night-vision drug."

At last they had room to stand and walk; the passage emerged into the open air through a hole in a rocky hillside. Boris realized with dull surprise that night had indeed fallen again; he had been all day in the cave.

"We'll be safe here, for a while," Brenda whispered. "All alone." She put her arms around him.

He was so dulled with thirst and fatigue and weary pain that for a moment he did not understand what she was doing. Then with a jolt of surprise he gripped her shoulders and pushed her away, looking into her face.

"Boris, please, I can't help myself. Here." She started to take off her coverall.

"No," he croaked. It was the damned Thought-Water, of course, making her do this. She had been leaning toward loving him, and the Water had pushed her. "Water," he croaked, looking round the starlit forest. The only animal urge he could feel at the moment was thirst.

"Boris!" But then she followed him downhill, limping on her bad ankle. "The river's this way." Her voice sounded as if she was weeping.

When he came in sight of the Yunoee, he staggered toward it with only elementary caution, and threw himself down on the bank. He thrust in his head, and drank and swallowed. He emerged with sharpened awareness of all his pains and problems, but again able to think clearly.

"Now, Boris, please. Love me."

"Brenda, honey, I've got to run for my life. There's no time. It's the drug making you do this now—"

She gave a little scream of frustration and shame, and her hand slapped across his face. "You filth! I risked my life to save you!"

"Brenda—" He hesitated. Would she come with him? Should he drag her along? There was her bad ankle. And if they caught her with him, likely they would kill her. If she stayed here, Magnuson might protect her. They didn't know she had sneaked into the cave.

Brenda made her own decision. "Go on, run! I'll stay here where there are *men!*"

And she collapsed, sobbing.

64

BORIS BENT over her, and kissed her once. "Good-by," he said, and started running away from her, dodging among the trees as if flint points were already hurtling at his back—as they might well be, at any moment.

When he had seen enough of the sky to get his bearings from the stars, he set his course northward, at right angles to the easterly direction of the colony. Some of Red Circles' men would go east to cut him off, but he would try to circle them and hide from them.

At the moment, the important thing was to put distance between himself and the Warriors' Village. So far, the grassy footing was easy, and Boris made the most of it. When daylight came, he would hide and rest, and think about scrounging food and improvising shoes.

Boris took stride after stride through the night, and there was no sign of pursuit yet. He came to a ridge, and climbed it, avoiding any way that looked in the starlight like a path, for beside a trail on this rim would be an ideal spot for a sentry. *Red Circles*, he thought, *you'll have quite a chase before you catch me, giving me this much start. In fact you'll find to your surprise that you can't catch me at all—positive thinking is the thing.*

From the top of the ridge, Boris looked back. Now there were torches coming among the trees, but they were scattered widely and uncertainly, and he had a quarter of a mile on the nearest of them. He rested for a moment, and then moved north into the hills.

Boris expected Magnuson to join the pursuit. Once through the ordeal and in the tribe officially, Magnuson would be a great Kappan chief, and Boris expected him to have no tolerance for heretics. If Morton and Kaleta survived the test, they would doubtless join the hunt too, wanting Boris kept silent about their smuggling.

Boris held his course northward, angling a little east. His pursuers seemed not to be prospering, for he saw no more torches. They would finish the ceremony, probably, and wait until dawn, before starting an all-out search.

His way led him downhill, and he came to a stream, prob-

ably the same river that wound through the villages. Boris drank again, deeply, and told himself to hurry on without delay. But he really needed rest, and he sat down for a moment beside the star-reflecting water.

A vivid flash of memory came, a picture of Jones fighting in the cave, transfixed by a spear, and Boris's head jerked up in alarm. He had dozed into sleep, sitting slumped over on the bank of the murmuring stream. Gods of Space, he had more than dozed; the eastern sky was gray. He jumped to his feet in a near panic, and stood turning his head this way and that, looking and listening; but no one was near. He sighed with relief. He would find a place to hide during the daylight hours and move on again at night.

He waded into the stream and bent to drink again.

The stream here had a faintly fishy taste. Well, what was so strange about that? Probably there were a number of things that could make a stream taste that way—fish, for one.

The Yunoee flowed quiet and dark around Boris's knees. He waded upstream, stooping now and then to let the river bathe his stiffening little wounds, and wash the dried Kappan blood from the spear he carried.

Dawn was becoming a fact. Boris tasted the river again; there was no use denying that here it savored faintly of the Water of Thought. That was one taste he was never going to forget.

He came to where a tangled thicket grew down to the water's edge, and probed his way with the spear into the midnight gloom of the densest growth, and settled down to rest.

When the ordeal ended, at dawn, Magnuson went with the other survivors to a joyful welcome—somewhat marred by Brazil's escape—in the Warriors' Village. Their wounds had been treated, and the new members of the tribe drank and ate and rested. Before allowing himself to relax, Magnuson first saw the new man, the one-handed hominid, safely housed in the pen where he had been one of six confined animals the day before. Planning the new man's protection and education, Magnuson fell asleep.

He was awakened by a not-too-gentle prodding, and saw a figure wearing a groundsuit standing over him. Startled, he jumped to his feet.

It was Morton's face inside the helmet. "Magnuson, you're coming with me. They haven't caught Brazil yet, and we can't let him reach the colony. I can run him down easy in this suit if I can get on his trail, but I need some guides and trackers and I need you to boss them and interpret."

Magnuson thought about Brazil. "Yes, he should be caught," he finally said.

"Damn right. I'm glad you see things straight for once."

Jane, excited, came running up to them. "You'll catch him, won't you? And what about Brenda? She couldn't be with him, could she?"

"You jealous?" Morton grinned. "Red Circles tells me little Brenda's just sitting out in the woods, all by herself. I told him to let her stay there as long as she's out of our hair for a while. She can't run away with that ankle."

Magnuson realized that Jane and Brenda had both been given the Water of Thought for the first time. And Morton! Again Magnuson would have to deal with a madman in a groundsuit.

"How do you two feel?" Magnuson asked.

"I'll feel fine when I get Brazil in these." Morton raised the suit's armored hands, and smiled. "Surprised to see me dressed up? Why, you told me the whole tribe would be my brothers now. Nobody stopped me putting it on."

"Go catch him, then," said Jane, her fingers twisting nervously at her hair. "Why should *she* ever have him?"

"Come on, Professor," said Morton.

"All right, all right, I'll come with you. Where's Kaleta? I'll have to leave some instructions for him."

"In there, still sleeping it off. Hurry up!"

Magnuson entered the hut and shook the mayor awake. "Kaleta, can I trust you to do something important?"

"I can hardly move."

"You needn't move much. I've got to go with Morton, and my hominid is in the pen, here in the village. I don't expect any of the villagers will attack him now, but, just in case, I want you to guard him. Nothing must happen to him. And see that he has food and water. I've treated his wounds already. Watch over him until I get back."

"Awright. When I wake up."

"You can sleep in front of the pen. No one will bother you."

From outside, Morton shouted, "Get the lead out, Magnuson! I'm takin' a regular war party north!"

Setting out with Morton and six warriors to track down Brazil, Magnuson glanced back into the empty-looking village. Kaleta's plump form was stretched in sleep beside the pen; above him, the one-handed hominid reached out through the palings, as if asking some patient question.

Boris awoke to find the sun near the zenith. He was ravenously hungry, and nibbled the leaves and juicy stalks of a likely-looking plant. While awaiting his stomach's judgment on the plant, he unraveled some strings from his net-garment, and tried binding big leaves to his feet to serve as sandals. He feared that the service life of leaf-sandals was likely to be almost zero, but no better materials were available. So far he had been lucky in that his hike had been mostly over easy grass. Tonight things might well be worse.

His stomach was growling with nothing worse than hunger, so he ate more of the leaves and stalks. Some trees grew up through the thicket, and under their loose bark Boris discovered some grubs which were no doubt rich in protein and fat, and which turned out to be quite palatable to an experienced planeteer who thought of something else while he swallowed. Boris did not need to approach starvation before he could suppress his civilized tastes. Today even raw and hairy food meant strength and life, and he meant to live.

After eating enough to take the edge off his hunger, and trying some improvements on the sandals, Boris rested again. It was nearly dark when he heard men's voices, evidently moving along the opposite bank of the stream. He thought they were speaking in the villagers' language, and he waited motionless until after they had faded out in the distance.

It was nearly six days now, he computed, since Jones had pointed an energy rifle at him and compelled him to swallow the Water of Thought. It was a day and a half since the ordeal had started, and doubtless that was over by now. For nearly twenty Standard Hours Boris had been free, and that would not sit well with the Kappans, nor with Magnuson, nor with the smugglers. A massive search would be under way for the defector from the fraternity. Magnuson or Kaleta or Morton might be wearing the groundsuit, in the search.

Probably they had a copter available, too, but it would not help them much above this high forest.

He had a substantial start on his pursuers, and a real chance. He decided to wade on upstream as far as possible, then leave the river and start moving in a great circle toward the colony. In three or four days he might reach it.

When it was quite dark, Boris slid from the thicket into the water again. When he drank, he was again aware of the taste of the Water of Thought, faint but undeniable. He couldn't puzzle it out now; he moved on.

Within a quarter of a mile, he ran into rapids and waterfalls, as he had more or less expected. He had to climb from the stream, and, looking back, he got a nasty shock. There were lanterns behind him, near the thicket where he had spent the day. He had used up strength and time, and moved himself a dozen miles further from the colony, but they were as close on his trail as ever. No doubt he had succeeded in scattering and worrying his tribe of enemies, but that did him little good.

There was a reasonable path following the course of the river, and he took it upstream. If he struck off through the brush he would slow himself down and leave a plain trail. Not to mention his feet. The leaf-sandals were falling apart already, as useless as he had feared they would be. Tonight, he thought, my feet will give out.

He looked up at the stars. The Space Force ship was now three days overdue, and might very well be in orbit around Kappa now, but then again it might very well be three more days in arriving. And when they arrived, they would hardly start their search during the hours of darkness. These were not very positive thoughts he was having, but they were the best he could do at the moment.

It was a nightmare of a night. All through it, four or five lanterns stayed on his trail in the dark. At last the undergrowth thinned out, and he could move away from the riverbank and start a false trail or two. Sore feet and all, he thought he gained a little distance on his pursuers, but at dawn he did not dare try and hide. He found himself following the spine of a high wooded ridge, and he just kept moving along it. He could go downhill, and hope to find a peaceful stretch of the Yunoee, or another stream in which to drown his trail; but if he missed finding an escape, the hunt-

ers would come down on him like an avalanche. He didn't think he could climb another hill.

Having just admitted that to himself, he came to a place where the ridge he was following angled higher. A sketch of a path led upward, and in the soft dust were several sets of prints of what looked like bare human feet. The sight raised some hope in Boris; to enter the territory of another tribe could mean a chance for him.

Somewhat to his surprise, Boris found that he could still walk uphill, at least in this soft dusty trail. His feet had once been strong and sure, and they might someday be useful again, but right now he would prefer not to know them. Then, too, there were things called water, and food, and rest, but Boris had more or less forgotten what they were like.

Scion of the Martian Brazils, famous bon vivant and adventurer, adjudged not quite human by Red Circles, scion of the Kappan Circles . . .

He was getting lightheaded, and all he had to do now was faint and roll back downhill; that would fix everything nicely. Boris gained a small rise in the trail, and stopped to breathe. Looking back, he could see the warriors coming, only two hundred yards behind him now. There were ten of them, and one had something over his eyes as if to shield them from the light. So, one of them had taken the night-vision drug, that was how they had tracked him through the night with only torches to light his trail. It seemed unfair.

Boris climbed on. He had to pause for rest after every second or third step, and each time he stopped he glanced back. The warriors saw him, all right, for they pointed at him, and waved their weapons as if to urge one another on. But still they advanced hesitantly, making no great speed. Could they possibly fear him? Did they think he had magic powers which had let him escape the ordeal?

Gritting his teeth and gripping his spear, Boris kept going. They weren't going to take him prisoner. No, not again. His hunters gained on him, but reluctantly. Maybe from down there he looked like a man walking deliberately, contemptuous of his pursuers. Maybe if he turned and walked toward them they would run.

He glanced back once more, and nearly fell, for his hunters were indeed retreating, backing away with nocked arrows and leveled spears. Boris looked uphill, and saw the hominid

tribe coming down in a slow semi-circle, dozens of them, armed with stones and crude clubs. He faced back immediately toward the retreating hunters and hurled his spear after them, staggering with the effort. The spear fell short, but the gesture just might suggest to the hominids that his heart was in the right place.

About half of the hominids charged downhill past Boris, howling at his pursuers, who turned and fled. The others surrounded him, yipping and jabbering about him, not knowing what to make of him. These were no dead-eyed quarry beasts. It seemed to Boris, groggy as he was, that these might very well be men. He made a planeteer's gesture for communicating with primitives, and aroused some interest. The hominids formed a loose squatting circle around Boris, and took turns jabbering. They shooed insects, and panted and yawned, showing their human teeth.

Boris's head was spinning, but he kept on making gestures, and tried a few words of this and that, being careful not to sound like a villager. His audience gaped unappreciatively. To blazes with them all, and also with the idea of preserving a show of something or other. If he was going to die here, it would not be while standing on these feet. He sat down in the dust, and began to examine what was left of his soles.

From somewhere downhill came cries and shouts that sounded like a fight in progress. Most of the crowd lost interest in Boris and charged off in that direction, only three or four staying behind to watch him.

He would try to ask them for water. Because the sun was so hot . . .

He was being carried, his head on a leathery shoulder, other arms and shoulders supporting his body. Hominid smell was thick about him. Overhead, treetops flowed by at a fast walk. Boris's mouth was wet: it seemed water had been poured on him, and he had a memory of recent choking and swallowing. It was dim here under the tall trees, though what little sky Boris could see was still bright with daylight. The trail he was on was narrow and twisting, overhung by many branches. His unspeaking bearers were carrying him into some secret fastness of the dim green forest.

Twenty-four hours after drinking the Water of Thought, Brenda felt its madness leaving her. When she was sure, she got to her feet and limped through the woods back toward the Warriors' Village. Now she could face Morton or Kaleta or Magnuson without fear of hurling herself at them like a love-starved spinster in a bad comedy.

Her obsession had been one of love and lust for Boris, and she could see now how she had almost killed him by trying to help him. And then, when he had to run for his life, she had slapped him. But he knew what the Water of Thought was; he would understand and forgive her; though the Water seemed to be easier on Earth-descended women than on their men. After one day of it, she wondered how Boris had endured it for five.

Several times during the day, parties of scowling warriors had come upon her in the woods, only to jabber contemptuously and hurry on, almost ignoring the alien female with the flat forehead, close-set eyes, and what they must think disgustingly soft skin.

But what mattered was that Boris had not yet been captured. The last search party, outward bound and looking even angrier than the first one, had passed Brenda not ten minutes ago.

Brenda hugged that knowledge as she limped slowly into the village. She had considered trying to get away and reach the colony, but she could not walk ten miles a day with this ankle. And she wanted to stay where she would know if anything happened to Boris.

A few children played in the dust of the village common, and women passed to and fro, stolidly engaged with their eternal chores. Brenda was one of the tribe now, and the women nodded to her and smiled across the barrier of language.

"Brenda!" It was Jane, her face showing relief, running toward her. "Brenda, honey. Oh, I'm glad you're all right."

"Where are the others?" Taking the weight off her ankle, Brenda sat down on a log which served the village as a bench.

"Your boyfriend is gone."

Brenda tried to appear surprised. "He got away?"

Jane's eyes searched hers. "Maybe you know about it already. All the men were wild about it, and Don was worse than any of the Kappans. Magnuson, too. They're all out chasing after Boris, but they haven't caught him." Jane, her face troubled, sat down beside Brenda. "Eddie was killed, in the ordeal."

"I'm sorry."

"Yes. He was married, anyway." Jane pulled her arm from Brenda's touch. "Honey, I have to confess something. It must have been that drug that made me do it. When I heard that Boris had gotten away, I—I was hoping that they'd catch him. In fact I ran around here screaming like some terrible . . . I wanted to see him dead, and you too, just because he was yours, and you had something I didn't." Jane began to cry. "I don't suppose you can understand."

"Oh, Janey, it *was* that awful drug. I know. It made me do things—"

The two small town girls who had grown up together sat side by side trying to comfort each other, both of them crying.

"Where's Mayor Pete?" Brenda asked finally, dabbing at her eyes and looking around the village.

"Oh, I wish I'd never heard of him, or Don Morton either. I knew they were both rotten, and still I played along with them. When that terrible business in the cave was over, they were proud of themselves like nasty little boys, like savages. They proved they were tough, and they didn't care that another man was murdered."

"They had to drink the Water of Thought, too."

"Don't make excuses for them, Brenda. Don never was any good, and the mayor isn't, not any more, since he got in with Don. I guess I'm no good, either."

Pete Kaleta peered around the corner of the hominid's pen, looking across the village common at the two girls, who were now crying on each other's shoulders again. Probably they were set to talk and weep the rest of the day. They were not likely to interfere with anything he did.

The hominid in the pen reached out through the palings to touch Kaleta's coverall; Kaleta brushed the single leathery hand away with distaste.

73

"So, we belong to the same club now," he said aloud, looking at the hominid. Both bore practically the same ritual wounds from the ordeal. "I hope you feel as lousy as I do."

The pale eyes looked back at Kaleta with what might be frustration, as if the creature wanted to talk to him and almost knew how.

Kaleta turned away. Since the ordeal he had not been able to think for long of anything except what he had seen in the Temple Village, a few miles away—a vat, filled with many gallons of the Water of Thought.

The interstellar criminal syndicate would pay a fortune, a vast fortune, for the contents of that vat. And now the warriors were all gone from the villages, Magnuson and Morton were gone, Jones and Brazil were out of the way. There was no one between Kaleta and the wealth in the lower village.

The copter was still parked down there near the Temple Village. Magnuson believed himself to have the only power key for the copter, but Magnuson was not as smart as he thought he was. Kaleta had hidden an extra power key inside the copter's cabin, and he had also concealed weapons there.

It was not likely that Kaleta would ever get a better chance than this. He could walk downstream right now, to the copter, and arm himself. Then he could raid the undefended temple, and fly away with buckets full of the Water of Thought. He would hide the stuff somewhere near the colony, and when the Space Force came he would put them on a false trail and try to keep them away from these villages. There were great risks involved, but the possible reward was worth any risk.

Kaleta saw himself safely away from Kappa and his nagging wife, amid the fleshpots of Earth or Planet Golden, allowing beautiful women to spend his money.

He drew a deep breath, and found that he had made his decision. He would do it; he would gamble everything now. A helpful idea immediately suggested itself, and Kaleta smiled and opened the door of the hominid's pen. Let the creature wander away. Then Magnuson, returning here, might think Kaleta had gone chasing after the escaped hominid. Or, Magnuson might even blame the villagers for both disappearances. Either way, there would be a diversion.

Without waiting to see whether the hominid took immedi-

ate advantage of the unlatched door, Kaleta turned and walked calmly away, as if he was just going into the woods to relieve himself. The few Kappan women and children in sight ignored him; he didn't think Jane or Brenda were looking at him at all.

Once the trees were solidly around him, Kaleta quickened his pace. Going downhill, he hoped to be able to reach the Temple Village in two hours or less.

He stumbled awkwardly as he emerged from the woods onto the riverside path, and cursed. He was still worn out, and aching all over, from the ordeal. He had had only about six hours sleep before Magnuson awakened him. Morton in a groundsuit was another good reason for Kaleta's getting out; he didn't trust Morton a bit. But the main reason was the Water of Thought, and the price that the Outfit would pay for it.

He would get away with twenty gallons if he got a drop; maybe he could get a lot more. He could force some of the Temple Villagers to help him. All Earth-descended men probably looked alike to them, and he might easily manage to blame his actions on someone else. There were all kinds of possibilities and dangers in his plan, that would have to be worked out as he went along. But he could not turn down this chance of wealth, because nothing else mattered.

His legs were weary already, but he still walked quickly, sliding and scrambling down the steeper places in the path. As a member of the tribe, he expected no trouble from any Kappans he might meet. Even Magnuson almost trusted him now and that was the biggest joke yet. Magnuson was clever but blind about his obsession with ordeals and weeding-out the unfit, wanting to be God and decide who could live and who couldn't, creating men from baboons.

It was strange, thought Kaleta, how everyone else among the Earth-descended had been mentally twisted by their draughts of the Water of Thought. Jones driven to give up everything else for another drink of it. Brazil paralyzed. Magnuson probably confirmed in his pseudo-religious fanaticism. Morton? Kaleta had hardly seen Morton since the ordeal, but now he looked over his shoulder and shivered slightly. Morton in his right mind was bad enough.

And the two girls had acted strangely. A collection of nuts, all of them. It seemed that he, Pete Kaleta, was the only one

75

who had not been unbalanced by drinking the Water of Thought. Probably that was because he was the only tough-minded realist among them to begin with.

Could he be certain of his own sanity? As he hurried downstream now he frowned, trying to step back mentally and view his present actions with objectivity. His basic goal, realistically enough, was wealth. Very well. Then it was only logical for him to steal the most valuable property within reach (which happened to be the Water), hide it, and later on sell it. Of course it was a dangerous plan, but you never gained anything really important without taking risks.

After he had somehow weathered the inevitable Space Force investigation, the smart thing would be to smuggle his stolen Water off the planet in small batches. He had contacts with crew members on various trading ships who would be eager to do a little illegal business.

He would be careful and not try to leave Kappa himself to enjoy his wealth, at least for a long time. If need be, he could forego the fleshpots and continue to put up with his wife's nagging. Once wealth was his, nothing else would bother him greatly.

Maybe Morton and Magnuson and Brazil would eliminate one another. That would help a lot, not having to try to kill them himself or cut them in. And the girls would have to be put out of the way somehow; that was sad, but there it was. They were all dangerous to Kaleta's wealth.

Anyway, when he had surmounted all such dangers in one way or another, he would smuggle his stolen Thought-Water off planet in small batches and have his payment smuggled in, in installments, just as the Water went out. He would arrange to be paid in bills of high denomination which would take up little space and so could easily be hidden.

Puffing with effort, his feet hurting, Kaleta still smiled and maintained his rapid pace downhill. His vision of wealth, before vague and abstract, had now become concrete. He could almost see the money, the dozens of crisp bills coming into his hands. Possibly he'd get away with thirty gallons of the Water today, and possibly the Outfit would pay him five million dollars for that much. Maybe just the first installment of his payment would be half a million. He would bury it in the woods, somewhere fairly near the colony. Interstellar currency was made to last, physically, and it would stay

buried years and years and still be fresh and crackling whenever he went to dig it out and fondle it. He could almost see that first payment of half a million right now, he could see the numbers and the zeros on the bills—

A rock tripped him, and he sprawled painfully on the path. He cursed and scrambled to his feet and hurried on.

After he had stolen and sold this first barrel-full of the Water of Thought, collecting his first five or six million, what was to prevent him from raiding these villages again and again, and getting away with more and more of the stuff? Maybe the Space Force could be put off somehow. Maybe he could bribe someone; even a Tribune. Kaleta grimaced. He would try that only as a last resort, for bribing anyone important would mean giving up a large portion of his wealth. A crooked Tribune would be very greedy. Kaleta groaned aloud, hurrying through the woods. It seemed he was doomed to be forced to share his money, with Morton or with someone else.

A sudden thought stopped Kaleta in the rocky path, and made him face back upstream. The real wealth, the source of the Water, was somewhere up there. Immediately after the ordeal, he and the other new members of the tribe had been told something of its secrets. Most of what had been revealed was magical nonsense about this and that, but one secret was that the Water of Thought was obtained by raiding the territory of the Forest People, north of the villages. Kaleta had been too groggy to think or care about it then, but now he saw it offered unlimited possibilities for the future, when he had weapons and a copter, and time.

But the vat in the temple was a sure thing, and when he had it emptied he could go on with further plans. Kaleta faced downstream again, and hurried on.

Now the Workers' Village was just ahead. A branching trail joined in here, and along it were approaching a few kilted men, dragging with them a half-grown hominid, gagged by a stick tied into its mouth, its arms bound. The men were laughing and pleased with themselves; evidently they had just caught a beast which would be useful in the quarry. When they saw Kaleta they stopped and stared at him, letting him pass the trail intersection ahead of them.

He waved and smiled at them, as he would have done on meeting Kappans near the colony. He half-understood

these villagers' speech, but now he did not try to say anything. All he wanted was to pass these men without alarming them.

He succeeded in this, and in another minute was entering the Workers' Village. The few people he saw were working, and paid him little attention. Trying to look like a man on a casual stroll, he stopped at the village well, where the river water came up mudless after filtering through twenty yards of sand. Taking his time, Kaleta drank from a gourd hung at the well, smiled at some watching children, and walked on along the downstream trail.

When he was a couple of hundred yards below the Workers' Village, he looked about to make sure he was unobserved, then waded out into the Yunoee. If he had all his directions straight, the copter should be only half a mile from him now. It was hidden at the edge of a landing clearing in the woods on the other side of the river, just a minute's walk from the Temple Village. Probably there would be a Kappan guard or two watching the copter, but Kaleta now had the wounds of his ordeal to prove he was one of them. The half-wit fraternity, Brazil had said. Right now Brazil was probably wishing he had joined.

The river, nowhere more than a stone's throw wide, was not swift at this point. Kaleta did not even bother to remove his light boots, though he had to swim a few yards near the center of the channel. Then he was wading again, reaching the opposite shore, and climbing out. No one was in sight except a few kilted laborers who were a long way off, and paying him no attention. He walked away from the river, across a cultivated field, and then into woods again.

He located the copter landing with little trouble. It was just a little natural clearing whose two or three obstructing trees had been hacked or burned away. The copter was just where Kaleta had last seen it—pulled back out of the clearing, under high trees whose canopy of branches would make it invisible from the air. There were two guards; not fierce warriors, Kaleta saw thankfully, but a pair of robed priests who looked as if they did not know what to do with the clubs in their hands. Evidently all of Red Circles' men were busy chasing Brazil.

Kaleta walked calmly out into the clearing. He smiled

78

and waved to the priests when they saw him; they were muscular youngsters, and he would have to be careful.

"I must enter bird," he said—or tried to say—in their language, as he walked toward them. He pointed to show what he meant, and continued to smile.

The two regarded him with some dislike, he thought, but they were not really suspicious. They seemed to be uncertain about the duties of guards, and jabbered between themselves, saying something about the chiefs. Finally, they made way for him to approach the copter.

Still smiling, Kaleta stepped past them. He opened the door to the cabin and felt under the front seat, letting out a breath of relief when his fingers found the machine pistol and the spare power key exactly where he had hidden them. There were also extra clips of ammunition for the pistol, which he brought out and stowed in a pocket of his coverall.

He climbed into the copter and looked over the controls. Everything was in order, ready to go. Now all he had to do was collect his cargo.

As he hopped down from the copter and approached the guards with the gun, his hands were shaking. He had never killed anyone before, and he felt almost sick at what he was going to do. But then he visualized the money again, and saw these two Kappans standing between himself and it.

The pistol made a low, ripping sound, like heavy cloth tearing. One burst, and then another. It was not loud, but the two young Kappans were twitching on the ground, amid a great deal of blood. Kaleta saw that he had used up half a clip, and reloaded. Now his hands were steady. He dragged the riddled bodies into the bushes, out of sight, and kicked leaves over the blood.

So far, so good. Now, should he fly the copter to the village? But that would attract the attention of everyone in the area; and, as he recalled, there was no good place to land in the village itself. He made sure there were no bloodstains on his hands or clothing, stuck the pistol inside his coverall, and started briskly down the path toward the Temple Village.

The path took him near the edge of Great Lake, which was as calm as ever, rimmed by distant green hills under the greenish Kappan sky. Lake and hills and sky made a peaceful scene, and Kaleta stopped for a moment to look at

it. Why did life have to be the grim and ugly thing it was? But there was no getting around it, the game of life had to be played by the rules of harsh reality.

A few seconds' walk took him past the spot where Brazil had jumped out in the groundsuit, to disarm Morton and him. Kaleta smiled; no interference this time.

His smile grew broader as he entered the Temple Village; it was, if anything, more nearly deserted than the other two. Kaleta walked straight to the temple, and entered. He found no one in the first chamber. In the room where the Water of Thought was buried, an old priest and a young one were fiddling around at the altar. They looked up as Kaleta came in, and they were astonished when he went straight to the sunken vat and pulled aside the cover. The priests shouted angrily at him, and he drew the pistol, wondering if they even knew what it was.

The older man came forward, waving his arms and yelling, and Kaleta shot him, knocking him back across the room. The young man just stood still, gaping, frozen with shock.

Against one wall were stacked some wooden buckets with fiber handles, clean and painted utensils, possibly used by the brave warriors who raided hominid territory for the Water of Thought. Kaleta held out a pair of the buckets to the frozen young man. He cursed the young man with no effect, and had to kick him before he would move.

"Fill them! Like this!" Kaleta got himself a third pail, and filled it from the vat. He would be able to carry only one, having to keep the pistol ready.

At last the young man got the idea, and obeyed. Kaleta prodded him toward the exit. "Go on! No, stupid, take the pails with you! Carry them!"

A woman saw them come out of the temple. She saw what they were carrying, and ran away screaming before Kaleta could decide whether or not to shoot at her. It was too bad, but he would probably have to do some more killing before he got away.

"Go, that way. Go on!" Kaleta urged his coolie through the village. The Kappan moved ahead slowly, carrying two buckets dripping with the Water of Thought, stopping every few feet to look back in unbelieving terror, as if he expected Kaleta to vanish at any moment. Kaleta snarled at him and jabbed him on with the pistol.

"Don't slop that stuff around, you—" But if he hit the man, more of the Water would certainly be spilled. They made slow progress, but the village seemed empty, as if the only effect of the woman's screams had been to scare the remaining people away. It seemed to Kaleta that it took him an hour to urge his trembling, laden captive as far as the copter.

Fortunately, the young man had set down the buckets before he saw the four dead hands of the two guards protruding from a thicket; at that sight, he went completely to pieces. Kaleta shoved him aside, and carefully hoisted his twenty or twenty-five gallons of wealth into the rear of the copter, a pail at a time. He found a sheet of sealing plastic in the copter, and wrapped the pails to prevent any further spillage. Everything was working out.

He hopped down from the copter, meaning to shoot the only potential witness who might identify him, when there flashed before his mind's eye the picture of those other empty pails inside the temple.

It was agonizing. There had been a lot of Thought-Water left in the vat. Should he attempt another trip? The delay would mean risking what he had already gained.

Maybe he could make ten million dollars today.

Kaleta grabbed the blubbering youth by one arm, and instead of shooting him, slung him staggering back toward the village.

"We go again. Hurry!" Kaleta made the youth run, and ran beside him. At the edge of the village Kaleta had to stop for a moment. He was still weak from the ordeal. If he fainted now—

But the vision of the ten million dollars was plain before him, and he knew he would not faint.

"Come along, hurry!"

The village still looked empty of people; Kaleta gasped with relief. Only the old priest's dead body inhabited the temple. Kaleta handed two more of the pails to his unwilling partner, and again took another for himself.

This time the Kappan youth knew what was wanted, and moved a trifle faster, filling the pails and starting out of the temple again. He kept shooting fearful glances at Kaleta's pistol, but he was starting to think again, and Kaleta watched him carefully.

81

Kaleta felt a rising certainty that he was going to make it; he could almost smell the money. From here on it was downhill. Even if half a dozen warriors came at him now, he thought, he could fight them off with the pistol, and get away.

They got out of the village and traveled the long-seeming path again, past the lake. They were halfway across the landing clearing when Kaleta heard a boy's voice shouting. A half-grown robed youth ran out of the forest near the copter, Red Circles gasping four steps behind him. Kaleta's porter set down his buckets and fell on his face. Red Circles had a bow and arrow in his hands, small things that it seemed a child might use for practice. The angle was wrong for Kaleta; if he shot Red Circles from here, some of the bullets could hit the copter, and drain priceless wealth from the Water-laden buckets stowed inside.

Kaleta sidestepped for a better angle. The bow twanged, and the little arrow came so swiftly that it was sprouted between Kaleta's ribs before he could try to dodge.

He looked down at the arrow in surprise, found he could not breathe, and dropped his pistol. He managed to carefully set down his pail full of the Water of Thought before he fell.

IX

DON MORTON DUG in his metal-shod feet and took a grip with his servo-powered gauntlets on the trunk of a sapling. He bent his legs, lifting, grunting with the strain. With a mighty ripping sound, roots snapping like shots, the young tree gave up its hold on the soil.

It was a satisfying feeling. Morton straightened up, waving the tree easily as a feathered wand. "There. I'm getting pretty good, huh?"

Magnuson was busy with a pair of binoculars, and did not answer at once. He and Morton were alone, for the moment, atop a ridge somewhere near the hidden headwaters of the Yunoee in hominid territory. The six warriors accompanying them as trackers on the search for Brazil were out hunting down an evening meal.

Ever since the ordeal, it seemed to Morton that Magnu-

son's behavior had been even more arrogant than usual, as if he deliberately wanted to anger a man. Now, he still seemed not to have heard what Morton had just said to him.

"How about an answer, huh?"

At last Magnuson put down the binoculars. "If the other party's report is true," he said, "the hominids could easily have killed him."

Talking about Brazil. Changing the subject without answering. Was this man trying to get himself killed?

"*I said, I'm getting pretty good with the suit!*" Morton roared, turning up his helmet's speakers to amplify his voice. "*Answer me! Answer!*"

Magnuson looked vaguely sick and uneasy. "I'm sorry," he said. "Very sorry. Yes. you are getting very good with the suit. When you find Brazil, he won't talk to you the way he did last time."

"Damn right he won't." Morton cracked the tree over his armored knee, and threw the shattered wood away. "And I don't believe the hominids got him, either. I'm gonna get him."

Brazil was the kind of guy who liked to get into one of these superman suits himself and then push people around. Morton remembered Brazil disarming him, and then laughing at him, back in the Temple Village. And then Brazil had somehow escaped from the cave of the ordeal, and had doubtless run away laughing again, while Morton had had to stay there and suffer. . . .

"I'll kill him," Morton vowed. "A guy like that. I'll break his arms and his legs, and then his neck, when I get these hands on him." Morton raised the steel fingers that trembled in sympathy with his rage; oh, this suit was a wonderful thing!

"Yes." Magnuson heaved a tired sigh, and sat down on a log. "In another day or two we may find him."

"Any idiot knows that: we *may* find him." Morton felt weary himself; he had worked hard today, practicing with the suit, and climbing cliffs and trees to look for Brazil. And the world seemed to be against him as it had always been.

Ever since the start of the ordeal, when he had tasted the Water of Thought, all the causes of just rage that Morton had endured in his lifetime had seemed to take on doubled force. The Water of Thought was good stuff after all, for a

83

real man; it just made him see clearly the way things really were.

The Water had made Morton fully aware of all the injustices heaped upon him, and during the ordeal his rage had been so great and pure that for a while it had made him meek. Morton had endured the sufferings of the ordeal with what amounted to calm patience, because that was the only way he could survive to enjoy revenge. When he had finished Brazil and gotten back to the village, Morton was going to look up the warrior who had tormented him during the ordeal, and devise for him some elaborate, slow, and horrible death. Morton wanted to spend a lot of time and thought on that project, not to hurry it.

Thinking of his enemies, Morton was unable to stand still a moment longer. He spun around, pacing nervously this way and that, armored hands flexing.

"Oh, sit down," said Magnuson peevishly. "Better save some of that energy."

That tore it. With the gorilla-strong arms of the suit, Morton grabbed Magnuson and hauled him to his feet. He aimed a backhanded slap at Magnuson's face, but at the last instant stopped it almost completely. He was going to need Magnuson yet for a while.

Magnuson fell back over the log. He lay there with his mouth bloody, conscious but making no move to get up.

"Why don't you stop making me mad?" Morton demanded. "You just keep asking for trouble."

"I'll try to stop."

Magnuson's cold eyes were uncomfortable things to face, and Morton turned away from them. "Where are those gooks?" he wondered aloud. "They're supposed to be hunters, and it takes 'em all day to catch one animal. I'm gonna see what they're up to." He trotted heavily away, down the hill.

When Morton was out of sight, and he was alone, Magnuson struggled wearily back up to a sitting position on the log. He spat out some blood, and tested his loosened teeth with tongue and fingers. It was a narrow, dangerous path he had to walk with Morton, every moment, until the effect of the drug had worn off. And even after that, Morton would still be deadly dangerous in the suit; Magnuson would never be able to trust him.

And yet Morton had come through the rite of passage, had proven himself as a man.

Magnuson shook his head. Morton's case proved only that real men could do bad things—as Brazil's proved that apparently strong, complete men could have fatal, hidden flaws that showed up only under the X-ray probing of the ordeal.

Magnuson was certain that only by such ritual testing of all its men could galactic civilization save itself from decadence. To help the cause of Man here on Kappa, Magnuson had stolen, lied and worked with the dope-smuggling scum of that civilization, making himself a criminal in its eyes. He had interfered in Kappan affairs, and he was prepared to commit worse crimes, to kill Brazil or anyone else who failed the test of manhood—but if civilization survived in the galaxy, Magnuson felt sure of being remembered as one of its saviors. And it struck him as ironic that two planeteers, members of that civilization's elite Space Force, had failed Man's test.

Magnuson remembered his first drink of the Water of Thought, which he had taken about a year ago. It had been part of his first initiation. Then, in the peculiar Kappan way, he had become a shaman without first becoming a member of a tribe. On that day, after he had taken the drug, while the drums pounded and the chant soared, he had seen with new and overpowering certainty how right and necessary was the work he had already chosen to do—to pull the Kappan hominids up into the human status for which some of them must be ready. This almost mystical certainty had continued during the four or five days it had taken him to arrange his own disappearance and flee to these villages. Then, though he never began to doubt, the transcendent quality of his belief in his work had abruptly faded.

Now, he realized his good fortune in having had a strong mind already committed to the truth before he drank the Water of Thought. Then, during his first weeks among the villagers, he had taken a good deal of interest in the drug. But he was no biologist and no chemist, and in those early days the Kappans had not trusted him with free access to the Water-vat in the temple. Soon his work with the quarry-hominids had absorbed him, and he had thought less and less about the Water. He had not taken a second drink of it until just before the ordeal, when all the candidates drank.

It had been a pleasant surprise to find that his earlier draught had evidently given him immunity; if that was the usual case with Earthmen, the crime syndicate was due to suffer a disappointment, which made Magnuson feel better about his involvement with them.

Now, the Water of Thought interested him hardly at all. On Kappa or on Earth, the key to Man's future lay in his deliberate evolutionary selection of himself, not in drugs.

Oh, to get back to the Warriors' Village, where the new man-hominid waited, new intelligence in his eyes, living proof who must convince the Space Force that Magnuson's way was right! Oh, in the name of Man, if only Kaleta was taking care of the hominid!

At the foot of the ridge, the suited figure of Morton reappeared, accompanied by the six warriors. There was water down there, a small tributary of the Yunoee. It would make a good place to camp for the night.

Morton waved for Magnuson to come down; it might be fatal to irritate Morton again. Magnuson stood up with a sigh, and began to descend the hill.

Before opening his eyes, Boris tried to remember where he was. He knew he was sitting on grassy earth, his back propped against a tree. Oh yes, the picnic. Brenda was so beautiful—

An unearthly voice jabbered nearby, and memory returned with a rush. Boris cracked his eyelids open. A daylight scene in the shady forest. Nearby and in the middle distance, a number of gray, two-legged forms moved about, apparently not concerned with Boris.

Had they carried him here to be guest or dinner? They had given him water, which was a most hopeful sign. Boris thought things over before he moved so much as a finger or completely opened his eyes while his accumulated physical discomforts were still soothed by warmth and inertia.

At least he had escaped the villagers. Jones was dead, and the other Earth-descended men might be. Ironic if Magnuson was killed in the ritual he loved so well, but Magnuson would survive if anyone did.

And Brenda—at the thought of her, Boris opened his eyes fully, and straightened up with a groan from his leaning

position against the tree. He might as well find out at once what the hominids intended.

A few of the gray figures noticed his movement, and turned toward him, showing mild interest. There was no general alarm, no cry of alert. What jabbering took place was between individuals. Watching and listening, Boris got a strong impression that it was genuine though primitive speech.

He could not call the place around him a camp. The hominids who had driven off the villagers had carried rocks and branches as weapons, but here not an artifact was in sight, not a lean-to, a fire, a bed, a shred of clothing or an ornament. With only the remains of his net-garment, Boris could feel overdressed among these leathery nudists.

On other planets he had seen primitive people who lived almost this simply. But something was wrong in this Eden, something was missing. A small hominid crowd had accumulated and was watching Boris with curiosity before he realized what the odd thing was. There were babes in female arms, but no other pre-pubescent children anywhere in sight.

He started to get to his feet. Slow movement kept him from startling his primitive audience. He began a routine of friendly gestures.

He towered a bit unsteadily over the crowd, which averaged about four and a half feet tall. Seen like this, in their own world, they were not ugly creatures. Somehow the thickness of their grayish, leathery skins was perceptible, and not unattractive.

As he went through the sign-language meant to demonstrate his admirable qualities of good will and fearlessness, Boris became especially aware of one individual in his audience—a male, taller than the average and probably a little older, if silver in hominid hair meant age.

The others seemed to make way for him with slight and probably unconscious movements. Boris paused in his presentation and looked at this individual who took the opportunity to toss something toward Boris. Boris found himself catching and holding the raw hind-quarter of a small mammal.

The haunch did not smell especially good, but at least it was fresh, and Boris's stomach rumbled approval. He made a thank-you gesture, peeled away some fur, bit, chewed, and swallowed.

The food-giving one said something to Boris. Boris wished him good health in return. In his planeteer's judgment, the odds that these were men had just risen enormously. Near-men might use tools to fight and hunt; but when a dominant male went about handing out food instead of grabbing it, it seemed a safe bet that the sometimes blurry-looking line at the border of humanity had been crossed.

So today's dinner was not where a planeteer was eaten but where he ate. The raw meat tasted better than grubs, though not a whole lot better. Boris stopped gesturing and enjoyed his food.

The food-giver alternately smiled and frowned, as if considering the obvious language problem. Or perhaps he was only stretching his face.

Before the attempts at dialogue could resume, a real monkey-troop alarm was called. The hominids surrounding Boris all scrambled away in one direction, jumping and shrieking. The food-giver ran with the others, trying like any leader to get ahead of his followers as soon as he was sure where they were going.

It seemed that a war party, or something like one, was returning. Boris could not recognize individuals, but he guessed it to be the group, all male, who had gone skirmishing after the village warriors. Several of the arriving hominids were wounded, and two of them were being carried by others. Of the two, one had a disabled leg and clung to a stretcher improvised from a springy branch. The other looked dead.

There was a great deal of jabbering, and Boris was almost forgotten in the excitement. He noticed that the dead hominid was receiving more attention than the wounded ones, and moved into a position where he could watch what was going on around the corpse. He could pick out no chief mourner, but it seemed to be an indignation meeting.

People as primitive as these were probably quite non-aggressive, but it still made Boris uneasy to be a lone outsider when they were angry about something. It was a time to be unobtrusive but not timid, and that was a balance hard to strike for a man who stood two feet taller than the crowd and came from a different planet.

But Boris was almost ignored for the moment. Here came a man with an edged stone in his hand, and Food-Giver

beside him, making their way through the crowd around the corpse. They squatted down by the head of the body, and the man with the rough hand-axe went to work on the neck.

This was intriguing. Boris watched closely with a hardened planeteer's interest. He thought he knew what was coming, for he remembered the hacked-open hominid skull he had seen in Magnuson's laboratory.

Now there were almost a hundred hominids gathered around the dead man, watching, but Boris's height still let him see. The head came free, and was more or less peeled. Then the man with the hand-axe turned the skull upside down and attacked the base, enlarging the *foramen magnum* to get at the brain.

Boris was expecting a ritual cannibalism of the brain, but there was nothing of the kind performed now. He missed some of the details of what was being done, but what he did see astonished him. Perhaps half a cup of clear liquid, only faintly tinted with blood, was drained from the skull into a gourd held ready by Food-Giver.

And that appeared to be that, for the present. The crowd began to disperse. Boris saw that some of them were weeping, but this did not surprise him. Here, observing the hominids in their natural state for only minutes, he had already seen enough to convince himself of their human status.

The question was, what had been drained into that gourd, and what was going to be done with it now? Was it some kind of lymph? Boris had a wild and horrible suspicion about that liquid.

Some of the females were now gathering closely about the dismembered corpse. Boris did not wait to see what they would do with it. Wincing along on painful feet, he followed Food-Giver and a couple of his aides, who were walking away with the gourd.

They took it without ceremony a couple of hundred yards through the woods to a small clearing centered by a smoldering pile of logs. Possibly lightning had once fired a dead tree here, and the embers had been fed and maintained since then.

At the edge of the blackened area stood a cairn of rocks, and a couple of hominids were already busy pushing the smoldering fire that way, leading it to the cairn with a lure of fresh dry wood. Others had gathered large, thick leaves,

89

which were now wrapped around the gourd. Then the gourd was settled on the cairn, positioned carefully not where it would cook, but where it would be heated. One man squatted down, keeping an eye on the fire's progress; the others drifted away.

Boris was thirsty, and limped downhill, following the lay of the land toward the probable location of a watercourse. No one hindered him, which was reassuring, though he had no plans for immediate flight. He would have to eat and rest, and do something about improvising shoes—if not pants—before starting once more for the colony.

At the foot of the slope he came upon the small stream he had expected to find; he wondered if it was the upper Yunoee. He lay down at the edge of it and drank, and felt a chill as if a snake had struck at him from the water. This stream was, though much diluted, the Water of Thought.

The stuff could hardly run in every river on the planet, so this evidently was the Yunoee. The farther upstream he got along it, the stronger was the taste. Down at the villages, it was ordinary river water. What would be found at the source?

For a few minutes Boris sat there, cooling his sore feet in the stream, and telling himself that mere survival presented him enough problems. Then his curiosity won out, and he began to hobble upstream along the bank. There was a waterfall close ahead, a high slender curtain of crashing spray.

Studying the bank on behalf of his sore feet, Boris's eye spotted an arrowhead; then another a few feet farther on. Red Circles' men might once have been here.

In a nearby bush was a broken pail, with a rotted handle of twisted fiber. Where had Boris seen the like before?

In the temple of the lower village, he remembered. Pails like this one had been piled near the buried vat of the Water of Thought.

He tasted the river again. The unforgettable flavor was there; now it grew stronger with every few yards he advanced, to the very foot of the waterfall. But still it was a flavoring only, not the strong Water itself.

Climbing the rocks beside the fall was a hard job, but Boris took his time. In one crevice he found bones that might

have been a village warrior's skeleton before animals had chewed them.

He gained the highest rock and sat on it, getting his breath, looking ahead on a level at a green meadow of Eden. Above the narrow fall, the river was a long and sinuous spring-fed pool amid a park of stately trees. When he had rested briefly, Boris walked through the lush, well-watered grass, near the pool. All was so peaceful that he thought of serpents.

It was not a serpent's head that rose from the grass at the very edge of the water. The head belonged to a half-grown hominid, who had evidently thrown himself down to drink.

Boris made a peace gesture. The boy stared back at him for long seconds, and then rolled over toward the water and drank again, as if deeply thirsty. Boris wondered if he might be sick. He was the youngest hominid, except for unweaned infants, that Boris had yet seen in the forest.

The youth took his time drinking. At last, with a sigh and a gurgling belch, he rolled back to look once more at Boris. Something in the look gave Boris the snaky chill again.

Boris stepped carefully toward the pool, meaning to taste it. But for all his caution, the young hominid was alarmed. The hominid was a gaping boy no longer, but a startled ape, leaping up heavy with drink, grabbing a fallen branch as a weapon, hooting and snarling wordless threats. Boris stood still.

Another hominid torso rose from the tall grass on the other side of the pool, this one showing the budding breasts of a young female. She hooted a questioning response to the male. And she too had been drinking, for silvery drops fell from her chin.

Boris stood quietly waiting. He was not physically afraid of the two small ones, but he wanted no misunderstanding with the tribe. Soon, the head on the other side of the pool bent down again to drink. The young male on the near side was not so easily placated; he still crouched, baring his teeth and growling.

Then a thing happened that was perhaps one of the ordinary miracles of the universe; but Boris was to remember it with perfect clarity for the rest of his life. Somewhere in the hominid brain a critical synapse closed; the hominid body stood a little straighter and a man looked out of the

hominid eyes, and distinctly spoke some words which sounded like a slowed-down version of an adult hominid's jabber.

An answer came, from behind Boris. He whirled; Food-Giver stood there, a club held with apparent absent-mindedness in one hand. Food-Giver was only five feet tall, but his arms were heavily muscled; Boris had a rough moment or two before he could be sure that Food-Giver was not annoyed with him.

The young hominid dropped his branch and sighed, as if he had understood Food-Giver's words, and had been reassured by them. Then he sprawled again at the edge of the pool to drink.

Food-Giver stood watching Boris. Cautiously Boris stepped to the edge of the pool, bent, and cupped up a few drops in his hand. It seemed he was committing no offense. He tasted it; it was the Water of Thought, nearly as strong as what he had been forced to drink from Jones's stone bottle, and again before the ordeal.

Boris sighed, and started away from the pool, heading downhill out of Eden. If he could, he meant to rest and eat and think for a day and a night. He was very weary and there was much to think about.

Food-Giver threw aside his club and walked beside him.

X

GETTING FOOD, or what passed for food, posed no great problem. The moment Boris showed an interest in anything eatable that a hominid had, some of it was handed him. It was not that he was regarded with any special favor; the hominids did the same thing among themselves. It was not surprising in an extremely primitive culture. Food-Giver had probably achieved what dominance he had simply by being a better provider than anyone else. Boris dug up some food for himself, lest he lose all status. He even managed to give away a couple of juicy roots and a few fat grubs he felt no reluctance to part with.

At night the tribe bedded down under the trees, mostly paired male and female. Boris found a comfortable spot near the edge of the fire-clearing and when he woke during the night made himself useful and kept warm by adding a log

or two. The leaf-wrapped gourd still waited on the cairn, and he was careful not to disturb it.

It was morning, and Food-Giver was prodding him awake. Grunting and stiff, Boris arose from his grassy nest, and saw at once that something was up. Four or five of the graying elders of the tribe were inspecting the gourd.

Evidently deciding that it had been warmed enough, they took it off through the forest. Boris's feet felt better, and he kept up with them. They looked at him curiously, and talked about him, but made no objection. By a roundabout way that avoided any steep rock-climbing they reached the pool of the Water of Thought, and poured into it, carefully but without ceremony, half the contents of the gourd. Then Water from the pool was added until the gourd was full.

Back at the fire-clearing, a gathering of the younger males awaited the elders and Boris. Attention was centered on the gourd. Things were solemn. Boris was willing to fade into the background, until it became obvious that he was expected to stay.

There were no drums or chants here, but still what followed was ritual, the first Boris had seen among the hominids. The young men sat in a semi-circle facing the leaders, and Food-Giver motioned Boris to take the place at the end of the young men's line. The gourd was handed to the man at the other end, who took a sip and passed it on to the next. Each man sipped in turn, and the gourd moved down the line from hand to hand.

Well, it hadn't killed him before he knew what it was; and there was no way to avoid it now. When the gourd reached him, Boris was ready. He touched his lips to the stuff inside.

It was the Water of Thought and nothing else, far stronger than he had ever tasted it before. What did the clear Yunoee have to do with hominid craniums? Almost absently, Boris handed the gourd to Food-Giver, who stood before him with what might be termed an expectant expression.

Food-Giver pushed Boris's hand back. Food-Giver raised his own empty hands in a pantomime of a man draining a cup to the last drop.

Well, Boris's second deep drink, just before the ordeal, hadn't seemed to affect him at all. What with his drinking from the tainted river, he might be building up an immunity.

There was a good cupful left in the gourd, and like a good diplomat Boris drank it all.

The taste was not bad, but it was very strong.

With that, the meeting was over, and the council returned to personal problems of root-digging and flea-scratching. Boris found that his hosts had shared other things besides food and drink with him, and walked to the river to drown some of the gifts or persuade them to leave.

After some success with that job, he started doing ingenious things with a flint point, some green tough bark, and a couple of strings from his shredded net. Planeteer's survival school had not been wasted on him.

Before he could complete the first moccasin, he knew he had a fever which was rapidly getting worse. He tried for a while to keep on working, and then gave up and threw himself down in the shade; he was burning up, and getting light-headed. Damn the Water of Thought. Jones had been feverish from drinking a lot of it. What now, plenty of bed rest?

He tossed restlessly on the grass, wondering if he dared go to the river and cool himself. Someone came to sit beside him, and he looked up to see Food-Giver.

"I hope you can talk soon, Swimmer-With-Berries," Food-Giver said.

"Soon, but I feel sick," answered Boris, abstractedly, speaking the hominid language. The jabber felt strange on his tongue, and yet not strange. Then Boris sat up, staring in awe at Food-Giver, who looked back at him in mild alarm. "Great Gods of the Galaxy," said Boris softly in Space Force-Colonial. There were no hominid words for that.

The fever leveled off before he became delirious, though all he could do for it was lie in the shade and hope. Food-Giver and some of the others stood or squatted around him, now and then questioning him softly and mournfully—or rather, questioning Swimmer-With-Berries, who had died yesterday from a villager's spear thrust. Of course Boris was still Yellow Monster, his original self, but as the newest male around he had been chosen to bear the reincarnation of Swimmer.

Boris fairly well understood these things without asking, for he found himself now possessed of a profusion of hominid

94

memories besides his new knowledge of the language. And yet, fever and all, he still knew himself as Boris Brazil; there was for him no real confusion of identity, no sense of an alien personality crowding him inside his skull.

Food-Giver (which was a correct title) and the others asked polite questions of Swimmer-With-Berries. Had it been painful, they asked, to die?

Not very, Boris remembered. He could plainly recall looking down at his own gray leathery chest, watching his own ebbing blood, glimpsing at his feet where his failing hands had dropped the rocks he had carried into the fight. He remembered seeing the tall yellowish monster who had thrown a spear at the villagers. Much farther back, he remembered himself at other sessions like this, asking the traditional mourners' questions of the newly dead, who were merged again through the Water of Thought with the living.

It was Boris who remembered all these things. Around him now were not old friends talking with Swimmer-With-Berries, though they thought of themselves that way. They were still Kappan hominids talking with a Mars-born planeteer. Swimmer was dead and gone, but he had left parts of his memory like segments of recording tape in Boris's brain.

Food-Giver and the others chatted of old times like cronies at a wake. Boris could not recall everything they spoke of, and this did not surprise them. That was the way the Water worked; some of the departed one's life was always lost to death.

But Boris now had Swimmer's memories of many everyday routine things, of eating and mating and fighting, and Boris searched those memories now for information.

There was a scene where a young female was being ritually buried, and rows of hominid faces looked at Swimmer as his hands scooped earth into the grave. There had been tears then on Swimmer's face, but there was no emotional content for Boris in this or any of the other memories.

The earliest of Swimmer's memories was one in which he lay by the Sacred Pool, drinking and drinking. His belly was bloated with the Water of Thought, but it was still pleasant to drink more.

Of course. Young hominids after being weaned ran free in the forest, on the fringes of the tribal territory, and survived as best they might. No adult tried to teach them anything,

95

for they were not yet real Thinking People, they were Dark People, like other animals. And sometimes the hated villagers trapped the young ones, and took them to a terrible place where they were tortured, and made to spend their lives in moving useless stones. There they remained Dark People forever because they were kept from the Sacred Pool.

About the same time that a free young wild one grew into the power of sex, the taste of the Sacred Pool, which had been repugnant to him, suddenly became irresistibly attractive. For long days the young ones lay by the banks of the pool, drinking until their bellies bloated, hardly stirring themselves to eat. Then there came a time when the taste of the Water no longer pleased them greatly. Then they came and joined the tribe, bringing with them the powers of speech and thought, and the tribal memories.

The tribal memories? Why, of course.

Now that he thought of it, Boris could remember himself in a female hominid body, gathering sweet roots along the base of a great ice wall that blocked the upper end of a valley—

As a planeteer, Boris recognized the great ice wall as a glacier. He could remember the looming size of it, and feel again its cold breath on his leathery hominid skin, as if he had passed it yesterday.

Was that scene ten thousand years old? Boris knew at least that much time had passed since glaciers scoured these subtropical valleys.

Restless with his fever and awed by what was happening to him, Boris got up and walked unsteadily away from the mourners. He went down to the Yunoee and splashed its water on his fevered face. The Yunoee was cool, but Boris had no memory of its ever being frozen, even when the glaciers were near. All adult hominids knew that its Sacred Pool had to be defended. It was the Water of Thought, a River of Thought that flowed in the brains of men, generation after generation.

After drinking the Thought-tainted water, Boris scooped up a shaky palmful and held it close to his eyes.

Hypothesis. A microscopic organism—call it the X-bug —lives and thrives and reproduces in the Sacred Pool. Some X-bugs are carried out over the fall, but for some reason they

die or lose their potency as they drift downstream; after a few miles, they are gone.

A hominid drinks from the pool. Suppose the X-bugs resist digestion and are taken into the drinker's bloodstream live. Suppose they have an affinity for the brain, and suppose that they become a loosely integrated but necessary part of the hominid brain, serving some critical synaptic function and also bringing information that is henceforth available to the hominid as memory. And also, while in the brain, they record some part of what the hominid experiences.

Boris discarded his handful of water and started groggily uphill again. He rather liked his theory. There were the planarian worms of Earth, one of which could acquire part of the simple learning of another by eating the educated one's minced body.

How could the X-bugs keep storing up new data, century after century, and still retain at least a substantial part of the old? Perhaps the X-bug reproductive process started each new individual with half its data-capacity blank.

Boris was not a biologist, only a feverish and beaten-up jack of all trades; but he thought that his theory could not be far from the truth.

The doctor, back at the colony, had said that Earthmen and Kappans were remarkably alike, biologically. But after all, Earthmen were not meant to imbibe their memories and the neural connections of their speech centers. When an Earthman drank the Water of Thought, the X-bugs must rush to his brain and there raise frustrated hell until the body's defense system did them in. A Kappan of the villagers' species who drank the Water probably experienced the same thing in a milder form—they spoke of trance, and racial memories. But it was small wonder that the Water of Thought caused an Earthman mental unbalance.

The mental effect of Boris's first drink had been so powerful that he had noticed no physical effects. But Jones had been feverish. Come to think of it, Jones had said things suggesting that he had picked up hominid memories with his draughts of Water. Then after four or five days, each of them had recovered. Boris had regained his freedom, and Jones had discovered that the object of his fanaticism no longer satisfied him.

97

Perhaps their first drinks had given them a certain immunity, for their second drinks, at the start of the ordeal, had had little or no effect. Kaleta and Morton had taken their first drinks when the ordeal started, and were probably still crazed in one way or another.

And Brenda—Gods, he had to get out of here and help her, or at least find out what was happening. But at the moment he was glad to be able to reach his shaded nest again, and sink weakly down into the grass.

"I am sick," he told Food-Giver. Food-Giver offered him half a mouse. Boris waved it away and closed his eyes.

Why had the third drink sickened him if he had been immune to the second? Well, the third had tasted much stronger than the other two, and he had been forced to drink more of it. If his theory was correct, the third drink had brought X-bugs to his brain in such concentration that the data they carried somehow became available to him. Skin-grafts could be made to take from Kappan to Earthman, Doc at the colony had said.

But this time, though the drink had been stronger, Boris had not been mentally unbalanced by it. Maybe his psyche had actually been strengthened by that first bout of temporary madness—another interesting theory. The Water of Thought was going to keep a lot of research people busy for a long time.

Magnuson was a scientist; but he had swallowed the Water, and then apparently had never tried to work on it.

Wearily puzzling about Magnuson, Boris fell into a fevered sleep. The mass animal-screeching of hominid children awakened him. Swimmer's memory knew that particular sound to be an important warning, and brought Boris jumping up from sleep. His first clear impression was that he felt much better. His fever was breaking, and he was in a cold sweat.

Boris ran with the tribe toward the distant sounds of alarm, picking up a club as he went. A couple of adult scouts who had gone out to investigate now came hurrying back to where the tribe was assembling.

"There are six villagers coming," one reported.

"And another monster, like this one," said the second scout, pointing to Boris. "And yet another monster, who has no face or hair, but shines all over like the sun on water. They are all

coming this way along the river, four or five shouts from here."

Food-Giver turned slowly to Boris, as if asking silently for expert advice on the subject of monsters.

Boris's fever was gone. If his theory was right, the last living cells of Swimmer-With-Berries had been repelled from Boris's Earth-descended brain, and were food for phagocytes in his alien circulatory system.

But Boris found that he still understood the hominid language. With a second's thought, he could still see the glacier, though perhaps some of the detail had been lost. Evidently his own brain had somehow re-recorded much of what Swimmer's cells had tried to bring it.

"I know this monster-who-shines," said Boris. "I think he and the other have come to find me and kill me."

"If they come with the villagers, they must be our enemies too," said someone. There was general agreement.

Whoever was in the groundsuit would not be a real expert in its use, and would doubtless be demented in some way by the Water of Thought. In some aggressive way, probably, since he came hunting.

Boris asked, "Did one of the monsters have shaggy hair on his face and head?"

"Yes, the one who did not shine and had much hair, darker than yours."

Magnuson. That meant Morton or Kaleta was in the suit; and Morton was the tough one. If it was true that the Water of Thought pushed a man toward his weakness, Morton might easily be afflicted with blind rage. This suggested a plan.

Boris interrupted a strategy conference. "This shining monster is a very great fighter. Clubs and little stones will not hurt him."

There was an awed murmur; all eyes were turned on Boris.

Swimmer's segmented memories were unclear about something, and Boris asked for information. "Food-Giver, have The People ever attacked the villages?"

Food-Giver was probably astonished at having to explain any historical matter to Swimmer. But he was tolerant of monsters, and finally answered, "Yes, six father's-times ago."

"If we go to fight in the villages, the villagers will kill us," observed a large man standing nearby. There were grunts of

99

agreement. The Sacred Pool meant humanity to future generations of The People, so it would always be defended to the death. But what was the reason for fighting in an enemy village?

"I think today all their warriors are busy in other places," said Boris. "And if we go to the villages we will frighten their whole tribe very much, so tomorrow their warriors may stay home instead of coming here. But first there is the shining monster, who can kill us all if we let him."

Again there was murmuring; but Swimmer's word seemed to be trusted.

"I want two of you young men, the most agile, to come with me," Boris said. "We will fight the monster among the high rocks, two shouts below the Sacred Pool." It was a bend of the Yunoee he had never seen, but he could remember the place. "Then the rest of The People can easily drive off the six warriors and the other monster."

The Home Guard was much astonished; they were not at all used to such strong suggestions. For fanatically poor discipline, this army would have made Old American backwoodsman look like Prussian regulars. Still, this proliferation of monsters was an unheard-of situation, and Boris's try for leadership was therefore at least tolerable to The People.

"We know six villagers are coming," said Food-Giver, sticking conservatively to facts. "Maybe there are more. I'm getting ready to fight." He made no comment on the plans of yellow monsters. He might have argued jealously against such plans if his culture had been slightly less primitive, but leaders in the simplest societies of every planet rarely argued. Everyone did much as they pleased, anyway.

Boris called firmly for two volunteers. "You," he said. "And you. Will you come with me? And will you do as I say? We will have a hard fight, and a strange fight, against the shining monster. We will save many of The People from being killed."

The two young males he had chosen had youth in their eyes, as well as in their supple bodies. They came with him. They knew no more of groundsuits than of quadratic equations, and quite likely he was going to get them mangled; but he told himself it was for Brenda, if not for The People.

XI

"Now SOMETHING'S wrong with the damn suit," growled Don Morton, standing knee-deep in the rapids of the upper Yun-oee. The suit's left arm had developed some kind of a hitch in movement; he couldn't control it precisely any more.

Magnuson, breathing heavily in his effort to keep up with Morton, was ascending the steep riverside path. The six warriors were out somewhere ahead, scouting. Or more probably loafing, Morton thought.

"I said, there's something wrong with this!" Morton waved the defective arm.

"Yes." Magnuson nodded agreement. It was easy to tell what he was thinking, though.

Morton demanded, "I suppose you think I shouldn't have broken all those rocks back there. Well, they kept slipping under my feet. Why shouldn't I hit 'em?"

"You know more about the suit than I do," said Magnuson. "Damn right I do."

Morton scanned the hillside about him. Here, the hills were steep, the bones of rock thrusting up through the soil, into occasional crags and pinnacles. Oh, to catch one glimpse of Brazil, who was the cause of all this effort and trouble! When he got a grip on Brazil he would tear him into hand-fuls.

Magnuson had stopped to drink from the stream. When he got up, he had a funny expression on his face; he smacked his lips and looked thoughtfully upstream.

"Well, you got any more bright ideas?" Morton asked him.

"At the moment, no," said Magnuson, at once giving Morton his polite attention. Magnuson wasn't really a bad guy; ever since Morton had slapped him he had been polite and respectful. It just showed that people needed a bit of rough treatment now and then; it was good for them.

Morton drank, too, turning his head inside the helmet and sucking insipid water from the suit's tank. Blah. Maybe he should chance taking off his helmet, so he could get a real drink—

"Look! There!" Magnuson was crouched, his body tensed, pointing.

Morton whirled, sending up a spray of water. A few hundred yards away, a figure moved along a steep hillside. An Earthman, tall and blond and nearly naked.

Morton hesitated momentarily.

"Go after him!" urged Magnuson. He straightened. "There's something burning near there—see all the smoke?"

"So what?" Morton took some slow steps toward the distant figure. "I can get him!" Rage came to a focus. Running, the suit's legs ripped sheets of water from the river. Morton sprinted up the bank, smashing aside brush and saplings, his eyes fixed on his enemy, at last in sight. The figure soon vanished behind some rocks, as if Brazil had seen him coming. Morton exulted. Go on, run, try to get away! This time, I've got the suit!

Running in the groundsuit was an athlete's dream come true, a joy that Morton felt more keenly with every trial. Almost effortlessly he now made the rough hillside flow down past him. Rocks flew back like missiles from his heels.

He pounded along the top of a rocky ridge, toward the broken hills and pinnacles where Brazil had vanished. Something was indeed burning there, something big judging by the smoke-pall that hung between rocky hills.

Was Brazil signaling? Morton stopped, anxiously scanning the sky. There were no copters in sight.

Was the smoke some kind of trick? But he was invulnerable! Morton laughed, and flew on. At the end of the ridge, he recklessly leaped across a ravine; landing on the other side, he fell, sprawling and sliding among rocks. He was unhurt, but even a second's delay was maddening. Cursing and scrambling, he rushed on.

Here was the spot where he had seen Brazil. And now—there he was! The tall figure hurried away along a dangerous rocky slope, toward the heavy smoke. Morton saw now that the dark gray clouds rose from a row of fires banked with smoldering greenery along the foot of the hill. Did Brazil hope to confuse him with smoke? Morton laughed at the futility of such a plan, and hurled himself after his enemy.

Something struck a clanging blow against his helmet. On the slope above Morton, a hominid snarled and jabbered, hurling rocks down at him.

Morton growled in rage and charged the hillside. Loose

102

gravel and sand flew from under his metal feet; he fell, then slid down into the greasy-looking smoke.

The air inside his helmet stayed as fresh as it ever got, but it was difficult to see. Again, a thrown rock clanged from his suit. He saw no one, but he heard the chittering of his enemies, as if they were laughing at him.

Were hominids helping Brazil? That was fine, that would mean more targets for Morton's revenge. He stood up, trying to see through the smoke, smiling coldly. Let them laugh; let them think they might escape. He could afford to wait a little longer.

He climbed carefully, and when he emerged from the smoke found that he had gotten turned around somehow, and was on a different slope. Over there was the hominid—but here was another one on another peak. He tried to decide which one to go after first, while more rocks clattered insultingly around him. He started after the nearest hominid, and heard a shout behind him. Brazil was there, on another pinnacle, hurling rocks like an ape himself. So! Hominids forgotten, Morton reversed himself again. He had to go down through the fires to reach Brazil. When he had kicked his way through the smoldering brush-piles, he found his faceplate fogged over with greasy soot and adhering dust, so he could hardly have distinguished a crouching man from a boulder. He stopped, fumbling inside the suit. There should be a washing system for the faceplate.

A hominid raced by, not twenty feet away, and hurled some filthy-looking muck at Morton. It spattered all over him, and part of it hit his faceplate, obscuring his vision further. Morton roared, and gave chase. But where had the ape gone? He had to stop for a moment and get his faceplate cleaned. Forgetfully, he brought his left arm up in a wiping motion, to try to scrape off some of the mess. The erratic arm smashed against the faceplate glass and the helm just above it. That did it. In a frenzy, Morton pounded his own helmet again and again, with raging fists. The suit-builders had turned out junk, useless junk!

But the helmet and faceplate withstood the beating; and when Morton finally found the interior control for the washer, even it still partially worked, cleaning half of his faceplate.

He looked up and saw Brazil, rolling a boulder down at him. With a yell, Morton charged. He would catch the rock

and hurl it back, flattening his enemy like an insect on a wall.

The rock hit him before he realized it was too big to catch, on this loose footing. The boulder bore him downhill, and he screamed in terror as it bounded with him, rolling him among other rocks, shooting him finally against immobile masses of stone, with a clanging like the end of the world.

He lay gasping there for long seconds, before he could feel sure he was not killed or maimed. In fact he was hardly hurt at all, just bruised and with the wind knocked out of him.

"I'm gonna break your arms and legs, Brazil, and then your neck!" he called aloud, when he got to his feet at last. He knew his enemies were somewhere nearby. They would be laughing at him, and getting ready to roll more rocks at him.

Both sides could play that game! With a sudden inspiration, Morton picked up some small rocks, and looked around for a target. Where was Brazil? Now it was hard to see anything through this smeared and damaged faceplate. Morton would like to get his hands on the madman, the degenerate, who built this suit, and—

There was a hominid, looking down at him! Morton threw an egg-sized stone; it seemed to go like a bullet, but it missed the target, and whizzed away into space.

He could swear he heard them laughing. Maybe they were getting another boulder ready to roll down at him; he had better get back up to the top of a hill. He picked up half a dozen throwing pebbles, but his maniacal left arm dropped and scattered them, half way up the slope. Another rock hit him. Smoke drifted around him.

Morton was beyond rage. He made a crooning sound, like a lover singing. When he saw Brazil, he charged at full speed paying no heed to anything else. A wide chasm was almost under his feet before he saw it. Morton leaped desperately, and the edge of the far side struck him in the chest. He slung there with his arms, emptiness under his feet, and the suit's left arm failed him, just as Brazil hit him with another big rock. Then Morton was endlessly falling, bouncing and falling again, the world of rocks and sky spinning around him and suddenly going dark.

"Is the shining monster dead?" asked one of the young men with Boris.

Boris sat down shakily on a ledge. His hands were bleeding from the edges of that last rock, and his chest was heaving. It had been a very near thing.

"I doubt it," he answered. "But I think he will be tired of fighting us."

"It will take—" The hominid held up a hand against the course of the sun. "This long, for us to climb down and see if the monster is dead. If the river does not carry him away. I think he finished falling in the river."

"You are a good fighter, Yellow Monster," said the other hominid.

"Thank you. Let's leave the Shining One where he is. I want to lead some of The People downstream against the villages."

An hour had passed since Morton had gone charging away after Brazil. Magnuson was crouching behind a log, within earshot of the murmuring Yunoee, the six warriors scattered near him in concealed positions. Shortly after Morton had left, the hominids had launched a stone-throwing attack, but the villagers' arrows had driven them off.

Now all was quiet. Could Morton be still venting some fiendish vengeance on his enemy? Or had Brazil out-thought him and escaped him, or even found a way to defeat him?

Magnuson rather suspected the latter. It was hard for him not to admire a man like Brazil. Maybe Brazil hadn't simply broken and fled from the ordeal. Maybe there had been some deeper reason—

"Magnuson, someone comes."

The warriors were stirring, turning their attention downstream, to the south. Were the hominids trying to encircle and trap them?

But it was Red Circles who came into view on the riverside path. He was leading a strong war party, twelve or fifteen men, all carrying the painted buckets that Magnuson knew were used only on raids after the Water of Thought.

Red Circles came forward, walking tall, his eyes scouting the woods. He stopped, and Magnuson stood up to greet him.

"Magnuson, the Earthman Ka-le-ta is dead."

"What? How?"

Red Circles put a hand to his belt and pulled out a machine pistol, holding it awkwardly. "Ka-le-ta killed three men with this, and he violated the temple. So I killed him."

"What of the hominid-man?" Magnuson asked. "Be careful with that weapon; it is dangerous." He couldn't see if the safety was on. Kaleta must have had the weapon hidden somewhere; then he had been drugged by the Water—

Red Circles curled his lip at the mention of danger; but he held the pistol out to Magnuson. "Maybe you can kill some of the Forest People with this, Magnuson, though you have no skill with the bow. Maybe you will kill your hominid-man, for he has run away."

"Run away?" Magnuson took a step forward, almost grabbing at Red Circles. "Where? How do you know?"

"The pen stands open."

Red Circles would not lie, but his tone was insolent. Magnuson accepted the pistol, put the safety on, and drew himself up.

"Red Circles, you will speak to me with respect. The Spirit of Man speaks to this world through me, and that is a greater thing than you can understand." Magnuson knew there was no Spirit, no God, and there would be none until Man had evolved himself upward to infinite power. But Magnuson's work brought that moment closer, so he was not lying to Red Circles. Red Circles could not know these things as a civilized man knew them, so their weight was all with Magnuson.

The war chief scowled, but he could not steadily look Magnuson in the eye.

"We must find the man-hominid," Magnuson said. "He is one of our tribe now. Have you any idea where he is?"

Red Circles gave the Kappan equivalent of a shrug. "Who can say where a hominid might hide?"

"We must search for him."

Red Circles shifted his feet uneasily, but his voice was stubborn. "I and these men are busy. We are going to get more Thought-Water. Ka-le-ta defiled the vat, and it must be restocked at once, so we are going to the Sacred Pool, all the way upstream. Once you asked many questions about the Water of Thought, Magnuson. Now you are one of us, and you can learn all about it."

This time Red Circles would not knuckle under. Still it was plain that he wanted no quarrel, that he was trying to

persuade Magnuson. Once Magnuson would have needed no persuading; he would have made a great effort to discover the source of the Water of Thought. Even now, the idea was tempting. This would be his last chance for any such discovery, for tomorrow or the next day the Space Force would be here, and he would be under arrest.

But there was no time to spare.

"We go downstream," said Magnuson, putting his full authority into his voice. "We must track down the man-hominid, and keep him with us. He is proof of a very great magic, more important than the Water of Thought; he is a man made from an animal!"

"You go downstream, if you want. But I am chief of these warriors." Red Circles turned and shouted commandingly to his men: "We go up!"

Boris was beginning to suspect that he might, after all, be the dynamic-leader type, for he had gotten about twenty-five of the younger hominid men to follow him downriver against the villages. It was against all the Space Force rules to exacerbate local warfare, but he could see no other course that offered him so good a chance of getting his pursuers off his neck and, hopefully, rescuing Brenda. He was gambling that only a few villagers would be at home, that they would flee, and that casualties on either side would be at a minimum. He would gamble more than that to help Brenda.

"Run forward and make much noise when we come to the first village," Boris told his company. "Remember to look for a female monster; she is my friend."

His boys grunted cheerful assent; following a determined leader was a new and exciting game to them.

They charged whooping downhill, and took the Warriors' Village by surprise. As Boris had hoped, there was not a warrior home. The women and children evacuated the huts with miraculous speed, and went screaming panic and murder down the path toward the Workers' Village.

Thankfully there was no real murder, nor even injury; the hominids were not culturally advanced enough to enjoy pillage and rapine. They shrieked good-naturedly to urge the fleeing enemy on, and waved good-by with clubs.

"Remember, look for female monsters!" Boris led a hut-to-hut search, aided by those of his irregulars who chose to

107

help. It did not take long to make certain that Brenda and Jane were elsewhere.

All this was fun! The hominids willingly followed Boris downhill again.

"We will frighten another village!" he shouted, encouragingly, waving them on. He had a hard time keeping up with them now, though he had stopped to borrow a pair of some warrior's new moccasins, which were an excellent fit. Shoes were a higher invention than the wheel, and he meant to insist on the point at the next scholarly meeting he attended.

Boris and his army swept into the Workers' Village to find that panic had preceded them, and the huts and workshops were already empty of people. From the direction of the quarry came a querulous hominid yipping; not words, but the frightened monkey-call of the young, though in deeper adult voices.

"It is the Dark People," said the hominid standing beside Boris. In the next instant he ran toward the quarry, yipping a response. The others cascaded after him.

"Wait! Not yet!" Boris had not foreseen this. "We'll get them out of there, but not yet!"

He might as well have shouted to recall the wind; his army was gone. But he could not blame them.

Seemingly alone in the deserted village, he ran from hut to hut.

"Brenda! Jane!" In one hut he found a quivering mass of bedding, but his probing uncovered only an ancient and terrified villager.

He took the downstream path again, this time alone. For the thousandth time he scanned the empty greenish day for any sign of rescuing copters. But there was no use expecting help beyond what he could give himself.

He scanned the stream closely as he neared the Temple Village, looking for the spot where Magnuson had made him throw in the second groundsuit and the energy rifles. Magnuson had not realized that an energy rifle would not be fouled by submersion.

When he came to the place, Boris waded out into the dark water, searching the muddy bottom with arms and legs. The current was not strong here, and what he sought could not be far away. Unless someone had beaten him to it.

He went under water to examine a deeper part of the bot-

108

tom. When he came up for a breath, Morton was standing on the bank twenty yards away, wearing the battered suit, watching Boris.

"The river's not going to hide you," said the suit's speaker.

"Are you still drugged, Morton?" Boris asked. And just then his groping feet found the second groundsuit on the bottom of the river. Neck-deep in water, he stepped back, moving his feet this way and that, searching further.

"Oh no," said Morton. "It's worn off. I won't knock myself out anymore. But you know too much about our little business; I can't let you stay alive. You and the others can be blamed on the Kappans."

"Where's Brenda?" Boris asked. And just then his foot found one of the energy rifles. His actions concealed underwater, he scooped the rifle up with his foot, into his hands. But Morton was still too far away.

Morton smiled, and in a clear pleasant voice said, in obscene fantasy, just how he had disposed of Brenda. In the next instant Morton rushed Boris, charging with resistless speed into the water. He came so quickly that Boris fired without raising the rifle above the surface.

There was a needle-jet of steam, and the groundsuit sounded, loudly, like a struck gong. A tiny hole appeared in its front. Morton fell forward with a great splash as Boris dove out of the way. The suited figure floated, face down, hissing, and Boris felt a wave of warmed water pass with it. The back of the cuirass, where the power lamp rode, showed a blackened place the size of a saucer; the suit's radio would be useless now, even if a way could be found to get at it from outside.

Holding the rifle, Boris climbed again from the river to the path. For a little while, before the suit sank, he and Morton kept pace toward the Temple Village and the quiet expanse of Great Lake beyond.

The wave of panic before the supposed hominid onslaught had emptied this village like the others. Again Boris walked among deserted dwellings, shouting for Brenda and Jane.

Pete Kaleta's head greeted him from atop a pole fixed in the ground before the temple. With shaky relief Boris made sure there was only one such pole. Brenda and Jane and Magnuson remained unaccounted for. Boris entered the tem-

109

ple, and poked his head and rifle into the inner room. Four trembling priests stood before the Water-vat, holding spears more or less leveled.

Boris had as yet absorbed next to nothing of the villagers' language, but he tried.

"Woman!" he said, or meant to say. "Woman. Me. Mine." He swept his arm around, asking where.

At last one of the priests appeared to get the idea, and raised a pointing arm.

XII

RED CIRCLES AND his band were out of Magnuson's sight now, on their way upstream. Magnuson was walking alone in the opposite direction, back toward the familiar territory around the villages.

He had lived and worked in these villages for a year now. He recalled that last year's rainy season had been starting when he staged his disappearance; and even now he could see this season's first towering thunderheads in the eastern sky.

There were times when he wished he might have made some science as impersonal and plain as meteorology his life's work. But Man had called to him, giving him no real choice. He had buried himself in these hills; he had dedicated himself, even to the point of hunting for a man to kill him as part of the work. A strange way to serve the cause of Life. But not really strange when you saw it clearly, for death was a necessary part of life.

Civilization had much to learn about the need for a continuous weeding-out of its members. Magnuson would welcome his approaching arrest and trial, whatever the charges might be, because of the publicity. He meant to make his defense a lesson for civilization.

His defense would be based on the success of his work; he had raised an ape-like, gibbering thing to the rank of Man, and in the end the courts would not be able to deny the living evidence of that one hominid. Sooner or later, the work of refining humanity would go on, on every planet, and that was all that mattered.

When he came in sight of the Warriors' Village, Magnu-

son paused, sensing something wrong. The village looked completely empty. Seeing him, a couple of old women came timidly out from where they had been hiding in the bush, and in excited voices told him of great massacre and destruction by a thousand raging hominids, led by the yellow-haired Earthman who had so magically escaped from the ordeal.

Magnuson soothed the women as well as he could, and hurried into the depopulated village. No corpses and no damage were visible, though there were hominid droppings in several places. Making Brazil a leader of the enemy forces was indeed an imaginative touch. Of course it was possible that Brazil had seen the village empty and had dared to pass through it. Perhaps he had been fleeing from the animals.

The pen was undamaged, though its door stood open, and the one-handed hominid was gone. Magnuson had believed Red Circles, but seeing this for himself was still a blow. At least there were no signs of violence in the pen.

The hominid might possibly have gone back to the familiar laboratory-pen, near the quarry. Magnuson hurried in that direction, toward the Workers' Village.

From ahead of him, somewhere downstream, there came a sound as of a metal gong being struck, once. Magnuson paused, listening, but the noise was not repeated. Thinking vaguely that the wild hominids might be attacking the Workers' Village, Magnuson loosened the machine pistol in his belt and hurried on.

Food-Giver had followed downstream after the howling young men who had chosen to go with Yellow Monster. Food-Giver was not jealous—at least not consciously so—but he was curious. Yellow Monster said what he wanted done in a way that made a man feel it was wrong to do anything else. Even though Yellow Monster rarely gave food to anyone, the young men still followed him toward the dangerous villages, so there was great power in Yellow Monster somewhere.

It was wise to go slow when approaching the villages. Food-Giver carried a big club and was ready at every step to run for his life. When Yellow Monster and the young hominids ran shouting into the first village, Food-Giver stayed back and waited to see what would happen. Not much of anything seemed to happen; there were no sounds of fighting.

Food-Giver was not convinced. He skirted the empty

111

village suspiciously and slowly. The young hominids and Yellow Monster were now out of his sight, but his ears and nose told him they were going on downstream.

Remembering another raid of six generations ago, Food-Giver visualized the location of the next village. He was drawing near it when he heard a call like that of hominid children in distress, but in deep adult voices. It came from ahead and to his right.

"The Dark People," Food-Giver whispered aloud. He took a tight grip on his club. He was alone, and afraid, in enemy territory, but he could not ignore that cry. He was a leader because nothing meant more to him than helping his people, and now the Dark People were calling for help.

Food-Giver had a generations-old memory of their place of torture, a deep senseless hole dug into stone. He knew where it was, and he moved with slow caution toward it.

Ahead he saw a couple of elderly villagers in kilts hurrying in frightened silence through the woods. They did not see him, and he could have killed them. But a noise might bring others, so he hid and waited for them to pass. Then he went carefully on toward the quarry he remembered but had never seen with his own eyes.

Very slowly, sense alert, he came out of the woods near the lip of the quarry. Here he found much hominid sign, and recognized the scent of one or two individuals. He interpreted the tracks to mean that the twenty-five young men, or most of them, had here turned north again toward home, scattering back through the woods and taking with them other hominids who could only be the Dark People.

Food-Giver sighed with relief. All this was good, very good. The villagers had been robbed of their slaves. The Dark People could be given to drink from the Sacred Pool, and thought would come to their eyes and tongues, and they would be Real People. The tribe had been strengthened. Yellow Monster and his strange powers had done very well.

Moving forward to peek down into the quarry-pit, Food-Giver saw three gray figures huddled together far below him. He saw that they were not bound or penned up. They were alive, and free to climb out, but still they stayed in the pit.

"Hey there!" he shouted to them, forgetting caution for a moment. "Do you want to be Dark People always?"

112

But they only huddled together and stared at him, as if they wanted him to go away.

So. If they refused help, he would not force it on them. He would go home. He had gotten only a few paces from the quarry when he saw among the trees a thing he did not remember. A strange big hut, not such as the villagers made but built of the branchless bodies of many trees placed close together. Curious as always, he approached it. The area smelled little of villager, but strongly of both monster and hominid. That seemed a friendly combination to Food-Giver, and he was emboldened to go closer.

There was a dark hole, like a cave, let into the cleverly arranged log-pile. Inside, someone moved, making timid sounds.

The freshest smell was hominid, so Food-Giver dared to go to the door and look inside. A one-handed male hominid was there, bedraggled and frightened-looking. Food-Giver noted the recent small wounds that marked the other's body, and stared at the old scar that ended the arm-stump. It was astonishing how neatly the hand had been removed, and how the owner had survived such a loss.

Then Food-Giver remembered to be courteous. "Are you Dark? Or do you think?"

The eyes of the one-handed hominid were strange and wild, as if thought flickered up and down like firelight behind them. His mouth worked uncertainly. "I . . . I . . . I . . ."

"Maybe you drank once and no more from the Sacred Pool," said Food-Giver. "That's not enough. You will come with me and drink more." Food-Giver tried to talk the way Yellow Monster did, stating positively what should be done. It seemed that such a method might accomplish great things. "Also you probably need food and ordinary water."

Something small squeaked and scuttled in a corner of the cabin. With an unthinking flash of movement Food-Giver knocked obstructions aside and struck at the rat with a hunting thrust of his club. The noise and sudden movement made the one-handed one scream and cower away into a corner.

Food-Giver had just made certain of the crippled rat when there were running footsteps outside the cabin. He turned sharply, but the breeze brought only a fresh whiff of monster. Food-Giver waited expectantly.

113

Walking quickly past the rim of the quarry, Magnuson peered down. Sledges and ropes and tools were scattered carelessly. There had been a hominid raid, evidently, and the kilted overseers and workers had fled. But three of the quarry hominids were still in the pit, perhaps because they knew no other place, perhaps because fear of their masters still held them when their masters were gone. Their upturned faces, expressionless as those of cows, followed Magnuson as he walked along the rim. I will not fail you, Magnuson thought, looking down at them. I will yet raise you up into the sun.

There came a sharp clatter and thump from ahead of him, and a hominid scream. Inside his laboratory! If the wild ones were in there, and the one-handed man—Magnuson ran forward. He found the machine pistol ready in his hand.

The one-handed hominid was huddled down in a corner, and looked up beseechingly as Magnuson burst in. Before Magnuson could say or do anything a big wild one lunged at him out of the gloom.

The automatic pistol hammered out a deafening repeated concussion in the enclosed space. One-Hand screamed once more, and was silent, cowering away from the noise. The wild one was hurled back across the room, and torn nearly in half. A table had already been upset, and a murderous club lay on the floor.

There were no others. Shakily, Magnuson lowered the pistol. He had come just barely in time, it seemed, but the new human life was safe. .

Something curious struck his eye, and he prodded with a toe at the nerve-twitching gray hand that had almost reached him. Half the body of a rat lay beside the hand. Curious.

Boris, still following the direction in which the priest had pointed, halted when he reached the edge of the clearing and saw the copter under the trees on the other side.

"Brenda?"

"Boris?" Her blessed head appeared in one of the copter ports, and was joined a second later by Jane's. "Boris, this thing won't fly; the controls are all smashed. But whoever did it forgot the radio. I got a message off half an hour ago, when the villagers all ran away. The colony took a bearing on us; they're sending an armed copter. Oh, you look so

funny in that little net. But you're alive . . ." Brenda began to sob.

Boris kissed her, gobbled half of an emergency ration he found in the copter, kissed her again, ate the other half of the ration, found a spare coverall and put it on.

"Since I look so funny, let's start hiking, ladies. I don't trust any offers of rescue."

He went first, with the rifle ready; Brenda was just behind him, her limp almost gone. They had made three hundred yards east along the lake shore when the copter from the colony arrived and picked them up.

A week later Boris walked once more across the common of the Temple Village, through pouring rain. Now the landing clearing was full of copters, and the muddy villages swarmed with Space Force men. The cruiser had arrived at last and was in orbit above the greenish clouds.

In the middle of the common, Boris came to a villager who stood still as if too bewildered to shelter himself. The steady rain had washed the colored clay from his powerful arms, but Boris knew him. When Boris made a peace gesture, the war chief only looked the more bewildered. After a brief sullen stare he turned and walked heavily away, a man whose normal world had been yanked out from under him, never to return.

Some of Earth's old primitives had believed that a rain such as this fell to mark the death of a great chief. Magnuson was no dead chief; he sat alone in his well-built hut, his face tired but showing an inner content.

He looked up without much surprise, as if Boris had been in his thoughts. "Brazil. It wasn't personal enmity that made me help them to hunt you. You understand that?"

"You mean Morton forced you?"

Magnuson hesitated. "I won't say that."

"You mean it was for the cause. The purification of mankind."

Magnuson folded his hands on the table before him. "I told you once that none of us matter, much, as individuals."

Boris shook his head slightly. "Anyway, I've already given my statement to the Tribune. Have you read it or heard it?"

"No. I've been ordered to stay in this hut. They'll charge me formally when I've obtained counsel." Magnuson was sit-

115

ting while Boris stood, but still Magnuson seemed to be looking down at him. "You know, my hominid is alive and well."

"Your hominid?"

"I think I may claim credit for him. There are Space Force people examining him now. The day before the Space Force came, I succeeded in teaching him a word or two of speech. So you see the rite of passage was effective."

Sure now that Magnuson did not yet know the truth about the hominids and the Water, Boris stood there feeling weary, and found that he had no wish to destroy the smiling assurance before him. It would be short-lived before the Tribune's coming wrath, or it would perpetuate itself by sliding completely into self-delusion.

Magnuson said, "I was only just in time to save him from a wild one, you know. I wonder what name he'll choose, when he understands about names."

" 'Food-Giver' is a good name," said Boris. "Might call him that."

"I don't believe I understand."

"No, I don't believe you do." Boris had just come from viewing Food-Giver's corpse. There had been no one to open the skull properly and in time, to drain and preserve the observations of his generous life for coming generations of his people.

His grunting, flea-picking, much abused and cheerful people. Nasty, virtuous, and short. They were Boris's people now, in a real sense, and he meant to do what he could for them in the future.

But Boris could also remember Brenda being led into this village, to this hut, helpless in the hands of those who might have killed her in their greed and lust. And Magnuson cutting the cord that bound her hands, throwing the cord aside, cursing whatever bound human beings, whatever stunted them or made them less than perfect.

"Magnuson, I'll do what I can to help you. You've drunk the Water of Thought several times; you may have been still under its influence."

"No, we both know the effect soon passes. My actions here have been sane and responsible. The credit or blame is mine."

"The big charge will be manslaughter, or maybe even murder." Boris could not stay in the hut any longer, and walked out into the rain.

116

Behind him he could hear the proud, dedicated voice: "Why, I don't see how they can base that. I didn't kill Jones. In fact, no one can now deny that I have *created* a new human life form . . ."

Back from a trip to hominid territory, where he had introduced the Tribune's men as friends, Boris found Brenda waiting for him outside the colony's main gate. She wore a rain hood, which he lifted to kiss her. She snuggled up against him.

So young. Never been anywhere, really. Such a small-town girl. In the last week he had seen her hunger for children and home-making.

Boris experienced a terrible sinking feeling, akin to drowning. Visions of future responsibilities rose before him, but he was helpless, as if again in the grip of the Water of Thought.

"Listen." He started to walk with Brenda in the rain. "I'm a planeteer. I'm stationed here and there, and I'm moving around all the time. I've never been married. I've never wanted to settle down—before. Do I have to struggle through this whole speech before you say yes or no?"

"Last time you said no to me."

"You little—that was because . . . *Are* you going to say no?"

"No," she said.

Here's a quick checklist of recent releases of

ACE SCIENCE-FICTION BOOKS

F-titles 40¢   M-titles 45¢

If you are missing any of these, they can be obtained
directly from the publisher by sending the indicated sum,
plus 5¢ handling fee, to Ace Books, Inc. (Dept. M M),
1120 Avenue of the Americas, New York, N. Y. 10036